A door marked

Hawker

A door marked
Hawker

Nigel Milliner

The Book Guild Ltd

First published in Great Britain in 2016 by
The Book Guild Ltd
9 Priory Business Park
Wistow Road, Kibworth
Leicestershire, LE8 0RX
Freephone: 0800 999 2982
www.bookguild.co.uk
Email: info@bookguild.co.uk
Twitter: @bookguild

Typeset in Centaur MT

Printed and bound in the UK by TJ International, Padstow, Cornwall

ISBN 978 1 91087 834 7

British Library Cataloguing in Publication Data.
A catalogue record for this book is available from the British Library.

To Nix, the artist.

CHAPTER 1

The almshouses in Fentonmar were built in 1887, as announced proudly by the numbers carved into granite under the eaves and, if anyone was still in doubt as to which millennium this referred to, the letters AD followed. The building was squat and solidly constructed of local stone and the first floor had the benefit of a covered balcony, supported from below by four sturdy, rounded granite pillars.

Although always referred to in the plural by locals the almshouses were in fact a single building, now divided into six separate dwellings and occupied by poor and needy elderly denizens of the parish. As a building overseen by the Almshouse Association it complied with that organisation's code of practice, as safeguarded by a meeting in the chapter house of Southwark Cathedral in 1946. There was a local warden who ensured that the elderly occupants – who considered this their home for what remained of their lives – maintained their dignity, freedom and independence. The three ground floor flats had front doors, all painted navy blue, which opened directly onto Fore Street, but access to the upper flats was from rather steep concrete steps at the rear.

On one particular late evening, at the time of year when spring is bursting damply to give way to summer, a single light glowed a dull orange through unlined curtains drawn across an upstairs window; just sufficient illumination to colour the raindrops that quivered from a sagging and blocked launder. Just to the right of the lighted window a twist of ivy leaned inwards from a downpipe and tapped gently against the pane. If one stood below in Fore Street and looked really closely one would have seen faint flashes of light from active television screens in two of the upper rooms.

From somewhere within the building a radio or CD player was

producing muffled organ music, which at two minutes after eleven that night was the only sound to be heard in the street outside the building. It was, after all, the time when most elderly people sank into their beds for a peaceful night's sleep.

The figure lurking down below behind one of the pillars knew the exact time, because the clock by the butcher's shop further up Fore Street had struck the hour two minutes earlier. She wore a black cloak and hid her face behind a luminous death mask, the only feature identifying her gender being her long, black-painted fingernails.

She drew back further into the darkness as a car rounded the corner below the almshouses and proceeded noisily up Fore Street in third gear. Once the car had passed, the black figure leaned out from behind the pillar and gazed expectantly down the road towards a small car park at the T-junction. It was unnecessary, but she looked at her watch anyway. Four minutes after eleven. The others were due at any minute.

The organ music stopped abruptly and she craned her neck towards the balcony above. The light should go out soon.

At ten minutes after eleven it went out and as if on cue she heard the van's engine as it approached slowly from the Truro road. There were no headlights and the driver must have killed the engine before reaching the car park, because she could hear the van's tyres quite distinctly as they hit the gravel surface and then came to a halt a few yards in.

She ran her tongue over dry lips and then reached under her cloak for the flask that pressed against her right hip. As she tipped the flask against her mouth she could just make out the rumble of the van door being slid open. They'd better have all the gear, she thought: there'd be no hanging about once they'd started.

In fact it all began slightly earlier than originally planned, because one of the three figures now running towards her up Fore Street kicked a metal dustbin as he wrestled to control the banner he was carrying. The lid slid off and hit the low stone wall by the adjacent house. The banner carrier paused as if to pick it up and was loudly sworn at by one of his companions.

Behind one of the stone columns the dark figure in the death mask raised her arms in frustrated anger as the first of the trio arrived, breathing hard from his brief exertion.

'You two ... other side of the street ... hold the banner out,' she rasped. There was no further need for silence or subterfuge.

She drew a small megaphone from under her cloak and then motioned for the third person to stand beside her. She pushed the mask back and took another quick swig from the flask before switching on the volume control. The man beside her, who wore a dog mask, gave her a nod and she raised the megaphone to her lips. The pair on the other side of the road then moved apart to unfurl and display the banner. *Animal Slayer*, it read and, in smaller letters at the bottom, *VAG*.

Death's Head cleared her throat, lifted the mask to spit and then pointed the megaphone skywards.

'Murderer!' she shouted and the harsh metallic amplification cut through the stillness of the night. Then, with greater gusto, 'Murderer! Killer of innocent animals!'

This was the signal for one of the party to begin banging the fallen dustbin lid against a wall and the other two to start a prearranged chant. The theme was the same as the one delivered through the megaphone.

For a few seconds nothing happened. Then a light came on: the same one that had been doused shortly after eleven, and then another on the opposite side of the street. This response encouraged the quartet in the street and the volume went up a notch.

A window opened and a pale elderly face peered anxiously around a curtain. One of the members of the protest group threw an object up towards the balcony and it thudded against the wall. The face disappeared rapidly and the window slammed shut. The thrower's head went back and he bayed out a harsh mocking laugh.

Death's Head became bolder now and she moved to the centre of the street to deliver her next blast from the megaphone.

'Shame. Animal killer. Vivisectionist!' she bellowed, stumbling slightly over the last two syllables. She turned and spat again as another light went on above and this time a voice crackled out from the almshouses.

'Shut your bloody noise and go away! We've called the police.'

One of the banner carriers laughed again and resumed the chant with his mate. The fourth member of the protest group picked up a clod of grassy earth from the roadside and hurled it up in the direction of the voice.

'Police won't come this time of night, you bastard,' he yelled back. 'Go and sort out your friend along there. He's the one who's broken nature's law.'

Death's Head, the group's leader, looked sideways at her colleague, nodded vigorously and lifted the megaphone to her mouth.

'We know who you are and *you* know why we're here. If you don't stop supporting the animal killers we'll be back again ... and again ... until you do.'

This must have been the signal for the short campaign to come to an end, because the banner holders came together and quickly furled it around the poles and the fourth man threw another missile. This one was harder and better directed and the sound of breaking glass drew a clearly audible scream from behind one of the windows. Death's Head switched off her megaphone, drew down her mask and whirled her arm in a circular motion.

'Time to go!' she shouted across the street and began to run down Fore Street towards the parked van.

Her three colleagues set off after her, but one of the banner carriers tripped over a pole and sprawled awkwardly onto the road. He swore loudly and scrambled to his feet, shaking off a helping hand and quickly got into his stride.

Emboldened by the sudden silence, one of the almshouses' residents came out onto the balcony and peered short-sightedly down the street. He put on his glasses in time to see the van's lights come on and its rear door being slammed shut. The van's gears ground into reverse and it made an untidy turn before lurching into the main road in the direction of Truro.

'Christ, what was that all about?' the elderly man said, glancing left and right, but no one else had ventured onto the balcony. The orange glow of a street light glinted off his faded shiny dressing gown, which he now drew more tightly around his middle. He gave an involuntary shudder and then turned back towards his balcony door. As he did so his slippered foot knocked against a hard object.

The old man frowned and clutched the balcony rail before bending down to pick up the object. His back protested as he reached down and he groaned at the effort. An unexpected voice from the gloom of the adjacent balcony startled him as he straightened.

'What's that, Harry?'

'God! Don't do that, Mavis, it's bad enough all this other business going on without you creeping up like that.'

'Sorry. Is that something those hooligans threw?'

Harry shuffled over to the partition railing as he squinted at the object. Down below a few people had gathered and were talking in hushed tones. One man was reading from a crumpled leaflet, while two others bent their heads to listen.

'Yes. It's paper wrapped round a rock by the looks of it.' Harry began to unwrap the missile and a large stone fell from his hands onto his foot. He gave a slight yelp and then opened up the paper.

'Here, give it to me,' Mavis rasped as Harry tried in vain to focus on the printed words. She straightened the spectacles on her nose and cleared her throat.

'*Vivisection Action Group (VAG)*,' she read and then exclaimed, 'Ooh, that's not very nice.'

She held the pamphlet up for Harry to see a picture of a monkey with its brains spilt onto a slab in what appeared to be a laboratory. Harry did not need his glasses to take in the gruesome image and he flinched.

'What's it say after that?'

She paused to look over the balcony as a car came up Fore Street with a blue light flashing on its roof. It came to a halt outside the almshouses and both front doors opened simultaneously.

'Better late than never,' Harry muttered and then turned back to face Mavis. She adjusted her glasses again and read on.

'*We, the members of the VAG deplore the abuse and mistreatment of animals in the name of medical science and make it our duty to expose all those who* directly, or indirectly, further the execution of this despicable practice.' She paused, shifted her position to allow more light to fall on the page.

'Is that all then?'

'Patience.' She gave him a stern glance and then continued. '*This includes those who invest in companies or businesses that deal with or promote the practice of animal murder for scientific purposes and we possess a list of names of such investors.*'

She stopped suddenly and let out a startled exclamation.

'What is it?' Harry's attention was now divided between what his neighbour was reading and the activity below. The two police – a man and a woman – were talking to some of the people who had ventured out of their doors. Harry could see five of them from where he stood. Two were in their dressing gowns, but the others were still in their day clothes.

'Dear me.' Mavis held a hand to her cheek.

'What?' Harry turned back to her.

'It says here … *Your name is on the list and we know where you live.*' She stared wide-eyed at Harry. 'That sounds threatening to me.'

'Yer, but who … who're they talking about?'

'I dunno, Harry. I've no shares in anything.' Then she added rather plaintively, 'Not even Tesco's.'

'Me neither.'

And, as if expecting to see a targeted shareholder standing out amongst their neighbours below, they both turned to gawp at the group in Fore Street.

One police officer was making notes, while the other started lining up the almshouse for a camera shot. She stopped shuffling around and then there was a flash as she took the photograph. Two more shots and then she turned back to talk to the man standing at her side.

'Do you think we should show them this?' Mavis asked, holding the leaflet as if it were a used piece of toilet paper.

'No,' Harry replied emphatically and then pointed to the street below. 'There's dozens of 'em floating around down there. They'll soon pick one up.'

'Well, if it's not me, nor you, who do you think they're at?'

'Dunno.' Harry scratched his chin and stared glumly at the scene in Fore Street. He noted that the policewoman was now looking up at him and he raised a hand self-consciously. 'I expect they'll want a statement from us.'

'Well, I can't tell them much.'

'Nor me, Mavis. Buggers woke me out of a deep sleep. I was having a lovely dream too.' He gave her a saucy grin. 'It was about that weather girl ... what's 'er name?'

'Harry!' She gave his arm a playful smack. 'Well, I'm going back to bed. Enough excitement for one night.'

Harry sighed. 'Yer, me too. Hope this don't happen too often. 'G'night, Mavis.'

'Night, Harry.'

The two shuffled away from the railing and disappeared back into their respective bedrooms, pulling doors closed in unison. For them the play was over, although the curtain had not yet come down on the final act.

In Fore Street the remaining players in the night's drama also gradually dispersed and front doors slammed with an air of finality. The policeman who had been reporting back to headquarters now turned and murmured something to his colleague. He bent to pick up a leaflet and glanced at it briefly before stuffing it in a pocket and then moving across to the car. As they drove off in the direction of Truro the clock at the top of Fore Street was striking midnight.

One light remained on upstairs in the almshouses for several minutes after the police had left and through a crack between curtains it illuminated a clod of mud, which was now sliding inexorably down a windowpane like some grotesque garden slug. From behind the sanctuary of their owner's room a pair of wary eyes followed the slug's progress until it finally plopped onto the balcony.

Only then did the eyes blink.

CHAPTER 2

The ancient village of Fentonmar is located some four miles inland from the nearest Cornish coastline, but nevertheless its claim to historical importance has strong connections with the sea: hence Fore Street. Until the silting up of the River Fal, towards the end of the sixteenth century, ships would sail up the Carrick Roads and then on through the Roseland as far as Fentonmar's wharf. From there imported goods would be offloaded and then local produce such as wool and tin taken on board for export.

The town, as it was five centuries ago had its own Member of Parliament, several churches, a manor house a mile up the hill and even a castle. It was a thriving community of farmers, miners and merchants until the time came when it ceased to be viable for increasingly larger ships to navigate the Fal. After that Fentonmar very rapidly withdrew from the fast lane of commercial activity. One of its churches was demolished, the castle gradually crumbled, people moved away as employment became scarce and it even ceased to be a parliamentary constituency in its own right. Today the manor house is merely a footnote in Hals county history of Cornwall and a nineteenth-century farmhouse stands on its site.

However, there remain in the village significant vestiges of past glory: not in the form of architecture, but in the layout of the former town's thoroughfares. There is still a back lane, where carts once trundled their wares to the rear of assorted dwellings. And then there are small offshoots leading nowhere from Fore Street, like insignificant twigs sprouting from the main branch of a tree. Today they would be referred to as cul-de-sacs, but no doubt when first developed they afforded an element of privacy to local merchants, who chose to build their houses slightly away from the noise and the mud of Fore Street. Now there are several houses located along these short side roads, some of them small terraces and some brick or stone built detached dwellings of modest size.

One of these stumpy lanes, near the top of Fore Street, is named Dowr Row, although this was probably a misnomer as it was not quite the last row in the village. There was one other opposite the church at the top, which probably indicated ribbon development at some point in Fentonmar's history. Whatever its origin, Dowr Row is not now at the end of the village.

There are only four houses in Dowr Row, one a thatched two-bedroom stone cottage and the other three slightly larger slate-roofed and stucco-fronted. Jack Mitchell, who lived with his wife in one of the slate-roofed houses, had often threatened to chip away at the stucco in order to reveal the stone walls he was convinced lay beneath the render. However, potential cost, time, and his wife had combined to put this project on hold: maybe permanently.

It was soon after nine o'clock in the morning two days after the almshouses incident and Mitchell was checking his emails when he heard the doorbell ring. He glanced up for a moment and then chose to ignore it, hoping Catherine would deal with it, but suddenly he remembered she was still in her nightdress in the bedroom. He cursed and pushed his chair back. Even if she was dressed he guessed Catherine would be in no fit state to greet visitors.

Mitchell padded down the stairs as the bell rang again. A short plump woman wearing a clerical collar stood with her arms behind her back when he opened the door.

'Hello, Jack, sorry to intrude so early,' the visitor gushed. 'Bit of a problem and I have to be in Bodmin by ten. Can I come in?'

He gave her a lopsided grin and stood back. 'Of course, come in Jane.'

Fentonmar's vicar made a big show of wiping her feet on the doormat, stepped into the hall and looked about as if it were her first time in the house.

'Come into the office.' He held out an arm, directing her towards the small room immediately off the hall. It was warmer in there and Catherine was less likely to barge in unexpectedly than if they were in the kitchen. 'What's up?'

The Reverend Jane Stokes hitched up her skirt and sat in the battered old armchair that was his concession to visitors to his office.

'Would you like coffee?'

'Thanks, but no time.' She leaned forward and fixed him with her dark, shiny pebble eyes. Her thin lips parted and her brow furrowed as she organised her opening gambit. Mitchell, now reclining on the other chair, recognised the symptoms, but resisted the urge to smile.

'You heard about the fracas down at the almshouses, I presume?' The bottle-dyed fringe bobbed independently as she spoke.

'Yes. Protest from some sort of animal rights group I hear.'

'So it seems ... from the literature they left drifting around Fore Street.' The frown deepened in disapproval and she drew her lips tightly together. There was a long pause as she constructed her next sentence. Something thumped onto the floor of the bedroom directly above and Mitchell's eyes swivelled upwards as if expecting to see the cause through the ceiling. The Reverend Stokes seemed not to notice.

'Jack, I don't think this was a random protest. I don't believe Fentonmar was chosen for that ugly display just by chance. No, I think it was an organised attempt to intimidate a member of our community.'

'Oh? Who?'

She pursed her mouth and the wrinkles on her forehead became more pronounced. 'I could be wrong, mind you, but I'm guessing they were targeting Dorgy Pascoe.'

'Dorgy? Why him?' he chuckled. 'What's he done to bring on the wrath of the bunny huggers?'

'Don't make light of it, Jack.' The vicar's round face and intense dark eyes admonished him. The rays of morning sunlight glinted off the fringe of her copper-coloured hair and Mitchell, not for the first time, found himself fascinated by the contrast of the untamed tresses and the dog collar.

'Sorry. Quite right. But,' he shrugged and repeated, 'why him?'

'I'm not sure, but he's the only one at the almshouses who has reacted to the attack.' She shifted her position rapidly and held her hands out, palms facing each other as if describing the length of a fish. 'No, they all reacted in one way or another, but what I mean about Dorgy is that he's just gone into his shell. Won't talk to anyone, won't leave his room.'

'You've tried, obviously.'

'Yes, both me, the police and a counsellor. He's just bottled up.' She tilted her head and the dark eyes bored into his, as if anticipating the obvious next comment.

'So, what do you want me to do?' He showed his teeth in an engaging smile. 'I presume that's why you're here.'

'Well, you know him as well as anyone. He's had … shall we say … a complicated life and one suspects he's a bit fragile. You know … not equipped to cope with a shock to the system like that. So, I was wondering if you would find the time to have a talk with him.'

So that was it. He sat back in the desk swivel chair and squinted towards the window from where he could see the silvery bark and fresh young leaves of the birch Catherine had planted last autumn. A couple of sparrows were busy hopping from one flimsy branch to another, perhaps demonstrating a natural excitement regarding the imminence of summer. He thought for a moment longer about his heavy workload and then turned back to face the vicar.

'I talk to him when he goes to the pub and I suppose we have a shared interest in old Cornwall, but I don't see that qualifies me as a bosom pal, Jane.'

'There's also the fact that you're a church visitor, Jack,' she said softly in that cotton wool voice favoured by the clergy when they are trying to press a point without seeming to do so.

He laughed and tapped the padded plastic arm of his chair in a gesture that admitted defeat. It was something he had almost forgotten. Months earlier he had agreed to visit village folk who might, for whatever reason, be in need of company. It was his consolation offer on refusing Jane's request for him to join the Parochial Church Council, but to date his pastoral services had not been called upon. *Sorry, God, but what was I thinking when I agreed to do this?*

'OK, Jane, I'll give it a go. But, what if the old boy won't talk to me either?'

'Then you'll have done all you can and we'll just have to keep an eye on him.'

'When might be a good time?'

'It's up to you.' She shrugged and the dog collar rode up her stubby neck. 'I know you're busy, but he's not going anywhere.'

Jack sighed. 'I'll check the diary and if it's clear I'll try this afternoon.'

She smiled and reached out to pat his arm. 'Thank you, Jack. I'm sure if anyone can get to the root of Dorgy's problem you can. Now I must dash off to Bodmin.'

She popped up from the chair like a puppet that has had its strings pulled and the sparrows flew off at the surprise movement. Jack rose more slowly, wondering silently what he had let himself in for. He saw the vicar to the front door.

'Bless you,' she beamed at him and then hurried up the short pathway to her waiting car.

Jack turned back into the house and pulled the front door closed behind him. He looked up and saw Catherine standing at the top of the stairs. She was still in her nightdress.

'You OK?' It was a familiar question, almost rhetorical.

She nodded and continued to stand there, hair dishevelled and eyes reacting defensively against sunlight that shone through the front door's clerestory windows.

'That was Jane,' he said as he walked on through the hallway, without waiting for a reply.

He picked up his fleece jacket from a chair in the kitchen and went back into the hallway.

'I have to go out for a bit. Maybe an hour,' he called out, but she was no longer standing there.

When Jack Mitchell reached the almshouses later that day he looked around before going to the back entrance, but there was no remaining evidence of the siege, as some locals were now calling the night-time incident. He nodded to an elderly resident as he pushed open the heavy wooden door. Inside a lone bulb hung under a simple plastic shade above the bare concrete of a small hallway. There was no matting at the bottom or carpet on the stairs and Jack reflected that ancient skulls would crack like coconuts in the event of a tumble down the steep stairway that loomed ahead of him. Jack shook his head ruefully. It seemed that the only concession to health and safety was a wooden handrail along one side of the staircase.

He pressed a timer switch, a light came on at the top of the stairs and he went up onto a long, cheerless landing. There were doors to the left and to the right and each was numbered with a metal alloy screw-on digit of the kind sold by old-fashioned hardware shops. He noted that a couple of doors were also named, presumably to suggest some kind of defiant individuality. The door he sought was the last on the left and he just had time to note that number one had *Hawker* painted crudely at eye level before the timer switch popped and the landing light went out. Lord help the less fleet of foot, he thought, as he knocked loudly on the door.

As he expected there was no response, so he knocked again and stood back in anticipation. Still silence from the other side.

A door at the far end of the landing opened slowly and Jack could make out a nose and a pair of spectacles peering around it. A hand crept out and pressed the timer switch. Once more the stark landing was alight.

'Dorgy's not in to anyone today,' a phlegmy voice volunteered.

Jack squinted into the distance at the half face.

'Is that Mrs Harris?' He was certain it was. 'It's Jack Mitchell.'

'I know who you'm be my dear, but Dorgy's still not coming out for anyone.'

Jack took a few steps along the landing. 'Is that just today? Or has he not spoken to anyone since the disturbance?'

'Took in his milk yesterday, that's all.' Mrs Harris coughed and the rattling sound echoed off bare walls. 'Won't talk to no one.'

'Thank you.' Jack turned back to number one and said over his shoulder, 'I'll just try once more.'

He waited until he heard the end door close and then prepared his knuckles for another battering. This time he followed it with an inducement.

'Dorgy, it's Jack Mitchell,' he shouted. 'I've got something for you. Pint of Rufus Craggs. You must be parched in there.'

No reply.

'You won't come to the pub, so the pub must come to you.'

This time, after a few seconds, there was a distinct shuffle from the other side of the door and then a voice, low but distinct. 'I don't drink bottled beer.'

'It's not bottled, Dorgy. It's straight off the tap, but it'll go flat soon if you don't let me in.'

Just then another door opened behind him and a curious face peered around the frame. Jack glanced back, irritated at the intrusion, and gave a rapid wave of dismissal at an inquisitive individual. A grey beard took the hint and closed his door again.

'Don't drink on me own neither.'

Jack smiled. The voice came from immediately behind the door.

'Neither do I.'

Now he heard the grating of a key turning in the lock.

Jack took a step back and cradled the two-litre milk container against his chest. The door in front of him eased open and Dorgy Pascoe stood there, unshaven, wearing an expression halfway between defiant and uncertain.

'May I come in?'

Dorgy did not reply, but took a backward step and gave Jack a faint nod. The moment his visitor was in the room he closed the door swiftly and turned the key, then swivelled back and his eyes settled on the milk container.

'I'll get glasses.'

He shuffled across the room in carpet slippers and through a doorway that led into a kitchenette as Jack did a quick sweep of the room. Apart from the kitchenette door there was another beside it and he assumed it opened onto a bathroom of sorts. There was no other evidence of washing facilities. A glazed door at the far side of the room from where he stood gave light from the balcony and he noted a smear of mud, now dry, disfiguring one of the lower panes.

The main room had an unmade bed in one corner, a utilitarian chair with padded seat and wooden arms, a small round table and, incongruously, a heavy roll-top desk near the balcony door. The table had an upright chair pushed tight up against it and what looked like the remains of breakfast utensils littering its surface.

Dorgy came back into the room clutching two glasses. He stopped and looked about him hesitantly.

'You'm better sit there.' He indicated the armchair and then turned to look at his bed with a faint expression of distaste. 'I'll go there.'

'Here, hold out your glass.' Jack had the top off the plastic bottle. 'Not too early for you?'

'Nooo.' Dorgy gurgled as he tipped his glass slightly for the frothy brown liquid to slide in. 'I b'aint had a drop for days.'

Jack filled his own glass and sat where instructed. He settled the container beside his chair and smiled at the old man, who was now tipping beer down his throat.

'Who sent you then?' Dorgy had a crafty look in his eye as he wiped the back of his hand across his stubbly chin.

'I wasn't *sent* by anyone. Jane suggested I might try to talk to you as you'd sent everyone else away.'

'Jane Stokes?'

'The vicar, yes.'

Dorgy grunted and his shoulders gave an involuntary lurch. The old man didn't approve of female vicars, although he was only an irregular churchgoer. He looked down at the glass and then raised it to his lips. Jack did the same and then waited.

'So, what do want to talk to me about, Jack Mitchell?'

'About the trouble the other night … why it's upset you so much. And if there's anything we … I …can do to help.'

Dorgy turned his head slowly to look out of the window, as if he were recreating the disturbance in his mind. His gnarled arthritic fingers twisted and fidgeted against the glass and one of his slippered feet tapped gently on the faded green carpet.

Jack reached down to the plastic container. He was rapidly writing off the afternoon in terms of other tasks he had planned.

'Not sure I want to talk about it,' Dorgy murmured, so low that Jack only just heard the words.

'Those hooligans seem to have frightened you more than they did the others.' Jack got up and poured some more beer into the old man's glass. 'Why was that, Dorgy?'

Dorgy looked down at the floor and muttered something.

'What was that?'

'They was targeting me,' he repeated more distinctly. 'Not the others. That's why.'

'How do you know?' Jack, genuinely perplexed, began chasing through his knowledge of Dorgy Pascoe's past, but could think of no connection the man might have had with animal experimentation that would warrant an attack by an animal rights group.

'They knew where I live.'

'Maybe, but that still doesn't explain why ...'

Dorgy held up a hand. 'You mean well, Jack Mitchell, but there's nudden you can do about it.'

'Listen, Dorgy, if you're right and these people are hounding you then there is something that can be done. This is a civilized community and if one of its members is being harassed by some fanatical group of people, then the law must put a stop to it. It's as simple as that.'

'Oh, yes,' Dorgy snorted. 'So, who are they? The police can't catch phantoms you know. They can't stop under my window all night, every night, waiting to catch 'em you know.'

It was plain that the old man was becoming agitated. He began rocking gently and the movement slopped some beer on the crumpled blanket of his unmade bed. Jack saw that it might not be long before any further meaningful conversation would come to an end. He waited a minute and then picked up the plastic container.

'OK, Dorgy, if you don't want to talk about it, then there's no more I can do for you.' He stood up. 'Here, you can have the rest of this.'

Dorgy stopped rocking and hesitated for only a moment before reaching out and taking the container. He muttered a word of thanks.

Jack stood for a while looking down at the bedraggled figure on his unmade bed and wondered if he should try just once more to prise something helpful from him. From their casual meetings in the pub, on a bench at the cricket ground or in passing on Fore Street Jack realised he knew little about the man's history. What kind of a name was Dorgy anyway? It was Cornish for badger, wasn't it? He knew that the old man had once been an artificial inseminator, working at most of the local livestock farms; a member of both the Fentonmar cricket and football teams; and once married. In fact Jack had discovered the married bit simply by spotting a stone in the church graveyard one day. Dorgy had never referred to his late wife in the course of conversation and neither had he referred to any offspring. At least, Jack reflected, not in his hearing. How little we know about others, he thought, even though we talk for hours about the world and how to put it straight. Do we all have some things in our lives over which we are constantly guarded?

'Dorgy,' Jack thrust his hands into his pockets, 'if you don't want to tell me why you think those people targeted you, perhaps someone closer to you? Do you have a son, or daughter maybe?'

It was as if Jack had prodded him with a stick. The close-cropped grizzled head rose sharply, thick grey eyebrows lowered over his watery eyes and he fixed his visitor with a grim stare.

'Don't you bring 'em into it.'

'Who? Your children?'

A long pause followed and Jack thought he had heard Dorgy's last word on the matter.

'No,' came the eventual reply. 'I meant any of my family.' Then there was an even longer pause. 'Got no daughter ... nor son ... not any more anyways.'

'I'm sorry to hear that.' Jack removed his hands from his pockets. It was time to go. He had done all he could think of to help the old man, who was obviously suffering from some kind of private torment. He nodded his farewell and then turned to leave. He was certainly no nearer finding out why this bedraggled old man might be the target of animal rights activists: if indeed he was the target. Jane Stokes could be quite wrong. Maybe he had simply been frightened stiff by the attack.

'Not your fault, Jack Mitchell,' Dorgy said, his voice rising as if in absolution. 'It's just the way of the world.'

'Yes, I suppose it is,' Jack replied, surprised at the unexpected piece of off-the-wall philosophy. 'Well, Dorgy, when you feel up to it I'll buy you a pint at the Plume.'

He turned the key and left then, with Dorgy Pascoe staring morosely at the near empty plastic milk container.

'Not a great success there, Mitchell,' Jack mumbled to himself as he pressed the switch for the stairwell light. Perhaps it was a mistake, he reflected, to take on the role of parish visitor: obviously he did not possess the knack of friendly persuasion.

CHAPTER 3

A week went by following Jack's visit to the almshouses and although spring was well advanced the weather conditions were not about to acknowledge that fact.

The dying days of April actually brought with it a drop in temperature and heavy rain cascaded for a couple of days non-stop. This created streams on the highways, washing them with the remains of winter's roadside detritus and blocking road drains along the way. Launders filled and gardens, barely drying out from winter storms, became sodden once more. Then, when the rain stopped, wind blew in from the south-west, causing further problems along the coast. People grumbled about the council's failure to clear the drains, but in fairness, it would have made no sense to tackle that job until the weather had relented.

Meanwhile, Jack had immersed himself in a tricky back duty tax case, where HM Revenue and Customs had challenged the returns of a local builder. This involved unravelling figures for the past six years and trying to construct a case from the faintest of paper trails. As a result all of his other clients had been put on hold and there certainly was no time for pro bono work, such as visiting needy locals. He had given Jane Stokes a report of his abortive visit to the almshouses, but had left her in little doubt that he would have to pass on pastoral work in the near future.

It was a Tuesday afternoon and he was staring out of the office window at the sad looking silver birch sapling, when there was a knock at the side door. In actual fact he assumed there was a knock, because it was the neighbour's dog's barking that alerted him to the arrival of a visitor. He returned his attention to the pile of papers on his desk and then to the spreadsheet on his laptop screen.

Catherine was in the house and he left her to deal with whoever it was.

He was in the middle of making an entry on the spreadsheet when the office door opened and Catherine put her head around it. Jack frowned as he looked up at her.

'You've got a visitor.' She glanced at his desk. 'Shall I tell him you're busy?'

He laughed at the irony of her understatement and then paused to examine her more closely as she stepped into the room. She was carefully coiffured, smartly dressed and seemed in an exceptionally buoyant mood.

Jack sighed. 'I suppose it depends on who it is.'

'Dorgy Pascoe,' she whispered and he noticed light glinting off her lip gloss.

'Dorgy!' He pushed his chair back and stretched out his legs. 'Well, I suppose if he's walked all the way up here, you'd better ...'

'I'll show him in then.'

She started to leave.

'Catherine,' Jack stopped her. 'Going somewhere?'

'To a séance with Madame Absinthe,' she replied huskily with a smile.

'No, seriously.'

'You've forgotten. It's the second Wednesday in the month.'

'Ah, the Old Cornwall Society. But, hang on, that's not until this evening. Why the ...?' He waved his hand airily above his head.

'Just getting ready. Can't spend all my life looking like an old bag, you know.' She blew him an exaggerated kiss. 'I'll fetch Dorgy.'

Jack continued to stare at the open door, puzzling once more at what he should be doing about his wife's increasingly erratic behaviour. It had become a worry to him that other people might begin to notice, if indeed they did not do so already. Selfishly, such a situation presented a potential embarrassment to him and an indignity for her, but the answer had to involve recognition of the delicate balance between total denial and her eventual self-awareness. Any action somewhere in between would surely exacerbate the problem enormously.

He was still pondering the problem when there was a gentle knock on the door and Dorgy stepped into the room. In his left hand was a brown envelope that he held like an unexploded bomb. He had shaved, after a fashion, and wore a donkey jacket over what looked to be a clean yellow shirt. His weathered face wore the same tortured look that Jack had seen the previous week, but since then something had obviously given him the courage to venture outside the security of his realm.

Jack stood up.

'Take a seat, Dorgy. Good to see you out and about again.'

The old man pulled the visitor's chair closer to Jack's desk and sat down cautiously.

'Sorry to come in on you like this, Jack Mitchell. Should have made an appointment, but I don't know what to do about this.'

Dorgy held up the envelope with a look of distaste playing round his crinkled mouth.

'Inland Revenue?'

'Revenue and Customs is what it says. I've never had one o' these 'ere forms before and I don't know what to do. I'm a pensioner. I don't owe no tax.'

Jack held out his hand and Dorgy gave him the envelope.

'It's a self-assessment tax return,' Jack confirmed, pulling out the form. 'I wonder what's triggered this. Do you have any income other than the state pension?'

'Just a small one from my employer, but they stop the tax their end.'

'And that's all? Absolutely no other income?'

'A dividend thing used to come sometimes, but that stopped a long time ago.'

Jack tapped the form gently against his keyboard and peered intently into Dorgy's rheumy eyes. 'What dividend was that, Dorgy?'

'Used to come regular for years from the company employed my old dad. He had quite a lot of shares and 'e passed 'em down to me.'

'UK company, is it?'

'Think so. Calls itself limited anyway.' Dorgy's brow furrowed. 'Except now they call themselves something else.'

'What do you mean? They changed their name, or they were taken over?'

'Oh, I don't know about bein' taken over or anything, Jack Mitchell.' Dorgy coughed and phlegm rattled around deep in his throat. 'All I know is the dividend stopped coming in regular. I never asked why.'

Jack leant back in his chair and unfolded the tax return. The screen saver began dancing around so he shifted the mouse. His half-completed letter sprang back on the screen as if to taunt him.

'Well, if it's a UK company any dividend would have carried a tax credit. And, as you're not a higher rate taxpayer there shouldn't have been any more income tax to pay. So, that still doesn't explain why HMRC has sent you a return.'

A glance at Dorgy's face told him that the old boy was not keeping up. The eyes had narrowed and his shaggy head nodded slowly, but there was no sign of comprehension there. This would have to be kept very simple indeed. Jack looked down at the form again.

'Dorgy, this is dated ninth February. Why've you left it so long before bringing it to me?'

The old man looked down at his feet and his mouth moved soundlessly. After a few seconds he looked up slowly, shrugged and then looked away again.

'Never mind. We've got until the end of October.'

'So, you won't have to put yourself out too much?' Dorgy had found his voice again.

'No, it doesn't look like more than a few minutes' work once we have all the papers. Don't worry about this, but I'll need your help in producing the stuff. Do you still have it all?'

'Should have. I put all the important papers in my desk,' he said proudly.

'Good. Then you pull them out and I'll come over and we'll get this form filled in. It should only take a few minutes.'

Dorgy's lips twitched into a thin smile. '"Tax don't 'ave to be taxing", eh Jack,' he said, quoting HMRC's lame slogan.

'That's right, Dorgy.' Jack stood up to signify the meeting was at an end. 'Except don't tell that to everyone, or I'll lose most of my clients.'

Dorgy rose with a loud click from his knees and then glanced back at Jack's desk enquiringly.

'Leave the form with me. I'll bring it over when I come.'

'Right.' Dorgy paused again and shuffled his feet in the time-honoured manner of one embarrassed. 'Now, your charges ... I'll pay whatever ... I mean how much ...?'

'Oh, don't worry about that. I won't be billing you. It really won't take much of my time and it'll be a pleasure to help you.' He placed a guiding hand on his new pro bono client's back. 'You can buy me a pint in the Plume some time.'

Dorgy muttered some phrase of thanks that Jack didn't catch and then began to make his way towards the back door.

'This way. The front door's quicker.'

The old man picked up his cap from where Catherine had left it.

'Oh, by the way,' he rested a hand on the doorknob, 'any further problems with the animal rights people?'

A defensive film immediately shot across Dorgy's eyes.

'No.'

'So, maybe that's the end of it.'

'Mebbe.' Dorgy eyed the door as if willing it to open.

'Well remember, if you do decide to talk about it ...'

The old man merely nodded and then moved forward as Jack opened the door. A gust of wind greeted them and Dorgy grabbed at the rim of his cap.

'Oh, just one more thing, Dorgy.'

He stopped, but did not turn around.

'What's the name of the company?'

Dorgy turned then, looking puzzled. 'Company?'

'The one that employed your father.'

'Oh, that. It was Life Solutions. Worked for them until he died.'

'Never heard of them.' Jack smiled and raised a hand. 'I'll call round in a few days then.'

Dorgy nodded and swivelled round to walk up the path.

As Jack closed the door and returned to his office he realised he had asked the wrong question. He needed to know the name of the company that had acquired the one that had employed Dorgy Pascoe's father.

Jack saved the letter he had been writing, brought up his search engine and keyed in Life Solutions. And there it was.

Founded in 1919 by biologist brothers Simon and George Towan this company carried out experimentation on animals for the furtherance of medical advancement. Operating from a laboratory near St Dennis in Cornwall the company began research and development under contract to small pharmaceutical businesses, later expanding to consultancy work for government agencies.

The small laboratory, originally a converted farm building, expanded as the business grew and by 1930 there were thirty employees. By that time the company had secured international research contracts and also offered a comprehensive range of clinical development services. It had achieved government approval of a large range of new medicines and provided services to pharmaceutical, crop protection and chemical companies. Some selected products achieved US Department of Agriculture approval and also became available worldwide. Scientists employed by the company became well known in scientific circles as lecturers and contributors to many scientific journals.

Simon Towan, also a noted philanthropist and art collector, died in 1959. At that time the shares of the private limited company were wholly owned by the Towan family. George Towan, who remained unmarried, died in 1970 and it is believed that he left his entire shareholding to long-standing and loyal members of the company's staff. This created a rift within the Towan family and eventually, in 1983, Life Solutions was sold to the international pharmaceutical company, Gammarbo Sciences Plc., for £52 million.

There was more, but that was enough for Jack Mitchell. He sat back slowly, still staring at his screen. Gammarho. One of the most significant, influential and progressive pharmaceutical companies in the world. And incredibly it looked like Dorgy Pascoe owned a chunk of it.

Or did he? Jack read again the bit about George Towan's bequest: *his entire shareholding to long-standing and loyal members.*

Suddenly he had an irrepressible urge to see those share certificates and also to know why the dividends had stopped.

A few minutes earlier a frightened old man had pottered into his study with a brown envelope and now, suddenly, it would appear that the same old man could be a shareholder in a leading pharmaceutical company: one that carried out animal experimentation.

There was now little doubt in his mind that the animal rights activists had been targeting Dorgy Pascoe.

CHAPTER 4

'Hi, Dad.'

Jack completed the swing of his axe and brought it down slightly off-centre onto the sycamore log, splitting it neatly in one blow. He laid the axe aside, wiped the dew from his brow, and turned to greet his daughter.

'Hello, love. You're home earlier than I expected.'

He crossed the chip-strewn floor of the log shed and kissed her loudly on the cheek.

'Woke early so managed to catch the first coach down.'

'So how did you get here from St Austell?' He wiped his hands on a rough piece of towel. 'You should have given me a call.'

'I got a lift from a guy who was going this way. Anyway, battery's flat on my mobile.'

'Again,' he chuckled. 'Never mind, you're here. Come in and have a drink. Have you seen Mum yet?'

They left the shed and walked across the grass towards the back door.

'Not yet.' She jerked a thumb at the rucksack on her back. 'Still carrying my hump. Came straight round here when I heard the chopping. Anyway, why're you cutting logs now?'

He laughed. 'Well, summer's been delayed ... and I need the exercise.'

Jack pushed the side door open and she went in, slipping the rucksack from her shoulders and onto a bench. He paused and then laid a restraining hand on her arm.

'Come into my office before you say hello to Mum.'

He glanced up the stairs as they made their way to his room. As he shut the door she turned to him and widened her eyes mischievously.

'Very mysterious.'

He gestured to the armchair and then sat down opposite her.

'Remind me ... when were you last home?'

'Not that long ago. Early spring. Just before I went back up to uni. Why?'

He lowered his head and a frown line appeared as he examined his fingernails. Looking up again he said, 'Before you left, did you notice a change in your mother? I mean did you see anything strange in her behaviour?'

It was her turn to frown and she pushed back a stray lock of her wavy auburn hair.

'Not really, Dad. I mean, she's always been a bit off-the-wall, hasn't she.' She shrugged and the hair flopped forward again. 'I mean, she's always ploughed her own furrow ... if that's the right expression.'

He gave her a wan smile.

'I know what you mean. The seeds of eccentricity have always been there, but ...'

'Is there a problem, Dad? Has she not been well or something?' She began picking at a loose strand on the arm of the chair.

'At the moment it's ... well, I'd say it's more of the *or something*. Small oddities in her behaviour. A sort of remoteness at times. Look, it might be nothing at all, but without making it too obvious, while you're here just ... observe.'

'You're worried, aren't you?'

'No, no, not ... not really worried ... yet, but I would appreciate your view.' He stood up quickly. 'Just don't make it too obvious. Now come and have a drink. I'll tell Mum you're here.'

She didn't stand up immediately, but stared earnestly at her father's face. It was a kindly face, but slightly careworn, with expressive creases that came to life according to his current mood. It was a face still youthful enough for her to imagine what a brother would look like, had he not died in early infancy.

She stood up and followed him out of the room.

The three of them lunched together in the small lean-to conservatory at the rear of the house. The morning sun had been strong enough to warm the room without the assistance of any artificial heating and in fact the automatic ceiling window would have opened had Jack not set the programme on manual. The warmth had activated the cluster flies that had lain dormant through the winter and in moments of silence during the meal their coordinated drone sounded like a warming up for the coming seasonal change.

To Jack's surprise Catherine was firing on all cylinders and had prepared a delicious roast shoulder of lamb and their daughter's favourite pudding, lemon meringue pie. She kept up a steady stream of bright conversation during the meal and showing no sign of the waywardness Jack had hinted at earlier. Several times he glanced at his daughter, trying to gauge a reaction, now feeling guilty that he had drawn attention to his concern. Perhaps he had misjudged the situation?

'And are you finding any time for leisure, darling, or is all work, work, work?' Catherine asked as she folded her napkin neatly beside her plate.

Jack's eyes narrowed as he watched irritably. Why does she always do that during the meal? Fold, lay down, pick up, unfold, put on lap, over and over again. He sighed.

'I think it's the other way around, Mum,' Rowan laughed. 'I try to find time for work between leisure. It's pretty hectic.'

'So that's what we're paying those massive fees for ... your playtime,' Jack exclaimed.

'Come on, Dad, you were at uni. You know what it's like. There are just so many lectures in a day and the rest is ... well, networking.'

'Networking, eh? In business that's jargon for oiling the wheels, hoping for a contract to come along. What's it mean for you?'

Catherine, unfolding her napkin again, leant towards Rowan. 'More pudding, darling?'

'No thanks, Mum,' she replied, then turned back to her father. 'Not contracts, just socialising. I'm doing the work necessary for my degree, but there's so much else going on. I'd be written off as a real spod if I spent most of my time ... what did you call it? ... sporting the oak?'

'No, of course you must have some fun, darling,' said Catherine, who had never been to university. Her fun had been spent at a finishing school in Switzerland: a finishing off school, Jack called it. A few years earlier they had travelled to Basel to see it, only to find it closed and now an apartment block. Finished off once and for all, Jack had said.

'Yes, sporting the oak,' he said and then added ruefully, 'Maybe you're right. I ended up with a third and didn't exactly excel at any sport.'

'Except the oak.' Catherine said airily.

'What?'

'You said you sported the oak.'

'Oh, I see. Sorry,' he replied, without enthusiasm.

Rowan, smiling, looked from one parent to the other and then pushed her chair back. 'Coffee anyone?'

'Only if you're brewing up the real stuff. How about you, Cath?'

Catherine gave him a strange look: as if noticing for the first time that he was sitting opposite her, and then her eyes twinkled a smile. 'I think I'll just go up for a post prandial rest, so no thanks to coffee. I'll be down a little later.'

'I hope so, otherwise I'll have to dig you out,' Jack chuckled. 'Coffee for two then, Rowan.'

Catherine gave a half yawn, waved airily and made for the stairs. He got up and joined his daughter in the kitchen.

'Business studies going well?'

'Business management actually, Dad.'

'Is there a subtle difference?'

She ladled some Blue Mountain into the percolator. 'I'm just splitting hairs. Yes, it's all going well. It certainly beats pure accounting for interest.'

He laughed. 'Well I certainly think you made the right choice there. Can't have two in the family.'

'If you had your choice again, what degree course would you do?'

'Oh, I don't know now. There are so many to choose from: over four hundred courses where you are aren't there?' He took two mugs down from a cupboard. 'I'd probably have done something totally absorbing and totally useless in terms of finding a worthwhile job afterwards.'

'Like?' she pressed.

He shrugged. 'I suppose something arty – history of art – both my interests combined.'

It was her turn to laugh. 'And with interests like that you became a chartered accountant! That doesn't stack up, Dad.'

'I know, but at least it's brought me a good living … and paid for your school fees, young lady.'

'And you're now your own boss, having made a pile in the city.'

'Oh, come on, darling! Hardly a pile. There was a good opportunity to jump ship and I'd accumulated a healthy pension pot, that's all.'

'Only teasing.' She patted his arm and then turned to the boiling kettle. 'So, what are you working on just now?'

'The usual. Some challenging tax cases. People who ignore the long arm of HMRC until it's nearly too late. It keeps the brain agile and brings in some beer money.'

'Any pro bono work?' She pushed the percolator plunger down. He hesitated. 'A little.'

It must have been the inflection in his voice, but she stopped what she was doing and looked quizzically at him.

' … and?'

'And what?'

'I get the impression there's something behind *a little*, that's all.'

He smiled and pushed the mugs towards her. 'You seem to know me too well.'

'Well, I am your daughter.'

'Come into the sitting room.' She poured out the coffee and followed him out of the kitchen. Before sitting down he stretched above the fireplace and straightened the oil portrait of Catherine that hung there, looking into its eyes for a few seconds.

'Have you heard of an anarchic bunch calling itself the Vivisection Action Group?'

She sat and placed her mug carefully on the round table beside her chair. 'Yes, of course. There are a few members at uni. They go off and protest where there are companies involved in animal vivisection. Why?'

'Are you a member?'

'No. I might sympathise with the cause, but I'm too into other things to get actively involved. What's this about?'

'Unfortunately they don't restrict their targeting to experimental companies. It seems that their latest victims are shareholders of those companies too. And a pretty cheap and cowardly way of putting over their prejudices that is as well.'

'That's a matter of opinion, Dad. Investors in companies that carry out such barbaric activities must expect criticism.'

'Even when those shareholders are old, defenceless and vulnerable?'

'Even then, they must know what they have invested in.'

'Do they?' He leaned towards her and repeated, 'Do they?'

'Well ... they must,' she said with decreasing conviction. 'Surely most people know what they've invested in.'

'Ha!' he rocked back in his chair. 'How little you know about people and their affairs. Yes, there actually are folk who not only don't know the business of the companies they put their money into, even more surprising, there are those who don't even know what investments they own!'

'How can that be? Companies send out statements. Dividends are paid. I know from my business studies that there's a lot of ignorance on financial matters, but ...'

'OK, only a very few don't know what they own, but I assure you they exist.'

There was a long pause and during that time they both heard a tap being run upstairs. This was followed by the warning bleeps of a vehicle reversing up Dowr Row.

'So, it sounds as if you have come across one of these unfortunates,' she said softly.

He nodded. 'Do you remember Dorgy Pascoe?'

'Of course. He lives in the almshouses. Is it him?' She sounded disbelieving.

'It is he. The vicar came to see me a short while ago to say that she believed he was in shock – not quite her words, but that was what she meant – after the almshouses had been targeted by the VAG. I don't think many of us knew who the hell they were, but they kindly left leaflets scattered all over the village to enlighten us. Anyway, Jane asked me to visit Dorgy to see what it was all about and, if necessary, give him some kind of comfort.'

'Oh, yes, you're a church visitor, aren't you?'

'Well drop the *church* bit. In a weak moment I agreed to visit the old and lonely in our parish. Some of them anyway.'

'Good for you.' She smiled and pushed her hair back. 'And good for them too, I expect.'

'So, I went to see the old boy. He eventually let me in, but verbally he wouldn't open up at all. Wouldn't tell me a thing. But, a few days ago he came to see me with a tax return to complete.'

'Ah, the pro bono job.'

'Exactly. I wasn't too pleased actually as I've got quite a lot on just now, but I couldn't turn him away ... especially after I found out why he's been sent the return.' Jack shook his head slowly at the memory. 'It seems the old chap has shares in a public company he didn't even know exists, let alone know what the company does.'

'How intriguing.'

'Have you heard of Gammarho?'

'Of course. Major pharma group. Probably in the top half dozen in the world. Don't tell me Dorgy ...'

'Dorgy is a shareholder and possibly one of some substance.'

Rowan put a hand to her mouth as Jack began to give her the full story as gleaned from Dorgy Pascoe. At the end of it she sat back and looked wide-eyed at her father.

'So, such financial innocents do exist,' she exclaimed. 'Do you know yet how much his investment is worth?'

'I've done a rough calculation, but it's based on an assumption and I could be thousands out.'

'OK, but based on your assumption?'

He closed his eyes for a few seconds as he recalled the figures.

'Well, the surviving brother, George Towan, owned fifty per cent of Life Solutions and according to the site data he left it all to long-serving employees. And here's the big assumption. As far as I can establish, the company employed about fifteen people at various levels, so let's assume that they were all eligible under George's definition of long-serving. The company was sold to Gammarho for £52 million. If you forget about any taxes and other debt obligations then George's fifty per cent would have been worth £26 million. Divide by fifteen and you get nearly £3.5 million. You see there are a lot of assumptions there. For example we don't know in what proportion George's legacy was shared out.'

'But still, that adds up to a whopping amount for a man like Dorgy Pascoe.'

'It's a tidy sum for anyone, let alone Dorgy.'

'Do you know how many Gammarho shares that equates to?'

'You mean Dorgy's part?'

'Yes.'

'No, not yet. I haven't checked to see what Gammarho's market price was back in 1974.'

'I still can't understand how anyone can have that kind of investment — especially if it was left to him by his father — and be totally ignorant about it.' She linked her fingers together. 'When are you going to see him again?'

'I haven't contacted him since he was here with the tax return, but I intend to after the weekend. I've really been too busy to follow it up yet.'

'Do you think he'll have a lot of tax to pay?'

'That depends on a number of factors. My hope is that it doesn't expand into a back duty case. The old boy might have spent all of the dividends he's received.'

'How far back can the tax people go?'

'Normally six years, but ...' He shrugged, '... if they suspect any kind of fraud it could be many more years than that.'

There was the sound of a lavatory being flushed above, followed by the closing of a door and muffled footsteps. Jack turned towards the sitting room door.

'Well, that rest didn't last long.'

That effectively put an end to discussion about Dorgy Pascoe and his inheritance. Rowan stood up and collected the coffee mugs. She paused beside her father's chair and looked down at him.

'Dad, I didn't actually notice anything odd about Mum's behaviour. Certainly not at lunch.'

'No, true, but the moods do come and go.' He grinned at her. 'I expect she's making a special effort for your visit.'

'Or, could you be imagining things?

'Maybe.' He stood up, easing his shoulders as they both headed out of the room. 'I sincerely hope so.'

That afternoon, with the tide low, they all went for a walk on the beach. There had been a spring storm two days before and seaweed was piled high in wavy rows along the high water mark. The weed was still wet and it now glistened brown and polished under a weak setting sun. A few people were spread along the length of the half-mile expanse of sand, many exercising their dogs and some just strolling and breathing in the fresh salty air. A clutch of gulls gathered at the water's edge, keeping a wary distance from other beach visitors. Away from the shore, but close enough to read its harbour marking, a fishing boat lolled in the light swell as a couple of fishermen tended their pots.

Catherine and Rowan strode out arm-in-arm chatting away and occasionally stopping to examine something that the tide had washed up. Jack took up a position just behind them, observing all about him, trying not to think about Dorgy Pascoe's inheritance.

Rowan decided to return the following evening and Jack drove her to the coach station as a thin mist rolled in to meet the dusk.

'If VAG were targeting Dorgy,' she said, turning to him after a period of silence, 'how did they know he's a shareholder of Gammarho?'

He changed gear and gunned the accelerator to pass a farm vehicle.

'It's not that difficult to access the names of members of a public company'

'That doesn't seem right. Shouldn't the records of ... what are they called? ... registrars be secure?'

'They should be. I mean, if you want to ask about your own

shareholding there are all sorts of checks, passwords and so on that you have to give before anything is divulged. But, I suppose, a fanatical organisation like VAG has equally fanatical moles inside registrars' offices whose fanaticism outweighs their duty to shareholders.'

'Oh, I see. But they're not all fanatics, Dad. They're mostly ordinary people who feel strongly about the cruelty of vivisection. The dumb animals that suffer have no other defenders, so they feel justified in protesting.'

'Simple protesting and petitioning in a civilised way is acceptable, but terrorising defenceless old people simply because they own shares in a pharmaceutical company is not. And I'm afraid that this kind of extreme behaviour is often the outcome when people become immersed in single interest groups ... they develop a warped and irrational perspective of priorities.'

She couldn't help laughing. He raised an eyebrow and glanced at her. This was a generational difference of opinion, one that appeared frequently in their discussions, but it was never going to be an issue of lasting division. They had too much respect for each other.

As they approached the outskirts of St Austell she fumbled in her pockets until she found her ticket. She pulled down the sun visor and checked her face, once again pushing back the stray lock of hair.

'Dad, I've been thinking.'

'Yes?'

'You say that Mum has been acting strangely recently.' A pause. 'Patrick would have been twenty-one last month. Do you think ...?'

He turned left at the red brick bank building and drove slowly past some parked taxis.

One of them pulled out just ahead and he eased back.

'Do you know, that never occurred to me. I'm ashamed to say that I'd completely overlooked that date. That year even. It's not that I've wiped him from my memory. How could I? My only son ...' He looked at her with a pained expression. 'I'm sorry.'

'It's just that mothers ... you know.'

'No, no, you could be right. Maybe I've been blind to the situation.' He arrived in front of the station, parked the car in the only available slot by the entrance and turned off the engine. 'Thanks for mentioning it.'

'I might be completely wrong, but it's a possibility.'

'No, darling, you were right to bring it up. I really should have been more aware.'

He sat, still gripping the wheel and Rowan stared at a small pulse that throbbed on his hand. Rowan looked at her watch: ten minutes before the bus was due to arrive. It was always late, but she had no inclination to stay in the car until it came. It suddenly reminded her of being taken back to school all those years ago. Her father was still staring ahead, temporarily caught up in some reverie and she wondered again if Patrick would have looked like him.

'Look, Dad, don't wait for me.' She reached into the back seat for her rucksack. 'I'll go into the waiting room for a coffee.'

He blinked and turned to her with a faint smile. 'OK, if that's what you want. Have you got something to eat on the journey?'

'Mum made some sandwiches.' She leaned across and kissed his cheek.

He squeezed her arm gently. 'Thanks for coming down to see the old folk. Always appreciated.'

She opened the door and stepped out onto the still damp tarmac. He lowered the window and she bent down to look in. 'No problem. And let me know about Dorgy and his shareholding.'

'Not sure I can do that,' he laughed. 'Client confidentiality.'

'What, even with pro bono work?'

'Even with pro bono work. Have a safe journey.' He started to raise the window and then shouted after her, 'And don't leave it so long before you come again.' But she was already on her way to the waiting room.

He watched her through the glass for a few seconds and then started the engine.

As he drove out of the station yard, he reflected: yes, Patrick would have been twenty-one.

CHAPTER 5

He paused halfway up the stairs to adjust his hold on the papers he was carrying, which was just long enough for the timer switch to click off the ceiling light when he was three steps from the top. Being daytime a mean streak of natural light oozed through a grubby skylight, otherwise he would have been stumbling in the gloom. What, he wondered, did the less able and much older residents make of this sorely inadequate system?

Dorgy had no telephone, neither landline nor mobile, so Jack realised he was visiting speculatively. Standing now outside the door marked *Hawker*, he knocked three times and stood back.

He gave it thirty seconds and then banged again, this time more forcefully. A door opened, but it was the wrong one. He turned to peer down the corridor.

'Hello Mrs Harris.' He never knew whether or not to address her as Mavis. 'Do you know if Dorgy's in?'

'Young Jack Mitchell is it?'

'I don't know about young, Mrs Harris, but yes, it's me.'

She nodded as if he had answered the correct password. 'Haven't seen him today, so I can't say where he's to.'

'Pity. There's something I need to talk to him about and I thought he might be expecting me.' He looked at Dorgy's door again and then turned back to Mavis. 'Do any of you on this floor have telephones?'

'Not telephone lines, no, but Harry there,' she pointed at the door between them, 'he has a mobile telephone. It's an Orange.'

Jack resisted the urge to smile. In the kingdom of the blind, the one-eyed man is king, so Harry obviously had the communications seat on the upstairs throne in the almshouses.

'You wouldn't know his number would you?' He knew it was a pointless question.

'Nooo.' She sounded shocked that such a question should be put to her. It was as if Jack had asked her for Harry's inside leg measurement.

'Right. Well, I'll just have to try some other time. Thank you Mrs Harris.'

It must have been the sound of their voices passing to and fro along the bare corridor, because, just as Jack was turning to press the timer switch for his descent, the door to *Hawker* swung open.

'There he is,' Mavis Harris exclaimed triumphantly, but rather unnecessarily, as if it were she who had conjured Dorgy from his lair.

'Thank you Mrs Harris,' Jack repeated and then nodded a greeting to the figure in the doorway. Without waiting for an invitation he stepped inside and Dorgy closed the door rapidly.

'Not much gets past Mrs Harris,' Jack said over his shoulder as he removed his jacket.

'Oh, she'm alright.' Dorgy gave a gurgling chuckle. 'She'm our neighbourhood watch.'

'Have you known each other long?'

'Yeeees.' He dragged the word out as if to emphasise the number of years. 'Boy and girl almost. She were at our wedding.'

'Funny then that you should both end up in the almshouses.' He bit his lip as soon as the words came out. The term *end up* might well be accurate, but it was not the most tactful way of putting it. And then, as Dorgy started to reply, Jack suddenly realised that he actually had no idea how old Dorgy Pascoe was. Maybe he really wasn't an old man at all: just a man who looked old through natural wear and tear.

'We been jogging along nearby ever since, so not so funny really.'

'No, I suppose not.' He turned and looked expectantly at the roll-top desk. The old man had not yet asked him why he was there. 'Now, Dorgy, shall we get down to business?'

'You come about the tax return business then.' It was a statement.

'That's right. Sorry to come unannounced, but as you've no phone ...' He shrugged.

'That's alright, Jack Mitchell.' He rolled back the desk top like a conjuror revealing his latest trick. 'I been expecting you any time this week. It's all here.'

'Excellent. Shall we look at the papers here, or ...?' he looked around the room for somewhere else to settle.

'Here will do, if you just bring up that chair.'

Jack pulled over an upright chair from near the window and as he did so noticed that the remains of the mud clod were still smearing the glass. Perhaps the old chap wanted to leave it there as a reminder. Or maybe he had just forgotten about it. He sat down and took out a pen.

'Now, what I need to do is to record all your sources of income for the tax year ended fifth April. Some might have had tax deducted at source, so we need to note that as well.' He pulled a face at the disorganised array of papers that lay on the desk and then turned to Dorgy. 'We'll start with your pension shall we?'

For the next few minutes Jack thumbed through dockets, statements and some correspondence, until he was satisfied that he had sufficient evidence of his pro bono client's yearly income. Dorgy was receiving a state pension and also an occupational pension from his former employer. The latter was not great – a little more than he received from the state – but together they pushed him into the lower tax bracket. This liability would presumably be covered through his tax coding, but now the proverbial elephant in the room loomed large before him.

'Now, investment income.' Jack flicked through the papers, but couldn't find what he was looking for. 'Have you got any dividend warrants from Gammarho, Dorgy?'

'Gammar who?'

'Gammarho. The company that took over Life Solutions,' he said with a touch of impatience.

'Oh, they! Sorry, I still can't get used to ... yes, they're in here.' He reached across the desk and pulled open a small drawer that was stuffed full of assorted papers.

Jack glanced at him. Gammarho acquired Life Solutions in 1983 and the fellow still wasn't tuned into the company's name.

Dorgy was now grunting while he shuffled the papers, clearly unable to interpret what it was Jack needed.

'Shall I take them?' Jack asked gently and reached over. 'We probably won't need more than about four of these, but let me check the dates.'

He was prepared for something out of the ordinary, but he could not help a sharp intake of breath as he pulled out the most recent dividend warrant. A quick glance at Dorgy, but the man seemed quite unmoved by Jack's reaction. In fact he was now staring out of the window. The slim piece of paper trembled slightly in Jack's hand.

Dorgy Pascoe was the registered owner of 110,000 Gammarho ordinary shares.

Dorgy suddenly turned away from the window. 'Sorry, I should have asked. Would you like a mug of tea? This looks like it might be thirsty work.'

Without waiting for an answer he rose and straightened his back. 'I'm putting the kettle on anyway, so ...'

'Yes, that would be nice, Dorgy,' he heard himself reply, but he was still staring down at the company's dividend warrant. He flipped over a few more papers and found the previous statement was in fact an election form, requiring the shareholder to opt either for a cash dividend or for the equivalent value to be reinvested.

'Right. I'll be a few minutes.' Dorgy shuffled off. 'Milk and sugar?'

'No sugar, thanks.'

One hundred and ten thousand shares.

He had checked the market price before going out and it was hovering around £16.56, slightly down on the day so far. He pulled out a pocket calculator, tapped in the numbers and then sat back wide-eyed. The old man – if indeed he was old – who had just gone somewhere to brew up a mug of tea, seemed to be quite oblivious of the fact that he had shares in a public quoted company worth in excess of £1,821,000. Shares in a company whose name he could not even remember. Shares until recently he did not even seem to know he owned. In the twenty-first century, how was this possible?

Even anti-vivisectionists had a better knowledge of Dorgy's shareholdings than this innocent did, because it was now obvious beyond any doubt that was why they had targeted him with their mud bombs and taunts.

One hundred and ten thousand shares.

He examined the warrant. This one was dated 31st March and was the final payment for the year. He thumbed back through the pile and found two earlier election statements. In total the annual dividend amounted to 36 pence. He did another calculation. Not an outstanding yield, but with the number of shares Dorgy owned it produced £39,600 for the year.

Jack couldn't help himself. He started laughing quietly at the absurdity of the situation. Oh, yes, Dorgy, you will have a tax liability. It was a couple of minutes before he realised the millionaire himself was standing behind him, wearing a slightly bemused expression.

'Dorgy, I think you'd better sit down before you drop that tea down the back of my neck.'

He reached out and took one of the mugs and Dorgy then eased himself onto his chair. Jack placed the steaming mug on an old envelope, well away from the other papers, and began to search for the right way to launch into what was to be a searching enquiry. Like a faithful but slightly dim family dog the old chap sat sipping his tea and watching Jack's every expression.

'Do you actually know how much this is worth?' Jack began, slowly waving one of the dividend warrants in front of a pair of unblinking eyes.

A few seconds passed before Dorgy replied. It was as if he suspected he had been asked a trick question and was fearful of trapping himself in Jack's snare.

'I don't rightly know, Jack Mitchell. There's a lot of shares there, but I've never checked their worth.'

Jack stared at him. It was entirely probable that the man did not even know where to look for the value of Gammarho shares. Perhaps he didn't know the difference between a private and a public quoted company. He decided to lower his level of expectation even more.

'Do you want to know how much they're worth?'

'Suppose I'd better ... if it helps you do the tax form,' he replied through an embarrassed chuckle.

'Well, it won't help complete your tax return, but I'll explain later why the value is important. Now, I suggest you put that tea down before there's a spillage.'

Dorgy shrugged, but did as he was told.

'Okay.' Jack cleared his throat and began. 'You are the registered owner of 110,000 ordinary shares in Gammarho, a publicly quoted pharmaceutical company. Publicly quoted means that the shares are listed on the London Stock Exchange and are traded daily. By traded I mean the shares are being bought and sold by the public, by institutions, other companies, pension funds etcetera. The buying and selling sets a price, like any other goods in a free market.' He paused. 'Are you with me so far?'

'I think so ... except,' he scratched his head, 'how do they buy and sell? I mean it's not like a cattle auction, is it?'

'No, not quite like an auction, because you're not bidding directly against another buyer. The price is set according to whether there are more buyers than sellers, or vice versa.' He felt this was heading off at a tangent, so returned to the main theme. 'Buying and selling is usually done through an agent, called a broker, but these are details. I'm just trying to set the scene for how your shares are valued in the market.'

He raised his eyebrows and peered encouragingly at his audience. Dorgy was nodding slowly, like one of those naff dogs that hang from rear-view mirrors. That was probably as good as it was going to get, Jack thought, so he continued.

'The price of each Gammarho share this morning before I came out was about £16.50, so if you multiply that by the number of shares you own ...' He paused like a compère about to announce the winner of a competition. '... the result is about £1.8 million.'

The silence was complete. At that moment even the road outside was empty of passing traffic. Jack thought for a moment that Dorgy had stopped breathing. Perhaps he had, because after a good half minute had passed he suddenly sucked in a gulp of air.

'Pounds?' he whispered and then made a big performance of clearing his throat.

'Yes, pounds, not pence. These shares are worth over £1.8 million.'

'Bloody hell, Jack Mitchell, that can't be right.' He was now shaking his head vigorously. 'Why didn't he tell me what they're worth? Why didn't anyone tell me?'

'Why didn't who tell you, Dorgy?'

My old Dad, that's who!' he exclaimed and Jack found it hard to conceal a smile. 'He passed them shares on to me and never a word about what they're worth.'

Dorgy was suddenly showing signs of agitation, rocking back and forth and clenching and unclenching his fists. It was if his late father had dealt him a cruelly unjust blow rather than enriching him beyond his wildest expectations. Jack reached out and laid a hand on the old man's trembling arm.

'When did he die, Dorgy? When did your father die?'

'What?' He seemed to be rapidly tipping over the edge of reason.

'Your father, Dorgy?' Jack repeated calmly. 'Take it easy now. Can you remember the year your father died?'

Dorgy stopped rocking and focused on Jack, as if surprised to see he was still there. A small line of saliva was running from the corner of his mouth and it slipped to his chin when eventually he spoke.

'Course I remember. He died five year ago.' He was calming down now. 'Why?'

'Only five years ago? I thought ...'

'He was ninety-six,' Dorgy said as if explaining something to a child. He took out a soiled handkerchief and wiped his chin.

'Good Lord.' Jack shook his head. 'So, did he leave these shares to you in his will?'

'Nooo. He didn't leave no will. He had nothing to leave anybody ... except his old pocket watch. The one he got from Life Solutions.'

'But the shares, Dorgy. For God's sake, that's hardly nothing.'

'No, you don't understand, Jack Mitchell.' Dorgy had regained his composure and was now chuckling in a kind of staccato cackle, his tobacco-stained teeth showing like tree stumps through the undergrowth of his three-day stubble. 'He gave them shares to me years before he died. He thought he was going to pop his clogs when he was eighty-three ... he had a bad chill one winter ... so he made them over to me. But he never said what they was worth. He did it all legal like and had the shares written over to me ... his only surviving child. That's how I got 'em. I knew what the company did, so that's how I knew they were shouting at me that night. But I thought it were Life Solutions, not Gammerwatsit.'

Jack's mouth was half open as he took in this vital information. He felt at last that he was beginning to hack his way out of a jungle of obfuscation. He didn't reply immediately, but looked down and began searching through the assorted Gammarho papers. It was probably more than fifteen years ago now, so there was little chance of it being there. And so it proved. He put the papers down and looked up at Dorgy.

'When your father transferred the shares to you, did he ask you to sign anything?'

'Well, I dunno.' He scratched his chin with an unkempt fingernail. 'It were a long time ago. I can't rightly remember. I mean, I might have.'

With emphasis on the word *might* he appeared satisfied that he had absolved himself of any guilt by way of forgetfulness, so he inclined his head to one side waiting for Jack's response.

Jack glanced at the mug at the side of the desk. It was no longer steaming.

'What I'm getting at, Dorgy, is,' he resumed cautiously, 'were you asked to sign any kind of mandate? That means an authorisation to the company to accumulate shares to your holding rather than receive dividends. This is an important point, because I can't find any dividend vouchers amongst these papers that predate the beginning of last tax year.'

'Mandate?' He grinned rather foolishly. 'If I did and it's not there now, then I don't know where it's to after all these years. I haven't always been in the almshouses you know. Moved around a bit before I come here, so maybe they got lost, or something.'

'OK. Can you at least tell me when you started getting dividends from Gemmarho?'

'Ah, that I can. Last autumn it was. I got a cheque. Then another came a fortnight ago. That was very nice, I can tell you.'

I bet it was, Jack thought.

Suddenly out of nowhere a handsome cheque arrives from a company you've never heard of. Wouldn't any normal person question this? No, he mustn't think of old Pascoe as being anything other than normal. Simple and incurious maybe, but not abnormal. But, why did the company suddenly start to pay dividends after so many years? All he could think of was that the warrant had lapsed and Dorgy had ignored an application for it to be renewed.

Try another tack.

'Did your father never receive dividends from Gammarho? After all, he'd owned them for many years before he passed them over to you.'

'No, he never said. Don't think he did though. He wouldn't have known what to do with the money anyways.'

Jack smiled. 'And do you, now that nearly £40,000 a year is coming in?'

'Haven't spent a penny of it yet, Jack Mitchell,' Dorgy announced proudly. 'Saving it up.'

'What for? Round the world trip?'

Dorgy gave no verbal reply, but threw back his head and hooted with laughter. The old chair he sat on creaked alarmingly and he slapped his wiry grey hair with a gnarled hand. Jack just watched him and marvelled that such a naïve individual could make his way through the complexities of the twenty-first century unaided. Maybe now he couldn't. If word got out that such an innocent was sitting on that sort of money the sharks would surely soon start to smell blood.

'Right, I tell you what I think has happened,' Jack said as soon as the old man had stopped laughing. 'Your father, for whatever reason, must have asked you to sign a mandate as a condition of accepting his gift. If that was the case ... and I can't think of any other reason why you would not have been receiving dividends ... then I suspect that mandate came up for renewal last year. If you ignored it then the default would have been that the company assumed you wanted dividends instead of rolling up further shares into your holding. Does that sound reasonable?'

Dorgy opened his eyes wide and gave an exaggerated shrug. Silly question, Jack Mitchell. When Gammarho took over Life Solutions in 1983 Pascoe senior might have signed a warrant instructing the company to have dividends rolled up, but he suspected that now he would never know what happened some years after that.

'Well, we'll go with that premise anyway.' Jack began to gather the relevant documents together. 'So, now I can at least complete your tax return from what I've got.'

'Thank you, Jack Mitchell, and I'm sorry it's taken up so much of your time.'

'Oh, don't worry about that, Dorgy.' He smiled. 'It's actually been rather interesting. An education you might say.'

'Well, I hope you've all you need there.'

'I should think so.'

They both stood up and as Jack began filling the folder he'd brought a thought occurred to him. It wasn't in his brief to raise the question and maybe Dorgy would take umbrage at being asked, but he felt it was a loose end that he must try to tie.

'By the way, Dorgy, have you made a will?'

The old man stared at him and Jack met his gaze. For a few seconds they looked like two fighters, each waiting for the other to throw the first punch. Then Dorgy dipped his mouth and gave one of his dramatic shrugs.

'Yer, I made a will.' His eyes narrowed. 'Why d'you ask?'

'That's good, because you've now got a fair sized fortune to leave someone.' He tied the string around his folder. 'If you die intestate ... that is, without leaving a will ... your next of kin will inherit. But you say you have no direct next of kin. It's not my business to ask who will benefit, but without a legally binding will ... well it could become messy.'

'No, I've taken care of that, don't you worry.' He began to move towards the door. 'And the extra won't mek no difference. I've taken care of it.'

Yes, Jack thought, interesting was certainly the right word for the afternoon's work, but something still remained unexplained. He wasn't sure why, but it was one more thing that he had to know before he left. He stopped at the door and turned to Dorgy.

'Well, now we can guess the reason for the VAG harassment, can you tell me why you couldn't talk about it before?'

With that simple question he obviously touched a tender spot. Dorgy drew in a long breath and avoided Jack's direct gaze. He now stood awkwardly with one hand on the door knob, his lips twitching silently. Then suddenly he seemed to make up his mind.

'No.' Jaw muscles were working under the stubble. 'No, Jack Mitchell, it's nothing I can ... no.'

'OK. If you still don't want to talk about it ...'

And that was it. Shame to end on that note, he thought, as they parted with merely a terse nod of the head from Dorgy Pascoe: not even a *thank you* for all the pro bono work. Jack was barely out of the door when it closed sharply behind him. It struck him as being a very strange reaction to a straightforward question.

Jack pressed the corridor light and walked slowly down the stairs.

Back in his study he reached out and picked up the burbling telephone.

'Hi, Dad.'

'Hello, darling.' Jack pushed his chair back and prepared himself for a conversation with his daughter. It could be short and to the point – usually something to do with money – or long and rambling: the latter if she was bored and had nothing much to say to her mother.

'How are you?' She sounded slightly out of puff.

'I'm fine. Keeping out of trouble, you know. Sounds as if you've been on the treadmill.'

'No, nothing so energetic, but I've just run up the stairs from the library.'

'So, what's new, since you were here?'

'Ah, well I have some information for you. You remember we

talked about the VAG ... the Vivisection Action Group ... when I was home a couple of weeks ago? You thought they might have been targeting old Dorgy. Well they've started getting active around here and a couple of them have been arrested for criminal damage.'

'The same ones you told me about?'

'Yes, two of them. The others got away, but these two were grabbed by security guards as they were cutting wires on a perimeter fence.'

'Where was this?'

'A laboratory not far from the university. The VAG discovered that they're carrying out experiments and were trying to liberate the animals ... or so it's said.'

'Is the lab connected with Gammarho?'

'I really don't know. It operates under another name, but it might be connected with Gammarho.'

'And do you know if they'll be prosecuted?'

'I think so. The company won't want the publicity of course, but at the same time they can't be seen to be letting VAG and their supporters get away with vandalism. It's a sort of Greenpeace situation.'

'So, are you suggesting that VAG is becoming more active nationally? Or is the timing of this just coincidental?'

'I'm sorry, that's another don't know. I just wanted to tell you, in case it ties in with anything going on down in Fentonmar.' He heard her slurp. 'And has there been another incident down there?'

'No, all quiet on this front. But I have established from talking to Dorgy that he was their target. I have no doubt about that. I'm not researching VAG in any way, but I am intrigued to know exactly how they found out he's a Gammarho shareholder.'

He was on the verge of telling her just how substantial a shareholder he is, but reined back just in time. Confidentiality applied equally to pro bono clients. Also, if members of the VAG organisation were connected with the university, that could be where the client list mole resided. Best that Rowan knew little of Dorgy's affairs. He thanked her for the information and then switched tracks onto more general topics.

As Rowan talked on about university activities, people she'd met and parties she'd been to, Jack studied the world outside his study window. The new birch leaves were now fully out, but in contrast many of those shed the previous autumn now lodged along the top of the privet hedge which bordered their stone wall. He disliked that hedge and would have rooted it out long ago in favour of an escallonia, if only he had had Catherine's support. He disapproved of privet, not for any botanical reason, but simply because to him it represented suburbia. In its own environment, along with Japanese flowering cherry, he would not have given it any consideration whatsoever. But here, in rural Cornwall, it was simply out of place. Now at least escallonia had a flower and grew ...

'Dad? Are you still with me?'

'Mmm? Yes, of course.'

'Next time I'll talk to Mum. At least she listens when I'm prattling on,' she sighed. 'By the way, how's she been recently?'

'Oh, not bad, but I'm keeping an eye on her.' He saw no benefit in mentioning the half-empty bottle of gin in the airing cupboard; the strange letter she was trying to compose to the constituency MP; or her new obsession about the neighbour's overhanging clematis. These things would pass in due course, before another eccentricity would appear. Yes, he would keep an eye on it.

'That's good,' she said dubiously. Then, just as he thought the conversation was reaching its natural conclusion she added, 'By the way, those two VAG protesters I told you about ... apparently one of them comes from Cornwall.'

'Wow, your grapevine really is working well. Whereabouts in Cornwall?'

'Camborne, I think. Do you think there's some connection with your lot?'

'Who knows? I have no idea how the network of a protest group operates, but it's quite possible. I'll bear that in mind if we have another incident.'

'OK, Dad. Must dash now. 'Bye.'

'Bye, darling.'

Jack swung his chair back into action mode. He had completed Dorgy's return in draft and now just had to verify the figures before he got the man's signature. It was nearly time to visit the almshouses again.

CHAPTER 6

A fine drizzle was being driven almost horizontally across Fore Street by a steady north-westerly as Jack made his way, head down, towards the almshouses. Some unswept rubbish scurried around in huddles at the edge of the pavements and the hanging sign outside the convenience store advertising hot coffee within rocked to and fro at the whim of the wind. Apart from an unaccompanied dog that scurried homeward hugging the walls of the terraced houses, there was no one else in sight. Or, almost no one.

Jack was almost alongside the store, trying to keep his hood from being yanked back by a playful gust, when an equally rain-proofed figure stepped out from its door.

'Jack! Just the man. Come inside for a minute.'

The Reverend Jane Stokes seized his arm and practically pulled him into the store. He bent down to straighten a stack of wire baskets and then moved over towards the magazine stand.

'Hello, Jane. Filthy day.' He glanced up at the wall clock. 'What can I do for you?'

'Jack, it's Dorgy.' She glanced over his shoulder and lowered her voice. 'I've just come from seeing Mavis and she says he's in quite a state.'

'Why? I'm just on my way to visit him myself.'

'He's been burgled.' Her eyes bulged as she reported the news.

'Good grief! What on earth could he have that anyone would . . .?' He stopped himself.

'I know. It makes no sense, unless it's a case of mistaken identity.' She shook her head and raindrops flicked across his face from her hood. 'First the animal rights people and now this. It really is too bad.'

'How did they get in?'

'Jack,' she looked reproachfully at him, 'you know that place. There's no security. Anyone can walk in.'

'I know, but his room ... he always keeps that locked.' He recalled the grinding of a key in the old man's lock when first he was admitted.

'I'm no expert in the field of burglary, but I don't think those locks would present a challenge to someone with the right tools.'

'So, they didn't even need to force their way in?'

'Doesn't seems so, no.' She stood back to allow a customer to pass.

'And now he's upset again.' He glanced down at the damp briefcase. 'Do you know what they took?'

'No. He wouldn't ... or perhaps couldn't ... say. And the funny thing is that he's quite insistent that the police are not involved.'

'You asked him, I presume?'

'No, he wouldn't see me, but Mavis says he's absolutely adamant. No police. He wouldn't explain why.'

Jack looked down at his damp shoes: the same reason why he wouldn't speak about the VAG harassment, he thought. Only this time it was even more directly personal.

'Do you think he'll see me? I've got some papers for him to sign.'

She dipped her mouth, opened her eyes wide again and shrugged. 'You can but try, my dear. You can but try.'

He smiled. 'I'll do that. And thank you for letting me know.'

She nodded, patted him on the arm and then moved swiftly to the door. 'Tell me what happens,' she called over her shoulder as she stepped out onto the pavement.

He left the shop and headed on down Fore Street.

Jack stood outside *Hawker*'s door and was about to knock when a slight sound made him turn and peer down the gloom of the sparse corridor. Mavis Harris's oval face was framed by the yellow glow that showed little more than a slit through her doorway. They stared at each other for a couple of seconds before Jack grabbed his opportunity.

'Mrs Harris,' he whispered down the landing as Mavis began a retreat into her burrow. 'Could I have a word?'

The old lady paused and then opened the door a little wider. Even in the poor light he could see her fleshy cheeks reddening guiltily: she had been caught snooping. He held up a pacifying hand as he approached.

'I'm glad to see you,' he said reassuringly. 'May I talk to you for a minute about Dorgy?'

She glanced quickly over her shoulder and Jack thought she already had a visitor, but then he guessed she was merely concerned at the state of her room. He doubted that old single people like this had many visitors, at which thought it was his turn to feel guilty. Had he not given an undertaking to visit the lonely of the parish?

She was looking at him again uncertainly.

'I was just going in to talk to Dorgy about a form he asked me to fill in for him.' He pointed to the briefcase as proof. 'But the vicar told me about the burglary and it might be a good idea to talk to his neighbour first.'

'Vicar's just been here, not an hour ago,' she said, still guarding her door.

'I know. I saw her in the shop. So I'm just wondering if you or perhaps Harry ...?'

'No good talking to Harry, my 'ansome. When his aid's off he's deaf as post.' She still stood her ground.

'Well then, if I could talk to you ...' He smiled. 'May I?'

'Alright then.' She gave a little sigh and stepped aside. 'Come in then. Would you like a cup of tea?'

'No thank you, Mrs Harris. I won't be long.'

'Suit yourself, dear.' She padded into her room and then turned to him with a scolding face. 'And it's Mavis. Mrs Harris is far too respectful for the likes of me.'

She cackled and then waved an arm in the direction of a floral patterned armchair. It looked suspiciously like one that they had taken to the tip last spring. He must have stared at it for too long, because she said, 'Very comfortable. It belonged to my mother.'

'Ah.' He sat down.

She fussed around a couple of cushions on the chair's smaller partner and then lowered her broad beam uncompromisingly onto it.

'Now Mr Mitchell, you want to ask about Dorgy Pascoe.'

He nearly said *call me Jack*, but decided to save that for another meeting. He settled the briefcase by his chair.

'Jane Stokes says that he's shaken up by the burglary, but he won't report it to the police. Why do you think that is?'

'I really don't know.' She frowned deeply and turned her gaze to a black porcelain cat that perched on the mantelpiece. 'I've knowed him for many years, but still he'll only tell you what he wants to tell you. Very private man is Dorgy.'

'Have you talked to him at all since it happened?'

'Oh, yes. I took him a cup of tea ... to calm his nerves, you know.'

He nodded, as if understanding the recuperative powers of a hot cup of tea.

'And he said nothing? He didn't tell you what had been stolen, or disturbed?'

'No. Just drank the tea quiet like and thanked me when he'd finished.' Then, with a spark of recollection. 'Oh, he did tell me to keep my door well locked, but of course I always do. Now I think I'll have another lock put on an' all.'

'Very wise.' Now for the vital question. 'Tell me, Mavis, did you see or hear anything at the time this happened?'

'No, more's the pity. I was out at a Seniors' do at the hall and it must have been then.' A chubby hand went to her cheek. 'And to think he might have been waiting and watching for me to go out.'

'You don't miss much then.' He remembered her reputation as a one-woman neighbourhood watch.

She cackled again; a scratchy high-pitched laugh that nevertheless conveyed a self-deprecating wit. 'You calling me a nosey parker then?'

'Not at all. Everyone should look out for their neighbour.'

'That's what I say.' She looked him approvingly. 'But I'm sorry I can't help with anything else.'

'That's alright. And Harry? You say he's deaf?'

'That's right. Wouldn't hear even if that Concorde came right overhead.'

He didn't break the news to her. There probably were some who still thought that distant clay mining explosions were Concorde breaking the sound barrier.

'So no chance that he heard anything?'

'He only puts his hearing aid in to talk to someone ... or to listen to his organ music.'

'Organ?'

'He used to be the organist at St Rumon's and I think he misses it. Had to give up because of the arthritis.'

'I see. Do you know if he heard anything on the night the animal rights people came?'

'Yes he did, because he'd been listening to his music at the time. He and I stood on the balcony to see what the row was about.'

'Did Dorgy come out on the balcony too?'

'No, he stayed in. Least I didn't see 'im come out.'

There was silence between them then and Jack knew he would get nothing more of interest from her. He gripped the chair and heaved himself up with a grunt.

'Well thank you for your time, Mavis.' He reached down for his case and then jerked a thumb towards the door. 'Do you think he'll let me in?'

She hefted herself up at the third attempt and then straightened her dress. 'It depends on his mood, my dear. You can but try.'

Mavis led the way to her door, opened it and stood aside.

'Good luck,' she said and then added awkwardly, 'I enjoyed our little chat.'

The door closed again before he could reply and he heard the chain going back. It was if she were telling him that she wouldn't be watching this time. He smiled into the greyness of the landing and then turned to walk the few strides to *Hawker*.

For the second time that afternoon he paused at the door, but this time to bend down and inspect the lock. There were no abrasions around the keyhole and clearly no indication that there had been a forced entry. But it was an old-fashioned mortise type that would present no challenge to someone with the right set of tools ... if there was no key engaged on the inside.

He reached up and rapped firmly on the bare oak door.

'Dorgy, it's me, Jack Mitchell,' he shouted.

When there was no reply, or indication of movement towards the door he raised his voice a decibel. 'Come on, Dorgy, open up. I've got some papers for you to sign. We can't complete the tax return until it's got your signature on it.'

He had already decided that he wasn't going to move until he'd been admitted. The old man's intransigence had begun to try his patience. He had his own life to lead, work to do and other fee-paying clients to attend to. This old fellow might have had a couple of upsets in his otherwise tranquil daily life, but that was no real reason for expecting him, his pro bono adviser, to jump as and when it suited.

Still nothing from inside.

'Dorgy, I'm staying here until you open the door. I'll set up camp if necessary.' He stepped back, leaned against a wall and began tapping a foot loudly against the skirting board.

Nearly five minutes must have passed and he was running out of tunes to whistle, when suddenly the key turned in *Hawker's* lock. The door opened slowly to reveal a pitiful sight.

If Dorgy Pascoe normally had any personal pride in his appearance it had slipped badly since Jack had last seen the man. He stood there now with his wiry hair unkempt, unshaven, shirt not tucked into his trousers and the face of impending doom. Jack stared at him for a second or two and then stepped into the room without a word.

Dorgy closed the door and locked it again. He followed Jack over to the antique desk.

'You got papers to sign,' he stated bluntly.

Jack flipped open the briefcase and pulled out the tax return.

'That's right. Sit down and we'll go through the figures first.'

He glanced at Dorgy and flinched. The man didn't smell too fresh either.

'Go through the figures.' Another dull statement.

Jack spread the papers out and started to explain each number that he had extrapolated from the data he'd been given, pausing occasionally to check that Dorgy was keeping up. He couldn't be sure that he was, because the reactions were minimal: just the occasional mumble or grunt. At least there were no objections.

At the end of it Jack turned to the old man. 'Now it's your turn. At the bottom of the form here you have to enter your date of birth and here your signature. I'll date it when I send it off. We have plenty of time.'

He handed Dorgy a pen and then pointed to the form. The old man looked at the pen, then at the form. He coughed loudly and some flecks of spittle blotted the page. He dabbed at them with a crumpled sleeve. Jack checked the time and then turned his gaze to the weather outside. The drizzle seemed to have stopped, but greyness persisted. Even with the advancing season he reckoned dusk would come early today.

When he turned back the form had been signed and Dorgy was holding the pen out to him. With his grim countenance he somehow made it look like a weapon: a mini rapier. Jack smiled, but not at that metaphor; more in relief that the simple task had been executed. He began to collect the papers together.

'Thanks, Dorgy. I'll obviously leave all of your basic documents here, but don't lose them. Just in case the Revenue needs to check them later.'

'Will I have tax to pay?' The wary dark eyes, red rimmed with tiredness, searched Jack's face.

'Oh yes, but I think we always knew that ... just not how much.' He reached out and tapped Dorgy on the arm. 'But don't worry, it won't break the bank. You've not spent any of it, so there should be no problem there.'

'Right. And when will I have to pay up?'

'Not for a long time. By the end of January next year.' He closed the case and stood up. 'My only concern now is the situation regarding earlier years. But we'll tackle that one if and when.'

Dorgy stumbled slightly as he stood up and as he steadied himself on the side of his desk for the first time since entering the room Jack realised that his client had been drinking. Up to that point he had deliberately avoided mentioning the burglary, because that would have betrayed a trust. Dorgy had not opened his door to discuss that particular problem, but now, seeing the distress in the man's whole demeanour, he felt the subject could no longer be ignored.

Jack made as if to leave, but then turned and faced the old man.

'I'm sorry to hear about the break-in, Dorgy. The vicar told me about it this afternoon.'

The crumpled face simply stared back at him.

'Never spoke to the vicar.'

'So, how did she know about it if you didn't report it to the police and you've been holed up here since it happened?'

'Must have been Mavis told the vicar,' he said petulantly.

'She's the only one you told?'

'That's right. Should've knowed she's spread it all over the village.'

'I don't think that's fair Dorgy. She's an old friend ... just worried about you.'

Dorgy acknowledged that observation with a sideways jerk of the head and a twitch of the lips. He looked pointedly at the door, but Jack was going nowhere just yet.

'So, did they take anything? Anything missing?'

'No.' A sly expression crept slowly over the unshaven features. 'He didn't find what he was looking for.'

Jack stared at him.

'How do you know what they were looking for? In fact, if nothing was stolen, how do you even know there was a burglar?'

'Oh, he was here alright. Papers on my desk moved around, and that drawer,' he pointed at the base of the desk, 'look, it's not pushed right back in.'

'You think he was searching for something in your desk then?' Jack noted that he had fallen into Dorgy's gender assumption without question.

'Yes, but that's an antique desk, given to my father by old Mr George.' He winked. 'It has secret places. And I know you'll keep that to yourself, Jack Mitchell.'

Dorgy then moved purposefully to the door and it was plain

that he intended to say no more. In fact, from the stone face that the man suddenly adopted, Jack got the impression he had already said too much. He followed.

'Thank you for all you've done for me, Jack Mitchell.' He managed a half smile as he opened the door. Jack nearly stretched out for a handshake, but at the last moment simply patted the old man on his sleeve, then turned and left.

A few days later he had occasion to regret not shaking Dorgy Pascoe's hand.

CHAPTER 7

'I'm thinking of going away.'

Jack looked up in surprise. Catherine had not spoken a word during the entire meal and he had not felt inclined to break the silence. It happened like that quite frequently these days: their respective thoughts running along parallel lines, but never achieving a mutual touching point.

'Oh? Going where?'

'A couple from the WI are planning a trip to China in the spring and I thought I might join them.'

'China!' Jack carefully manoeuvred a fish bone to the front of his mouth and then placed it by the others on the side of his plate. The fish van's battered cod that evening had proved to be an abuse of the word *filleted*. 'That's a hell of a long way from Falmouth.'

'What's Falmouth got to do with anything?' she demanded irritably. 'Falmouth isn't the centre of the universe you know.'

'It might well be to those who live there.' He smiled, but there was only a frosty grunt in response.

'What is it about China that appeals to you? It's a big place.'

She stared at him suspiciously.

'Don't patronise me, Jack.'

'For God's sake, I'm not patronising. You've made a big announcement, so I'm just asking.'

'I don't have the details yet.' She began fiddling nervously with a fork. 'Probably the Great Wall amongst other things. You can see the Great Wall from space, you know.'

'I know.' He laced his fingers and rested them on the edge of the table. 'I've seen the pictures.'

'So you also know how much of China there is to see.' She carried on playing with the fork as she eyed him defiantly.

'Have they asked you to join them?' Jack asked as he prodded a chip into a small puddle of tomato sauce.

She looked down at the table and her hand folded around the fork. 'Not as such. Not yet anyway.'

'So,' he took in a deep breath, 'you're just hoping . . .?'

She didn't move for a few seconds. Then suddenly she dropped the fork, seized both sides of her half-empty plate and in what seemed to be a single movement lifted it from the table and brought it down with force. The plate, part of a set from her mother, split neatly down the middle at the point where it met the discarded fork and several peas scampered across the table, like prisoners escaping from an open jail.

Catherine glowered down at the parted Crown Derby as if furious that she had failed to smash it into smaller pieces, then, as Jack looked on with his mouth half-open, she jumped to her feet, knocking her chair over.

'Christ! I'm sick of being cooped up in this miserable little village. Don't you see? I've got to get out. Anywhere far away . . . anywhere.' She turned and fled towards the stairway.

Jack was on his feet. 'Catherine! Darling . . .'

But she was running up the stairs, sobbing.

The phone began to ring.

'Oh, fuck!'

For a second he made as if to answer it, but then turned and followed his distraught wife. As he reached the top of the stairs her bedroom door slammed shut and then he heard from down below a message being left on the answering machine.

Jack, it's Jane Stokes. Something's happened. Could you call me back as soon as possible?'

He paused outside the closed door and listened. From the other side came the sound of rummaging, interspersed with the odd sob. He tried the handle, but the door was locked.

'Catherine, open the door please.'

There was no reply, so he knocked gently and repeated, 'Open the door. This is silly. Let's just talk about what's bothering you.'

Still no answer, but the rummaging had stopped.

'Come on Catherine, I can't talk to you through a locked door. If it's something I've done ... or not done ... I want you to tell me about it.'

This time there was a reply, but too muffled to make out the words.

'What's that, darling? I can't hear.'

Something inside the room hit the floor with a heavy thud.

'I said,' she shouted hoarsely, 'I'm going to bed.'

He stared helplessly at the door handle and then let his head fall forward until it rested against one of the white-painted panels.

'OK then. We'll talk in the morning when you're rested.'

There was silence from the room. He straightened up and sighed.

'I might go out for a while,' he murmured.

He turned to go and then paused, calling back at the door, 'I'll sleep in the spare room tonight.'

There was an unintelligible murmur by way of response, so he shook his head and set off down the stairs in search of his jacket.

It was a fine spring evening and the air was fresh with a faint scent on damp daffodils and newly cut grass as Jack crossed the path from the front door to the garden gate. It was less than a five minute walk from there to the Plume of Feathers in Fore Street and he strode purposefully in that direction, passing the still-open convenience store on the way. Although the store's window was randomly posted with advertising notices, he thought he could see one of the assistants waving from inside, as if to attract his attention. He put his head down, paid no attention and quickened his stride.

He nodded at a couple who stood outside the Plume's entrance enjoying their smoke in earnest silence and went in.

The heavy door with frosted glass upper-work clumped closed behind him as he approached the bar. Being a weekday evening there were few people there. Although spring was at last into its full stride a log fire burned eagerly in the grate and a skinny middle-aged woman stood close to it clutching a glass of red wine. Her companion, who Jack knew as Stan, was gesticulating energetically as he explained some recent event. By the way she kept glancing glumly over his shoulder she did not seem particularly impressed.

Further along the bar, on his usual perch, sat Walter Cartwright, proprietor of a small and unprofitable antique shop. He was a single man, apparently once married, but now living alone above the shop with his unpredictable terrier. The dog now lay just below its master's feet at the base of the stool on which he sat.

At a corner table, littered with the detritus of a finished meal, a couple of women were in earnest conversation. From the way in which their heads arched forward like fighting cocks no doubt a serious session of character assassination was in progress. Jack glanced at them and smiled as he swung himself onto a bar stool.

'Evening, Jack. How's things?' Walter's floridly genial face cracked into a welcoming grin.

'Pretty shitty, Walter. You?'

'Had a sale today, so mustn't complain.'

'Well done. I hope it was that ghastly oil painting that's been leering out of your window for weeks.' He turned to wink at the young man behind the bar. 'Pint of Tribute please, Phil.'

'No it bloody well was not, more's the pity. That one's destined for a boot sale, I think.'

'Tried eBay?'

'Not yet. But I will if I could find a way of describing it.'

Phil pushed the frothing glass across the counter as Jack fished for some cash in his pocket.

'Well, all sorts of crap sells on eBay, so maybe you'd be lucky.'

'I'd stand a better chance if I knew who'd painted the thing.' Walter frowned into his glass.

'If it's not signed you could just make up a name. It's a pastoral scene, so what about Constable ... Bert Constable?'

Walter gave a wheezy chortle and downed the rest of his drink.

'I prefer Trevor Gainsborough. There's a comely lass under the tree, if you hadn't noticed,' he said and began fumbling in the pockets of his battered Barbour. Jack took the hint and pointed at the empty glass.

'Top you up?'

'That's very civil of you, dear boy.' He pushed his glass towards the barman.

They watched the amber liquid flow as Phil eased the pump handle back and forth. One of the women from the corner approached the bar with two empties, while a young waitress trotted busily towards their table to collect dirty plates.

Jack passed a note across the bar and Phil turned to the cash register for change. He glanced over his shoulder and saw that Stan and the woman had moved away from the fire. The heat must at last have penetrated to the skinny woman's bones.

'By the way, Jack,' the barman said as he handed over the change, 'Jane Stokes was in here earlier looking for you.'

'For me? Did she say why?'

He suddenly remembered the telephone message back at home.

'No, but she seemed a bit hot and bothered.'

'Probably about old Dorgy,' Walter offered as he took the top off his beer.

'What about him?'

'Haven't you heard? He fell down the stairs at the almshouses.' Walter paused for a cough. 'He's in Treliske Hospital.'

'Oh, hell. When did this happen?'

Walter gave an exaggerated shrug and looked quizzically at the barman.

'I think it was some time during last night. I heard they found him this morning at the bottom of the stairs.' Phil said as he moved over to where the woman was waiting to be served.

'Damn! Jane phoned earlier, but I didn't pick up.' Jack drained his glass and stood up. 'Sorry, Walter, got to dash.'

Walter waved a hand airily as Jack zipped his jacket and made for the exit.

Back in the house he speed-dialled the vicarage number and then glanced at the hall clock. It was nearly ten.

'Jane Stokes.'

'Jane, it's Jack Mitchell. I'm sorry I missed your call earlier.'

I was just having a domestic with my wife, he thought.

'Oh, Jack, at last. It's about Dorgy.' She sounded out of breath, but then she was always on the move at speed. 'Mavis found him at the bottom of the stairs this morning and he's in a bad way. The poor man might have been there half the night for all we know.'

'That's dreadful, but can't he say when he fell?'

'Jack,' she lowered her voice, 'he doesn't know anything. He was unconscious when the ambulance arrived and he was still out when they got to A&E.'

'You mean he's in a coma?'

'Quite possibly. I don't know yet, but I was at the hospital this afternoon and he's still not come round.'

He sat down slowly, wondering what was expected of him. Why had the vicar been so keen to make contact with him of all people about the old man's accident? It wasn't as if he was a relative or even a close friend.

'They've moved him to a ward, I presume?'

'Yes, they had to make a bed available in A&E.'

There was a long pause, as if she was waiting for him to ask the next question. Eventually he obliged.

'Why me, Jane?' He raised his eyes to see if anything had changed upstairs, but all seemed to be as he had left it.

She let out a long sigh, as if glad that at last he had asked the right question.

'Look it's late, but could you come round to the vicarage early tomorrow? It's just that when Mavis found him he was still conscious. Well, sort of. It didn't make any sense to her, but Dorgy seemed to be trying to tell her something and she's sure he mentioned your name.'

He didn't reply to that.

'Hello. Jack?'

'Sorry, Jane, I ...' He cleared his throat. 'You say he mentioned my name?'

'Yes, so Mavis says. I know you've been doing some work with Dorgy recently, so I thought if you were to go to the hospital the sound of your voice might ... you know ... get through to him.'

'Well, I'm willing to try, if you think it could help. But I can't imagine why he would mention my name. Maybe I should talk to Mavis first.'

'By all means, but I would really like to speak to you before you do anything else.'

There was an inflection in her voice that persuaded him to accept the invitation. He glanced up the stairs again and then ran a hand over his hair.

'Okay, Jane, what's a reasonable time for you?'

'Milo's off to the garden centre before eight-thirty, so any time after that would be fine.'

Milo was Jane's husband. He was officially retired from whatever it was he did in Penryn, but now worked three days a week at a garden centre near St Austell. The couple had no children and plants seemed to be his substitute for progeny. They certainly had the neatest and most colourful garden in Fentonmar.

'Alright, Jane, I'll be there before nine.'

'Good. Thank you.'

He wished her a good night and cradled the phone. A quick check with his diary told him that there was in fact an appointment at ten, but he couldn't imagine the meeting with Jane Stokes would last that long.

Jack wandered slowly into the kitchen, filled a glass with tap water and then made his way upstairs. He paused at the bedroom door and gently tried the handle. It was still locked, but he could just make out the sound of muted snoring from the other side. He stared accusingly for a few moments at the handle and then moved along the corridor to the guest bedroom.

The next morning Catherine came down the stairs soon after eight and settled herself at the kitchen table opposite Jack, smiling at him as if nothing had occurred the previous night.

'Sleep well, darling?' She reached out and dragged a cup towards her across the table.

'Yes.' He looked up from the newspaper. 'You?'

'Like a log ... or some other immobile object. You've made a pot of tea. How thoughtful.'

He continued to stare at her as she filled her cup. She was in a light and airy mood: as if adopting a completely different persona from the troubled and truculent one of the evening before.

'You really shouldn't lock your door at night. I might have needed to come in.'

'Why?'

'Why come in? Well,' he shrugged, 'to check that you're okay, for example.'

She threw her head back and gave a short caustic laugh. 'Why would I not be okay, Jack? Just because I was in a bit of a huff last night? You surely didn't think I was going to do anything stupid, do you?'

He didn't reply, but his silence was answer enough.

She leaned back in her chair and, after examining his face with wide-eyed amazement, laughed again.

'Really, Jack, you do take things too seriously sometimes. We're all entitled to the odd mood you know.'

'Perhaps, but I wish I could judge when yours are coming on.' He drank the last of his tea and stood up. 'I have to be off now.'

'Not permanently I hope,' she giggled. 'Not going off in a sulk?'

'I rarely sulk, Catherine. No, I have a meeting with Jane. Dorgy's had an accident and she wants to talk to me about it.'

'Oh, I'm sorry to hear that. What happened?'

'I don't have any details yet. That's why I'm going to see Jane.' He took some used breakfast items to the sink. 'I'll tell you more when I come back.'

'Why you, Jack?'

He smiled. 'I asked her the same question. I should be back before lunch.'

'I might not be in.'

'That's okay. I'll make a sandwich or something.'

He knew there was little point in asking where she might be if not at home. Recently she had started making these announcements before anything was actually arranged and then, if nothing came up, she would go out later anyway. If he asked where to, she was often evasive.

As he pulled on a light jacket he pondered the problem, knowing that at some point it would have to be tackled professionally. But not today.

The vicarage was a plain square building set back from Fore Street, up a short and narrow unmade lane. A climbing rose covered the stuccoed white painted wall to the left of the main entrance and its buds looked pregnant with promise for the new season. Jack pushed open the front garden gate and its hinges squawked in protest. A ginger cat that had been sitting on a pile of cuttings in a wheelbarrow jumped off and bounded away around the side of the house.

She must have been waiting for him because the door opened before he was halfway up the path.

'Come in, Jack.'

'Morning, Jane.' He stepped into the hallway and waited for her to close the door. 'Bad news about poor old Dorgy. Have you heard anything this morning?'

She ushered him into the square room at the front that served as her study, or consulting room, as she liked to call it. Its walls were papered with the kind of pattern that you can sit and make shapes of, if you have nothing else to do. Once, during a cramped PCC meeting, Jack had made out a profile of Neville Chamberlain.

Her computer stood on a small oak table in the corner and a few narrow chairs were scattered around randomly on a faded Indian rug. Jane waved her hand magisterially over the array of furniture and Jack sat down.

'Coffee or tea?' she asked.

'No thanks, I've just had breakfast.'

'Lucky you. I've been up since six-thirty.' She sat opposite him and looked down at her hands. 'Dorgy's not come round yet.'

'In Treliske I presume?'

'Yes. Intensive care.'

'Oh, God. That bad.'

She looked up and frowned, running a plump forefinger inside her dog collar as if it were trying to throttle her.

'Yes, he took a pretty bad knock to the head. But that's not why I asked you to come over.' The finger moved swiftly to flick back some stray hairs overlapping her forehead. 'I told you that Mavis found him?'

He nodded.

'She'd been away from home last night ... went to visit her

sister in Probus and slept over. Her brother-in-law dropped her off at the almshouses early this morning on his way to St Mawes. He runs a shop down there, I think. The first thing she saw when she opened the door downstairs was Dorgy lying at the bottom of the stairway with a pool of blood round his head. You can imagine what a shock it gave her.'

'Poor woman. And Dorgy, was he ...?'

'... conscious? Yes, just about.' She was still gazing earnestly into his eyes. 'That's when he mentioned your name.'

'Are you sure? Or, I should say, is Mavis sure. She must have been in a state of shock.'

'Oh, she was ... and still is. In fact I've been giving her some counselling.'

Jack raised an eyebrow.

'Yes, I am a trained counsellor. It goes with the many facets of my job.'

'Of course. So, is she at home now?'

'She is, but I don't intend to leave her on her own for long.'

Jack looked across the room at the shape of a snarling dog just to the left of Neville Chamberlain. For some reason he suddenly felt ill at ease.

'So, what was it he said to Mavis? Or perhaps, I should say *thought* he said?'

'Well, as you can imagine he'd probably been lying there for several hours. No one would have heard him from upstairs even if he had been able to call out. Certainly not Harry anyway. Mavis said at first she didn't know if he was alive or dead. But just as she was about to go off to make a 999 call he stirred and began muttering. She put her ear close, but couldn't make out what he was trying to say. Then suddenly, according to Mavis that is, Dorgy said ...' – Jane grimaced as if she had just sucked a lime – '... *tell Jack Mitchell 'tis in ivy.*'

Jack's face gave an involuntary twitch of surprise. 'Makes no sense. Is she absolutely sure she heard right? You say she was in shock.'

'Well, there's no doubt she was shaken up finding the old man like that, but she's quite adamant that's what she heard him say.'

Tell Jack Mitchell 'tis in ivy. Jack scratched his head. 'It's not even a sentence.'

'I know. Maybe it was all he could manage.'

'And he said it twice?'

'So Mavis told me.'

'I've got to talk to her, Jane.'

'Not for a day or two you won't. On top of the shock of finding Dorgy in that state she now blames herself for not acting faster to get help.'

'Poor woman.' Jack stretched his legs out across the rug. 'I'll leave it for a few days then. But can you tell me what happened after that?'

'Well, as you know, she has no telephone so she went to one of the downstairs flats – they hadn't heard anything either – and made an emergency call from there. An ambulance arrived in about twenty minutes, but by then Dorgy had passed out again. They stretchered him aboard and then belted off to Treliske.'

'And was he conscious at any of that time?'

'No. It's as if the effort of talking to Mavis was too much. He was right out by the time the ambulance arrived.'

'And who informed you? Mavis?'

'Yes. She was in quite a state.'

'And the police?'

'Police?' She looked shocked at the suggestion.

'You're assuming it was an accident, Jane, but ...' he shrugged and tilted his head.

'Oh, Jack, surely you can't be suggesting that it was anything but an accident? These are old people and accidents like that do happen.'

'Dorgy wasn't as old as you might think.'

'Maybe not, but he drank.' She placed emphasis on the last word as if invoking the Devil's name.

'I still think certain details should have been noted formally. I mean, if he dies – which God forbid – I should imagine there'll have to be an inquest.'

She frowned and then stared at him critically. Her mobile phone began to buzz, but she ignored it and eventually the noise stopped.

For the first time since entering the room Jack became aware that there was utter silence in the rest of the house. One would expect some sort of sound from an active vicarage: telephone ringing somewhere, choral music from the kitchen, dog pattering about or doorbell jangling. Nothing.

'Of course, you're right,' she said softly. 'Perhaps we should have notified the police.'

'Sorry, it's just me being the eternal pessimist. He'll probably come round with a sore head. He's a tough old boy.' He had tried to sound cheery, but somehow the words were hollow.

'I know he's tough, but that's probably the only reason he didn't die immediately as a result of the fall.' She stood up abruptly and walked to her window and added pensively, 'I wonder what he meant.'

'We'll soon find out ... when he wakes.'

She turned to face him. '*If* he wakes.'

'You really think there's a chance he might not.'

She didn't reply, but gave an almost imperceptible shake of the head. Jack paused for a moment and then glanced at his watch. He stood.

'I'd better be on my way. No doubt you have a busy day ahead too.'

Jane turned and went to the door, her long skirt swishing as she walked.

'Yes, that's how it is.' She opened the door. 'Thank you for coming over, Jack. You see now why I didn't want to discuss this over the phone.'

'Bugged is it?' he teased.

She chuckled. 'You never know. Some of my parishioners have some very shady secrets.'

As they reached the front door a car pulled in through the vicarage gate. Milo had returned with a load of potted plants on the back seat. She turned to him. 'I'll keep in contact with Mavis and let you know when she might be in a fit state to talk to you.'

'Thanks. Meanwhile I'll go over to the hospital and try to see Dorgy.'

'Good luck.'

He passed Milo on his way out and offered to help unload the bags of compost piled into the car boot. The offer was not accepted, so he carried on back up Fore Street. The day had turned warm and bright.

Jack turned off the busy roundabout and onto the access road that led to a small retail park and Treliske Hospital. A yellow cherry picker was parked half onto the grass verge, which added to the slowness of traffic movement. One man in a day-glo jacket stood at the bottom of the machine while his helmeted mate busied himself with a small chainsaw fifteen feet above the ground. Several severed pine branches lay scattered beneath.

Eventually he arrived at the hospital car park and followed an ambulance to the end, where he turned into a vacant slot. He switched off the engine and sat staring ahead at the entrance. He hadn't brought anything for Dorgy because he wasn't expecting the old fellow to be in a fit state to take in anything consumable. And now he wondered what he would say to him if he were to find him awake and alert. He watched a car pull up outside the hospital entrance, sighed and then opened the door.

He went in the main entrance, past the vending machines and magazine racks, and searched for a reception area. The young woman behind the partition stopped writing and looked up at him. He gave her Dorgy's name. She smiled briefly at him and then began tapping into her computer. He did not expect encouraging news and she did not disappoint him.

'Mr Pascoe is in the intensive care ward.' She glanced back at the screen and then adopted a sympathetic face. 'I'm afraid he's not regained consciousness, so there's really no point in going to see him.'

'I see.' Jack hesitated, then added hopefully, 'Is it possible then to have some kind of informed medical update ... an opinion as to when he might ...?'

'Are you a relative?' She looked him over as if assessing Jack's connection with the comatose patient.

'No, just a friend,' and then added with a lopsided smile, 'and his accountant.'

Neither of those categories carried much weight apparently,

because she merely regarded him sympathetically and advised him to leave it for today and phone in tomorrow for a report. He accepted this advice, thanked her and then went out to the car park ticket machine. As he fed coins into the slot he felt a heavy weight of pessimism sweep over him, which had nothing to do with the exorbitant cost of his short stay at the hospital. How long can someone be unconscious and then fully recover? Some people survive for months, even years, in a comatose state and then make a complete return to normality, but that was rare. Dorgy was neither young nor a particularly fit man.

He left the coin machine kiosk as a squabbling middle-aged couple arrived. Neither of them had enough cash in coinage to feed the machine. He moved swiftly across the tarmac before they waylaid him for assistance.

The cherry picker had moved on down the road and was now parked near the exit, making it difficult to see oncoming traffic. He looked right and then took his chance, accelerating out towards the roundabout.

On the way back to Fentonmar he stopped at the large stationery store on the outskirts of the city. The car park was crowded and he slipped the car into one of the few available spaces. He walked over to the store entrance, went through the automatic doors and looked around.

He collected a plastic shopping basket and made for the computer section, picking up a couple of inkjet cartridges from the wall racks. Further along he collected a packet of A4 paper and a few ballpoint pens.

He was about to return to the cash desk when a row of specialist legal documents caught his attention. Amongst them were pro forma wills: the simple kind where all one needs to do is fill in the items to be left and name the beneficiaries before having it witnessed. He imagined it was the sort of document that Dorgy would have bought if he wanted to avoid the expense of a solicitor drawing up something more formal. That is, assuming Dorgy had left a will at all. He had claimed that he had, but had given no clue as to where he kept it.

He stared at the will form for a while. It wasn't all that the old man had not told him either. But now, if Dorgy didn't pull through, he, Jack Mitchell, was in the privileged position of knowing the old man owned an extremely valuable slice of Gammarho shares.

Then a small trickle of doubt began to filter through. Was this knowledge in fact unique to him? Certainly the animal rights protesters had found out, but might Dorgy have told anyone else? Maybe someone closer to home? Surely anyone who went to the trouble of drawing up a will would also want a blood relative or close friend to know it existed. And what about the witnesses to the document? Although it was not necessary to tell witnesses what they were signing, it was quite possible they would also be in a position to confirm the existence of a will.

He moved on to the cash desk, paid for his goods and left the store. It was after four o'clock and late afternoon homeward movement had begun. It seemed to him that more and more people were working flexi hours these days. Good for them and their home life, he thought, but a pain for those just wanting to pass through Truro city. But in spite of the traffic he was back in Fentonmar in twenty minutes.

He stooped down to pick the scattered mail from floor and then automatically looked up the stairs. Was Catherine not in? If she wasn't it would be quite normal for her to have stepped over the mail on her way out. Normal? No, not normal, but perhaps in keeping with her increasingly unpredictable behaviour. He closed the front door and was about to go to his study when he heard a faint sound from a room above.

'Catherine?' he called out.

No reply, so he called out again, this time louder.

He dropped the letters on the hall table and went up the stairs. Her bedroom door was ajar, so he pushed it wider and stood staring at a scene of utter chaos. For a few moments he thought they had been burgled. The window was open and a light breeze was moving the half-closed blind around so that it occasionally knocked against the pane. He crossed the room, stepping over discarded clothes, pulled the blind up and closed the window.

Turning back to face the room he slowly took in the random disarray before him. Clothes lay scattered on the unmade bed, with more on the floor and also over the back of a chair. The wardrobe door was open and only a few wooden hangers remained unadorned on the rail.

Her dressing table was littered with assorted make-up bottles, together with brushes, a comb, a pair of nail scissors and, teetering on the edge, a paperback book. Carefully avoiding the clothes he went over and picked up the book. He turned it over to read the title.

One Hundred Days in Peking by Doris Smallbone.

He put the book down again and exhaled slowly. So, the new-found China obsession was still on. He took one more look around and then left the room, pulling the door closed behind him. This situation called for another discussion with Rowan.

The blinking light on the answerphone caught his eye as he dropped the letters on his desk.

'Jack, it's Jane,' the breathless message began. 'Sorry not to catch you. It's bad news about Dorgy I'm afraid. He passed away this afternoon. Give me a call when you can.'

He sat down heavily and stared at the telephone.

Poor old bugger, he thought. Somehow the news wasn't really a surprise, but what a miserable way to go. He must have gone within minutes of his visit to the hospital. Or, had he already died by the time he arrived at reception and they had not by then been informed? It didn't matter either way now. He switched his gaze to a pile of papers at the corner of the desk.

Tell Jack Mitchell 'tis in ivy. What did he mean? It wasn't even as if the almshouses were covered in the stuff.

He leaned over, picked up the phone, paused for a moment and then stabbed in the vicarage number. After a few rings Milo picked up.

'She's at the front door, Jack. Just getting rid of an agitated parishioner.' Milo was not known for his diplomatic skills. 'I'll call her.'

Two minutes passed.

'Hello, Jack.' The same breathless voice. It seemed that

Fentonmar's vicar did everything at the gallop. 'Thanks for calling back. Desperate news.'

'It certainly is. I was there this afternoon, but wasn't admitted.' He leaned back and the swivel chair creaked. 'They contacted you direct I suppose?'

'Yes. He had a massive brain haemorrhage and there wasn't anything they could do.'

'But I thought they'd scanned for that kind of damage.'

'I know, they did, but apparently this can happen at any time after a severe head injury. The delay can be minutes or even days. It's so sad.'

'He never regained consciousness I suppose?'

'No. I checked with the nursing staff.'

'So what happens now? I mean, does he have any relatives that you know about?'

She sighed and he could visualise her pushing back that stray lock of hair. 'I really don't know, Jack. Mavis Harris knows ... knew him well, so I'll talk to her.'

'He had a son.' Jack frowned as he said it. 'But Dorgy told me he'd died. At least, I think that's what he meant.'

'I'll talk to Mavis,' she repeated.

'Did he have no visitors in hospital?'

'I didn't ask, but possibly not as only a few people knew he was in there.'

'I think I'll ask the hospital. It might be important.'

'Maybe so, but you know what has to happen now?'

'Yes. A post-mortem.' He looked up sharply as his front door slammed shut. 'And probably an inquest after that.'

'Almost certainly.' She made a clicking noise with her tongue. 'And it looks like you might have been right about police involvement.'

'I think it's usual before an inquest.'

There was silence between the two of them and at that moment his study door opened and he turned to see the bedraggled figure of his wife standing there.

'And when that's over,' Jane said with another sigh, 'I'll have to make funeral arrangements.'

'Yes, of course you will,' he replied vaguely as he stared at Catherine. 'Look, Jane, I have to go now, but I'll be in touch soon. Oh, and I also need to talk to Mavis ... whether or not she's still in shock.'

He rang off before the vicar could launch into another sentence and leaned back in his chair.

'Where the devil have you been? You look like you've been rolling in the undergrowth.'

'Nearly right. I've been walking the dog,' she replied archly.

His eyes narrowed, observing her closely before saying slowly, 'But we haven't got a dog, Catherine.'

'I know that, Jack.' Her hands went to her hips and she jerked her head in the direction of the neighbouring house. 'Their dog.'

'I see. Did they ask you to?' To his knowledge she had never done this kind of thing before. In fact he was fairly certain that she didn't even like the neighbours much.

'No.' She looked down at her skirt as if noticing its dishevelled state for the first time and then began brushing it lightly. A few small pieces of vegetation floated down onto the carpet. 'It got into our garden somehow and it ... well, it just looked as if it wanted a walk.'

He laughed. 'So, where did you go?'

She moved over to the window and began plucking some yellowed leaves from the house plant on the sill.

'Do you ever water this, Jack? Look at the state of it.'

'Where did you go?' he repeated.

'The footpath from Back Lane to Corbett's farm.'

'But that's completely overgrown. No wonder you look like that. It's a wonder you didn't tear your clothes on the brambles.'

'I know it's overgrown ... now.' She laid particular emphasis on the last word. 'It's a bloody disgrace that the council should let a public footpath get into that state. No wonder no one uses it.'

'Chicken and egg, I'd guess. They don't cut it back because no one uses it.' He smiled up at her. 'Why don't you bring it up at the next parish council meeting?'

'I probably will.' She dropped the leaves into his waste basket and turned to leave. 'I'm going to tidy up.'

'By the way, talking of tidying,' he called after her, 'what's with all the scattered clothes in our room?'

'Having a clear-out. I need to know if I have the right clothes for China.'

He shook his head. 'China! So, you're still planning on going?'

'Yes, I am.' Her abrupt reply was shrill and defiant as she made for the door.

She had gone before he could say anything else and as he sat staring at the closed door he pondered futilely once more as to what he should do about Catherine. Eventually he turned back to face the papers on his desk.

'I wonder if she returned the dog?' he murmured.

CHAPTER 8

Detective Sergeant Clive Bray sat on a stool by the bar of the Plume of Feathers, his huge right hand enveloping a pint of Proper Cornish. On the bar beside the glass lay a crumpled bag containing a few crumbs of the pork scratchings he had just finished eating. Beside him sat Dennis Fowler, a local builder, and together they were deep in discussion about the roadworks that were in progress on the way to St Mawes.

In point of fact most of the discussion was coming from Fowler, who, in spite of his diminutive stature, rarely talked more than a couple of decibels below a shout. And once in full flow it was difficult to turn him off. Now he was haranguing Bray about the damage that the extended works would have on his trade further down the Roseland peninsular, not to mention upset to the tourist business at that time of year and how a fire engine had been held up for ten minutes by the temporary lights two miles south of Fentonmar. Clive Bray just nodded and grunted as he stared down at his half-finished pint. Although none of these inconveniences were in any way his responsibility he was accustomed to bearing the brunt of the locals' ire. It just went with the job.

Jack Mitchell walked in on this diatribe. It was a couple of evenings after the dog-walking incident and he now stood and glanced around the room to see who else was there before going up to the bar. He smiling at the young barmaid and nodded as she reached out and held a glass enquiringly under the Tribute tap. It was one of the benefits of being known in your local. He thanked her, paid for the drink and then positioned himself at the far end of the bar, where he could keep Clive Bray in full view.

Apart from his reputation as a talker, Dennis Fowler was also known for his weak bladder. Even in his cricket-playing days he would have to leave the field several times during an innings to relieve himself behind the pavilion. A pint-size man with a gallon-size thirst is what they used to say of him and, with age, the holding capacity had not increased. Consequently Jack did not have long to wait before he could seize his opportunity.

As Fowler slid off his stool and strode purposefully towards the gents Jack also made his move and went along to where a relieved looking Clive Bray sat.

'Getting an earful, Clive?'

DS Bray swivelled gracefully on the stool, still clutching his glass.

'Hello, Jack. Didn't see you come in.'

'Haven't been here long.' He glanced over the policeman's shoulder. 'I don't want to break up your chat with Dennis, but there's something I want to ask you about.'

The large square face immediately took on a defensive expression and Jack noticed the jaw tighten. Pub time was for relaxation and escape.

'I know you're off duty, Clive, but I need to ask someone who has the knowledge about a procedural matter.'

'Procedural?'

'Yes. Can you spare me five minutes?'

The policeman quickly weighed up the options and, hearing Fowler's voice from the far side of the room, quickly chose what he hoped would be the least taxing. 'Okay, Jack, but let's move over there.'

'Right.'

They crossed the room to a spare table near the gaming machine and sat down. Bray leaned back against the wall and inclined his head as if waiting for a suspect to make a statement.

'I suppose you've heard that Dorgy Pascoe died a couple of days ago,' Jack began.

'Yes. Tragic that.'

'Well, the point is that although it was probably an accident there'll surely have to be an inquest now. If he'd recovered and gone back to the almshouses all would have been well.' Bray frowned and Jack added quickly, 'I mean, of course the custodians of the almshouses would have copped a lot of stick for the state of the stairs, the poor lighting and so on, but Dorgy would have at least been able to resume his life there. But now he's dead all that's got to be reviewed far more rigorously.'

Bray began fiddling with a beer mat. 'And what's your interest in this, Jack?'

It was a perfectly reasonable question and Jack had asked it of himself many times. He was not a relative of the deceased, or even a close confidant, and he certainly was not enquiring in any official legal capacity. He knew that any answer to that question was bound to sound rather lame. He took a sip of beer as he gathered his thoughts.

'Up to a few days before he fell down the stairs I was dealing with Dorgy's tax affairs. He'd come to me and asked me to complete his return, which I did. He signed the form and I sent it off to the Revenue, but the matter hasn't been closed yet. I feel responsible for seeing it through, but I've not been in this position before.'

The policeman's face held no expression as he locked onto Jack's gaze, but after a few seconds there was an almost imperceptible nod.

'Fair enough. So, how can I help?'

'As I said, it's about the procedure now … in case I'm called upon for any kind of evidence at an inquest.' Jack reached out for his glass and took another drink. 'Can you tell me what will happen now that Dorgy's died?'

'Okay. As it happens I'm not going to be involved with this in any way … it's too close to home. But I can tell you what the normal procedure would be prior to an inquest at the coroner's court in a case like this. Firstly, there'd be a forensic examination.'

'How can that be,' Jack interrupted, 'when it's several days since the incident? Blood would have been washed away, stairs scrubbed etcetera.'

'True, but you'd be surprised what the forensic boys and girls can come up with, even after someone has had a clean up. There will always be something, however slight, that'll offer up some kind of a clue. A scratch mark on the wall from a fingernail for example. That could tell a story in itself.'

'How?'

'If someone is coshed at the top of the stairs he's probably not going to be in a position to try and stop himself falling. But if he's tripped he'll instinctively throw out his hands to arrest the fall.'

'I see. So the forensic team will be searching those stairs from top to bottom for any kind of anomaly that might be a link with Dorgy's fall.'

'Not just the stairs. The whole bloody apartment, the landing, windows, the lot.'

Someone arrived beside them and began feeding coins into the machine, so Bray moved his chair a bit closer.

'Then there's the ambulance team,' he added.

'Of course. They would have made some kind of report.'

'That's right. Even though they were there to try and save a life and get their patient to A&E as quickly as possible, they would still have noted the situation. You know ... position of the body, visible wounds, broken bones etcetera.'

'Would you expect them to have taken a photograph?'

'I would hope so. It's easy enough these days. Nearly everyone has a camera on their mobile.'

'Is that standard issue to paramedics?'

'Not sure. Certainly should be. It is for coppers.'

'And all this data is gathered together as evidence at the coroner's court. How long before the inquest is likely to take place?'

Bray shrugged his heavy shoulders. 'How long's a piece of string? Weeks ... months. It all depends on how much time is needed to gather the evidence before and after the autopsy. Also it might be necessary to trace possible witnesses ... that sort of thing.'

'Sadly there weren't any witnesses in this case,' Jack murmured into his beer.

'How do you know?'

Jack looked up sharply and then smiled.

'You're being a policeman now.'

'That's what I'm paid for.' He leaned towards Jack and lowered his voice. 'Can you tell me for certain that there were no witnesses?'

'No, of course not, but I'm assuming that if there were they'd have come forward by now.'

'You're a trusting soul, Jack Mitchell,' Bray chuckled. 'You'd be surprised at the lengths people will go to not to be involved. Even if there had been an innocent bystander at the top of the stairs when Dorgy went down, can you imagine what might be going through that person's mind after the fall? Self-preservation will be the first instinct. Will they think I pushed him? Best to stay clear. Mustn't get involved.'

'Come on, Clive, that's just too cynical an assessment of human nature. In this case a witness would probably have known Dorgy and instinctively would have wanted to help.'

'Maybe … or maybe not.' He glanced towards the bar. 'And, if the hypothetical witness was not a friend of Dorgy Pascoe?'

'Well, that's a different ball game, I agree.'

'That's why I'm a policeman.' His full lips spread into a broad smile, which somehow made them resemble a small brown banana. 'Now, would you like another drink, Jack?'

He glanced at his watch. 'No thanks, Clive. I'd better go back. I've got a few things to sort out before bed. But thanks for the information. Very helpful.'

Clive Bray stood up and the table rocked slightly.

'That's okay. Let's hope it all goes smoothly now. We don't want anything messy, do we?' And with that he moved back to the bar counter.

'No, we certainly don't want that,' Jack said quietly to himself. 'We don't want messy.'

He drained his glass and pushed the table away to ease his legs through the gap.

On his way out some instinct made him glance back into the crowded room and for a second his eyes met those of a man sitting alone at the end of the bar. The man looked away immediately, but Jack had the uneasy feeling that he had been singled out for observation and that impression remained with him as he trudged homewards up the hill.

Next morning, soon after eight-thirty, Jack opened the front door, having just returned home with a copy of *The Times*. Catherine stood at the foot of the stairs in her dressing gown, her arms folded across her chest. She looked unhappy.

He stopped and looked enquiringly at her.

'What's up?'

'I am, that's what. And I'm not best pleased about it.' He looked down and noticed that she had on only one slipper. The toenails on her bare foot glinted red polish from the shaft of sunlight that streamed from the still open front door.

'Why?' He shut the door.

'Your friend the vicar phoned, that's why. Woke me up. She might as well move in the amount of time you two spend together these days.'

He ignored the comment and brushed past her on the way to his office.

'Any message?' he cast over his shoulder.

'Not via me there wasn't, but she probably wants you to call back.' She turned and set off up the stairs. 'I'm going back to bed.'

He stood still for a few moments, then sighed and pushed open the office door. The newspaper landed on his desk with a thud and a pen scuttled across the surface. He picked up the telephone and dialled.

'Fentonmar vicarage.' Jane's usual breathy reply.

'Jack Mitchell, Jane. Catherine said you called.'

'Yes, Jack, thank you for calling back.' A hesitation, then, 'Is she alright? Sounded a bit out of sorts.'

'Yes, she's fine. I think you woke her up, that's all.'

'Oh!' The single simple expletive seemed to sum up the situation and Jack smiled. No doubt it was a sin to be asleep after eight o'clock.

'What can I do for you?'

'I had a call this morning from a man I've never met,' she began cautiously. 'He wants to talk to me and he also asked if you could come along as well.'

He absorbed this information before replying. 'Ah, what man and what's he want to talk about?'

'He says his name's Nathan Pascoe and he wants to talk about his father. He wants to talk about Dorgy.'

'What?' Jack sat down. 'He says he's Dorgy's son? But Dorgy doesn't have a son. At least, that's what he told me.'

'I know. That's what I thought too.'

'So, what did you say to the chap ... this Nathan?'

'I agreed to see him. I couldn't doubt his word outright over the phone, but I did suggest he bring some credentials with him. I really had to do some very rapid thinking, I can tell you.'

'Sounds as if you fielded it pretty well.' But then, Jack thought, that must come with experience and training. Shock and surprise must surely be excluded from a vicar's repertoire of responses. 'So when did you agree to meet him?'

'He was quite insistent that he sees me as soon as possible, but the earliest I can make it is next Tuesday.' He heard paper rustling at the other end. 'I must say he sounded rather a rough individual. Very little polish there, I think.'

He reached for his diary. 'What time on Tuesday?'

'Two o'clock, after I return from a hospital visit. Can you manage that?'

'Tuesday at two. Yes, it means I'll have to push something on a bit, but that shouldn't be a problem.' He wrote it down and then snapped the diary shut. 'Sounds mysterious, doesn't it?'

'Yes,' she replied, dragging the word out as if unsure whether or not mysterious was quite her scene.

'OK, Jane, I'll be with you then, if not before.' Then, as a sudden afterthought, added, 'By the way, do you have access to Dorgy's flat?'

'No, but the caretaker has a key. She lives in Fore Street. Why?'

'If we are to talk with this chap who claims to be Dorgy's son, it would be helpful if we could be armed with some props.'

'You mean some kind of proof of identity?'

'Yes, something that only a son would be familiar with. You know, a photograph, a letter or something of that kind.'

She hesitated. 'I might be able to persuade her to let me in, but rummaging through Dorgy's possessions might be another thing.'

'Nevertheless, it's something that has to be done sometime. I know neither of us has any authority yet, but at some point ... after an autopsy presumably ... I expect you'll be burying him. And another point, I have Dorgy's authority to access his papers for a follow-up on his tax return. So, we both have legitimate reasons for access.'

'Hmmm, I suppose so,' she said cautiously. Then, more positively, 'I'll see what I can do to persuade the caretaker.'

It turned out to be more difficult than they had anticipated to gain access to Dorgy's flat. Because the man had now died and as the circumstances of his death had yet to be determined the police had placed a strip of their tape across the door and had instructed the caretaker to prevent any unauthorised person from entering.

Jack had to use what leverage his position as Dorgy's accountant afforded him, but the police sergeant had remained adamant. Even though there was no suggestion at this stage that the flat was a crime scene, the forensic people were still dusting for fingerprints and any other unusual evidence they could find. In the end it was with great reluctance that the sergeant agreed to allow Jack in under supervision for the specific purpose of retrieving relevant papers, which he would have to sign for and then return on request if necessary. This greatly narrowed the options as to what he could remove as proof of Nathan Pascoe's identity, but he had to accept what was offered.

On the day before they were due to meet Nathan, Jack was greeted by a glum female police constable, who asked him for ID. That established, she trudged ahead of him up the stairs. He noted that a new and more robust handrail had already been installed and, when they reached the top, an electrician was working on the light control switch. He stopped what he was doing, wiped sweat from his brow with a sleeve and watched them silently as they passed.

The constable ducked under the tape and inserted the key. She fumbled around for a while and then muttered something about being the wrong key and began again. Finally the door swung open and she ushered him inside.

Jack stood for a few moments and rapidly took in the familiar layout and contents of the room. He had rehearsed this, knowing he would be restricted in what they would allow him to take.

Jane had suggested that they keep their interview with Nathan Pascoe as a matter between themselves until they knew exactly why he had called the meeting and Jack had gone along with this. As a result he knew he wouldn't get away with trying to sneak out items such as photographs, but if he could find something like a passport he reckoned he could bluff it with the constable. Then the thought of a passport made him smile: Dorgy had probably never left the country in his life.

He moved over to the roll-top desk and then stopped, turning to the constable.

'Prints? Mine will soon be all over the desk.'

'It's okay,' she replied, 'they've got those already.'

As she stood with legs apart and hands neatly crossed in front of her he suddenly realised that those prints that *they* already had would of course include his own. He very much doubted that Dorgy had dusted the place in his final hours. For no logical reason the thought made him feel uneasy. He stepped up to the desk, pulled out the chair and sat down. As he rolled back the top he sensed a slight movement from behind. Maybe she was surprised it was not locked? The top folded right back and settled with a wooden click.

He remembered from his visits to Dorgy approximately where the old man had kept certain papers and now he began a search for old employment payslips or any kind of document that only a close relative might be able to recognise. He soon found the former, but nothing else was coming up that might prove suitable. As the minutes passed so the search became more intense. Any moment now, he thought, she's going to call 'time'.

He stopped looking though the desk top area and turned to the drawers. Here there were even older papers, including newspaper cuttings, old bills old pipes, a tobacco tin full of paperclips and general detritus gathered from Dorgy's past life. He opened out one of the cuttings, glanced at it and then prepared to move down to the next drawer, when he heard her take a step forward.

'Lookin' for anything specific?' she drawled.

He turned his head. 'Anything that will make my life easier if and when the Revenue start asking for evidence of figures we declared on the form.'

He was banking on the mention of the voodoo word 'Revenue' doing the trick and it almost worked.

'Can't you just wait until they ask?'

He turned now to face her full-on.

'Constable,' he began, adopting a legalistic air, 'have you ever dealt with HM Revenue & Customs?'

'Not if I can help it.' She almost smiled.

'Well, let me tell you. It will take them at least a month to acknowledge receipt of Mr Pascoe's tax return and by then they will have been informed of his death. That will no doubt give rise to a series of searching questions, which will all have to be answered satisfactorily for his affairs to be formally settled before the Probate Office begins its work. This is something he employed me to do for him and I want to see it through with the minimum of hassle before I grow old.'

This time she did smile. 'Fair enough.'

'I'll only be another five minutes.' He turned back to pull out the third and final desk drawer.

This one contained items that had no right to be in a drawing-room desk. There were old instruments, which Jack assumed to be from Dorgy's specialised employment; a scrapbook containing pictures and news items from various agricultural fairs; a few pre-vinyl twelve-inch records; and three dog collars. He lifted the records and immediately shot a sideways glance at the constable. She was now far more relaxed about the situation and appeared to be staring at the house across the street. As a result she missed Jack's swift hand movement from drawer to his jacket pocket.

She turned back from the window.

'Isn't this the place where those animal rights people made a ruckus a couple of months ago?'

'That's right.' He closed the drawer and began gathering together papers he had selected. 'Upset these poor folk in the almshouses.'

'I heard it was 'cos one of them had shares in a vivisection company.'

'Maybe.' He rolled the desk top down. 'But really mean to target old people like that.'

He stood up and handed the papers over. 'Inventory time.'

She took the papers, sat down on the nearest chair and then proceeded to note on a pad the heading from each of the documents. Her radio began to crackle and squawk, but she ignored it and carried on writing. Jack buttoned his jacket and pretended to study a photograph of a prize bull that hung lopsidedly on the wall.

'There. That's all done.' She stood up and handed over the papers, which were now enclosed in a plastic folder that she had conjured up from somewhere.

'Thanks.'

He straightened the photograph, looked swiftly around the room and then headed for the outer door with the constable in tow.

Out on the landing the electrician was packing his tools away. He gave them a cursory glance as they passed.

At the top of the staircase Jack gestured for the constable to go down first and at the same moment had a fleeting glimpse of the door at the end of the landing closing silently.

'I'll be out in a few minutes.' He pointed vaguely. 'I've got to speak to someone down there.'

The constable hesitated, then accepting that her duty of supervision was over, nodded and set off down stairs. He heard the outer door slam closed just as he reached Mavis flat. There was no rehearsal for this so he knew he would just have to wing it: that is if she were willing to let him in. He took a deep breath and knocked.

Unsurprisingly there was no response. This time he knocked louder and longer.

'Mavis. Mrs Harris. It's Jack Mitchell. Could I talk to you please?' He stood with his ear close to the woodwork. 'It's important that I talk to you. I won't take long.'

Still silence.

'Mavis, you'll have to talk to me some time and it's probably better that we do it before the police come to ask you questions.' He then lowered his voice slightly. 'They'll have to do that you know, now that Dorgy's dead.'

In the silence that followed he thought he could hear footsteps slowly shuffling towards the door. He was right. The key turned and then the doorknob.

Mavis Harris peered through the gap permitted by the extended security chain. She checked that it actually was Jack on the other side and when satisfied she released the chain and opened the door.

'Thank you.' He smiled at her and stepped into the room.

She regarded him cautiously. 'Would you like tea, Mr Mitchell?'

'If it's no trouble, yes please.'

She padded off to her kitchenette and he chose a chair with its back to the window. Looking around nothing appeared to have altered in the room since his last visit, but then there was no reason why it should have. Her friend and neighbour down the corridor had died in tragic circumstances, but that was no reason why she should begin altering her life. While he waited he took the papers out of the plastic folder and began to leaf through them. There was nothing really useful there: they were mainly props for the benefit of the police officer. What was of greatest significance was inside his jacket pocket.

He heard the clink of spoon against china and then she reappeared with a steaming Coronation commemoration mug.

'Thank you.'

She placed the mug carefully on a coaster beside him and then sat down, watching him with what he considered to be an air of cautious defiance. It was not hostility, but there was about her demeanour the look of someone who will very soon have to defend herself. He knew he would have to tread carefully, but it was she who spoke first.

'You said the police …?'

'Yes, it's usual in this kind of case, Mavis. Where there's an unexpected death, routine questions will have to be asked, even where there are no obvious suspicious circumstances.'

He sipped the sweet tea. 'I thought I'd make it easier for you by talking about Dorgy before they do.'

'Oh. What do you need to know? I wasn't here that night you know.'

'I know you weren't, but as you found him at the bottom of the stairs I'm afraid that they will regard you as a key witness.'

'I suppose so.' The poor woman began squeezing her fingers together and it was clear that the shock of discovery remained vivid in her mind. 'Poor man, he was barely breathing.'

'It must have been terrible for you, but he did manage to speak, didn't he?'

She looked startled and her mouth opened, but she did not reply.

'Jane Stokes told me, but as far as I know she's confided in no one else.' He leaned towards her. 'He asked you to tell me something? Can you remember exactly what it was he said?'

Her lower lip was trembling and he thought at first she was not going to say anything. Then she cleared her throat.

'He said, *tell Jack Mitchell 'tis in ivy.*'

'Are you sure? I mean, could it have been *it's in the ivy?*'

'Could have been. He repeated it, but he was very faint. I think he was trying to stay conscious just to say that, because soon after he ...' She gave a strangled sob, pulled out a small handkerchief and blew loudly into it.

Jack sat back and looked down at his hands, waiting for her to compose herself. There was another blow and then she raised her head to look at him through watery eyes.

'Sorry.'

He shook his head, frowned and then fanned his hands to signify complete understanding at her loss of composure. 'You've had a terrible shock. I quite understand.'

'What do you think he meant, Mr Mitchell?'

He drew in a long breath and held it for a few seconds before replying. 'I really don't know. I was hoping you might be able to throw some light on it.'

She shook her head. 'Meant nothing to me. Maybe he was delirious.'

'That's always possible, but you said you thought he'd remained conscious just to say that.' He scratched his head. 'Are you sure he said *ivy*? Could it have been another word?'

'It was definitely ivy,' she said adamantly, pronouncing the word in clear Cornish dialect.

'Okay.'

His right hand slipped inside his jacket and he felt the edge of the stiffened paper. There seemed to be nothing to be gained by pursuing Dorgy's last words any further.

'And if you're wondering,' she blurted out suddenly, 'I've not told anyone else about what he said, other than the vicar.'

'I think that's a good thing, just for now. Best wait until things are sorted out.'

He smiled reassuringly. 'Now, do you mind if I ask you what you know about Dorgy's family?'

She looked surprise. 'His family?'

'Yes. You told me you've known Dorgy for many years, so presumably you knew his wife well.'

'Loveday? Oh, she were a lovely person. Some said too good for Dorgy. She came from a mining family over to St Dennis. Died youngish though. Cancer of the liver it was.'

She stopped abruptly and peered at him suspiciously, as if sensing that she was giving away too much information.

'That's very sad. And presumably he didn't marry again?'

'No. Never did. After she went he drew into himself.' She pulled herself up and adjusted the cushion behind her back. 'Mr Mitchell, forgive me for asking, but I don't understand why you need to know so much about his family.'

Jack was prepared for this. 'I was acting for Dorgy on his financial affairs when he died. Now he's dead there'll be further affairs to sort out.'

It sounded vague but credible and she accepted it at face value, simply nodding her head in time with the mantelpiece clock as it struck the hour. The room had an air of timeless mustiness about it: as if waiting patiently for its ageing occupant to move on. And when she did, all of the ancient treasures would go as well, making room for another deserving parish pensioner. He looked away for a moment as a budgerigar chirped from its cage and when he turned back he saw her anxious eyes observing him. It was as if she was trying to read his thoughts.

'My bird,' she said unnecessarily.

He smiled. No appropriate comment came to mind.

'Mavis, did Dorgy and Loveday have children?'

She frowned and looked down at her hands: hands that were now slowly patting her lap. He cocked his head and waited patiently for her reply. Eventually she looked up at him.

'Yes, they had a son,' she said tersely.

'One son? No other children?'

'Just one son.'

'Now, that causes me some confusion, because Dorgy quite distinctly told me that he had no son.'

'He said that?' Now there was a faint mocking twinkle in her eyes, as if they were at the beginning of a guessing game.

'Well, to be exact, I think his words were *not any more*. Did the son die then?'

'Nooo.' She chucked mirthlessly for a moment and then added vehemently, 'He didn't die.'

'So, what did he mean?'

She smoothed her dress with her age-wrinkled hands and gave out an exaggerated sigh. It seemed to say, *I've gone so far, so I might as well finish.*

'It's like this, Mr Mitchell. After Loveday died and, as I said, Dorgy withdrew into himself, the only person who was able to help him in any way was his son's wife, Rachel. The son, Nathan, was a sailor in the merchant navy and was away a lot, but even when he was home he didn't visit his father. Rachel and Nathan lived in Redruth at the time, so it wasn't that far for him to come over to Fentonmar, but they seldom did. Dorgy and Nathan were never close from the beginning. Maybe it was Loveday's fault or maybe Nathan resented the fact that his father let her illness take hold without doing more to have her treated. Whatever it was, their relationship just grew worse until eventually they never saw or spoke to each other. At least, not that I ever knew of.' She paused to dab her mouth with the handkerchief. 'I think it got worse soon after Nathan left the sea and took up a job with a builder in Redruth. And then the baby was born.'

She stopped.

'Baby?' he prompted.

'Rachel had a baby girl.' Her voice went up an octave. 'But Nathan wouldn't even let his father see his own granddaughter. That really hit Dorgy bad. And, to make it worse, Nathan then left Rachel and went off with some other woman.'

'He left his wife and child?'

'Left them to fend for themselves, yes.'

'Did Dorgy tell you all this?'

'Dorgy told me some, when he felt like talking, but I heard from other people too. Dorgy don't go blabbing about his affairs, but Rachel isn't one to bottle it up.'

'How very sad. Did Rachel and the baby have any support from family, or friends?'

'I think her parents – they'd moved to down St Just way – I think they helped for a while, but she was a proud girl. Determined to make her own way. Started a small business, something to do with fabrics, I think.'

'And does she still live in Redruth?'

'Yes. I still get a Christmas card from her every year and a few months ago I saw her in Penryn Street, when I was in Redruth.'

'Did you speak to her?'

'Just briefly. She were in a hurry to get somewhere. Looked well enough though.'

Jack closed his eyes as he assimilated this tale of family turmoil. He had his own domestic problem with Catherine, but the situation that Mavis had described, if accurate, was surely far worse. A father who had denied his son's existence through some unknown dispute in the distant past; that son apparently a neglectful ne'er-do-well; and his wife and small child abandoned to fend for themselves. It was a dysfunctional mess that put his current difficulty into perspective.

He opened his eyes and focused on Mavis who was looking at him quizzically.

'And what about Nathan?' he said quickly. 'Do you ever see him?'

'Nooo.' She said it instantly and with feeling, as if he had insulted her.

'So, as far as you know he never came to visit his father here at the almshouses?'

'Never. I told you, they fell out and Dorgy would have no more to do with him. As far as Dorgy was concerned he had no son.' She ended with an emphatic nod of the head.

'Okay.' He thought for a moment of pursuing the question of who fell out with whom first between father and son, but decided to let that go. The response would almost certainly be in a similar negative vein. 'But, would you recognise Nathan if you saw him today?'

Again she adopted the look of mild suspicion. It was as if she could not fathom the purpose of his line of questioning.

'I should think so,' she said cautiously, then added hastily, 'but I wouldn't want to see or talk to that man, not ever again.'

It was his turn to be curious.

'Why? Has he ... has he ever been unpleasant towards you?'

'He was no good through and through. He has a mean streak in him. I wouldn't trust him an inch. Treated Rachel rotten.'

'But people change, Mavis. You say you haven't seen him for years. You're talking about a young fellow, who might well have been wild and irresponsible, not a mature man.'

There was a long pause.

'He hasn't changed,' she murmured, staring down at the handkerchief clutched firmly in her wrinkled hand.

She knows something, he thought, but decided now was the wrong time to follow it up. Instead he drew the yellow dog-eared document from his jacket pocket. He opened the creased British visitor's passport and held it out to her so she could see the photograph. It was a lean twice-folded form on thick yellow paper; the kind of document usually issued to a child under the age of sixteen and for a limited period. This one was in the name of a boy five months short of his sixteenth birthday. He had dark unruly hair, piercing black eyes and a thin mouth arched downwards under a broad nose. There was a darkening under the nose that might have been the beginnings of a moustache.

'Do you recognise him?'

She said nothing, but took the passport from him as if it were explosive. It trembled slightly in her hand as she peered at the photograph.

'That's Nathan,' she said bluntly.

'I know. It says so. But, I was hoping you might be able to tell me if he's changed much as an adult. I know you say you haven't seen him for years, but are there any distinguishing features that would not have altered with adulthood?'

'I remember this,' she replied quietly, tapping the passport. 'Loveday wanted him to go with a school party to France. She was very ill at the time, but she still wanted the best for her son and had saved up the money. She wanted him to ... to better himself, have some culture, that she and Dorgy never had.' She looked up at him and her eyes blazed for a second. 'He went, but he never acquired no culture. And he certainly never bettered himself!'

He nodded, allowing time for her recollection to settle back into its box, before repeating, 'But would you recognise him today from that photograph?'

'If I haven't seen him, how would I know?' The reply had about it the triumphant air of someone who has spotted a trap and sidestepped it. 'And anyway, Mr Mitchell, why is it so important that you recognise Nathan now?'

He hesitated as a slow-moving tractor rumbled past the house. It was going up the hill, probably pulling a heavy load, and one of her windows reverberated in harmony with the struggling diesel engine. Mavis scowled at the window and the budgerigar gave an excited chirp. The noise passed on by and she shook her head as she turned back to face him.

'Why is it important? Because I need to be sure I'm talking to the right man when we meet.'

'You're meeting him?' Her eyes opened wide in alarm. 'Why?'

'A man claiming to be Nathan Pascoe contacted the vicar and

asked to meet her. He also requested that I be at that meeting. Neither of us has a clue as to why he wants to meet us, but, if he is Nathan, then it has to be about his father's death. Now, I would like to go to that meeting with some kind of assurance that the man I'm talking to isn't an opportunist, a con artist or the like. That's why, Mavis.'

'Oh, I see.'

'So, can you think of any way we might be sure it's him?'

She put her head to one side and stared at the ceiling lamp. Then suddenly the arthritic fingers snapped together as a flash of inspiration hit her. She held the passport to one side so that the natural light from the window fell on the photograph.

'He had a scar near his ear. He got it playing rugby for the Reds.' She squinted, holding the boy's image closer to her left eye. 'No, it's not there, so this must have been taken before the accident.'

'A deep scar? Not one that would have faded with age?'

'Yes, very bad it was. Needed lots of stitches. I'm sure you should still be able to see it today.'

'Unless he's grown a beard.' Jack grimaced at the thought.

'Then there's the ears.' She was now entering into the spirit of the exercise, twisting the yellow document left and right as she scrutinised the boy's every facial feature. 'See, his ears have no lobes. They just go straight down into his head.'

He couldn't help chuckling at the old woman's description.

'Look.' She was holding the document out for him to see.

'You're absolutely right.' He took the passport from her. 'And ears are one feature that don't change much with age.'

Mavis Harris now appeared very pleased with herself. She pushed her glasses further up the bridge of her nose and sat back with a smug look on her face. 'I should have been a detective, like the one who was here yesterday.'

He had just returned the passport to his inside jacket pocket and his hand froze there.

'A detective was here?'

'Well, I assumed he was. It was a policeman anyway, from Truro.'

'What did he want with you?' He withdrew his hand slowly.

'Asked questions about the night Dorgy fell down the stairs, that's all. I said I wasn't here, so couldn't help him.' She shrugged and the glasses slipped back down her nose. 'He made a few notes then left.'

Of course the police would have questioned her, but it was strange that she hadn't mentioned it earlier. The moment Dorgy died they would have had to be involved. As Clive Bray had explained the forensic people would have come in for a thorough examination and the neighbours would have been interviewed. All of the neighbours.

'Presumably the policemen talked to Harry as well?'

'Oh yes,' she chortled, 'but they wouldn't have got much out of him. Deaf as a post is Harry.'

'But not when he's wearing his hearing aid surely?'

'No, not then, but he never wears it around the flat. Unless he's watching TV and then he can't hear anything else anyway, he turns it up so loud.'

'That means he didn't hear anything the night Dorgy fell?'

'That's right, my dear. And anyway it was probably late into the night and he would have been asleep.'

Jack made no comment at that observation, but mulled over her assumption of the time Dorgy had fallen. Why would he have been out on the landing after other residents of the almshouses were asleep in their beds? What would have persuaded him to leave his flat in the dark and then to lose his footing at the top of those stairs? And yet, if he had fallen earlier, someone from one of the flats below would surely have heard something. There would have been a noise, such as a cry or a loud thump.

'Mavis, would Harry know Nathan if he saw him today?' He hardly knew why he asked that question, but it seemed significant nevertheless: a tying up of a loose end perhaps.

'Nooo. Harry never knew Nathan. In fact I'm not sure he knew Dorgy before he moved to here.'

Jack nodded. It was time to go. He stretched an arm to glance at his watch.

'Well, sorry to have taken up so much of your time, Mavis, but it's been very helpful.' He stood and the old lady began to struggle to her feet.

'No, please don't get up. I'll see myself out.'

'I need to lock the door, Mr Mitchell.' She wavered for a moment, clutching the back of the chair, and then shuffled over to the door. The bird chirruped as if to say goodbye. 'I hope that Nathan behaves himself when you meet.'

'If it is Nathan.' He smiled at her as he slipped through the door and into the corridor. 'Goodbye and thanks again.'

The door closed and he heard the key being turned in the lock, followed by the security chain clicking into place. He thought she was wise to be cautious until all the unknowns had been resolved.

He reached the bottom of the stone steps and waited for a few seconds to see if the light remained on. It did, so at least some good had come of Dorgy's tragic end. He stepped out into the back yard and the door clumped closed behind. He reached back and gave it a push, but it had self-locked: another improvement.

Jack walked out of the yard, his shoes crunching on some dead cordyline leaves that had dropped from a neighbouring tree. They seemed to be an apt metaphor for the ageing inhabitants of the almshouses, one of whom now Zimmered into the yard from the lane. He nodded at her and she gave him a baleful stare in return.

As he walked the incline up Fore Street to his home he speculated as to where this was all leading and what Nathan Pascoe might want of him. One should not prejudge, he thought, but Mavis had painted a picture of rather an unsavoury character. He was not relishing the prospect of their meeting.

He reached Dowr Lane and stopped abruptly in front of his house. The gate was open. Only one person left it swinging off the catch, in spite of constant reminders. He went through, closed it behind him and grinned to himself as he opened the front door.

'Rowan?' he shouted from the hallway.

'In the kitchen, Dad.'

He took off his jacket and hung it from the end of the bannister and was about to go into the kitchen when she came out to greet him.

'Well, we weren't expecting you. What's happened?'

He gave her a hug and then stepped back, studying her face.

'Nothing's happened. I've not been rusticated or anything like that.' She glanced over her shoulder and lowered her voice. 'I need to talk to you about Mum, that's all.'

'Ah.' He looked past her towards the kitchen. 'Is she here?'

She nodded.

'Okay, I'll just check in and then we can talk in my office.'

He let go of her shoulder and moved away towards the kitchen.

Catherine was sitting at the pine table that stood in the middle of the room. In front of her was a plastic bowl and beside that a jumble of unwashed potatoes. Then rather bizarrely beside the potatoes, near the corner of the table, was a hairdryer. She didn't look up as he came into the room, but stared vacantly at the bowl.

'Hello darling,' he said with as much levity as he could muster. 'Sorry I've been so long.'

She looked up then and he could see she had been crying. Her hair was tousled as if it had been ploughed by careless fingers and her eyes were red-rimmed.

'Rowan's here,' she said dully.

'I know. I met her in the hallway.' He pointed at the potatoes. 'Can I help with those? It looks enough to feed an army.'

She turned her gaze to the heap of King Edwards as if seeing them for the first time.

'Not an army. Not in this house anyway.' She reached out and picked one of them off the table and dropped it disdainfully, mud and all, into the bowl.

He stood over her awkwardly, not knowing how to react. Then, hearing a small noise behind him he turned his head and saw Rowan. She gave him a knowing look and then stepped over to her mother.

'Mum, come on. Leave this to us. Go and have a rest upstairs.' She put a hand under Catherine's arm, coaxing her to her feet. 'We'll call you when it's ready.'

To Jack's surprise Catherine pushed her chair back and rose to her feet. He stood back as Rowan guided her mother towards the kitchen door. Meekly compliant, Catherine allowed herself to be led to the stairs as Jack watched, feeling rather helpless.

He was still in the kitchen, scrubbing a potato in the sink, when Rowan returned a few minutes later. He put the brush down and dried his hands.

'Did you manage to get her to bed?'

'Yes. And I got her to take a sleeping pill.'

'Good. Well done.' He hung up the towel. 'Now come and tell me, what made you come down?'

They left the kitchen and she followed him into his office.

The sun was now at its zenith and dappled shadows cast by the small birch tree outside danced hypnotically across the furnishings. Jack reached up and pulled a cord to half-close the blinds and then sat down. Rowan eased herself into the visitor's chair and glanced around the room.

She knew this room well. It was his sanctuary and workplace, but also somewhere he had always encouraged her to visit at any time she had something important to discuss, both as a girl and more recently as a woman. Little had altered in there. The furniture was spare and the carpet wearing thin in places. The same family photographs hung on the wall alongside a framed professional certificate. In fact the only change in the room in recent times was the computer and even that was no longer state of the art technology.

She glanced at the mantelpiece inlaid over a blocked-off fireplace. The oak cased clock that chimed the hour with a delicate tintinnabulation was still there. It had been left to him by his father: the grandfather she never knew. She turned back to face him. He was studying her affectionately, with a faint smile in his brown eyes.

'Well?'

'I guess it's a daughter's intuition,' she began. 'Nothing definite. Perhaps something you said over the phone, or something in Mum's voice when I spoke to her recently, or the birthday card she sent last week.'

'But your birthday's not till August.'

'Exactly.' She frowned and then swept a hand over her hair. 'What's going on, Dad? Something's definitely not right with her.'

Jack leaned back and his cheeks puffed out as he exhaled. He was about to enter unfamiliar territory, but he knew Rowan would instantly detect obfuscation in anything he said. She was too astute to be fobbed off with red herrings.

'The plain fact is that I don't know what your mother's problem is, Ro. It's true she's been behaving oddly for some time now, gradually becoming more ... erratic, you could say. I just put it down to mild depression, brought on by God knows what, but as soon as I get a few things tied up I plan for us to take a holiday. Perhaps go off to the sun somewhere. That might do the trick.'

He paused. Rowan was shaking her head slowly.

'I don't think it's that simple, Dad. I don't think it's something that can be put right with a holiday.'

'Look, darling, whatever the problem is, it's not as if she's gone completely off the rails. She's not chewing the carpet or anything like that.' Noting the hint of frustrated anger in his voice he checked himself and raised an apologetic hand. 'I've known cases of bipolar disorders and also people with deep depression and your mother is nowhere near being in that category. I think we just have to be patient and ... well perhaps I should try to be more understanding in the future.'

It was a lame ending and he knew it.

'Dad, I'm no expert myself, but I really think a little more than patience and understanding is called for here. There's no question in my mind that Mum has some kind of mental hang-up and these things can only get worse if they're not dealt with in the early stages. We must do something before it gets worse.' Her voice cracked as she implored him. 'You have to face it and get her to go to an expert. I don't know if it's a counsellor, a psychiatrist or whatever, but she needs a specialist, and soon.'

Father and daughter searched each other's eyes, both knowing that what she had said was the unavoidable path to follow. Eventually he nodded. It was the all-seeing wisdom of the only child: the only child who should have had a brother.

'I'll talk to Dr Dodsworth at the surgery and ask if he can recommend someone. Meanwhile I'll try to give your mother some closer attention.' He raked his head a couple of times and looked towards the window. 'The problem is that I'm particularly busy just at this time. It's not going to be easy.'

'No one said it would be easy, Dad,' she snapped. 'It's never easy when someone in the family needs help. If you won't do something soon, then I'll simply have to.'

'I said I would, so I will, but it will mean some juggling of priorities.'

'Isn't that what life is about, Dad? Juggling priorities? So, when it comes to getting professional help for your wife ... well, I know where mine would be.'

Rowan's normally pale freckled cheeks had reddened with her emotional outpouring and Jack could not help smiling in admiration at her daughter's spirit. Some young people have doubts about right and wrong and agonise desperately as to how they fit into the world order. Not so Rowan Mitchell. There were few shades of grey in her life. Black was black and white was white and now that a course of action had coagulated in her mind, immediate action had to be taken. She had spoken. There is the time in a parent's life, he thought, when a lecture from one's offspring simply had to be accepted. He looked at her pensively.

'Well, Dad, what's so important that it can't wait until you see about Mum?'

He rubbed his chin. 'Well, apart from the usual client workload, there's this Dorgy Pascoe business.'

'Dorgy Pascoe? But you told me you'd finished his tax work? Didn't you? And anyway, he's dead now.'

It sounded brutal the way she said it, but he knew no malice was intended.

'Yes, he's dead, and that's part of the problem. There's nothing definite yet, but I have a feeling that Dorgy deceased is going to give me more of a headache than Dorgy alive.'

'Oh, come on Dad, you're not involved in any way. Why should there be a headache?'

'Well, for a start there'll be an inquest and as someone involved in his affairs up to shortly before his death I'm sure to be called. Then there'll be questions from HMRC about his affairs.' He stopped, lowered his head and added, 'And then there's this meeting with Nathan Pascoe.'

'Nathan Pascoe?'

'Mmmm.' Jack looked at her. 'Nathan Pascoe. Dorgy's son. Or, at the moment, a chap who claims to be Dorgy's son, wants to meet me and the vicar. We have no idea what he wants, but I've agreed to the meeting anyway.'

'Well, that is intriguing. I didn't know Dorgy had a son.'

'He had a son alright, but Dorgy led me to believe the fellow no longer existed. Now we just have to make sure the man who turns up isn't an imposter.'

'Why should he be? It's not as if there's anything to be gained by claiming to be the son of an old man who lives in a grace and favour home. Is there?'

He did not reply, but turned his gaze again to the window. A light breeze was shaking the new birch leaves. The swallows, recently arrived from their treacherous journey from Africa, were flashing enthusiastically around the sky. In a few hours they would be making way in the evening sky for the resident bats. He had never established where in the house they lived, but he was fully aware that he shared his home with them. In fact, in this crazy ecological world, they probably had more right to live there than he or Catherine did.

Catherine. Time for action.

'Dad?'

He arched his eyebrows and turned back to face her.

'That all sounds very interesting, but surely not more important than tackling Mum's problem.'

'No, darling, of course it's not.' He stood then and stretched. 'I will get on with it, beginning tomorrow. Now, how about preparing some lunch?'

'What me?' She laughed and adjusted her jeans as she left the chair.

'No, of course not.' He put an arm on her shoulder as they left the room. 'Both of us.'

As they passed the bottom of the stairs Jack glanced up.

'Do you think your mother will be up for something to eat?'

'Unlikely. I gave her a full dose. She should be out all afternoon.'

He grunted and pushed the kitchen door open for her.

'Now, tell me what you've been up to.'

CHAPTER 9

Jack tried to persuade Rowan to spend the next day with them, but she insisted that she had to return before she missed any more lectures. So, after he had checked on Catherine and given her breakfast he insisted on driving his daughter to St Austell station, rather than wait for a local bus.

He saw her onto the platform, but she told him not to wait for the train to arrive. Her final words were a reminder of the promise he had made in the office, saying that she would be checking on him. He had laughed as he gave her a parting wave.

Catherine had risen from her afternoon sleep with a headache, possibly caused by the dose Rowan had administered, but seemed otherwise to be in a stable mood. It was like that, he thought: one day up, the next down. But perhaps soon the mood swings would become more frequent. Rowan was right: the time to take remedial action was now.

The return journey was slow, with a tractor holding up the morning traffic, but after he parked the car he went straight inside and looked up the surgery number. After cutting through the usual recorded options he got the receptionist and made an appointment with Dr Dodsworth. Catherine was busy watering some plants in the front porch, so he left her to it and went to put the kettle on.

As he sat in front of his computer sipping from a steaming mug he felt enveloped by a warm feeling of virtuosity. He had taken the first small step as promised. Why, he wondered, had it taken his daughter to prompt him to do what was now so obvious? It surely wasn't that he had been so busy. It was simply that he had been in denial: too close to see what was under his nose.

An hour passed and he was making good progress with some

complex preparation for a hearing before the General Commissioners when the office phone rang. It was the vicar.

'Jack,' she launched straight in, 'he wants to meet us tonight. Can you manage?'

'What? We were scheduled to see him at two. Why's he put it back?'

'I don't know. He just said he can't make it earlier.'

'Hang on a bit.'

Jack flipped open his diary and confirmed that the evening was free. He also knew that Catherine would be at home.

'Okay,' he sighed. 'Where and when?'

'He wants to make it seven-thirty in the Plume.'

'The *Plume*? That's going to be a bit public for a meeting, isn't it?'

'There's a small meeting room at the back. He says he's arranged it with Len.'

'Oh, so he knows our landlord. Fair enough, I'll be there.'

'Good. I've had to rearrange something, but I do want to get this over with.'

'I don't suppose he's said what it's about yet. I'd like to be prepared, if possible.'

'I would guess he wants to talk to me about funeral arrangements, but why you at the same time ... no idea.'

'Well, we'll soon find out. See you at seven-thirty.'

He rang off, thought for a while and then reached for the temporary passport that lay on top of a pile of Dorgy's papers. He opened it and stared at the photograph as if trying to identify any additional feature that might remain in a grown man. Thinking of his own adolescent image and comparing that with the face he saw in the mirror each day he realised there was only a slim chance of any recognisable comparison. He replaced the passport and switched his concentration back to the work in hand.

They ate mainly in silence that evening. Jack had volunteered to prepare the meal and they sat down to eat it just after seven. He had spent much of the day in his office, taking a brief break to walk to the shop for a couple of pasties at lunchtime. Catherine was not particularly fond of pasties, but as they were fresh from the baker and the pastry was not too thick she did not complain.

Without making it too obvious he had studied her at odd times during the day, trying to judge her mood. Mostly she was going about various domestic duties quietly, replying to his comments rationally, but volunteering little herself. There had been no further mention of the fanciful trip to China or any other oddities and he began to wonder if Rowan and he had exaggerated her state of mind. After all, he reasoned, many women of Catherine's age suffer a mild form of depression as they come to terms with their change of life.

'Who are you going to see?' she suddenly asked as he reached out for the water jug.

'Nathan Pascoe.' He ignored the fact that he had told her already. 'He's Dorgy's son. Or so he claims.'

'How will you know?'

She suddenly seemed alert and interested.

'Good question. I've spoken with Mavis Harris, who knew him as a young man, and she's given me a few pointers.'

'Well, good luck.' She even managed a wan smile. 'Do you know what he wants to talk about?'

'No idea.' He rose from the table. 'But I hope to find out in a few minutes.'

He bent down and kissed her lightly on the cheek. She smelled of lavender soap.

'Will you be alright for an hour or so?'

'Of course.' She opened her eyes wide as she looked up at him. 'I usually am.'

With a gentle pat on her shoulder he turned and left her sitting at the table.

The evening was warm and there was the smell of early summer about it. Someone nearby had been mowing grass and Jack breathed in its tangy fragrance. The lights still blazed fluorescently from the convenience store and he glanced through the open door as he passed by. Someone was hunched over the counter busy checking her lottery scratch cards. She had probably been doing that every week for years and never won a penny. How sad, he thought, that those who could least afford to do so wasted their meagre disposable cash on such a forlorn hope. But that was it: hope triumphing over expectation.

He reached the Plume of Feathers and stepped in. The main bar area was sparsely populated, but he expected that for early on a weekday evening. Walter Cartwright was sitting at the bar next to a young woman wearing a well-worn fleece jacket and drinking something yellow from a long glass. They appeared to be discussing an object that Walter was holding delicately in his left hand. Further down the bar counter sat another regular who in fact was so regular that he was more of a fixture. Jack nodded to him and caught the barman's eye.

'Anyone in the side room yet Phil?'

'Jane Stokes. Came in about five minutes ago.'

'Thanks. I'll take a pint in with me.' He pulled a note from his wallet. 'Has she got something to drink?'

'A flagon of holy water.' Phil's eyes twinkled at his witticism as he pulled at the pump handle.

Jack checked the room again and then looked back at the door. Their man was late.

'When a fellow comes in looking for us, send him in please, Phil.'

'Will do.'

He took his beer and ducked under the low door lintel as he went into the side room. Jane was sitting on the padded seat next to the fireplace. The fire would not now be lighted until autumn and a large bowl now stood on the hearth, displaying an array of plastic flowers. Jack smiled at her and drew up a chair.

'Well, no show yet,' he said as he settled down.

'It's only just after half past. And he is coming from Redruth.'

She said this as if describing a journey of immense distance and he smiled again.

'This is very odd, don't you think?' He gave her a quizzical look. 'How should we play it?'

'Straight I suppose, Jack. I'll hear what he has to say and then deal with it as best I can.'

'Yes, that's fine for you. He probably just wants to talk to you about funeral arrangements, but what about me? I have no idea what he wants of me, but if it's anything of a legal nature I'm not going to volunteer a word until we know for certain that he is Nathan Pascoe.'

She gave him a wide-eyed stare. 'Do you think there's doubt?'

'Well I would think so. A chap we've never heard of comes out of the blue shortly after Dorgy's death claiming to be his son. He could be anybody ... an opportunist imposter.'

'But why would he? It's not as if there's anything to be gained from Dorgy's death.'

Jack's jaw tightened as he picked up his glass. If only you knew, he thought.

'Nevertheless, I went to talk to Mavis to see if she could give me a clue as to his identity.'

Jane blinked at him a few times before replying.

'You went to see Mavis? So, did she know ...?'

She stopped abruptly and they both turned to look up at the door as it swung open.

He stood there, pint glass in hand, regarding them with dark unblinking and expressionless eyes. His head was shaven, but that might have been more to disguise a deeply receding hairline rather than as a statement of the current fashion. Or then it might have been just to save money on a haircut. The sallow face carried a growth of beard, which probably represented about four days without shaving as opposed to an attempt at designer stubble. But even with that covering and the artificial light in the room Jack could detect the white line of ancient scar tissue from left ear across the top of a prominent cheekbone. A small gold cross dangled from his right ear.

Jack recognised him instantly as the man he had seen in the pub a few nights earlier. He stood, pushed his chair back and offered his hand in greeting.

'Nathan Pascoe, I presume?'

'That's me.' He came towards Jack, looked at the hand dubiously and then held his out to be shaken. 'And you are Mr Mitchell?'

'Jack Mitchell.' He let go of the man's damp hand and gestured towards Jane. 'This is the Reverend Jane Stokes, vicar of St Rumon's Church.'

'Y'oroight?' He addressed Jane with a Cornish greeting, but did not offer a handshake.

Jack sat down again and surreptitiously wiped the palm of his hand along his trouser leg.

'Grab a chair.'

The man dragged one with curved arms across to where they sat and reached out to put his glass on the table. Jack noted the large hands with unkempt nails and a very swollen knuckle on a middle finger. They were hands that knew only manual work. There was no artistry in those sausage-shaped fingers. When he stretched his arm out, what looked like the tail of a snake appeared in blue ink from under the receding shirt cuff.

He appeared in no hurry to say anything, but fumbled in a pocket of his jeans, bringing out a multi-folded piece of paper. This he opened out laboriously, placing it on the table and smoothing it with the side of his hand. Jack recognised it immediately and resisted an urge to smile.

'Just in case you had doubts,' the man said, 'this is my berf certificate.'

'Thank you.' Jack picked it up. 'It's best to be sure. You see, we didn't know Dorgy had a son until you contacted us.'

He ran his eyes over the document: subject's name; date and place of birth; parents' names. They all seemed genuine. He handed the flimsy paper back and the man folded it again.

'Do you remember where you went on holiday when you were fifteen?'

The question was asked innocently enough, but completely out of context it took the man by surprise. It took him a few moments to refocus and then a sly look crept across his weather-worn face.

'What kind of question is that?'

'It's just that I know and I wondered if you do.' Jack arched an eyebrow. 'Do you?'

The glare Jack received was undoubtedly intended to be

unfriendly, but he could see that the man was searching his memory for the answer.

'Well, it must have been the year me mother packed me off to France,' he replied hesitantly, like a speculative contestant in a TV quiz show. 'What's it to you?'

'We have to be certain as to your identity before we go any further. I'm sure you'll appreciate that. I think personal recollections are probably more reliable than birth certificates these days.'

The man's features relaxed slowly and eventually he nodded.

'Well, pleased to meet you, Nathan Pascoe. And what can we do for you?'

Pascoe's features returned to their default bland as he turned to Jane. He tugged lightly at the gold cross and Jack wondered if it had been painful inserting it through the gristle of his ear.

'Vicar,' he began awkwardly, 'I'm not a churchgoing man, but my old man had a lot to do with this parish and I know he'd like to be laid to rest here.'

Pascoe coughed and took a quick sip of his drink. He looked as if he had rehearsed that short speech and was now wondering if it had come out right.

Jane, who had spent the past few minutes studying Pascoe, put a hand to her dog collar as if to adjust it. 'Well certainly that can be arranged, Mr Pascoe. Your father was not a religious man either, but he often helped with church functions – perhaps not lately – but as a long-time resident of this parish he certainly is entitled to be buried at St Rumon's. There are of course the usual formal procedures to be followed and there will be a burial fee.'

A sudden change of expression crossed Pascoe's face. It looked like one of relief. He swallowed and licked his lips.

'Oh, I thought it was going to be more complicated.' He coughed again and Jack guessed from the nicotine-stained fingers that he was desperate to light up a cigarette. 'So, how much is the fee?'

'If the service is to be at St Rumon's the PCC will charge £360, some of which goes to the diocese, and then there's the undertaker's charge. That will depend on what kind of burial you choose. I presume you're looking for a burial rather than cremation?'

'I dunno. Maybe cremation, but Dorgy'd want a stone somewhere.'

'Well, a gravestone would only be appropriate if he were to be buried. But a small plaque in the churchyard would be perfectly acceptable in the case of a cremation. I would add that gravestones don't come cheap, Mr Pascoe.' Jane sat back and placed her hands on her lap.

'Okay, so what we looking at? Five hundred, a thousand?'

'Rather more than the latter, I fear. Funerals are rather expensive these days, but if he's buried you could cut the cost with a ... lesser coffin.'

Pascoe started chewing one of his ragged nails as he considered the options. Jack's eyes flicked from one party to the other, as if watching a miniature tennis match. Eventually Pascoe arched forward, his heavy eyebrows meeting in the middle and slapped a hand on the table.

'What the 'ell. He's my dad. I'll give 'im a good send off. Never mind the cost. Just don't put 'im in no cardboard coffin.'

Jane Stokes laughed out loud at that. 'There's no question of cardboard, Mr Pascoe. They can cut the cost of the casket without going that cheap.'

He straightened and the heavy brows sank lower over his eyes. It was clear that he resented being laughed at, even by a priest: maybe especially by a priest. His hands disappeared under the table and Jack heard the crack of knuckles.

'Okay then, I'll contact the undertaker and we'll work something out,' he said after a few moments' reflection. 'Can you give me a name?'

'Of an undertaker, you mean?' Jane seemed unfazed by Pascoe's petulance.

'Yes, an undertaker.'

A pen and a sheet of paper appeared from somewhere and she wrote down the name of a local undertaker. He took it from her without comment.

'I've also written my phone number there, so contact me as soon as you've had the all-clear to inter your father.'

He looked puzzled. 'All-clear? What d'you mean all-clear?'

Jack cleared his throat.

'There has to be an autopsy before Dorgy can be buried ... because of the nature of his death.'

Pascoe glowered at him with his mouth half-open, but there was also an element of alarm in his eyes.

'A post-mortem you mean? Why? It's quite clear how he died ain't it?'

'Yes, it's quite clear that he died as a result of falling down the stairs at the almshouses, but the authorities can't just leave it like that without investigating how and why. Surely you can see that?'

Pascoe continued to stare at Jack as he took in this information, the scar tissue becoming more pronounced as the surrounding cheek reddened. He was breathing deeply and clearly trying to contain some inner turmoil.

'I assure you it's quite normal practice where there's a sudden death of this kind,' Jack added.

'Normal practice,' Pascoe repeated with exaggerated precision.

'Yes, there'll be a full medical examination and the report will be produced at the inquest.'

'Oh, for Christ's sake!' he exploded as he seized the arms of his chair. 'Anyone would think 'e'd been murdered. What the 'ell do they need an inquest for?'

Jane began to say something, but Jack quickly put out an arm to stop her.

'Look, Mr Pascoe. If your father had been ill and under regular medical supervision before dying peacefully in his bed, no autopsy or inquest would be necessary. As it is that's not how he died. He was not under medical supervision at the time and he fell down the stairs in the middle of the night, apparently with no witnesses. So, of course everything that can be done to find out why he died that way must be done and carried out by the experts. As I said, it's regular practice and not something that's in any way unusual.'

Jack held the man's stare, but he did not find it easy. There was a lot of hostility there.

'Right.' Pascoe's jaw muscles were working hard, but the

breathing had eased. He also relaxed his grip on the chair. 'So, when does all this 'appen. When can I bury my old man?'

'That's in the hands of the pathologist, but it can't be long now. I'm sure it'll be straightforward.'

Jack cast a sideways glance at Jane, but she didn't seem ready to add anything. In fact she was taking a sneaky look at her watch.

'That don't really answer the question,' Pascoe grumbled, 'but I guess I'd better get in touch with the 'ospital.'

'Good idea. Now do you have anything else to discuss with the vicar?'

'No, not for now.'

Taking her cue Jane stood up abruptly and picked up her empty glass. She flashed a sympathetic smile at Jack and then turned to Pascoe.

'I'll also be in contact with the hospital, Mr Pascoe, and when all the formalities are over I'll be in touch about the funeral arrangements. Meanwhile I suggest you talk to the undertakers.'

'Okay.'

She waited a second for some kind of thanks for her time and advice, but as none was forthcoming she said goodnight to Jack and quickly left the room. As soon as the door closed he turned his attention to Pascoe, who was now working at his teeth with a matchstick.

'Now, Mr Pascoe, what can I do for you?'

'You sorted Dorgy's tax for 'im, din you?' There was no preamble.

'Yes, I prepared his tax return.' Jack frowned at him. 'But how do you know that?'

''E must have told me.' Pascoe stared defiantly.

'But I heard you two had fallen out and hadn't talked to each other for years.'

'Well, maybe someone else told me. What's it matter. I just 'eard somewhere.'

Jack heard the knuckles crack again under the table. There was no denial about lack of dialogue between father and son, but it seemed almost incredible that he could have obtained that kind of information from anyone else. Who else, he wondered, would Dorgy have talked to about his tax affairs?

'Was it from Mavis Harris perhaps?'

'Look, what's this? The third degree or something?'

Jack locked his fingers and leaned back in the chair, trying to make up his mind about this surly son of Dorgy Pascoe. He could get up right away and say that he was uninterested in whatever it was the man needed to talk to him about, or he could just accept the boorish manner and wait to find out. Some time later he was to regret that he ignored his instinct to walk away. Instead, after a few seconds' reflection, curiosity inclined him towards the latter option.

'Alright, never mind how you heard. Yes, your father asked me to prepare figures for his tax return after he received one from HMRC … that's Revenue and Customs.'

'I know who they are.'

He ignored the abrupt reply.

'So, how does that lead up to what you want to see me about?'

'Well, Mr Mitchell, if you've done his tax return then you must know more about my Dad's financial affairs than anyone.' Pascoe stopped and raised a thick black eyebrow for confirmation. Jack's frown deepened, but he nodded.

'Quite possibly. His current financial affairs anyway.'

'In that case you are probably best placed to work out 'is worth for the probate people. Would I be right?'

'Probably.' Jack repeated, suddenly seeing where this was going.

'Mr Mitchell,' Pascoe leaned close enough to Jack for him to smell the stale tobacco on his breath. 'I want to hire your services to settle my father's estate. That's the word ain't it … his estate?'

'Yes, estate is the right word,' Jack replied quietly. 'But why me, simply because I did his tax return? It would be more usual to employ a solicitor to obtain probate.'

'No, I don't want no solicitor. My Dad never had any time for them and neither do I. They're bloody expensive and take too long gettin' anything done.'

'And you assume that I won't be too expensive or take too long?' Jack smiled at the unintended crassness of the man's assumption.

'No,' Pascoe slapped the arms of his chair, 'I didn't mean that. I'll pay a fair price at the goin' rate of course. It's just that you'd have a head start, knowing his affairs an' all. And also, operatin' on your own you could get things wound up quicker.'

'Actually the speed of winding up an estate is almost entirely dependent on the responses to searches and the workload of the Probate Office. You can't blame solicitors for that ... at least, not always.' He wondered how Pascoe knew he was a sole practitioner, but didn't press the point.

'Yeah, yeah, I see that, but how about it? Would you do what's needed to settle my Dad's estate?'

There were so many unanswered questions and so much about this man that was dislikeable. And yet, in spite of his charmless son, Jack still had a soft spot for Dorgy's memory. He wanted to see the old boy put to rest with everything sewn up neatly. Young Pascoe was right in a way: he had started something by dealing with HMRC on his behalf. Then there was his knowledge about the massive shareholding in Gammarho. This was the ticking time bomb at the bottom of it all and he wondered if Nathan Pascoe had some way of knowing about that.

Jack stroked his chin gently as he watched a fly struggle at the bottom of his empty glass.

Then, with a quick intake of breath, he reached a decision.

'Okay, Mr Pascoe, I'll take you on as my client.' He reached inside his jacket. 'Here's my card. Give me a call and we'll make a date for a meeting at my office to discuss details. The back of a pub's not the best place.'

Pascoe took the card and stuffed it into his shirt pocket.

'Thanks.' He gave a lopsided smile and the scar twisted upwards. 'I'll call you tomorrow. Is there anything I should bring along?'

'Not at this stage.' Jack paused. 'Unless you can lay yours hands on a copy of Dorgy's will?'

Pascoe was about to push himself up from the chair, but stopped abruptly with hands gripping its arms. A sly look crept across his features.

'His will?' The crafty expression gave way to a manufactured one of deep thought. 'I don't think my Dad ever made a will. Like I said, he had no time for lawyers, so I very much doubt he would have gone to one for a will. Does that make a big difference?'

'You don't have to go to a lawyer to draw up a will. You can buy a ready printed one at almost any stationers and you simply fill in the names of the beneficiaries and what you intend to leave them. The only important thing is to remember to have a couple of witnesses to your signature.' Jack studied the man's face closely as he added, 'Anyway, how can you be sure that your father didn't write a will?'

'No, of course I can't be a hundred per cent sure,' Pascoe had resumed his seat and a finger drummed nervously on the chair arm. 'It's just that he never mentioned one at any time, even when we was on good speakin' terms.'

'Nevertheless, you do realise that if I'm to act for you the first thing I have to do is to search Dorgy's effects to see if there is a will. Probate can only be granted where there is a will to prove. If there isn't one then the process is quite different.'

Pascoe shifted awkwardly in the chair and he started picking at one of his torn fingernails.

'So, what 'appens if there's no will?'

'Then the rules of intestacy will apply.' Jack stood up quickly, hoping to signal a termination to their discussion. 'Anyway, that's some way down the road. Give me a call and we'll go into details when we meet at my office.'

Pascoe scratched his head and then nodded slowly as he stared dubiously at Jack. The gold cross twinkled under the single bulb above his head. It seemed that he wanted to end the meeting only on his terms, but Jack was already at the door.

'Okay?' Jack could not bring himself to sign off with *it was nice to meet you.*

'Okay,' Pascoe replied reluctantly and rose from his chair. He didn't take his glass to the bar as he left the room.

Even before he stepped out onto Fore Street and a balmy starlit evening Jack was pondering the will situation. Young Pascoe had vehemently denied the existence of one, but Dorgy had definitely said a will existed. At least, that was what he remembered from an earlier conversation and he wished now that he had pressed Dorgy to be more specific.

A few minutes later when he pushed his front door open only the hall light was on downstairs, but it was clear that Catherine had gone to bed early.

Catherine: that was tomorrow's problem to tackle.

CHAPTER 10

Dr Dodsworth had expressed surprise that Jack had asked specifically for an appointment with her, as his usual, albeit rare, consultations were with one of her colleagues in the practice. However, once he had explained his dilemma regarding Catherine's state of mind she had been quite happy to listen and to advise.

He had been quite expecting some kind of Chinese wall to come down, with the doctor citing patient confidentiality or some such code of practice, but Dodsworth was clearly not a jobsworth practitioner. It probably helped that he and Catherine were well known in the parish and indeed they had met socially with some of the practice partners on occasions. In any event, rather to his surprise and relief, she was sympathetic and offered helpful advice as to what he should do next.

After a twenty minute talk he left the surgery with the feeling of relief that he had shared his concerns with someone who most certainly had been confronted in the past with patients, especially women, who were going through difficult phases of their lives and needed help in readjusting. The first thing to do, she had said, was to persuade Catherine to make an appointment herself so that there could be a frank discussion about her current troubles. But the important thing was for her to arrive at the decision herself to attend a consultation. It was stressed that extreme subtlety and diplomacy should be employed in helping her to make such a decision of her own accord.

Jack was pondering the strategy for this challenge as he drove into Dowr Row to be confronted with a refuse lorry blocking the lane. He pulled up at the end of the lane, preparing to wait patiently when through the closed car window he heard a raised voice: his wife's voice. He lowered the window and stuck his head out to get a view of what the altercation was about.

Catherine, just in his vision around the side of the dustcart, appeared to be haranguing someone whom he could not see. He closed his eyes and sighed, before getting out of the car and walking purposefully towards his house.

'Hello, what's going on?'

Catherine, who had had her back to him, spun around at the sound of his voice. Her hair was dishevelled and she was wearing an apron over what she called one of her 'day dresses'. In front of her, still clutching a black plastic rubbish bag, stood a burly refuse disposal operative wearing an orange overall and a bemused expression.

'Ah, Jack, you're here at last. Now, please tell this man to do his job and remove these.'

She pointed to a heap of material behind her and it took him a few seconds to realise that they were Catherine's clothes. Jack looked at the dustman and then back at his wife.

'Darling, I think you'll find that it is not his job to take away old clothes. They should be taken to a clothes bank, or if they're in good nick to a charity shop.'

He turned to the man for confirmation. His mate, the driver was leaning out of the cab window and grinning from ear to ear.

'That's what I've been telling the lady, sir, but she don't listen. Them clothes don't go into this cart,' the man practically wailed.

'What do we pay our rates for?' Catherine demanded. 'I ask you, is it right that council tax payers should have to run around the country doing the job that these people are paid to do?'

'Be reasonable, Catherine.' Jack took her firmly by the elbow and practically pulled her back towards their garden gate. 'They know their job and they have instructions as to what rubbish to take and what not to collect. Now come on, they have a job to do and we're holding them up.'

'You're just bloody weak, Jack,' she rounded on him. 'Weak and pathetic. It's time someone stood up for the right of householders and that somebody's certainly not going to be you.'

He tightened the grip on her arm and she struggled to break loose. As he eased her through the gate he turned and shrugged at the dustmen.

'Sorry about that,' was all he could think of saying, but the man in the orange overall was already round the back of the cart slinging in the black sack. The driver, still grinning, eased back behind the wheel, crunched into gear and carried on up the lane.

'Thank you for that public vote of confidence,' Jack murmured through gritted teeth as he led his wife up the path to their front door. 'Now I suggest you wait inside until I bring that pile of clothes back in and then collect the car.'

Before she could say anything he slammed the front door and marched back up the path. Subtlety and diplomacy were going to be a major challenge, he thought. This was going to be a job for a saint, and a saint he was not.

He went back to the end of the lane, backed the car out into Fore Street and, once the dustcart had trundled its way out, drove back to the house. That brief interlude helped ease his rising temper, so he gathered the clothes calmly and bundled them into the back of the car before going into the house.

Catherine was sitting on the bottom step, clutching her arm and staring miserably at the floor. He closed the front door and looked down at her.

'Now, what's all this with the clothes?' he asked gently.

'You hurt my arm,' she replied like a petulant schoolgirl, but still not looking at him.

'Catherine, you were behaving unreasonably and probably attracting the neighbours' attention with all that shouting.'

'That's no reason to behave like a bully.'

He thrust his hands into his pockets and glowered at her. He had never struck his wife and hoped that he never would, but just at that moment he felt like lashing out at something or someone. She had wounded him with her stinging insult in front of the dustmen and now, a few minutes later, she was resorting to cringing self-pity. Rarely had he felt more out of control of a situation and, what made it worse, this was his wife. It was the woman he still loved, even though she was steadily becoming enveloped inside an impenetrable cloud of turpitude and negativity. The challenge of persuading her to seek professional help suddenly looked like a very steep hill to climb.

There seemed no point in making any further comment, so he turned sharply and went into his office. Work presented the only therapy at that moment.

Jack was still at his desk working on a spreadsheet when the clock struck three. He had not even come out for lunch. So, it was a surprise when the door opened silently and he turned to see Catherine standing there, looking demure and contrite.

'Oh, hello. How long have you been there?'

'Not long.'

'Come in. Sit down.' He swivelled round and gestured at the chair beneath the bookshelves.

She hesitated. 'I'm not disturbing your work, am I?'

'Nothing that can't be put off for a while. Look, darling, I'm sorry I hurt ...'

'No.' She held up a hand and screwed her eyes shut. 'I've come to apologise. I ... I don't know what ...'

He leapt to his feet and gave her a hug, easing her over to the chair and sitting her down. He recognised in an instant that this had to be the time for the whole issue to come to the fore. It was as if she were having a lucid moment, with the cloud temporarily lifting. He went back to his desk and lowered himself onto the worn padded seat.

'It's not been easy for you recently has it? Don't you think we should talk about it now?'

She nodded, but said nothing. He noticed that she had made an effort to smarten her appearance, with hair brushed back and a pale blush applied to her lips. He had always loved those lips. The upper one was broad and straight, but the lower was generous and curved, giving them the look of a rather seductive pout. It was a pensive pout, not a grumpy one, and it sat proudly above her neatly rounded chin.

'Can you not tell me what's troubling you? I might be able to help, you know.'

She gave a deep trembling sigh and her hands folded slowly into fists. They were not tight fists that might suggest anger, but loosely folded, as if trying to conceal something.

'I don't know, Jack,' she began softly. 'It's as if some kind of deep gloom comes over me from time to time. I just feel desperate, as if I need to be somewhere else, or even someone else. Maybe I do become someone else. I feel so ... so, empty and pointless.'

'Why didn't you talk to me about it before?'

She shrugged. 'What could you do? What could you say to make things right again? I don't mean that in an unkind way, it's just that ... well you have your own work and I thought it's something I could sort out for myself.'

'You could have tried, rather than letting it all get a hold of you.' He was trying to avoid using the word depression, but also aware that it had to be addressed at some point.

'Jack,' her eyes suddenly blazed at him intently, 'do you think I'm going mad?'

'Good God, no.' He found himself genuinely shocked at the suggestion. 'Maybe suffering from a temporary loss of self-esteem, but nothing that some kind of medication can't put right.'

'Loss of self-esteem?' She managed a thin smile. 'That sounds like a euphemism for depression.'

'Well, I suppose that could be the explanation, but I'm no expert on these things.' He smiled back. 'Who am I to judge? All I'm sure of is that it's something that'll pass in time.'

The smile disappeared and she gazed at him silently through half-closed eyes for what seemed to be an age. Eventually those lips parted and she put a long finger to her cheek.

'I think you're a very dear man, Jack Mitchell, and I'm lucky to have you as my husband.'

'Wow!' he exclaimed at the unexpected compliment. 'What have I done to deserve that?'

'Not everyone would be so understanding.'

'Nice of you to say so, but I'm afraid that simple understanding isn't going to make you well again.'

Jack searched her eyes, trying to see what lay behind. They

were the same grey-blue eyes that he knew so well, but now there was a dullness to them: a film of fathomless sadness. She was making a big effort to rise above her depression, that was clear, but the grey fog of her personal torment seemed to enshroud her whole being. Not for the first time he felt helpless.

'Make me well again, Jack? What do you suggest?'

'Again, I'm in no position to advise, but I would suggest that you see someone who is.'

He raised his eyebrows, hoping for a positive response. At first there was none, although there was an almost imperceptible sag in her whole frame. Then she raised her head slightly; almost defiantly.

'A psychiatrist you mean?'

'No, that's not what I mean. What I'm thinking is that you make an appointment to see Dr Dodsworth and discuss with her how you've been feeling and she'll probably prescribe some appropriate medication.'

'Happy pills?' She managed a wan smile.

'Call them what you like, but if it works, wouldn't that be a good thing?'

She stretched out and patted him on the knee.

'Very delicately put, my dear.'

'Well, will you do it? Will you talk to Dr Dodsworth?'

'Okay.'

She said it in such a matter of fact way that it took him by surprise. He had been expecting resistance, or some kind of counter argument. It seemed that she had agreed too readily. It was the sort of easy acceptance to perform that someone makes when in fact they have no intention of fulfilling their promise.

'Good. That's excellent. So, you'll contact her in the morning, will you?' He glanced at his watch. 'Or, why not now? It's not too late to phone the surgery.'

Damn! He was being too eager, too gushing. This was a fledgling agreement: he had to give it a chance to fly.

The worry lines on her face had reappeared and her fingers were plucking nervously at the buttons on her shirt.

'Let's give it a day, shall we?' She looked pleadingly at him. 'After all, I'm a lot better today, aren't I?'

'This afternoon maybe, but if you want to leave it till tomorrow, so be it.'

Her sudden mood swings were unnerving, leaving him convinced that today would not be too soon for a doctor's appointment. Nevertheless, he had taken the first steps and not without some measure of success, so he thought.

He was just wondering how to wind up the session on a conciliatory note, when his desk telephone did it for him. He reached over for it.

'Sorry, darling. Business. We'll talk again over dinner. Let me know if I can help with anything.'

She got up slowly and made her way out of the room as he pressed the talk button. The caller didn't announce himself, but he recognised the uncultured voice at the other end.

'Mr Pascoe,' he replied without enthusiasm.

The castors gave a squeak of protest as he shunted his chair closer to the desk. As Pascoe launched into his request for an appointment Jack slipped the phone under his chin and reached for his diary.

They arrived at a mutually suitable time and day and then Pascoe rang off abruptly. It had sounded as if he had been talking from inside a large metal container.

Jack jotted down a few notes and then rocked back in his chair. He suddenly felt hungry.

CHAPTER 11

It was one of those days in Fentonmar when all the local traffic that could pass through at the same time does pass through at the same time. Or at least try to.

The school summer term was almost halfway through and busses of varying shapes, sizes and colours squeezed up Fore Street, meeting the empty busses going down Fore Street. Meanwhile those parents who choose to deliver their children on their way to work were having to manoeuvre around the busses and all this was going on at the same time as a large John Deere tractor was double parked outside the convenience store. No doubt the tractor driver's midday croust was far more important than Fentonmar's traffic easing.

Jack stepped out of the shop clutching a copy of the *Financial Times* and grinned at the sight before him. All that was needed now was for the mobile library to arrive for there to be complete gridlock.

He turned his collar up against the thin early morning sea fret that was blowing in from the bay and crossed the road. Nathan Pascoe was expected in half an hour, but with the current traffic situation he guessed his client would be late, whatever form of transport he chose to take.

Since their discussion in his study Catherine had appeared to be calmer and more rational, but had not been in a hurry to make an appointment with the doctor. Jack had let that drift for a day and then chosen a suitable moment to drop a gentle reminder of her agreement. At first she had appeared vague about the whole matter and it took some replays on Jack's part to bring her mind into focus. However, when that had been achieved and he had suggested that the surgery call could come from him, she had snapped at him that it was her business to do it. And, to her credit, that's what she did that morning.

He almost bumped into the paper delivery boy as he strode into Dowr Row, but managed a neat sidestep off the pavement. The lad muttered a hasty apology and rushed on to the next house. Jack hailed a neighbour who was about to get into his car on the other side of the road and then pushed open his garden gate.

Catherine's appointment was for five o'clock that evening.

Pascoe was late, as Jack expected, but it was nothing to do with traffic. He had come on a motorcycle, so had managed to weave through the congestion, but, according to him, there had been a long queue at the petrol pumps. In any event it was nearly ten o'clock when he pulled into Dowr Row. Jack, and probably several of his neighbours, heard the roar of the powerful Harley-Davidson as Pascoe gunned the throttle before switching off.

Catherine was arranging some early roses in the hallway as Jack passed her on the way to the front door.

'What on earth was that?'

'A client.' He opened the door and waited while Pascoe removed his helmet and other protective gear. 'Not the usual run of client perhaps, but a client all the same.'

'I suppose it doesn't matter as long as they pay.' She continued cutting and preening the flowers. 'Will he want tea?'

'No idea. I'll ask.'

Pascoe came up the path in a rolling kind of gait. It was the sort of walk that suggested a leg injury, or perhaps many years at sea.

'Y'oroight?' he greeted Jack, who stood back to let him in.

'Hello. Get held up in the traffic?'

That was when he explained about the petrol pump queue, but there was no real apology. He acknowledged Catherine with a nod and she in turn asked him if he would like some tea.

'Coffee please.' He laid his black ersatz leather jacket on the hall chair. 'Black and no sugar.'

He followed Jack's guiding hand into the study, looked around and then sat down.

'Been riding a motorbike long?' Jack manoeuvred his desk chair around so that they were facing each other. A pen and pad lay ready on a small table beside him. He had considered recording the interview, but then dismissed the idea as potentially distracting for his client.

'Since I were a boy. Started with a moped.'

That triggered some private recollection, because he gave a gurgling laugh and Jack caught sight of uneven, brown stained teeth. The companion to that soon reached his nostrils, in the form of a waft of stale tobacco.

He decided to cut short any further small talk and, after adjusting the position of his pad, came straight to the point of the meeting.

'Now, what do you know about the probate procedure?'

'Nudden really, that's why I come to you.'

'OK, we'll start at the beginning.' Jack tapped his pen on the pad. 'First and foremost I'll have to establish whether or not your father left a will.'

'I told you, he didn't,' Pascoe interrupted.

'I know you said that, but suppose I tell you that he claimed he had written one.'

'Then he's a liar. That's all I can say to that.'

'Forgive me for saying so, Mr Pascoe, but you cannot possibly know that for a fact. Of your own admission you've not spoken to or seen your father for many years, so how can you be so positive that he's not made a last will and testament?'

Nathan Pascoe's eyes glinted angrily and his jaw muscles were working hard. This is a man of mercurial temper, Jack thought, and not one I'd like to cross. But at the same time he was intrigued as to what was causing his new client to be so adamant on the subject of Dorgy's will. He inclined his head and made a face that he hoped would encourage an answer.

Pascoe slowly took control of himself and then, looking down at the floor, said lamely, 'It's just not something he'd have done. He weren't one for legal paperwork and that.'

'OK, that might be the case, but in law I have to do everything possible to establish whether or not a will exists. I assure you that it will not be possible to obtain probate without that research being carried out. You have to accept that I'm afraid.'

'OK,' Pascoe replied through a heavy sigh. 'So, how do you start?'

'We start by searching through the papers in his home. Then, if we find nothing there, we try to find out if it might be with a deposit holder.'

'You mean like a bank?'

'Yes, or a solicitor, even though you say he had no time for lawyers.'

'How d'you find that out then?'

'I advertise through public notices. You can see them every week in the local newspapers and you can be sure that those are also seen by bank officials and lawyers. Then, if all of that fails to produce a valid will I can then treat this as an intestacy case.'

'Intestacy?'

Jack was about to explain the laws of intestacy when it came back to him that they had covered much of this ground towards the end of their last meeting. Was the man slow on the uptake, he wondered, or simply being deliberately obtuse? He took a deep breath and was about to begin a basic explanation when the door opened and Catherine came in with a mug.

'Your coffee, Mr Pascoe.'

If she had been a horse Jack would have said she bridled at the point of reaching the seated Pascoe. Her reaction amounted to a mini recoil as she took a step back and held the mug out at arm's length. He took it without looking up at her.

'Ta.' He cradled the mug in both hands and sniffed at the contents.

Jack and Catherine's eyes met and he gave her a swift droop-mouth expression. She rolled her eyes, turned and closed the door quietly behind her.

'Right,' Jack resumed. 'The laws of intestacy are that where the deceased dies without leaving a valid will the surviving child or children receive the major part of the estate, after all outstanding bills have been settled. Do you have siblings?'

'Siblings?'

'Brothers or sisters.'

'Oh.' The expression was one of relief, as if Jack had implied he was afflicted by some dreadful disease. 'No bruvvers or sisters.'

'You were Dorgy's only child and he had no other from another marriage?'

'That's right. Anyway, he never married again after me Mum died and he never had another wife before that. There's just me.'

He said that with a triumphant air and then leaned back with a smirk. It was as if he had scored a goal against all odds. Jack looked closely at him for a few seconds, puzzled by the man's reaction.

'Well, under the laws of intestacy,' he continued, 'if you are the sole offspring of Dorgy Pascoe you will be the main beneficiary of his estate.'

'OK.' The smirk was still there.

'And do you have any idea what your father might have to leave?'

'No.' The answer was immediate and emphatic. 'He wouldn't have much. Maybe some savings from 'is pension and the furniture in 'is flat. No, Dad wouldn't have much to leave.'

'If that's the case,' Jack replied slowly, 'then it shouldn't take long to wind it all up. But, first things first. We have to search for a will.'

Pascoe, still appearing totally relaxed, was sipping at the coffee.

'OK,' he said again. 'How and when do we start?'

Jack leaned across his desk and took up a two-page document.

'We actually start with you reviewing this contract of engagement. If you can agree my terms, then sign it and we can begin. Take a few minutes to read it. I'll just fiddle around with a few things at my desk while you're at it.'

He handed the contract to Pascoe and then swung his chair around. He didn't really expect to find anything to deal with at the desk in the few minutes available, but leaving Pascoe in his office alone was not a favoured option. Behind his back he heard the occasional sucking of teeth and one grunt, but he carried on reading a letter that had arrived in the morning post.

Pascoe was not a fast reader and he was beginning to wonder

what next to do when eventually he heard the document being tapped on the table behind him.

'OK.' Pascoe cleared his throat and Jack swivelled around to face him. 'Seems oroight to me, but the fee's a bit steep, ain't it?'

'It's the usual rate charged for this kind of service and, I believe, quite competitive compared with many of the local firms. I won't take offence if you want to shop around.'

'No, they'd only have to do the ground work you've already covered.' He reached into a pocket and pulled out a pen: the kind sent out with charities' begging letters. 'I'll sign it.'

'Thank you.'

Pascoe handed over the two pages, which Jack signed and dated.

'I'm a bit tied up for most of today, so when can you come over to Fentonmar next so we can begin going through Dorgy's papers?'

Pascoe thought for a moment. 'Day after tomorrow I can be over 'ere. That okay?'

'That should be fine.' A quick glance at the diary. 'Make it in the morning. Shall we say ten o'clock at the almshouses?'

A shadow flashed across the man's face and there was a brief hesitation.

'Okay, if that's what you want. Ten o'clock.'

Jack left his chair and switched on the photocopier. The machine whirred into action and he eased the contract under the lid. He looked over his shoulder as the copy spewed out.

'What's your occupation now, Mr Pascoe?'

Pascoe was on his feet.

'Not in full time work at the moment. Bit of building with a friend in Camborne.'

Jack handed him the copy and made for the door.

'You used to be in the merchant navy, didn't you?'

Pascoe's dark eyebrows shot up.

'How d'you know that?'

'Same way as you know things.' Jack smiled and opened the door. 'Local talk.'

'Yeah, I was at sea, but that were a long time ago. When I left I did some steeplejack work for BT.'

Jack said nothing to that and Pascoe followed him to the front door as Catherine was coming down the stairs. Pascoe turned and looked up at her.

'Thanks for the coffee, missis.'

'You're welcome,' Catherine said, continuing her slow descent.

'Day after tomorrow, ten o'clock.' Jack repeated as Pascoe walked out. There had been no attempt at a handshake.

'OK.'

Jack closed the door and a few seconds later he heard the Harley-Davidson wake up with a roar. He smiled at Catherine and gave a faint shake of the head.

'I hope he'll be paying you well.'

'The usual rate.' He paused and said almost to himself, 'But this might take longer than he expects.'

'In which case, I hope he actually pays at all.'

Jack laughed and crossed his fingers.

'By the way, do you want me to take you to the surgery this evening?'

'I'm not an invalid, Jack,' she replied tartly. 'And if you're wondering if I've remembered, well I have. Five o'clock, as I told you. But I'm beginning to wonder why I agreed to go at all. I'm feeling fine now.'

'Now maybe, but what about tomorrow, or next week? Just let's stick to what we agreed was for the best. Yes?'

'Yes, yes,' she replied irritably and headed off to the kitchen.

Jack stood for a moment, then sighed and headed back to his office.

Something was troubling him about the meeting with Nathan Pascoe and it was not just the lingering smell of stale cheap tobacco.

Catherine drove off to her doctor's appointment somewhat reluctantly at ten to five. Even as she drove away Jack could not be sure that she would keep the appointment, such was the nature of her mercurial moods. He could only hope that she would be completely frank with the doctor if she did make it there.

She was not home by six and he was standing in the hallway pondering whether or not this was a hopeful sign, when the office phone rang. He turned and darted back into the room. He picked up and at first there was silence from the other end. Jack repeated his response and then, after a couple of seconds, there was some throat clearing.

'It's Harry 'ere,' came an elderly and uncertain voice.

'Harry?'

'Harry Charters from the almshouses.'

'Oh, Harry, of course. What can I do for you?'

'I need to tell you something. Been thinking about it. Decided it's the right thing to do.'

'Alright, Harry,' Jack replied cautiously. 'Do you want to tell me over the phone, or shall I come round to see you?'

'No!' He said it so emphatically that it brought on another bout of throat clearance. 'No, don't come 'ere. I don't want anyone to see you coming in to see me.'

'Sounds very mysterious, Harry, but if that's what you want ...'

'It is. I'm getting on now and I don't want any trouble, but I want to do what's right.'

'Of course.' Jack sat down and picked up a pen. 'So, what's on your mind?'

There was a long pause during which something started knocking against the old man's phone. Jack guessed that he was adjusting his hearing aid.

'Hello, you still there?' the old voice came across urgently.

'Yes, I'm here, Harry.'

'Got your number from the parish magazine.'

'Good thinking.' Jack looked at his watch. Catherine should have been home by now.

'Mr Mitchell, there was someone here that night. I saw 'un.'

'Which night, Harry?'

'The night young Dorgy went down the stairs. I saw 'un.'

'You saw someone at the almshouses ... you mean someone who didn't belong there ... on the night Dorgy fell?'

'That's what I said.'

'Why didn't you report this before? It might be important, Harry.'

Jack looked up as he heard a car pulling into the front yard.

'Like I said, I didn't want to get involved.' There was a quaver in the man's voice and it suddenly occurred to Jack that he was scared.

'What made you want to contact me now? And why not the police? You know they were there after Dorgy died.'

'I'm not one for going to the police. I knew you was looking after Dorgy's business, so I thought about it and decided to tell you.'

The front door opened and a few seconds later a weary looking Catherine put her head around the door. He raised a hand in greeting and she pulled a face before retreating.

'OK, so what exactly did you see?'

'I didn't hear nothing, you understand? Didn't have my 'earing aid on. Just saw.' He coughed. 'I was standing on the terrace outside my room taking the evenin' air ... couldn't sleep see ... when I saw this figure out of the corner of my eye on the pavement below.'

'What was he doing ... this figure?'

'He was just suddenly there is what I mean. I didn't see him walk up or down the road, so he must have come from somewhere.'

Jack closed his eyes and put a hand to his forehead. Was the old boy hallucinating? Was he wasting his time with imaginings brought on by delayed trauma? Whatever: he decided to play along.

'Then what happened? Where did he go after that?'

'He looked around sort of furtive like, then just scarpered down the hill towards the car park.'

'And you think this was a man?

'Oh, yer. Well, I'm pretty sure it were a man. Or maybe it were one of they animal rights people come back.'

'I see.' Jack thought for a moment. 'Harry, I know you say you don't want to get involved, but did you know there might have to be an inquest into Dorgy's death? In fact I'm sure there will be and this kind of information might be important if one is held.'

The only sound from the other end was some laboured breathing.

'Harry?'

'I knew I should have kept it to meself. I shouldn't have called you, Mr Mitchell. I tell you I don't want to get involved with no inquest. Just keep me out of it, will you.' There was a note of panic in the old voice.

'OK, calm down now, Harry. I'll keep your name out of it if I can. Anyway, when the police came round, did they talk to you?'

A pause.

'Yer, they talked to me.'

'What did you tell them then?'

A longer hesitation this time.

'I told them nothing. Didn't lie. Just said I heard nothing and that's how it's going to stay.' More knocking on the line and then he added hastily. 'Got to go now.'

The line went dead. Jack stood for a while staring at the telephone, gently fisting his palm. What the hell was he to make of that?

Catherine was upstairs in her bedroom, sitting in front of the dressing table.

'Well, how did it go?'

She didn't turn, but raised her eyes to look at his image in the mirror.

'Pills, pills, pills.'

'What sort of pills?'

'Oh, antidepressant, calming, that sort of thing.'

'So, you did have a completely frank discussion with Dr Dodsworth?'

'Yes, Jack,' she said through a careworn sigh, 'open and frank. That's what you wanted, wasn't it?'

'Yes, darling, that's what we both wanted, if things are to get back to normal.'

'Normal! Hah.'

They stared at each other for while through the medium of the mirror, then Jack nodded. She had done what he had asked, so at least that was a start. But was it to be a start of a return to complete stability of her mind? Would menopausal depressant blockers do the trick? The cocktail in his mind was rapidly beginning to curdle: Dorgy, Catherine, Nathan Pascoe and now old Harry and his imaginings.

'I'm going out for a while. I'll cook supper if you like, but there's something I need to think about.'

He didn't wait for a reply, but left her looking forlornly at her own image.

Downstairs the phone began to warble as he was picking up the car keys from where she had left them, but he ignored it. When he stepped out and pulled the front door closed behind him he could hear the muffled tones of his own voice as the instrument kicked onto answer mode. He didn't try to analyse his motive: he just knew that he had to be out of there and somewhere else.

He drove down Fore Street and then turned left again at the bottom, heading towards Veryan Bay and an area of coast he and Catherine had favoured over the years. After a couple of miles he turned off the main St Mawes road into a narrow lane that would take him to the sea.

Until a few months ago he and Catherine had driven down there to a sloping field by the cliff overlooking Gull Rock. There they had spread out a rug after steering clear of sheep dung and thistles and then relaxed as they sipped a cool Chablis, watching activity out at sea. Not that there was much ever going on: maybe a fishing boat checking lobster and crab pots, a distant tanker heading for Falmouth or a couple of sailing boats leaning into the breeze. It didn't matter. They were not there for the action. They were there to unwind and to discuss everyday trivia or sometimes distant plans for some time after his complete retirement. Often they talked about Rowan, her future and how it might link in with their own.

But that was a few months ago.

As his involvement in local activities and business workload had grown and Catherine's world had folded in on itself, so their inclination to put it all into perspective on that hillside had withered. Now, as he parked the car in the rutted parking area by a disused quarry, he wondered if that part of their lives could ever be brought to life again.

Jack locked the car and stood for a few moments taking in the colours of the sea and found himself, not for the first time, wishing he had a son with whom to share his thoughts.

He crossed the lane and walked alongside a barbed-wire fence up the slight incline until reaching a gate. Stepping carefully across a cattle grid he reached out and unfastened the catch. A few sheep, ruminating rhythmically watched him with mild interest from the other side of the fence. He returned their baleful stare as he refastened the gate and then carried on up the track, which became narrower as it reached the peak of the incline. Thick unkempt gorse made an avenue of this part of the track and some early bright yellow flowers dotted randomly on the prickly stems. He might have imagined it, but he thought he could smell their delicate, almond-like aroma.

There was a stile at the top of the incline with a slab of slate imbedded in the rough ground at its base. Once he had hauled Catherine back when she was about to set foot on an adder as it basked on the warm stone. She had shrieked and the adder, awoken at the sound, had whipped off like a bent arrow into thick undergrowth. He thought of that incident now as he crossed the stile. Poor bloody adder. Life was full of ugly surprises.

A couple of times in past years, in mid-autumn, he and Catherine had found *their* field liberally covered in mushrooms. They had filled whatever container they had on them and taken them home for an omelette feast. Catherine had asked him if they were stealing from the farmer, or was it nature's bounty, like picking blackberries. Jack had not known the answer, but speculated that if the farmer had not planted them as crop then they were probably fair game for anyone. He had said he would check it on Google when they returned home, but he never had. Now it was the wrong time of the year for mushrooms and in any case he had lost interest in the ownership question.

He chose a clean spot and sat down, spreading his legs and rested back on his elbows. There were no animals in the field, but across the nearest fence he could see the inquisitive faces of two wild ponies as they reached over and chomped at some tufts of grass.

Out at sea the lowering sun was playing with the surface of the water, causing it to twinkle back at a few bulbous cumulus clouds that kept spoiling the game. A lone ship broke the horizon and he strained to identify it. Too much superstructure for a tanker and not flat enough for a loaded container ship. Possibly a cruise liner. Apart from that there was only a small Bermuda-rigged sailing boat in sight.

From his position he was unable to see the shoreline, but something below must have caused a disturbance, because a pair of oystercatchers suddenly shot into view, piping their shrill cry as they flew. Just as quickly as they appeared they then plunged down again to the rocks below. After that all was still and quiet again.

Jack plucked idly at the grass by his side as he tried to focus his thoughts and to analyse the cause for his sudden lapse into despondency.

His was normally a positive demeanour. He could ride out storms, whether domestic or in business and find answers for situations that would often cause others difficulty in resolving. But now there was a two-pronged attack: one he had no experience in dealing with and the other becoming murkier the deeper he became involved. Perhaps Catherine's instability was temporary; something that could be regulated with antidepressants. But, what if that were not the case? What if hers were the early warning signs of something more permanent? How would he cope if she were developing Alzheimer's? His mouth became dry at the very thought of it.

He slapped the ground angrily. Selfish, selfish man! If the worst scenario occurred, of course he would cope. He would have to. Many people say that the dreaded illness takes away the person they once knew and have loved, but they deal with it nevertheless. And if the illness became so bad that carers were needed, then so be it. One simply has to face it: there can be no running away.

One of the clouds slid across the evening sun and the sea stopped twinkling.

That was one problem. Then there was the increasingly puzzling Dorgy business.

Here was a man, Nathan Pascoe, who claimed not to have seen or spoken to his father for many years suddenly appearing to claim his inheritance. If Dorgy had effectively disowned his only offspring on what grounds would that person expect to be left anything when his father died? And why was he now so eager to claim what he clearly regarded as his birthright, when for all he knew Dorgy had next to nothing to leave?

But the spectre that lurked in the wings and which only Jack could see was the fortune in Gammarho shares. If it were not for that then tidying up Dorgy's affairs and obtaining probate should be a doddle. He could complete the whole thing in a few hours, collect a small fee from Nathan and then move on. As it was, because of the shares, there would have to be a detailed valuation of the remainder of the estate, possible weeks before the Probate Office settled matters and all the while Nathan Pascoe hanging over him with his tobacco breath.

And then that was only if there was a valid will in existence.

His elbows were beginning to cramp, so he lay back and tucked his hands behind his head.

The sun was dipping behind the hill behind him and cloud cover was increasing. The distant ship had passed over the horizon and the sailing boat had also gone. A few gulls wheeled above his field and he watched their apparently aimless flight as they manoeuvred to synchronise with the air currents.

Jack lay there for several minutes until an insect began crawling over his ear. He flicked it off and then sat up. Enough communing with nature: time to return to the real world.

He stood stiffly, brushed off his trousers and then looked around. The ponies were still foraging at the edge of the adjacent field and they regarded him suspiciously as he made his way back to the track.

When he arrived at where he had left the car a small white van was parked nearby, but no one was in sight. Next to the flag of St Piran stuck to its rear was a green ivy motif with some words underneath. At a distance of a few yards he couldn't read what was written, but the motif unlocked a thought.

Tell Jack Mitchell 'tis in ivy.

What did he mean? Why him and not someone else?

He gave the van a last glance before starting the engine and driving off.

The sun had gone for the day and he remembered he had told Catherine he would prepare dinner.

CHAPTER 12

Jack arrived at the almshouses just before ten, but there was no sign of Pascoe. He was carrying an empty brown leather briefcase in the expectation that there would be papers to take away after their search.

He had come directly from the home of the almshouses' caretaker, having picked up the key to Dorgy's flat. The woman was a very cautious gatekeeper, who had required documents of authorisation and proof of identity, even though she knew perfectly well who Jack was. Fortunately he had on him the terms of engagement signed by Nathan Pascoe and eventually the caretaker had handed over the key, muttering dire warnings regarding its return.

Jack now stood by the rear entrance to the building, wondering whether to wait upstairs or stay where he was, when suddenly Pascoe appeared from behind a shed in the yard. He crept out like a schoolboy emerging after a crafty smoke, or, more likely, like someone who did not want to be spotted by any of the residents.

Jack pulled open the door. 'Morning, Nathan.'

'Y'orroight?'

Pascoe had indeed been having a smoke and he now ground the butt end on the tarmac before crossing the yard.

Jack switched the light on as they mounted the stark staircase and once again he had an image of Dorgy plunging helplessly down to the bottom. If only, he thought, the handrail that he now grasped had been in place at the time. Surely someone was going to be pilloried for the lack of safety precautions? Where was health and safety when needed? Did they not carry out risk assessments in this place?

They reached the top and Jack pulled out the key. As he turned the lock he could hear Pascoe breathing heavily close behind him. It was clearly some time since he had done steeplejack work.

They went in. The room smelled stale and airless and someone had drawn the curtains closed. Jack moved across, pulled them apart and opened a window.

'Right, where do we start?' Pascoe asked. He had also brought a case of sorts: a supermarket "bag-for-life", which he dropped beside the desk.

'We're looking for a will, so I think the contents of the desk would be best to begin with.' Jack quickly scanned the room. 'I doubt that your father went in for wall safes.'

Pascoe looked at him, but there was no flicker of a smile. Clearly the man was here to do a job and that was all.

Jack placed his briefcase on the other side of the desk and reached up to turn on a lamp.

'We'd better do this together, so we don't miss anything. Remember, I'm also looking for anything connected with Dorgy's estate.' He pulled out a pad. 'I could have used a tape recorder, but jotting items down will probably be just as quick.'

'OK.'

Jack was fairly sure that nothing remained in the desk relating to Gammarho shareholdings or dividends, but if there were he wanted to be the first to spot them. This was not the time to tell Nathan Pascoe that he might soon be a rich man. The desk was not locked so he rolled back the lid.

It was never going to be a quick job and after an hour of painstaking searching – first the loose papers inside the writing area and then the lower drawers – the task was only half done. They were about to pull open the second drawer down when Jack straightened his back and turned to Pascoe.

'Coffee break? I expect Dorgy's got some in the kitchen. And you'll probably be wanting a smoke.'

'Yeah, sounds a good idea.' Pascoe reached into a shirt pocket and pulled out a cigarette he had rolled earlier. 'Thought they might have turned the electricity off. You know, for boilin' a kettle and that.'

'I don't think they can do it separately, in a communal building like this,' Jack called from the kitchenette.

Someone had thoughtfully cleared the fridge and then unplugged it, so at least there was nothing mouldering in there. Jack pulled open a store cupboard and with a cry of triumph took down a jar of Nescafé. The old stainless steel kettle began to boil and Jack, keeping a wary eye on Pascoe in the next room, poured the water into a couple of reasonably clean mugs he had found.

Pascoe was standing by the window staring down at the street when he returned to the desk. He flicked the remains of his cigarette out of the open window and came over to take the mug from Jack.

'Did you never visit him here?'

It was meant as an innocent question, but it was received as if some personal insult had been thrown at him.

'I told you, din I? We didn't speak. I never came 'ere.' The scar was turning white in contrast to the colour in his face. 'So don't keep askin' me that. OK?'

'Alright.' Jack held the angry stare. 'It was just conversation. Let's get on, shall we?'

They carried on, sifting, discarding and separating, mostly in silence. Occasionally Jack would ask Pascoe if he had any use for some item of memorabilia, but in nearly every case the man had no use or interest in anything his father had kept. Once they had found a sepia-faded photograph of a young woman standing beside an old farmyard pump and Pascoe stared at it for a while before slipping it into a pocket. Jack looked at him, but there was no explanation of who she was. He guessed it was his mother, but did not risk asking.

This went on until twelve-thirty and nothing of any great interest had come to light: certainly no will. Jack stood up and arched his back.

'Have you made any plans for lunch?' Jack asked. He certainly had no intention of sharing any of his break time with this surly individual.

'Got a pasty.' Pascoe nodded towards his plastic bag.

'Right. Well you have that when you're ready, but I'm going on till the job's finished. I promised the caretaker I'd have the key back to her by early afternoon.'

It was a lie, but he had no intention of leaving Pascoe alone in the flat for a minute. Even going to the lavatory was risky.

So Pascoe chomped his way through a cold pasty while he watched Jack shuffling papers and assorted detritus, occasionally asking for an explanation about something that emerged from the muddle.

It was nearly two o'clock when they finally came to the end of the bottom drawer, which signalled the conclusion of their exhaustive search. They had even located the four hidden pull-out compartments at the back of the writing area. These were vertically grooved to look like miniature Doric columns, but would probably not have fooled a six year-old child.

However, there were no treasures there either: only old letters, photographs and postcards. Jack sighed and nudged a discarded pile with his foot.

'Bugger all here of any use.' He looked at Pascoe. 'And certainly no will.'

'I told you there wouldn't be.' He was licking a Rizla and Jack had another sight of the stained teeth. 'Wasting our time,' he added, pulling out a box of matches.

'And I told you that this is something that has to be done.' He glanced vaguely around the gloomy flat. 'Where else to look in here?'

Pascoe stuck the cigarette in his mouth. It bobbed up and down as he replied.

'Pull out all the drawers in the kitchen. Clear the cupboards. Rip the place apart for all I care.' He squinted as he put a match to the thin cigarette. 'You won't find nothing.'

And that is what they did, short of actually ripping the place apart. At three o'clock, with Jack feeling hunger pangs, they agreed to quit. He found a black binbag in the kitchen and started to stuff the disposed contents of Dorgy's desk into it.

'Sure you don't want any of this? Last chance.'

Pascoe barely glanced at the heap on the floor, but shook his head and turned his attention to one of the paintings on the wall.

It was a watercolour depicting a sea scene behind a ruined engine house. It must have been done in early summer because the artist had dabbed what appeared to be pink thrift in the foreground.

'These pictures worth anything?'

Jack pushed the last of the papers into the bin liner and knotted it.

'I doubt it, but I'll get everything here valued ...' He paused and then added hastily, 'Just in case it's needed for probate. I know a chap in the village who does that kind of thing.'

Pascoe blew out smoke and turned his attention from the painting to look at Jack suspiciously.

'Qualified valuer, is he?'

'He's a specialist in antiques and the like, so this lot,' he swept out an all-encompassing arm, 'should pose no problem for him.'

Pascoe stood in thought for a while at this information, pursed his lips, and then nodded his acceptance. He looked down at the cigarette butt held between his fingers and scowled before deliberately dropping it on the faded carpet and grinding it under his shoe. Jack stared at him blandly, managing with difficulty to hide his distaste. He walked over to the window and closed it.

'So, what happens now?' Pascoe almost demanded.

Jack walked over to the door with the bin bag.

'I'll have to put a public notice in the *West Briton*.' He opened the door.

'Public notice? What will that say?'

'It's a requirement of the 1925 Trustees Act. In effect it will ask if anyone has a claim on your father's estate.'

'Bloody hell!' Pascoe exploded. 'That's inviting any Tom, Dick or 'arry to claim part of what's my inheritance.'

'Don't worry, there'll be very careful checks on the validity of any claims. And anyway, I'd be very surprised if anyone comes forward. They rarely do.' He moved out onto the landing and pulled the key from his pocket. 'I'll make sure your interests are protected.'

Pascoe was wearing a frown that creased his forehead in three deep lines. He was clearly unhappy at this revelation, but he followed

Jack silently down the stairs after the door had been locked. In fact he was so concerned at the thought of publicity that he failed to notice that the door at the end of the corridor stood slightly ajar. Jack saw it though and wondered once again if Mavis knew more than she had told him.

The two men parted company in the yard. Jack had no idea where Pascoe had parked his motorcycle, but a few minutes later he heard its roar as it set off down Fore Street. He heaved the bin bag over his shoulder and began his walk home, stopping on the way to return the key to the caretaker. This lot, he thought, will make a merry bonfire.

Catherine was out when he returned, so he went into his office, placed the briefcase by his desk and then sat down to compose a public notice. It wasn't something he had needed to do before, but the format was a standard one and, after checking that he had Dorgy's correct first name, he began.

CHARLES 'DORGY' PASCOE (deceased)
Pursuant to the Trustees Act 1925 any persons having a claim against or an interest in the Estate of the aforementioned deceased late of the almshouses, Fentonmar, Cornwall, who died ...

He stopped and cursed as the telephone rang. After glancing at the caller's number he let it go, keyed in the date of death and carried on.

... are required to send particulars thereof in writing to the undersigned within two weeks of this notice, after which date the Estate will be distributed having regard only to claims and interests of which he has had notice.

Jack completed the notice with his name and address and then emailed it to the *West Briton*. He sat and stared at the *message sent* advice for a few moments, as if expecting an instant response. Then, remembering that the *London Gazette* would also need a copy of the notice, he brought up a Word document file and repeated the text in letter format.

Job done so far, now what would emerge from Dorgy's past? In a strange way he found himself hoping that something or someone would come forward, if only to make life a bit more awkward for Nathan Pascoe.

He was contemplating the ways in which his newest client could get his comeuppance when he heard the front door close. Catherine was back.

'You completely ignored me,' she declared as she put her head around the office door.

'Oh? How and when?'

'I waved at you as I drove past in Fore Street. You didn't even look up. And what was in that bag? You looked like a hobo.'

He laughed and pointed at the bin bag in the corner.

'Dorgy's disposables. I've just spent an unpleasant and uncomfortable few hours in the company of Nathan Pascoe.'

She came into the room and looked curiously at the bag.

'Where did it all come from?'

'Nearly all from his desk. Nothing of any importance as far as I can tell.'

'But, surely Nathan must value some of the stuff Dorgy collected over the years? It can't all be rubbish.'

'Believe me, Nathan is not interested in memorabilia. All he salvaged from the entire contents of his father's desk was a photograph.'

'Such a shame,' she said softly, regarding the black bundle as if it were a dead animal.

'It's his choice.' He turned his attention back to her. 'And how are you feeling today?'

'Alright. Slept quite well.' She made an odd gesture, as if brushing away a fly and added, 'I've just been shopping in ...'

Jack stared at her as she struggled to recall the name of ... what? The shop; the town; the supermarket where she had just returned from?

'Truro?' he ventured.

'No!' she replied crossly. 'It doesn't matter.'

With that she spun round and left the room, closing the door loudly behind her.

Jack continued to stare at the space where she had been, his face creased with renewed anxiety. Nothing more was said about the lapse of memory, which, he reasoned, could have happened to anybody, but later that day he saw two bags of groceries by the larder door. Tesco bags.

Two days later, after a light early supper when they spoke sparingly, he excused himself and went down the road to the Plume.

He was in luck. The person he hoped to see was there at the bar, staring into a half-empty pint glass.

'Evening, Walter.'

'Ah, Jack.' The antique shop owner's face lit up as if he had been rescued from a state of eternal gloom. 'What'll you have?'

'Pint of Tribute please, but it's I who should be buying you a drink ...' He sat down and nodded to Phil. '... because, I'm about to ask you a favour.'

'Ask away.'

'Would you take on a bit of valuing for me? Usual fee of course.'

'Don't tell me ... old Dorgy's stuff?'

'Got it first time. There's very little of value, but I'll need it for probate anyway ... that is if we find a will.'

Walter Cartwright, although a bit of a barfly by reputation, was no fool. His ruddy face creased in thought as he pushed a glass along the bar to Jack.

'The old boy can't have left much. At any rate, well below the inheritance tax limit, so why the need to spend time and money on a formal valuation of his nick-nacks?'

'Probably no necessity for it at all, Walter. Just look on it as good housekeeping.'

'I see,' he said dubiously. 'So, I presume you've been appointed executor.'

'Yes, Nathan Pascoe's roped me in to do the clearing up. Do you know him?'

'No, I've not lived in Fentonmar that long.' Walter stroked his untidy beard. 'But, his reputation lives on amongst the older residents. Bit of a tearaway they say.'

'And age doesn't seem to have smoothed off many of the rough edges either.'

'He's not moving back here is he?'

'Not that he's said, but I doubt it. I don't think he's likely to move from Redruth.'

A contemplative silence followed for a few minutes as the two men paid attention to their ale. There was a murmur of conversation in the corner of the room and canned music drifted in from the kitchen area. Phil was busy rearranging liqueur bottles on a shelf.

'How soon do you want me to do the valuation?'

'Oh, there's no hurry. Dorgy's not buried yet. When's convenient for you?'

Walter pulled a bruised black leather-bound diary from his crumpled linen jacket and leafed through the pages.

'I've got a young assistant in on Thursday of this week, so I think I can leave him to mind the shop. How about ten-thirty?'

'That sounds fine. If I've something else planned I'll postpone it.'

He didn't hear the postman arrive the next morning, so Catherine picked the mail up as she passed the front door. She shuffled it, took out one addressed to her, then went across the hallway to Jack's office. He looked up from his work as she came in.

'Three things for you.' She dropped them on his desk. 'Doesn't look exciting.'

'Thanks.'

As she turned to leave it occurred to him that those were almost the only words they had exchanged that morning. Her mood had appeared brittle so he was reluctant to mention the antidepressant pills and to ask if she felt they were helping. Anyway, how would she know whether or not they were doing any good when she had barely acknowledged the existence of any problem to begin with? He knew he would have to face her with the question, but not just yet.

He glanced at the envelopes, pushed them aside and turned back to the screen. Just five more entries on a spreadsheet later his office phone rang. He glanced at the caller's number and then picked up.

'Jane, good morning.'

'Hello, Jack. Have you had something from the coroner's office this morning?'

'Just a minute.'

He spread the envelopes, picked one up and slit it open.

'Yes. It looks like a request to attend Dorgy's inquest.'

'I think it's more like a summons actually. Mine arrived this morning and it just occurred to me that they might like you along as well as a witness.'

'Well, it seems you were right, although I don't know what contribution I can make.'

'Dorgy's accountant ... one of the last people to see him alive ... an opinion as to his state of mind, etcetera. I would say you have a lot to offer.'

'It sounds as if you've been to these things before.'

'Oh, yes. Priest, police and social workers are in and out of inquests like ...' She tailed off, not being able to think of a suitable simile. 'Anyway, I presume you'll be free on the given date?'

He checked his diary.

'Yes, that day's clear. Should you and I talk before then?'

'No, I don't think that will be necessary. The coroner's line of questioning is unlikely to overlap between us.'

'Okay. I'll see you there.'

They rang off and Jack made a diary note before returning to work.

Later that day he Googled 'coroner's court' for background information.

CHAPTER 13

To Jack's surprise Walter Cartwright arrived at his front door just before ten o'clock on the morning they had agreed to meet. He was carrying a cheap-looking plastic briefcase which was tucked under a long brown raincoat. Pulled well down on his head was a dark fedora, which now glistened damply from an early morning fret. With his grizzly beard and ruddy cheeks he looked like an escapee from a Spaghetti Western.

'You're early.' Jack glanced at his watch. 'I thought we were going to meet at the almshouses after I collected the key.'

'Thought I'd catch you in your lair, old boy.' He took off the hat. 'May I come in?'

'Of course.' Jack stood aside. 'Would you like a coffee before we go?'

'That would be nice.'

Walter caught sight of Catherine at the far end of the hallway and gave her a wave. He removed the coat, hung it on a peg and followed Jack into the kitchen. Catherine had disappeared.

Jack filled the kettle and switched it on.

'Look, old chap, don't get me wrong on this, but,' Walter began hesitantly, 'is there more to this than meets the eye?'

He put the plastic case on the kitchen table and fixed Jack with his soft brown eyes. Jack stopped in the act of collecting two cups and met the gaze.

'What do you mean?'

'Well, I said in the pub that a formal valuation was unnecessary unless the estate's likely to exceed ... what is it? ... about £325,000. Now don't tell me Dorgy Pascoe left anything near that amount, eh?'

Jack stared at the kettle, willing it to begin its boil while he collected his thoughts. He had not expected to be challenged in this way.

'Alright, Walter, there's more to this than simply what we'll find in Dorgy's flat. However, I can't say any more than that at this time. There's an inquest coming up and until that's over Dorgy can't even be put under the ground. I'm sorry about the secrecy, but . . .' He shrugged.

'My dear chap, I quite understand.' He chuckled and his cheeks crinkled above the unkempt beard. 'I just had to establish that I was floating my canoe up the right creek, that's all.'

Jack smiled at the metaphor and turned back to the bubbling kettle.

'Very astute of you, Walter.' He filled a cup and passed it over. 'But please keep any suspicions you might have to yourself for now.'

'No problem, Jack. I'm sealed like a mummy's tomb.'

Quarter of an hour later they were heading down Fore Street, Walter rolling like a sailor and Jack keeping step beside him. They stopped at the caretaker's house and once more Jack had to persuade her of the necessity to enter *Hawker*.

'Officious woman,' Walter commented as they carried on down the street.

'Jobsworth,' Jack replied.

As they entered the yard Jack gave Walter a sidelong glance.

'Look, I do feel a bit guilty asking you to do this.' He pulled open the now familiar door. 'I'm no expert, but there's really very little of value up there.'

'Don't you worry about that, Jack. You never know what we'll find.' He followed up the stairs, breathing heavily. 'And I'll be able to suss the place out while we're here.'

'Why, do you think you'll end up here?'

Walter gave a great roar of laughter.

'I bloody hope not.'

Just as they reached the top of the stairs Jack saw a figure disappear into the room at the end of the corridor and the door quickly close.

'Who was that?' Walter was resting against a wall as Jack turned the key in *Hawker's* door.

'Probably Mavis Harris. Do you know her?'

'Can't say I do.'

'She seems very keen to avoid me for some reason.' They went in and he murmured to himself, 'I wonder why.'

'Good God, it smells like a morgue in here,' Walter exclaimed as he hurried across the room. 'I'll open a window.'

Jack turned on the ceiling light and its sixty watt glow highlighted a spider's web attached to the pale blue plastic shade. He glanced around the room, but nothing seemed to have been moved. Walter had taken out a thin note pad and was scribbling something in it. When he had finished he looked up.

'Okay, let's begin. What've got?'

'More or less what you can see. There are some paintings, prints and photographs on the walls. The furniture in here and then there's the kitchen … or do they call it a kitchenette? … but very little in there.' He pointed to the oak desk. 'That's probably the most valuable item in here.'

'Yes, that's a fine piece.' Walter went over and ran an appreciative hand down the side. 'I'll come to that last, after the rest of the tat.'

'Right. Do you mind if I leave you to it for a while. I'd like to talk to Mavis for a few minutes. That is if she'll let me in.'

'No, go ahead.'

He left Walter peering closely at a watercolour of St Ives bay.

There was no reply to his knock on Mavis's door, but that did not surprise him. He tried again, this time a little harder, and put his face close to the lock.

'Mavis, it's Jack Mitchell here. I need to talk to you. It won't take long.'

Complete silence from within.

'Mavis, I know you're in there. Please open the door. I need to talk to you about the inquest.'

The budgerigar began chirping, but there was no sound of movement. He sighed and was about to move off when suddenly the door opened a crack … just as far as the security chain would allow.

'About the inquest?' Wisps of her wiry hair fluttered in the gap as she positioned her face so that one eye could observe him.

'Yes. Has the coroner asked you to attend the hearing?'

He realised then that it wasn't a breeze that caused her hair to move about like that. The woman was trembling. The single eye was wide with fear and the fingers that now hovered over the chain were fluttering out of control.

'Are you alright, Mavis?'

She did not reply to that, but the trembling fingers seized the chain catch and released it. The door opened cautiously.

'You'd better come in, Mr Mitchell.'

The bird gave a screech as he stepped into the room.

The curtains were half-closed and most of the light came from a standard lamp that stood behind her high-backed armchair. A basket full of knitting wool was on the floor beside the chair and the garment she had been working on was draped over one of the arms.

She wore a long dress and a beige cardigan held together at the front by a single button. Her hair looked as if she had started to show it a brush, but had then abandoned the attempt. The overall picture was of a woman in some distress. It was not the self-assured person he had talked with only a few days earlier.

'Has something happened? You don't look very well.'

She hadn't invited him to sit down so he remained awkwardly in the middle of the room while she stood in front of him clutching her hands together. It was as if she was trying to calm the shaking.

'They want me to give evidence at the inquest.' The words tumbled out and he saw a thin line of dribble by the side of her mouth. 'Do I have to go?'

'Well, the coroner can call anyone he thinks can have a bearing on the case and it's not something you can refuse. When it comes to an inquest I believe they have even more authority than the police.' He put out a comforting hand and patted her arm. 'But you shouldn't let it worry you. It's not like a trial. The coroner simply needs to bring together anyone who can help to establish the exact cause of Dorgy's death.'

'But why me?' she wailed. 'I wasn't even here. I can't know anything about it.'

'You weren't here, but you were Dorgy's neighbour and you'd known him and his family for many years. You can talk about his frame of mind, his general health shortly before he fell and that kind of thing. You'll only be a kind of character witness, Mavis.'

'Is that all?' There was hope now mingling with fear in the old woman's voice.

'Yes, I'm sure of it. And don't forget you were probably the last person he ever spoke to.'

'But that didn't make no sense. It'll sound daft if I repeat what he said in front of the judge.'

He suppressed the urge to laugh. The poor woman was obviously confused.

'No, it's not a trial. He's a coroner, not a judge, simply trying to determine the cause of death. And if it makes things easier for you I'll take you to Truro on the day.'

'So, you've been called too?'

'I have and so has the vicar, so you won't be alone.'

She stepped back a couple of paces, grabbed the back of her chair and closed her eyes.

'Oh, that's such a relief to hear that, Mr Mitchell.' She opened her eyes again and put an age-spotted hand to her cheek. 'Such a relief. I was really scared.'

'Then I'm glad I came to see you.'

'And it's not a trial, you say? I won't be under oath or anything like that?'

'Not a trial, but you will actually be under oath.'

Her fragile confidence suddenly waned as fast as it had returned and she was looking fretful again, so he added quickly, 'But that shouldn't be a problem, surely? As you'll be telling the truth it's merely a formality.'

'No, I suppose so.' But she seemed far from sure about that.

'Look, I have to go now. There's someone in Dorgy's place valuing his possessions, but if you have any others worries, please contact me.' He put on his persuasive smile. 'Promise?'

She simply nodded, so he turned to leave.

'And I'll pick you up for the inquest.'

'Thank you, Mr Mitchell.'

'Not a problem.'

He turned back as the door was closing and caught a glimpse of something in those tired old eyes: something that his reassurances had failed to erase. He began to ask if there was anything else troubling her, when the door clicked shut and the chain went back up.

Walter was peering into one of the recesses of the oak desk when he returned to Hawker.

'Looking for woodworm?'

The antique dealer laughed and straightened up.

'No, no sign of infestation here. In fact it looks in pretty good nick. Well cared for.' He gave the desk an affectionate pat. 'Such a shame.'

'What is?'

'Well, a generation ago this piece would have commanded a good price at auction. Look at it. It's probably late Victorian, but with its raised gallery back and pigeonholes there's a lot going on.' He reached for one of the hidden compartments. 'And these fluted columns are merely fronts for secret caches, but no doubt you've already found them.'

'Yes, Nathan and I have been through them all. There was no treasure there.'

'But today,' he shrugged, 'today there's no market for these heavy dark wood pieces. The present generation with their smaller rooms want light furniture. They have no space for items that came from large grand houses and certainly not oak.'

'Of little value then?'

'Sadly. But you never know who's going to be at the auction. It only takes two to push the price up.' He began to look animated. 'I once went to an auction in London where the chunk of an Abyssinian frieze was being sold as part of a house clearance. From the home of a retired archaeologist, I think. Nobody thought it would fetch more than a porcelain chamber pot, but ... there were two Japanese gentlemen bidding.'

'So, how much did it go for?'

'I can't remember the exact sum, but I can tell you that you could have filled your house with porcelain chamber pots for what the winning Jap paid.' He turned to look at the desk. 'Yes, a great shame.'

'What about the rest of it? Anything else worth putting into an auction?'

'I liked a couple of the watercolours. Again, probably Victorian. Not my taste, but they might come back into fashion. The rest is junk. Put it on a stall at the next church fete.'

'Oh, they'll love me for that!' Jack laughed. 'I wouldn't even dare ask Jane Stokes. No, it'll probably be the tip.'

'What about Nathan?'

'I have no idea what sort of home he lives in, but I'd be surprised if he has any use for most of this clobber.'

Walter slipped the note pad into a pocket and then closed the desk lid.

'That's it then.' Jack went to close the window. 'I'll use your valuations for probate, but how do you recommend we sell … auction, privately, eBay?'

'I think local auction down at Par would be best. You don't want to get into eBay, with all the hassle of delivery.'

'Okay, I'll be guided by you.' He cast a quick look around. 'Right, shall we go?'

They reached the door when Walter suddenly stopped.

'Wait. I forgot to show you something. Come over here.'

He took Jack's arm and led him back to the desk. He rolled back the lid and slid out one of the columnar caches.

'Look at this.'

'What am I looking for?'

'No great revelation I'm afraid … just a small observation of detail. See that mark?'

Jack squinted as he leaned forward to peer into the narrow compartment.

'Yes. It looks like a scratch in the wood, that's all.'

'Aha! Walter exclaimed. 'More than a mere scratch, old boy …

it's a groove. And if you pull the compartment out completely you'll see another groove inside the cavity.' He pushed the compartment back into its slot. 'And if you pull the next one out you'll find two grooves on each and so on up the line.'

He stood up and looked enquiringly at his companion.

'A simple method, but essential for matching, should all of the drawers and compartments be removed at the same time.'

'There's nothing revolutionary in that, Walter, we do that with our drawers at home.'

Walter uttered a loud guffaw.

'I knew you'd be impressed.'

He was still laughing as they left the flat.

CHAPTER 14

On his way home Jack stopped at the store to buy a copy of the *West Briton*. Back in his office he flicked through the pages until he arrived at the public notices. His was one of four that week, but it stood out boldly enough.

He folded the paper and dropped it on a chair. He was not expecting anyone to respond. Who read those public notices anyway? Only public servants, lawyers and sad people.

He left the office and went in search of Catherine.

She was in the garden staring up at a tree.

'Hello, what you doing?'

Startled, she spun around.

'Jack, don't creep up like that.'

'Sorry, I didn't mean to creep.' He kissed her lightly on the cheek. 'Something wrong with the tree?'

'No, and that's the problem,' she replied petulantly. 'Whoever decided to plant this thing here?'

He looked at her, perplexed.

'You did, about eight years ago. You said you liked Japanese flowering cherry.'

'That's ridiculous, Jack. I hate these things, especially in a rural setting. They're so ... so urban. And when they come out in the spring they look like bloody candy floss.'

'So, you want it down?' he asked patiently, knowing he was right about the planting.

'The sooner the better.'

She was still eyeing the offending tree with distaste, as if in her frustration with life in general she had to find something or someone to blame. He wondered if she had stopped taking the tablets, but dared not ask.

'I'll put it on my list.'

He turned to go back into the house, but she had not had her last word.

'Something else for the dreckly list is it, Jack?'

She said something else, but he did not stop to catch what it was. All he could think of was that this was not the woman he married. It was not even the woman of last summer. This was someone who needed help to adjust.

He buried himself in work until the sun began to fade.

The next morning he was up early and left for Truro immediately after a hurried breakfast, so he and Catherine had little chance to converse. In any event she seemed withdrawn and he welcomed the excuse not to indulge in recriminations or any other unpleasant banter.

After going to the bank and a bookshop he walked up Lemon Street and then down Barrack Lane to the coroner's office. There he had a brief talk with one of the office staff about inquest procedure and also obtained a copy of their diary for the coming month. It confirmed that the case of Charles Pascoe was scheduled for 10.00 hrs the following Wednesday in the Municipal Building's council chambers in Boscawan Street.

Arriving back home he was not surprised to find that Catherine had gone out. Often he did not know where she went and often these days he did not ask. It wasn't that he didn't care: it was more that he was afraid of being accused of prying. Something that used to be simple and natural interaction between husband and wife had now become a matter of suspicion, which to his interpretation almost amounted to paranoia. It was a situation that he knew must not be allowed to continue, but one that currently he felt unable to resolve.

He sat for a while at his desk staring at the birch tree, reluctant to raise the stimulus necessary to begin work. Dreckly, he thought. I'll do it dreckly, after a cup of coffee. And that made him think about the hapless flowering cherry.

In the kitchen, waiting for the kettle to boil, he stood looking at the tree and wondering not so much how to cut it down, but where he would dispose of the wood. He drifted back to his office and was still in a mood of introverted nihilism when the telephone rang. It was Rowan.

'Hello, darling. How are you?'

'I'm fine, Dad. Just between lectures at the moment.' It sounded as if she was munching a piece of toast. 'I just wondered if Fentonmar's had any more VAG activity recently.'

It took a second for him to remember what VAG was.

'Ah, the Vivisection Action Group. No, not around here, as far as I'm aware. Why?'

'Because they've been active up here again. Broke into a lab on the campus last night, smashed up a few things and left slogans all over the place.'

'They carry out animal experiments at the university?'

'No, I don't think so, at least not on live ones, but one of the lecturers recently had a paper published in support.' Munch, munch. 'We can't think of any other reason.'

'That's a damned shame. What's being done about it?'

'The police have been called in and there are one or two sympathisers here who've been questioned, but so far no real clues. I was just wondering if there's any link to your lot down in Cornwall.'

'Well, the ones we had rampaging through Fentonmar in the spring have never been traced, so there's no way of telling. I expect there's some kind of network activity, but these people seem to be clever at covering their tracks.'

'Oh, well, I just wondered.'

'Sorry I can't tell you any more. I must admit I hadn't thought about it for a while.'

'Never mind. How's Mum been, by the way?'

He hesitated. There was no reason why he should feel guilt at Catherine's condition, but something nagged inside, telling him that he could have ... should have ... done more to help her. Especially after her visit to Dr Dodsworth. Now he would have to skirt around making that admission to his daughter.

'Not much changed since you were here last, I'm afraid. I did persuade her to go to the doctor and she was prescribed medication, but the moods ... well, she's still rather brittle.'

'It could just be the menopause, Dad. Something that'll pass in a while.'

'How long is a while? Months? Years? And meanwhile what do we do if it's something more permanent?'

She must have detected a note of desperation in his voice, because there was a long silence before she replied.

'Are you suggesting that there might be some kind of mental degeneration, like early onset dementia?' she practically whispered.

'How do I know, Rowan? It's a fine line to tread. I can't make her go to a specialist if it's against her will. I'd rather hoped that the doctor might have detected something, but maybe you'd say that's passing the buck. What the hell do I do?'

'I think all you can do at the moment, Dad, is monitor the situation. You know, make notes of anything erratic or unusual that she does and then, even if it means going behind her back, seek advice from a specialist. That's all I can think of at the moment.'

He looked at his daughter's image above his desk and smiled.

'That sounds like good advice, from a young but wise head.'

'It must be awful for you.'

'It's awful for both of us, darling, but I just hope we find the right solution in the end.'

There was another voice in the background and Rowan cupped her mobile to reply.

'I have to go now, Dad. Lovely to talk to you and try not to worry too much about it.'

'I'll try. And thanks for the advice.'

He put the phone down and shook his head. There was always a weak link in the armour that helped ward off life's problems and his had now been pierced. His wife, the one person closest to him, seemed to be steadily crumbling and he could not think of a way to handle the situation. Thank God for Rowan, he thought.

'Do you feel like going to the pub today?' he asked, not really expecting a positive response.

It was something they used to do regularly on Saturdays not so long ago. After dealing with a few necessary domestic chores he and Catherine would stroll down Fore Street and meet up with friends at the Plume. She would have a glass of chilled white wine – a Burgundy was her favourite – and he mostly drank a pint or two of bitter. They never knew who amongst their friends and acquaintances would be there, but it didn't matter: there would always be someone to chat to. Mostly they would stay for lunch, except in the high summer season when the restaurant filled with visitors. On those days they might have an extra drink and then walk back home to relax.

That was how it used to be.

'Well?'

'I don't think so.' She made a play of sorting some tableware in a kitchen drawer. 'I'm too busy for that.'

'Busy doing what?'

'I'm just ... there are things I need to catch up with, Jack,' she replied, flustered. 'You just don't seem to appreciate ...'

'Okay, but what about lunch? If you're so busy, can I get it?'

'Lunch?' She spun around and glared at him. 'Why are you talking about lunch when we've just had breakfast? For God's sake ...'

She dragged her fingers through her hair, turned and stamped out of the room. Jack watched her depart; a despairing expression clouding his face. He knew she had nothing pressing to do that day. It was all confusion in her mind; the very thought of making rational everyday decisions was proving overpowering. And it was getting worse all the time.

He continued to stare into the void of the doorway and an emotion crept over him that he had not experienced since their son had arrived stillborn. He felt like crying.

The sound of the letter box snapping shut was like a slap in the face. He went to the front door and picked up the morning's post.

Two bills, a begging letter from a charity and a grey envelope addressed in an uneducated hand. He took it all into the office and slit open the letter.

Dear Mr Mitchell,

I am writing this after reading the public notice in the West Briton about Dorgy Pascoe's death and inviting people with claims to come forward. Myself I have no claim, but I was the wife of Nathan Pascoe and I have a daughter who might have a claim to a part of what Dorgy left.

You will see from the address above that I live in Redruth and so does Nathan, but we do not have any contact between us and he has not spoke to me about his father's passing. Also above is my mobile number and I would be pleased if you could call me so that I could come and talk to you about any claim that my daughter might have.

I do not want anything for myself, but I am sure that Dorgy would want her to have somthing to remember him by.

Yours truly,

Rachel Coweth (was Pascoe)

He read it through again.

Something had come out of the woodwork and it was from an unexpected source. Or was it? He knew that Nathan had a daughter, because Mavis had told him so. According to the old lady Nathan had *treated them rotten* and left them for another woman. Rachel Coweth probably knew nothing of the laws of intestacy, so maybe this letter was no more than a bit of hopeful opportunism. But what also surprised him was that she should be reading the public notices on page fifty-six of the local paper, tucked in between the classified section and the sport. It made him wonder if she might have been expecting something of the kind to appear.

He also detected a strange thing about the phraseology in the letter. It wasn't the dubious grammar or the odd spelling mistake. Something else jarred. He asked himself once more, why would this woman think that Nathan's daughter might have a claim to part of Dorgy's estate?

He looked at the mobile number and then checked the time. Now seemed as good a time as any to make the call and it would also divert his thoughts from worries about Catherine.

Jack keyed in the number.

There was a long delay and he was anticipating the recorded message when a female voice answered.

'Yes?'

In the background there was the general hubbub of perhaps a crowded supermarket or a shopping mall.

'Is that Rachel Coweth?'

'Yes,' she replied suspiciously.

'This is Jack Mitchell, Dorgy Pascoe's executor. I got your letter this morning.'

'Oh yes?'

'Is this a bad time to talk? You sound busy.'

'Well, it's not good just now.' She sounded flustered. 'I'm in Asda.'

'Right, not good then. When can I call you back?'

'I'm nearly done. Just got to pick up something from the freezer. Give me a call in ... twenty minutes. I should be in the car park by then.'

'Will do.'

He rang off and then pulled out the file he had started building up on Dorgy's affairs. There were some basic facts that he had jotted down after his talk with Mavis Harris. Was there something she had said about Rachel Pascoe that he needed to know before they talked? He found the few pieces of information he was looking for and quickly read it through. There was very little. She and her baby had been abandoned by Nathan. She lived in Redruth and had a business of some kind, dealing with fabrics.

He waited out the remaining minutes of her twenty and then pressed recall.

She was ready for him and this time the voice came more calmly from the sterile silence of a vehicle's interior.

'So, you got my letter? I hope I did the right thing ... contacting you like that.'

'Absolutely. That's why I published the notice. And how did you manage to spot it, by the way?'

'Oh, I was looking through the ads for something and just turned to that page. The name just jumped out at me.'

'That's lucky. But, you did know that Dorgy had died, didn't you?'

'Yes, I heard.' He detected an unmistakable note of sadness in her voice. 'He was a nice man. Very kind to me ... a few years ago.'

Jack decided it was unimportant to ask how she had heard.

'Rachel, we need to meet. You've made a claim on Dorgy's estate, but there are a number of things we must talk about first.'

'Okay, I'll come to you.'

'No, I'd prefer to meet you where you live, if that's possible.'

She made a sound that might have articulated some kind of mild dissent, because it was a few seconds before she replied.

'Rachel?'

'I ... I'm just thinking. I work, see, so during the day's not good for me.'

'No, I appreciate that, so I was thinking of the evening sometime.'

'Well, if you must,' she said uncertainly, 'but I would have preferred to go to your place.'

It was suddenly clear to him. She didn't want anyone to spot him visiting.

'I understand, but you needn't worry. I'll come late and be very discreet. Now tell me your address.'

'Do you know Redruth?'

'I've been there a few times.'

She proceeded to give him the address and followed that by detailed instructions as to how best to get to it. There was still concern in her voice, but clearly acceptance now that he was in a position to dictate terms.

'I'd like to see you before the inquest on Wednesday next week. That really only gives us Monday or Tuesday. Any preference?'

'Inquest?'

The single-word enquiry suggested more that she did not know what it was rather than the fact that one was taking place.

'It's the coroner's investigation into exactly how Dorgy died. Standard practice after a sudden and unexplained death.'

'But I was told he fell down the stairs at his home. How is that unexplained?'

'No witnesses, he was in comparatively good health and it was in the middle of the night. All of those things need to be explained.'

'Oh.'

Jack pictured her staring out of a car's windscreen. Why, he wondered, were so many people apparently alarmed at the thought of the upcoming inquest?

'So, Monday or Tuesday?'

She took time gathering her thoughts. He heard a car's engine starting up and the lack of hollowness in the sound told him that she had opened a window.

'Um, Tuesday's best for me. Can you make it sometime after eight o'clock?'

"Course I can.' He wrote it down. 'And, will your daughter be there?'

'Why? Is it important?'

'As this affects her it would be preferable to keep her in the loop.'

'I can't say for sure, Mr Mitchell. She's nineteen and I can't tell her what to do no more.'

'I understand. My own daughter's about the same age,' he chuckled. 'But let her know I'm coming anyway and why.'

And that was how he left it: Rachel Coweth after eight next Tuesday. He sat back and thought for a while and then went out into the garden for some fresh air. The early summer sun had dried out the night time dampness and there was crispness in the atmosphere that he found invigorating. He breathed in and stretched his arms.

There was a slight movement to his right and he turned.

Catherine was slumped in one of the garden chairs that he had placed on the patio the previous week. There was a book lying on the ground beside her, carelessly arched as if she had dropped it. She was wearing sunglasses, so he couldn't tell whether or not her eyes were open. He stared at her.

'Lovely day,' he said to the shaded eyes.

A grunt.

'Have you decided about the pub? It might make a nice change for you.'

A mumbled response.

'I take it that's a no then. Okay, so I'll cut the grass then go off in about an hour. Join me if you change your mind.'

And that's what he did. But, she didn't join him.

Jack took the Scorrier road off the A30. It wasn't the most direct route into Redruth, but from the map it seemed the most sensible way to approach the area where she lived. In any event he knew that part well enough not to resort to satnav. There was a warren of small lanes and side streets to the east of the town so a postcode would probably be of little use. If he got lost he would simply stop and ask.

It was clear to him that Rachel Coweth was keen that no one should see him visiting her, but as the calendar was only about three weeks from the longest day it would still be light at eight-thirty. Therefore, once he had located her street he decided he would park around the corner and walk to her house. She had described it as a stone-fronted semi with a brown door.

He peeled off at the top of Mount Ambrose Road and carried on down the hill towards the railway station. Taking the next left after Drump Road he pulled in and took another look at the street map. Her road was not far from there so he drove on for another 200 yards and parked between a white van and a skip bin.

The houses here, even in the back streets of Redruth, reflected the towns auspicious past. Once the centre of mining prosperity many of the dwellings were solidly built three-storey buildings: maybe the homes of mining managers or tradespeople who had thrived on the town's prosperity. Now many of these houses had been converted into flats, with occasional office conversions or builders' yards alongside. Just below where he now stood he knew that Clinton Road boasted many fine houses, but one got the impression that the present occupants in an earlier generation would have been living in the attic and working below stairs. Redruth had become that sort of town. If it were not for the proud statue of a miner at the top of Fore Street and the Cornwall Studies Centre in Alma Place one would be forgiven for being totally ignorant of the town's great days.

He got out and locked the car. It was ten minutes past eight and he suspected that behind most of those tall windows eyes would be focused on whatever game show or soap was showing that evening. Apart from an old woman shuffling painfully along the uneven pavement behind her Zimmer frame there was no one about.

A few yards on he saw the entrance to her road. Here the houses were of a poorer variety and crowded together with no front gardens. Although stone clad and sturdy looking, these former miners' cottages gave off an aura of impoverishment. Cars of the kind that shy away from MOT tests were lined bumper-to-bumper on either side of the narrow cul-de-sac road, making him wonder how they ever managed to leave. There was no turning area at the top, so the only way out was to back into the broader road at the end.

Number eleven had lost one of its ones and only the screw that had formerly secured it to the brown front door confirmed that he had reached his destination. The rusting wrought iron gate uttered a grating creak as he pushed it open and from somewhere inside the house a dog began yapping.

Before pressing the doorbell he looked over his shoulder in both directions. He smiled at what seemed to be an absurd piece of subterfuge, but for some unexplained reason that seemed to be how Rachel wanted it to be.

He pushed the button.

At first there was no movement from inside, so he was about to knock when without warning the door opened.

She was a large woman, mainly around the hip and buttock region: probably the result of a poor diet and lack of exercise over many years. She wore trousers that strained against her thighs and a crumpled cotton blouse revealed a cavernous cleavage. Above a pallid complexion her hair was a tousled mass of peroxide waves with a strawberry streak down one side. It looked as if someone had sprayed it on with an aerosol can.

Jack had only a few seconds to take all this in as they appraised each other, but somewhere under the bloated features he could see the remains of a once pretty face. She was probably little more than forty, but she looked ten years older.

'Mr Mitchell?' she said after also carrying out the quick furtive street survey.

He put out his hand, which she grasped hastily and practically pulled him inside. The door closed sharply behind him and he found himself in a gloomy hallway lighted with a single unshaded low wattage bulb.

'Mrs Pascoe ... I mean Ms Coweth, nice to meet you.'

He nearly stumbled over a wicker basket by the door and as his eyes grew accustomed to the shadowy surroundings he saw other carelessly discarded obstacles scattered around. The dog, obviously shut away somewhere in the house, was yapping again.

'Sorry about the mess, Mr Mitchell. Please come this way.' She threw a glance over her shoulder. 'And it's Rachel.'

She pushed at a door to the right of the hallway and led him into the front room. The light was brighter in here, but the furnishings were depressingly shabby. A two-seater sofa looked like something rescued from the council tip and the other two armchairs were in little better condition. They were the sort with padded seats and thin curved arms. If invited to sit he decided to choose one of those.

There were curtains on either side of the bay window, but they were not drawn closed. The inevitable net curtains were the only barrier to prying eyes. The floor carpet was a mass of colours, most of which jarred with the puce and white striped wallpaper. Apart from a large dusty mirror the only thing hanging on the any of the walls was a print of Monet's water lilies. A small round table stacked with magazines and other papers stood alongside a forty-inch plasma screen television set.

'Is your daughter here, or did she decide to go out?'

'Kylie? Yes she's gone out.'

Had she arranged to go out beforehand or after she heard he was coming? He tactfully didn't ask.

'Pity, because this is all about her really.'

She didn't reply to that, but asked hurriedly, 'Would you like some coffee, or tea maybe?'

'Thank you.' He tried not to think about how hygienic the kitchen might be. 'I'd like some tea, if it's not too much trouble. Milk, no sugar.'

'No trouble.' She waved an arm at the sofa. 'Make yourself comfortable while I put the kettle on.'

Jack sat and scanned the room with a jaundiced eye.

There was a curse from the kitchen followed the clatter of something metallic falling on the floor. Thinking that it could be some while before the tea arrived, he got up and crossed the room to the overloaded table. The contents looked like refugees from a dentist's waiting room. A copy of the *Western Morning News* lay underneath a well-thumbed woman's magazine.

He picked up the newspaper. It was a few days old and the lead story recorded the rescue of a weekend sailor who had got into trouble off the Lizard.

He was about to put the paper down again when a smaller headline wedged down the right hand side caught his attention. *Animal rights group smash lab. See p 9.* It had to be Rowan's story.

After a quick glance towards the kitchen he flicked over the pages.

Page nine was there, but so was a gaping rectangle where the story had been cut out. There was the sound from next door of a spoon rattling the sides of a cup, so he hastily closed the paper and went back to his seat.

'There you go.' She thrust a large steaming mug at him.

'Thank you.'

Why put off until tomorrow, he read on the side of the mug and then, turning it around, *what you didn't want to do yesterday?*

When he looked up she was sprawled on the sofa staring at him expectantly.

'Is there any chance that Kylie might be back before I leave?' He took an experimental sip of the tea. It was drinkable.

'No way. She comes in all hours. Don't know what she gets up to sometimes.'

'Too bad. Well I'll go through it all with you and maybe you can let her know what we've discussed.' She nodded. 'Okay, I'll start by telling you what happens with a case of intestacy ... that is, when someone dies without leaving a will.'

For the next twenty minutes he covered the circumstances of Dorgy's death; explained the necessity for an inquest; told her about the search for a will; and finally outlined the circumstances in which Kylie might have a claim. She sat expressionless through most of this, but when he had finished a tightening of the flesh around her eyes suggested puzzlement.

'I think I've got most of that, Mr Mitchell, but what I don't get is why the public notice was necessary. I mean, it's not as if Dorgy was worth much, is it?

'The public notice is necessary because the executor has to try his best to flush out all claimants. So far you're the only one, but I don't know if Dorgy deposited a will with a solicitor or in a bank deposit box. If I ignored that possibility and went ahead assuming he'd left no will there would be an awful stink if later on someone came forward with a legitimate claim. Do you see that?'

'Yes, I understand that part, but, like I said, Dorgy didn't have that much to leave, so no one's going to create over a pittance.'

He drank some more tea and then carefully placed the mug on the floor by his chair.

'How do you know?'

'Sorry?'

'How do you know that Dorgy had only a pittance to leave?'

'Well, I ... I don't know ... I only assume,' she said, flustered. 'He was never a man of ... I mean it's not as if he won the lottery or anything.'

'Did you know him well enough to form that opinion, Rachel?'

To his surprise a red flush began to work its way up her stout neck and she tried to cover what he assumed was embarrassment with a chubby hand to her mouth.

'I don't know what you mean, Mr Mitchell,' she stammered. 'He was my father-in-law, so for the years I was married to Nathan I knew him as well as any daughter-in-law would.'

'But that state didn't last long, did it? I believe that soon after Nathan came back from the navy you two split up. Is that right?'

'Yes, that's right.'

'So, for the many years that passed between when you parted from Nathan and Dorgy's death he was effectively not your father-in-law.'

She squirmed on the sofa and giggled nervously.

'You sound like a lawyer cross-examining me.'

'I'm sorry, it's not meant to be like that. I'm just trying to establish a few things that might help me as Dorgy's executor.'

That sounded weak to him, but she seemed to accept it.

'Does that mean Dorgy might have left more than I thought?'

'It's possible, but I've still got a lot of research to do.'

'And you're saying that Nathan gets it all … whatever it is?'

'If there's no valid will, yes. He is Dorgy's only child, I believe.'

'And can that be challenged?'

'A will can be challenged in law, but I don't think there's any way of overturning the laws of intestacy.'

She suddenly ran the fingers of both hands through the strawberry-streaked mop of hair and turned aside to stare intently at the blank TV screen. A jumble of indecision seemed to be churning through her mind. Jack watched closely as he picked the mug from the floor. The tea was tepid, but he drained the lot. It was something to do.

'Would it make any difference,' she began slowly, 'if Nathan was not Kylie's father?'

For a moment he was stunned by the question. He hadn't been expecting a fast ball from this woman.

'Well, yes,' he replied, frowning. 'If she's not related to him then there would be no link to Dorgy and therefore no possibility of a claim of any kind. Is this a hypothetical question?'

Rachel didn't reply for several seconds and he was sure it wasn't because she was ignorant of the word *hypothetical*.

'Forget I asked that,' was her eventual reply. It was abrupt and emphatic.

He didn't pursue it, but neither did he forget it. People like Rachel don't ask such questions without cause or motive.

After that there was little else to discuss. He said he would keep her informed as to his progress and whether or not there were any other claimants. He also assured her that it was unlikely either she or Kylie would be called to the inquest. If the coroner had wanted them he would have issued a summons by now.

He got up, handed her the mug and shot a glance at the window. It was dark now and the street light cast its orange glow over the row of cars beneath.

'Do you mind if I use your toilet before I go?' He grinned self-consciously. 'That was a large mug of tea.'

'No, of course you can.' She turned to point. 'It's straight ahead at the top of the stairs.'

'Thank you.'

He went slowly up the stairs, aware that she was watching him from below. He didn't look left or right, but went straight into the bathroom and closed the door. Crouching low he peered through the vacant keyhole, from where he had a clear view to the base of the stairway. Rachel was no longer there.

Quickly he opened the door, stepped out onto the landing and then pulled the door closed behind him. There were two other doors on the landing: one open with the light on and the other closed with the letter K painted in red at eye level. He went across to the closed door, clenched his teeth and turned the knob. It wasn't locked, so he pushed it open and felt for the light switch.

His mouth opened in amazement. It was like a police operations room during a murder hunt: or more appropriately perhaps, the centre of operations of an obsessive collector. An entire wall was papered with news cuttings, photographs, posters, slogans and advertisements. The bed was neatly spread with a duvet, the cover of which featured badgers gathered in and around their setts. That was all that was neat. A pile of clothes lay on the floor by an open cupboard, a chair was heaped with magazines, a table was littered with cosmetic detritus and propped in one corner was a furled banner.

Jack knew had had only a few seconds to take all this in before arousing suspicion, so he flashed an image of it with his mobile and stepped swiftly back onto the landing. Back in the bathroom he darted across to the lavatory and gave it a flush, then noisily ran some water from the basin tap. He was halfway down the stairs when Rachel appeared from around the corner.

'Sorry about the delay. One of my contact lenses fell out in the basin.' He made a play of fingering an eye. 'Damned difficult to find again sometimes.'

She didn't comment, but turned her gaze to the top of the stairs, as if expecting to see something out of place.

'Have you lived here a long time?' he asked as they moved towards the front door.

'Most of my life. It was my father's house and I inherited it after he died.' She unlatched the door and added bleakly. 'Cancer.'

'I'm sorry. Such a cruel illness.'

He put out his hand and she took it hesitantly.

'Thank you again for seeing me, Rachel. And, as I said, I'll be in touch.'

'OK.'

The door closed behind him as he crossed the road and, when he glanced back at number eleven, he saw a light go on in the front bedroom.

The skip had not moved, but the white van in front had and its place had been taken by a battered pick-up. It took several manoeuvres to extricate his car from the slot. While he was doing this he caught sight of a faint red glow from the front seat of a builder's van on the other side of the road. It only lasted a second, the time it takes someone to draw on a cigarette, and all was darkness again when he pulled out into the road.

As he turned into the main road that would take him out of Redruth he looked into the rear-view mirror and noted that the van and its occupant had not moved.

It was after ten o'clock when he arrived home. He garaged the car and opened the front door quietly. But he need not have bothered. Catherine was still up and watching some inane chat show, where a couple of so-called comedians were showing off in front of an audience primed with laughing gas.

'Hello,' he said, putting his head around the door. 'Everything alright?'

'Yes,' she replied, not looking up. 'Why wouldn't it be?'

Okay, he asked a stupid question, but did it deserve a stupid answer? He stared at the back of her head for a few moments.

'I've had a bit of a tiring session with the client in Redruth, so I'm going to bed now. Do you need anything before I go up?'

She half turned now and he could see that she had applied some deep red lipstick. 'No, I think I can remember how to go up the stairs.'

'Right, then I'll see you in the morning.'

He turned out the porch light and locked the front door, trusting Catherine to deal with the other lights.

In the bedroom he pulled out his mobile and called up the photograph of Kylie's room. It had been taken in haste, so not a great shot, but he was able to zoom in on various parts of the display wall.

It was not possible to read any detail, nor identify any individual person, but some of the headlines stood out boldly. One of them was the report cut from the *Western Morning News* and there, above some lurid photographs of different species of animal, many in a state of distress, were the initials VAG.

CHAPTER 15

Mavis Harris was waiting for him at the front of the almshouses. She stood between two of the mock Doric columns staring anxiously up Fore Street as if not believing he would actually arrive at all, let alone at the promised time.

Jack pulled over and leant across to open the passenger door for her. He smiled as he saw her chosen outfit. This was to be a big day for her and she had dressed in what was probably her finest get-up: the same clothes that she would wear for a wedding or a funeral. It was just unfortunate that a pale blue woollen suit was totally inappropriate for a warm June day. As she struggled into the car he reflected on how hot she would be in the council chamber.

'Hello, Mavis. Alright?'

She wriggled into a comfortable position and then reached for the seat belt as they set off for Truro.

'Yes. And you?'

'Yes, fine.' He glanced at her. 'Now, Mavis, I know this is something new for you – in fact it's new to me too – but it shouldn't be an ordeal. The coroner is a professional man – he could be a lawyer or a doctor – and he will have conducted many inquests, so he'll be experienced in making people feel at ease. It's not a court case, so there won't be any pressure from a bullying counsel, or anything like that. Just listen carefully to what's being said and, when he asks you a question, just answer it simply and truthfully. No one expects any more than that from you.'

'How long will it last?'

'I've seen the rest of the day's schedule, but I don't know exactly. Probably about two hours. Only the complex cases last more than that.'

'You think this will be straightforward then?'

'Let's hope so.'

They sat in silence for a while as they both, for different reasons, continued to hope for a speedy conclusion to the morning's proceedings.

It wasn't until Jack turned onto the A390 that she turned to him and asked, 'Do you know who else will be there?'

'Not precisely. Nathan, of course, and the vicar, but I can't think who else could make a useful contribution.'

'What about the doctors?'

'I doubt it. What is usual is that the relevant medical people will have submitted written reports and these will be read out by the clerk.' He turned and grinned at her. 'Doctors are too busy to give up their time to attend inquests.'

'Mr Mitchell,' she said slowly with a faint tremor in her voice, 'there's something still bothering me.'

'Oh? What's that?'

'You know I heard Dorgy say something before he passed out ... you know, at the bottom of the stairs?'

'Yes, I remember.'

'Well, it made no sense to me then and it makes no sense now and I'm beginning to think ... well, that I misheard.'

'Mavis, you were quite sure you heard right when we talked. I even wrote it down. *Tell Jack Mitchell 'tis in ivy.* That's what you heard, isn't it?'

'I know, but that's what I *thought* he said. Suppose I heard wrong? If I heard wrong then I'll be misleading the court, won't I?'

'No, Mavis, of course you won't. That is what you believe he said and so all you can do is repeat it to the coroner if he asks. Dorgy was on the verge of unconsciousness, so whatever he said was probably nonsense in any case.' He reached out and patted her arm. 'It's certainly not something for you to fret about. All you have to do is say what you heard. Anyway, he might not even ask that question.'

Mavis was silent, but he could tell that he had not succeeded in putting her at ease.

A few minutes later they drove into the outskirts of Truro and Jack headed for the car park nearest to Boscawan Street. Beside him he could sense his elderly passenger's discomfort as she perspired in her woollen suit. It was unlikely that the committee room would be air conditioned.

He swung the car into the multi-storey and eased it into a space near the paying machine. Two hours or three? He fished around for some coins and then slotted in enough to cover three hours. Mavis was still unbuckling her seat belt. It was still only nine-forty and the inquest was not due to open until ten. He took the parking ticket and put it on the dash as the old lady hefted herself out of the car.

'It's only a five minute walk from here and we've plenty of time,' he said

As they walked at her meandering pace down the lane by the car park and then through Lemon Street Market he began to wonder how he would frame his own answers. He was still pondering this point when they arrived at the unprepossessing entrance to City Hall.

Jack held the door open for Mavis and she stepped inside cautiously, as if entering the Tardis for the first time. He nodded at the woman behind the information desk and then shepherded the old lady past the ranks of publicity leaflets, towards the winding stone staircase. It was slow progress to the top as she kept stopping to look at photographs of past mayors of Truro that lined the walls.

They were greeted at the gallery landing by the Inquest Support Service representative clutching a clipboard. She smiled at them, glanced down at the board and then turned to Jack.

'Good morning, are you here for Charles Pascoe's inquest?'

He still found it strange to hear Dorgy referred to so formally, especially as the craggy old fellow looked such an unlikely individual to be labelled Charles.

'Yes. I'm Jack Mitchell and this is Mrs Harris ... Mavis Harris.'

The assistant ticked off their names on the register and gave Mavis a toothsome smile.

'Good, thank you.' She indicated the row of seats along the wall outside the committee room. 'Please take a seat. If you need something to drink before we begin, there's a water cooler down the corridor.'

'Who is the coroner today?' Jack asked.

'Mr Callingham.' And then added respectfully, 'He's a QC.'

Mavis made a little noise and they both looked at her. The eyes betrayed the old woman's inner fears, but the astute assistant also sensed the situation.

'There's no need to worry, my dear. Mr Callingham is very gentle with his line of questioning and you'll find that he won't labour a point once he's got an answer.'

'There, nothing to worry about,' Jack whispered as he led Mavis to a seat.

As he sat down beside her Jack looked around. It was still early for the session, but they were not the first to arrive. A tall man in an ill-fitting suit stood by the cooler sipping water and staring into a glass trophy cabinet. From his bearing and close cropped hair Jack guessed that he was a policeman.

Sitting opposite were a couple of young women. One was overweight and trying to hide it by wearing a loose-fitting floral dress, parted in the middle by a wide leather belt. The other was slim and pretty with scraped back black hair, pale skin and an oriental slant to her eyes. They were deep in conversation, glancing occasionally at an iPad balanced on the floral lap.

Neither Jane nor Nathan had yet arrived.

He was about to say something to Mavis when a door opened onto the corridor and a grey haired man in a charcoal suit stepped out. He looked around him briefly and then headed over to where they sat. He introduced himself as the clerk to the court, asked who they were and then gave them a briefing on the court procedure.

It was during this briefing that Jane arrived at the top of the stairs puffing from the climb. She saw Jack and came over to them, standing behind the clerk until he moved off.

Jack stood.

'Cutting it fine, Jane.'

'I know. Traffic problems.' She nodded at Mavis and then looked around. 'Nathan not here yet?'

'No. I hope he's not forgotten.'

'Better not have. I believe there's a massive fine for not heeding a coroner's call.'

Their conversation was cut short by the return of the clerk and Jane stepped aside to hear what he had to say.

Jack was staring idly at the perspex ceiling high above the corridor, watching the blurred outline of a gull as it strode around, when the door opposite opened again. A small neat man came out. The clerk saw him, excused himself hurriedly and crossed the hallway to join him. The two of them then made their way purposefully across the hall to the heavy oak door marked *Committee Room*. The Inquest Support assistant gestured to the assorted gathering and the move into the room began.

The two women with the iPad were ushered to one side of the room where a row of chairs was stationed, the others were invited to sit at the table in the centre and Callingham QC took his position at its head.

The clerk took his place to the coroner's right and Jack sat next to him. Mavis shuffled into the chair close beside Jack and on the other side of the table Jane and the crumple-suited man took their places. The Support Service assistant sat as sentinel by the door.

Callingham took his time. He laid out his papers in two orderly piles, took off his glasses to give them a wipe and not until he had done that did he look up and study the group.

'Good morning.' He raised his eyebrows, peered over the top of his reading glasses and gave the gathering the benefit of a disarming smile. 'We're here today to look into the sad demise of Charles Pascoe, known I believe to all as Dorgy Pascoe, and to determine the precise cause of his death. Put simply, what I ...'

The committee room door opened, the Support Service assistant stood up sharply and Callingham's eyes narrowed as he focused on the cause of the disturbance. Nathan, unshaven and close-cropped, stopped in the doorway and looked about him.

'Sorry,' he mumbled as he was directed to the seat opposite Mavis.

When all attention had returned to Callingham, the coroner resumed.

'As I was saying, the purpose of this inquest is to examine the who, where, when and how leading up to Mr Pascoe's death. At the end of all the testimonies that we shall hear this morning I hope to be able to reach a definitive cause of the incident that led to his death and then to direct accordingly. If however I am not satisfied that we have heard all of the evidence available then we will adjourn, giving such time as is necessary to gather that evidence. Let us hope that will not be the case today.'

He turned to the clerk.

'Do we have the medical reports?'

The clerk opened a file and placed a large hand on an A4 sheet.

'Right. I'll ask the clerk to read the reports from the attending paramedic, from Mr Pascoe's doctor and also the autopsy statement.'

The clerk coughed, adjusted the spectacles that seemed too small for his broad face and began to read from his typed sheet.

The paramedic's report was brief but succinct. He and his colleague had attended the scene at eight-forty in the morning after being called to the location of an apparent fall down a staircase. The casualty's exact position at the base of the stairs was described in detail, even down to the angle at which his trailing foot was turned. The casualty, a white male of about seventy years of age, was unconscious, had bled profusely from a head wound and, after he had been stretchered to the ambulance, was found to have abrasions on arms and legs. It also seemed likely that some ribs had been fractured. The casualty's injuries seemed to be consistent with a fall from the top of the stairs. Although the precise time of the fall could not be determined, as the casualty was fully clothed it could be assumed that it was before he went to bed that night.

Jack glanced at the coroner for his reaction to that piece of deduction, but there was not a trace of irony in his expression.

There was some more detail after that, but Jack was now studying Nathan. The man was wearing a denim jacket over a red and black patterned shirt and his gold cross glinted under the bright ceiling light as he fidgeted with his fingernails. Was he not taking this all in, or was he deliberately trying to appear detached from the circumstances of his father's death?

Then, suddenly conscious of the stare, Nathan looked up and for a few seconds the cold dark eyes held Jack's in an uncompromising challenge. Jack didn't blink, but he gave a faint nod and then turned his attention once more to the clerk, who had now moved on to Dorgy's GP's report.

This again was brief. For a man of sixty-nine (not actually true, Jack thought: he would not have been that age until September) he was in reasonable health. Although he smoked moderately and suffered occasional bouts of bronchitis his heart was strong and his blood pressure normal. He drank alcohol, but apparently not frequently to excess. Since retiring from his occupation as a farm artificial inseminator he had taken little regular exercise, but was not known to have any physical restrictions in his normal daily movements.

The clerk stopped and turned to the coroner. Callingham took his cue and asked those around the table if all that was clear so far. There were nods from all those concerned, except for Nathan, who continued to pick at his nails.

'Very well, could we now have the hospital's report? As you are probably all aware, Mr Pascoe died in hospital a short time after admission and in the circumstances an autopsy was deemed necessary.'

The clerk adjusted his glasses once more and launched into the autopsy statement. This was longer and far more detailed in nature and, from some of the expressions around the table, caused some discomfort amongst the listeners. Jack, who tended to recoil at the sight of blood, tried desperately to listen to the words without conjuring up vivid images to accompany the script. It didn't help his concentration either to hear Mavis softly sobbing at his side.

Eventually the clerk reached the end of the statement. He closed his file and for a few moments there was complete silence in the room. It was as if the coroner were allowing Dorgy's spirit time to waft away into some ethereal resting place before he brought them all back to reality.

Mavis had stopped crying and was now blowing her nose. This seemed to irritate Nathan, because Jack caught him glaring at her from under his thick black eyebrows.

'We have now heard all of the medical evidence,' the coroner resumed, 'from which it would seem that none of Mr Pascoe's injuries was inconsistent with a tumble down the stairs. As you heard, the eventual cause of his death was a delayed and massive brain haemorrhage: something that it seems could not have been predicted, in spite of the head injuries and subsequent scans.'

There was something in the delivery of his last few words that to Jack appeared weighted with cynicism, but no one else seemed to notice.

The coroner now turned to Jane, who up to this point in the proceedings had been totally absorbed while staring at some point on the wall opposite.

'Reverend Stokes, you knew Dorgy Pascoe quite well I believe and spoke with him only a few days before his death. Would you please take the oath before I ask you a few questions about your perception of his state of mind?'

The clerk stood up and went around to where Jane sat.

'You can either take an oath on the Bible or read from the prepared statement, but,' he smiled, 'I would think you should have no hesitation in choosing the former.'

Jane stood, placed her hand on the Bible that the clerk held out and repeated the oath. She sat down again and gave the coroner her full attention as the clerk resumed his seat.

'Reverend Stokes, what is your assessment of Dorgy's frame of mind in the days before his fall?'

'He was always a quiet and reserved sort of character, sir.' Jack smiled: she clearly knew the correct form of address. 'He wasn't a regular churchgoer, but was always prepared to help with parish activities. I don't know if he had a wide circle of friends, but that was probably from personal choice. But it was only after the incident outside his home in the spring that his personality seemed to change and after that he tended to become more introverted.'

'Would you remind us of this incident and, if you can,

suggest why in your opinion it might have caused a change in his personality?'

Jane then went into a lengthy discourse on the VAG demonstration outside the almshouses and the fact that Dorgy seemed to become withdrawn after it. She, of course, knew nothing about Dorgy's shareholding in Gammarho, but her account of the happenings on that spring night made Jack's stomach give a lurch. It was suddenly obvious to him that when it came to his turn it would probably be unavoidable under oath for him not to disclose what he knew about the shareholding. Showing all his cards before these people in a public arena was the last thing he wanted to happen, but in a coroner's court there could be no refuge behind the screen of client confidentiality.

He looked across the room at the two women sitting against the wall and scribbling. My God, he thought. They had to be from the local press.

He was still scrabbling around his jumble of thoughts for some plan of damage limitation when Jane wound up her statement with an almost casual reference to the break-in at Dorgy's flat. The coroner inclined his head and eyed her over the rim of his glasses.

'This break-in ... a burglary, I assume you mean? Was anything stolen?'

'No, sir, as far as Mr Pascoe could see nothing was taken. There was some disturbance amongst his effects, but that was all. It was as if the intruder had been looking for something, but had gone away empty-handed.'

'I see.' He tapped his pen gently on the pad. 'And were any of the other flats broken into on that day?'

'No sir.'

'Well, thank you for that helpful résumé, Reverend Stokes.' He turned his attention to his order paper and then raised his head slowly until he settled his gaze on Mavis.

'Mrs Harris, you were the unfortunate person who found your neighbour, Dorgy Pascoe, on the morning after his fall. It must have been a terrible shock for you and something you will never forget,' he said gently, but Jack could almost feel Mavis trembling. Or was it he who was trembling? 'So, in your own words, would you please tell us what happened that morning?'

Once more the clerk proffered the Bible and, in tremulous tones, Mavis repeated the oath and then sat down heavily.

'I understand that you had been away from home for the night. Would you tell us what happened when you returned?' The coroner removed his glasses. 'Take your time, Mrs Harris … or, may I call you Mavis?'

Jack reached out and tapped her softly on the arm. She stirred, gave a sputtering cough and then drew herself up in the chair. Her big moment had arrived.

'I went into the almshouses yard soon after half past seven. I was early that morning because my sister's husband works up the road from Fentonmar and he always starts before eight and he gave me a lift in. When I pulled open the door at the bottom … it's hardly ever locked … I got the shock of my life, because 'e was lyin' there.'

'By "he" I suppose you mean Dorgy Pascoe?'

'Yes.' she said, looking at Callingham as if she couldn't have been talking about anyone else.

'And when you say the outer door is hardly ever locked, do you mean it can be locked if necessary?'

'There's three of us … two now … living up there and like as not we forget to take our front door key, so with no bell or nothin' we could be there all day or night knockin' to get in.'

'So, it is possible for anyone to walk in there at any time?'

'I suppose so, unless the caretaker chooses to lock it at night.'

'How often does she do that?'

'When she's feelin' teasy.'

A subdued burst of mirth spread around the room and the coroner turned to his clerk with an arched eyebrow. The clerk leaned towards him and whispered, 'Bad tempered, sir.'

'Ah. And how often might that be? You see,' he hurried on, 'I'm trying to establish in percentage terms the likelihood of the outer door to the almshouses being unlocked on that particular night.'

'Um, if I might ...' Jane had raised her hand like a schoolgirl who needs to catch the teacher's eye.

'Yes, Reverend Stokes?'

'I visit the almshouses on a regular basis and talk to residents both upstairs and down, so I do have a fair idea of how often that door is locked at night. In fact there have been concerns, which I have passed on to the caretaker, that there might be a security risk there.' Jane drew in a breath. 'So, I would say that the outer door is very rarely locked. Perhaps four or five times a year.'

Callingham finished making a note and looked up.

'Therefore one might safely assume that the door would have been accessible to anyone throughout the night that Mr Pascoe fell down the stairs?'

'I would say so, yes.'

'Thank you. No doubt the police have established this point in talking to the caretaker.' He shot a glance at the man on Jane's left. 'We'll pursue that point later.'

The room was becoming warmer and someone nearby was not using a very effective deodorant. One small window high above floor level had been opened, but it was not enough to circulate the air in the room. It was sufficient however to allow in the sound of the cathedral clock, which began to strike eleven.

The coroner was addressing Mavis again.

'You found Dorgy Pascoe lying at the foot of the stairs. What did you do?'

'It took a few seconds to get over the shock, but I bent down and felt 'is head. I don't know why ... maybe to see if it was still warm. 'Is eyes were closed but I could see a pulse on his neck and I knew he was alive. Then I saw all the blood and I near fainted.' She stopped and Jack turned to look at her. She seemed at that moment to be on the verge of fainting. The ever vigilant assistant was on her feet and by Mavis's side in a few seconds, handing her a beaker of water. Mavis drank gratefully.

The coroner caught the assistant's eye and beckoned her over.

'Is it possible to open another window?'

'Yes, of course. I'll fetch the pole.'

She scurried around the table and picked up a six-foot pole from the corner by her chair and returned to hook down one of the windows. There was a faint murmur of relief from the group, as if grateful for a pause in the intensity of the proceedings. Whether or not the small window would make much difference to the ambience of the room probably mattered little: it was a break.

Jack gave Mavis another glance. She seemed to have recovered.

'Very unpleasant for you, Mavis,' Callingham continued. It seemed to be an understatement. 'You say his eyes were closed, but did he at any time regain consciousness while you were with him?'

Mavis took a few seconds to answer.

'It were as if 'e was waitin' for someone to come ... as if all those hours 'e was holdin' on to speak to someone. Yes, I was about to go off to get help, when he opened his eyes and I saw 'is lips moving. I said *Oh, Dorgy, what happened*, but I couldn't hear nothing so I put my ear to his face.'

She stopped again.

'And what did he say?'

'It made no sense, my lord.' The coroner accepted his promotion without blinking. 'What Dorgy said, or what I thought I 'eard 'm say was, *tell Jack Mitchell 'tis in ivy*.'

She sat staring at the coroner, clutching her hands together and appearing to be expecting a reprimand for making a stupid statement. Jack turned his attention to Nathan and was astonished to see the man glowering at Mavis from across the table. The look could only have been described as one of overt hostility.

'We have it on record that that is precisely what you heard him say, but, on reflection, could it have been something else?'

'No, sir,' Mavis was now quite emphatic, 'that's what I 'eard 'im say. It might make no sense, but there's nothing wrong with my 'earin'.'

'I'm sure there isn't.' The coroner smiled at the old woman. 'So then you went off for help. Where did you go?'

'One of the ground floor residents has a telephone, so I knocked on 'er door. She was still in bed so I had to knock for a couple of minutes before she opened up. But when she saw Dorgy she soon woke up proper and made a call for the ambulance.'

'Did you attempt to move Mr Pascoe at all before the ambulance came?'

'I wanted to. To make him more comfortable like, you know, but the neighbour said leave 'im be. She's been to first aid classes, see.'

'She did the right thing. And how long was it before the ambulance arrived?'

'Not long. They were very quick really. Maybe about fifteen minutes, but I don't know for sure. I wasn't paying' much heed to time just then.'

'I'm not surprised. Now, when the ambulance arrived, what did you do?'

'I went into the neighbour's flat and she gave me some tea.'

'And that was the end of your involvement?'

'Yes, sir.'

He scribbled some more notes on a yellow pad and then laid his Parker neatly beside it and looked up.

'Thank you, Mavis. That's all been very helpful.'

Callingham consulted his papers again and then turned to the grey-suited man.

'Detective Constable Hill.'

'Hall, sir.'

The coroner looked down at his list and then back with a smile at the policeman.

'I'm so sorry. Obviously a mistype.' He made a hasty correction. 'Now, would you give us the police report of the incident?'

DC Hall stood to read from the statement card. He then sat and ran his hand over the paper in front of him as if ironing out any wrinkles before beginning to read out the findings of the forensic team. As they had not been called in until after Dorgy's death it was obvious that evidence might inadvertently have been compromised, but the entire area, including Dorgy's flat, had been covered as thoroughly as possible, including careful reference to photographs taken by the ambulance team. The eventual conclusion was that

Charles Pascoe had fallen from the top of the stairs without any evidence of third party involvement. There were signs from skin fragments that he had tried to arrest his fall, but without an adequate hand rail such an attempt would have been in vain.

It had been noted that the window onto the balcony at the front of the house was open on the night of the incident, but it had been established that that was not uncommon at the top of the almshouses, where the residents frequently went out onto the balcony.

Forensics had also examined the clothes that Mr Pascoe had worn that evening, but again there was no sign of any DNA other than his own. There were traces of recent alcohol spillage on the front of a cardigan, but, as the autopsy report had disclosed, he had been drinking a moderate amount of beer on the evening of his fall.

Hall stopped, folded the paper and looked up at the coroner.

'Thank you constable.' Callingham pulled at one of his earlobes as he focused on the policeman. 'You say that there is nothing suspicious regarding the open window onto the balcony, but what about the unlocked door below?'

'In terms of access you mean, sir?'

'Yes,' was the sharp response. It was the first sign of irritability that the coroner had displayed in seventy-five minutes.

'That was noted as a security risk, sir, but each individual door to the flats off the landing had locks and it is unlikely that an occupant would have admitted anyone they were unsure of. But, from a health and safety consideration we drew attention to the lack of a handrail on one side of the stairs, the inadequate lighting on the stairwell and the uncovered stone treads on the stairs.'

'I understand that those safety measures have now been taken in hand . . . alas too late for Mr Pascoe.' He leaned forward. 'But you say that the police investigation came up with no evidence to indicate that Mr Pascoe's fall was anything other than a tragic accident?'

'That is correct, sir.'

'Thank you constable.'

Calligham took a drink of water and then adjusted some of the papers in front of him. Without looking up he said, 'Mr Mitchell, would you take the oath please?'

Jack stood, took the Bible and repeated the clerk's words. As he resumed his seat he caught Nathan's eyes on him. They contained the same challenging glare, as if willing him to do his bidding ... whatever that might be.

'Mr Mitchell you were one of the last people to speak at length with Mr Pascoe. Would you tell us, please, what exactly was the nature of your dealings with him?'

'Yes, sir. I am a church visitor, appointed by the vicar,' he pointed at Jane, who nodded, 'to visit people in the parish ... usually elderly people ... as a pastoral service. They are usually people on their own, who might be lonely, or perhaps have suffered bereavement. Well, after Dorgy's experience with the animal rights protesters Jane, the vicar, asked me to talk to him and ask if there was any kind of support we could offer.'

'Forgive me for interrupting there, but what made you think Dorgy in particular was being targeted and not any of the other residents of the almshouses?'

'At the time we didn't think he had been singled out. It was just that the others seemed to take the demonstration in their stride. Dorgy didn't. He just went into his shell, or so it was reported back to the vicar.'

'I see. Please continue.'

'At first he was reluctant to see me. We didn't know each other well ... just nodding acquaintances in the pub ... so no reason why he should have thrown his door open to me. Anyway, eventually I did persuade him to let me in and we had a chat.'

Jack paused and smiled sheepishly at the coroner.

'I have to admit that I bribed him with a pint of his favourite beer.'

There was a ripple of restrained mirth around the room and even the coroner's eyes sparkled for a couple of seconds. Jack cleared his throat and continued.

'Once I was in his flat we talked generally, which led eventually into discussion about the demonstration. That's when he claimed that they were targeting him specifically. He was quite emphatic about that, but unfortunately he refused to give me any reason why and we left it at that. It wasn't until he came to see me several days later about a tax return he'd received that I found a rational reason for him being the demonstrators' target.'

Jack had been addressing his recollections directly to Callingham, but now he paused and glanced at Nathan. It was something he had been resisting, but some magnetic force suddenly compelled him to seek out those dark malevolent eyes in order to gauge a reaction. He regretted it instantly, because it betrayed his own weakness.

For a few seconds, seeming to Jack much longer, their two pairs of eyes locked in a one-sided combat. He was under oath and about to reveal publicly something about Nathan's father that he had not even discussed with the son. And Nathan's expression was now telling him that somehow he knew what was coming. Jack found himself fighting to hold his nerve.

'Mr Mitchell?'

He swallowed, licked his lips and then turned back to face the coroner.

'I made an appointment to visit Dorgy at his flat to go through his papers and help him with the return, although at that stage I could see no reason why a man of his means ... or so I thought at the time ... should be filling in a tax return at all.' He stopped to take a drink of water. It tasted stagnant, but it was wet. 'Then, to my amazement, I discovered that Dorgy Pascoe is the registered owner of a holding of ordinary shares in a major pharmaceutical company.'

There was a gasp of surprise from someone in the room, but it wasn't Nathan. Jack stole a glance at the journalists. They were scribbling furiously.

'And being ordinary shares I presume they bore dividends?' Callingham asked coolly.

'They did, sir. The Inland Revenue must have done a trawl and found that no additional tax had been paid on this income. Hence the tax return. But, what surprised me almost as much as Dorgy's shareholding was his apparent ignorance of its worth.'

Although this information was not directly relevant to the hearing, it seemed to have seized the coroner's imagination and he pursued the point.

'How do you think that came about, Mr Mitchell?'

It was too late to draw a line, so he went on to explain the historical events: Dorgy's employment and the takeover by Gammarho of the company his father worked for and the fact that Dorgy was an unworldly man, who simply had no knowledge of the value of his holding, nor of the fact that it was growing annually by the reinvestment of dividends.

Even Jane Stokes was now looking perplexed and, although the words were coming out of his own mouth, Jack could understand how it might all sound so implausible to those sitting around the table. But he avoided looking at Nathan again.

'And presumably the animal rights protesters also found out about Dorgy's holding?'

The coroner was right on the button, but then he was a QC.

'Yes, sir. It's not difficult to find shareholder lists of publicly quoted companies and this one has a history of animal experimental research.'

Callingham started rolling his expensive fountain pen between thumb and forefinger as he gazed pensively into the distance. One could detect a legal brain hard at work.

Eventually he stopped rolling the pen and pointed it at Jack.

'If Dorgy Pascoe was ignorant of the value of his own shareholding, what, in your opinion is the likelihood of any other third party being privy to this knowledge ... that is, apart from the animal rights protesters?'

It was a tough one to answer. Having admitted a few minutes earlier that he was not close to Dorgy, it might not ring true if he said it was unlikely that anyone else knew of the shareholding. But if he played safe and said that it was implausible that no one else in Dorgy's circle knew, it would throw the question open as to who might be included in that arena. And, in any event, how would his answer affect the ultimate verdict of the inquest?

Suddenly the room seemed to be a very small, stuffy and

claustrophobic place: a box with no exit and where Callingham and the rest of them now sat in the stalls waiting for his answer.

He took another sip of water and then looked down at the table as he replied.

'I got to know Dorgy better during our dealings over his tax affairs and I found him to be a very reticent and private man. Incredible as it may seem, I believe he genuinely had no knowledge of the value of his holding in this company and therefore I find it highly unlikely that anyone else amongst his group of personal friends and family had any knowledge of it either. I think it would have been out of character for him to have spoken about it with anyone else and that his shock at being targeted by the protest group was in no way feigned.'

He set his jaw and then looked up at the coroner. Please, he thought, don't ask for the size of the shareholding.

Callingham wrote something briefly on his pad and then lifted his head and met Jack's earnest stare with his own non-committal mask.

'Thank you, Mr Mitchell.' He linked his fingers and leaned forward. 'What then did you make of the subsequent break-in to Dorgy's flat? Do you consider that this was connected in any way with his shareholding?'

'No, sir. I discussed the break-in with Reverend Stokes, without mentioning my discovery of Dorgy's shareholding of course, and we could not think of any reason other than it being an opportunist burglary where the perpetrator found nothing of value. In any event it would not have benefited anyone to steal the share certificate, even if it had been there to steal.'

Callingham's brow wrinkled and he pursed his lips as he peered over his glasses. For a moment Jack was sure he was about to ask where the certificate was at the time of the break-in, but he presumably dismissed this as being irrelevant to the enquiry.

'I think that's all for now, Mr Mitchell, thank you.' He leant over to the clerk and a few words passed between them before he turned to address them all. 'We've been in here for the best part of two hours, so I think it would be a good idea if we all stretched our legs for a few minutes. If you would all go out into the corridor now and perhaps take a comfort break, I'll ask the inquest attendant to return you to the committee room in about ten minutes.'

He leaned his slim frame back in his chair and eased his shoulders while the witnesses pushed back chairs and began to shuffle through the open door. The policeman was the last to pass the attendant and he stopped to murmur a few words to her.

'Yes, of course,' she replied, 'I'm sure you won't be required again today.'

DC Hall turned and, like an animal that has been released from a cage, bounded gratefully down the winding staircase.

Just before the door closed again Jack had a glimpse of the coroner and clerk deep in conversation. He felt a tap on his elbow and turned to find Mavis looking up at him.

'Why didn't he call Nathan?' she whispered hoarsely.

Jack's eyes swept the corridor before answering. The man in question was at the far end drawing water from the cooler.

'I don't know. Maybe he felt there was nothing he could add to the information already provided.' He squinted at her. 'Did you want him to be questioned?'

'No!' Her reply was emphatic. 'No good would have come of that, I'm sure. He would just have blackened poor Dorgy's name.'

'You think so?'

'Yes. He's a mean one that Nathan.'

Nathan was now walking slowly back up the corridor so Jack moved away from Mavis and hailed Jane as she came out of the ladies' toilet.

'Well, what do you think the verdict will be?' he asked her.

'Oh, I do hope he's satisfied with what he's heard, Jack. If not then there will have to be another hearing and maybe next time with a jury.'

'That would be a bit extreme, wouldn't it? To summon a jury, I mean.'

'Probably, but if he decides for example that Dorgy's death was caused as a result of negligence on the part of the almshouse authorities, well ...' She heaved an exaggerated shrug and the dog collar rose up her neck.

'As you say, let's hope it doesn't come to that.'

They were silent after that, both buried in their own thoughts. To pass the time and also to exercise his legs he excused himself and wandered down to the water cooler. One of the journalists, the thin one, was standing there looking up at the perspex section of the roof

'It hardly seems adequate for a building like this,' she said as he filled a plastic cup.

'No, it doesn't look it, but I bet it's pretty tough stuff.'

'To let more light in, I suppose.'

'I reckon so,' He sipped from the cup. 'Are you from the *West Briton?*'

'Yes. It's my turn to do inquests,' she giggled. 'How do you think this one'll turn out?'

'No idea, but we'll find out in a few minutes.'

He flashed her a brief smile and then wandered back to the main group.

'Ladies and gentlemen,' the inquest attendant announced as she opened the committee room door, 'would you please resume your seats.'

They all began to shuffle back into the room, like reluctant sheep being penned at the end of a drive. As he pulled his chair in closer to the table Jack turned and gave Mavis a reassuring smile. Nathan was already seated and seemed to be deliberately avoiding eye contact with anyone.

When all was quiet and he had their attention Callingham QC surveyed the group.

Jack had managed to check the inquest diary and knew that they had already overrun the allotted two-hour session and that Callingham was due to hear another case at two o'clock. Whichever way this was going he reckoned the coroner would have to be brief.

'As you can imagine, every case that comes to inquest court is harrowing for friends and relatives of the deceased and this has been no exception,' he began, while studying his pen. 'As I said at the beginning of this case what I have to do is to hear all the evidence available and then decide the who, when, where and how before reaching a verdict. I have done that this morning and I thank you all for your contributions towards my reaching a verdict. For most it will have been the first time you have had to do something of this kind and I expect some of you might have found it a bit stressful.' He aimed a tepid grin at Mavis. 'However, your testimonies have helped me tremendously in reaching a conclusion.'

And the winner is ... the irreverent thought flashed through Jack's head.

'We have had the medical reports, we've heard the statement from the police, Mrs Harris's replies to my questioning and statements from the other two witnesses. I had decided not to call upon Mr Pascoe's immediate neighbour at the almshouse as he had already given a full report to the police and would have had nothing useful to add to these proceedings. So, I am satisfied that I have heard all of the relevant statements pertaining to events leading up to Mr Pascoe's death.

'Although there are some aspects of this case which might never be explained, such as why Mr Pascoe was on the landing so late at night, these, in my opinion are insufficient to influence my decision. There is also the matter of the lack of security and safety measures at the almshouse, but these have now been corrected and I hope lessons have been learned for the future.'

His verdict, once it finally came, was very low-key and delivered in a matter-of-fact tone of voice.

'It is my conclusion therefore that Charles Pascoe died as a result of a tragic accident and I am now releasing his body to the family for burial.'

There was a sudden hiss from Nathan and all eyes turned to him. His own eyes were blazing in what Jack later described as a look of wild triumph, as if his football team had scored a winning goal in extra time. Jack frowned at him. Having contributed nothing to the entire proceedings and being there presumably because he was next of kin, he was now displaying an unseemly lack of decorum.

Why? The verdict permitted him to bury his father, but why should that produce such a reaction?

The clerk was clearly embarrassed, Jane was shaking her head, but the coroner appeared unmoved and was gathering up his papers. Perhaps he had seen and heard it all before: different people react in a variety of ways.

'Thank you all.' It was the clerk, pushing his chair back, who gave the signal for dismissal and they began to file out.

Nathan was the first to leave the committee room and, looking at nobody as he strolled out, he began rolling a smoke as he made his leisurely way down the staircase, wearing a smug expression.

'What did you make of that?' asked Jane

'Well, he clearly had no love for his father, so I suppose he sees the verdict as a step nearer to his inheritance.'

'Yes, you managed to keep that close to your chest.' She smiled up at him.

'Client confidentiality, Jane. I wasn't likely to broadcast it around Fentonmar and neither did I want it to come out here. Unfortunately the coroner forced my hand.'

He said a brief word of thanks to the inquest assistant as they passed and then checked that Mavis was till in tow. She was following meekly a step behind them.

'I wonder if that information should have made a difference?' Jane murmured.

He stopped abruptly and looked directly at her and Mavis almost bumped into him.

'To the verdict, you mean?'

'Yes.'

'Should it have? You sound like Jane Marple, not Jane Stokes,' he laughed.

'Perhaps not,' she replied and began to go downstairs ahead of him. 'Perhaps not.'

No more was said about Nathan and his impending inheritance and outside the big blue doors in Boscawan Street they parted company: Jack and his passenger towards the car park and Jane Stokes heading off to the SPCK shop near the cathedral.

He was deep in thought, still pondering Jane's question, when Mavis grabbed his arm.

'Mr Mitchell, look there.'

He stopped and followed her gaze.

'What is it?'

'In the window there. It's Rachel and I think she's waving at us.'

He saw her now. She was sitting at a counter near the window of a coffee shop, with a hand raised, as if hailing a taxi. She was looking directly at him.

'Mavis, have you got something to do in the city ... shopping perhaps?'

'Well,' she replied slowly, 'not really, but I can always find something.'

'Thank you. It looks as if she wants to speak to me. I hope you don't mind.'

'No, I don't mind.' She looked at him suspiciously. 'I didn't know you knew her.'

'You remember where we left the car?' he said ignoring her comment. 'Well, I'll meet you there in half an hour. Okay?'

'Alright.' She shrugged and waddled off towards the Pannier Market.

Jack went into the café.

'Hello, Rachel.'

'I'm so glad I caught you, Mr Mitchell.' She swivelled off the stool, knocking a cup as she did so. A spoon clattered to the floor and Jack bent to picked it up.

'Can I get you another coffee?'

'No thanks ... or maybe yes ... it might be best to talk in here.' She was flustered.

'Okay, I'll get them. Cappuccino okay?'

She nodded and the strawberry streak did a little dance on her head.

When he returned with the coffees she was making an effort to smooth down her wild platinum locks with a long thin brush. She was not succeeding. He put the cups on the counter and drew up a stool.

'Thanks.' She cast an anxious glance out of the window before facing him again.

'Who are you trying to avoid?'

'Is it that obvious?'

He smiled at her and stirred the coffee. She hung her head and two folds in her neck joined up as one.

'Did you see Nathan leaving the Municipal Building?'

'Yes, he went out before us. Why?'

'Well, he's the one, I don't want him to see me ... specially not talking to you.'

'I saw him heading towards the bus station, so you should be alright. So, what's on your mind?'

She might have had many hours to rehearse this meeting and what she was going to say, but it was clear that she didn't know how to kick it off. She played with the coffee spoon and looked again out of the window.

Jack sneaked a glance at his watch.

'You know I asked you about Kylie's position when we met?' she began.

'You mean about her rights as a possible beneficiary?'

'Yes, and I said what would the position be if Nathan wasn't her father.' She was practically squirming and a faint flush tinged her full cheeks. There was another long pause. 'Mr Mitchell, I've never told anyone this before and I'm only telling you now because Dorgy's dead and because Kylie ... she's my daughter alright, but ... but she's not Nathan's.'

It was Jack's turn to look out of the window. He chewed gently on his lower lip as he took in this revelation.

'So, whose daughter is she?' he asked, still peering through the streaked glass.

When there was no immediate reply he turned back to face her. There was a smudge under her left eye where the mascara had moistened.

'Dorgy's,' she whispered.

She had said it so softly that he practically had to lip read.

'Dorgy's?' he repeated after a moment, as if to confirm that he had heard her correctly. 'Would you like to tell me how that came about?'

With a great sigh she relaxed. It was as though she had jumped the last hurdle in an obstacle race and was now heading for the finishing post. Suddenly there was no stopping her.

'Nathan was at sea a lot of the time during the early years of our marriage, so I was on me own much of the time. Dorgy was very kind and helped out when he could. His wife had died, so I also helped him. He didn't have that many close friends, so I suppose we comforted each other and helped each other out ... you know, how families do. Then, one night after we'd been to the pub, had a few laughs we went back to mine and ...' she shrugged. 'He was a good looking man and fit. I was young and lonely. I thought, what the hell ... and so it happened.'

Jack, mesmerised by this frank exposure of infidelity, drained his coffee cup and took a deep breath.

'Bloody hell,' he murmured, 'this cracks open a can of worms.'

She blinked and gave him a bland stare.

'But it makes a difference for Kylie, doesn't it?'

He blew out a sharp exhalation of air and scratched his head vigorously.

'My dear lady, that consideration is only one part of a whole string of events, but yes, it could make a big difference. But, before I raise your hopes too much let me list a few things that will have to be established.'

Her face took on a wide-eyed attentive expression.

'To begin with, I can confirm that under the Family Law Reform Act of 1969 illegitimate children have the right to inherit on the death of a parent, but,' he raised a cautionary finger, 'you will have to prove beyond doubt that what you have told me is true before Kylie can have any hope of inheriting anything.'

'Of course it's true,' she said indignantly. 'You don't think I'd lie on a serious matter like this. It took a lot for me to come out and tell you at all.'

'Rachel, I am not doubting your word. I am just telling you that you will be required to go through all kinds of hoops to establish legally that Kylie is Dorgy's daughter.'

'Well, for a start she was born barely eight months after Nathan came back on shore leave. I used to pretend she was premature but she wasn't,' she said slyly.

'Okay, maybe that can be established from hospital records … if they're still available.'

'And what about DNA?'

'Rachel, Nathan will have the same DNA as his father.' He raised his eyebrows at her.

'Oh, of course.'

From a mood of expectant euphoria she suddenly became downcast and now stared despondently at her bright red fingernails.

'Then there's Nathan's reaction to this news. Have you considered that?'

'How do you mean?'

'Suddenly finding that his only child might not be his, but his father's? And, if that is proven, having his inheritance halved? Surely you can see that he's going to fight your claim?'

'He'd fight his own shadow given the chance,' she said sullenly.

He checked the wall clock and then turned back to her. There was no doubt that it had taken a lot of nerve to reveal her dark secret for the first time and, whether or not it was true, one thing was certain: she was not the one who would benefit by it.

'Does Kylie know any of this?'

'God, no!' She said it so vehemently that a couple of people in the café looked their way. She lowered her voice to add, 'She doesn't even know Dorgy was supposed to be her grandfather.'

'What?' He stared at her incredulously. 'How can that be?'

'Like I said, soon after Kylie was born we broke up and Nathan went 'is own way. Dorgy kept in touch for a while, but for my sake, he said, he thought it best to stay away as she grew up. I think he was afraid of what Nathan would do if he found out 'is father was still seeing me.'

'You're telling me that Nathan might have suspected you were…?'

'Yes, he always did and that's the main reason for them falling out. So, from the beginning Kylie thought 'er grandfather was dead.'

Jack's face wore a pained expression. *God, what a mess other people's lives can be,* he thought. This was all going to take a lot of sorting out, but at least now he could see a few pieces of the jigsaw puzzle falling into place.

'I'll need to talk to Kylie. You realise that now, don't you?'

'Yeah, I suppose so.' She hung her head.

'It won't be easy for either of you, but it has to be faced some time.'

She nodded.

'But before that happens, there's another matter I need to be clear about.'

'Yes?'

'I know that Kylie is involved with the animal rights movement … the Vivisection Action Group in particular.'

Her mouth dropped open.

'How do you know that?'

'There are plenty of clues about your house, but never mind that. What I want to know is, if Kylie didn't know Dorgy was her grandfather, how did it happen that she was demonstrating with the VAG outside his home that night?'

It was a speculative shot, but she flinched, almost as if he had hit her.

'She *didn't* know it was her grandfather they was targeting. He was just a man who held shares in a big company that carried out animal experiments,' she whined. 'Honest, if I knew what she was up to I would have stopped her.'

'How could you have stopped her? You couldn't do that surely without telling her the truth about her conception.'

'I could have found a way. I didn't want Dorgy hurt, but I didn't know it was Fentonmar they was going to that night.'

'So, you *did* know of her active involvement with VAG.'

'Yes, but I 'ad no influence to stop it. In fact, in some ways I have a sympathy with what they're trying to do.'

'Until it directly affects the father of your child?'

'Yes. Until that happened. And,' she added defiantly, 'I honestly didn't know it was Dorgy's place they went to until long after.'

'How long after?'

'Oh, must be weeks. Someone from Fentonmar told me.'

'I see.' He looked at the clock again. His half hour was running out. 'But Kylie knew her target's surname ... the same name as her supposed father. Why didn't that make her stop and think?'

She surprised him by laughing.

'Mr Mitchell, do you know how many Pascoes there are in Cornwall?'

'Ah, I see what you mean.'

He looked up as a young woman in a green apron bustled up to the counter and snatched up their empty cups.

'Finished?' she asked brusquely.

'Yes thanks. We're leaving in a couple of minutes.'

The woman gave a curt nod and hurried away.

'Anyway,' Rachel added demurely, 'I think Kylie resented the fact that someone with that name should be dealing in such companies.'

It was his turn to laugh.

'So, you say your daughter thought she was simply harassing a man called Pascoe who happened to own shares in a pharmaceutical company, but was no kin of hers?'

'That's right.'

'And you found out about this harassment and realised the connection some weeks later.'

'That's right,' she repeated.

'But those *some weeks later* was before I went to see you in Redruth.'

'Yes ... So?'

'Then, Rachel, you've not been completely honest with me, have you?'

'Oh?'

'When we met at your house you led me to believe that you had no idea Dorgy had anything substantial to leave, but by that time you did know about the shares. So, why the deception?'

The red flush was rapidly returning.

'I ... didn't know what ... I thought it best to pretend I didn't know ... for Kylie's sake mainly.'

'Well, from now on I think we need complete honesty if we're to make progress with this. Alright?'

'OK. I'm sorry.'

'Good. Let's keep it that way. Well, I have to catch up with Mavis now, but I'll be in touch. I think we need to move this case along.'

He pushed off from the stool and went to pay for the coffee.

When he held the door open for her she hesitated, searching the street before making a move out of the shop. Then, as she passed him he suddenly had a thought.

'I take it this meeting was no coincidence?'

'You said the inquest was today, so I knew you'd be here.'

'I told you the inquest was today?'

'Yes.'

'Right.' He put out his hand and she took it limply. 'Well now, don't forget. I'll need to talk to Kylie and the sooner the better.'

She gave him a weak smile and a vague nod of the head, then turned and headed in the direction of the bus station. Jack stood for a few moments, watching her make her ungainly way up Boscawan Street. She had known about the inquest date and time, but she certainly hadn't expressed an interest in the verdict, and he found that odd.

When Jack reached the car in the covered parking area Mavis was nowhere to be seen. He checked his watch, to find that he had left her for nearly forty minutes. Surely she hadn't wandered off again?

He was about to unlock the car when a movement caught his eye and Mavis appeared from behind a pillar.

'Hello! Playing hide-and-seek?'

She hurried towards the car as fast as her bent legs would permit and pulled open the passenger door. Her face registered something close to fear.

Jack slid in behind the wheel and looked inquisitively at the old woman.

'What's up?'

'It's Nathan. He's been hanging about here, but I don't think he saw me.'

'Are you sure?' He started the engine. 'I saw him heading towards the bus station.'

'He was here alright. Talking to someone, then got on that bike of his and roared off a few minutes before you came.'

'So why were you still hiding?' He eased the car out of the parking space.

'I don't trust that man. He might have come back.'

Jack smiled as he pulled out into the sunshine.

'You can laugh, Mr Mitchell, but I don't like that Nathan. There's no good in him.'

'You know what they say, Mavis? That there's some good in everyone.'

She didn't comment on that, other than to grunt her scepticism.

He pulled out into the road and turned left towards the A390. Traffic was dense in both directions and the school holidays had not yet begun. He slowed to allow a yellow delivery van pull into the stream and at the same moment from the corner of his eye he saw a motorcyclist mount his machine up the side street to the right.

The rider had his helmet on, but the build was about right. It could have been Nathan, or maybe Mavis's paranoia was catching. The sighting occurred so fast that he had no chance of a second look. Now there were several cars behind him, obscuring any opportunity to see if the motorcycle was following.

'What did she want?'

Mavis's sudden question jolted his concentration.

He eyed the rear view mirror as he moved onto Trafalgar roundabout. There was a motorcycle, but the rider had a different colour helmet. Or was it a trick of the light? He switched lanes to get a better view and received a horn blast from a blue Audi coming up fast behind.

'She wanted to know how the inquest went, but didn't want to be seen by Nathan,' he lied.

'Huh! I can understand that.' He sensed her staring at him. 'I wonder how she knew about it?'

'What? The inquest?' It was best to play dumb. 'I wondered that, but it's not actually difficult to find dates of public meetings.'

She turned away then and stared straight ahead. Nothing more was said until they were a mile from Fentonmar. Then, as Jack slowed behind a tractor, he turned to look at his passenger.

'Mavis, tell me, has Nathan ever threatened you in any way?'

It was as if he had given her an electric shock. He actually felt her jump in the seat.

'Me, Mr Mitchell? Why would he threaten me?' she wailed.

'You seem to be scared of the man and people aren't scared of other people without good reason.'

'I'm not scared,' she replied in a voice that had sunk a couple of octaves. 'Well, not zackly scared. It's just that I don't like 'im … never 'ave, since when he was young. An' if I can avoid meetin' 'im I do.'

'But you would tell me, wouldn't you, if he ever threatened you in any way?'

She was silent.

'Mavis?'

'I would, but I can't think why he would threaten me.'

She sounded completely unconvincing, but he decided to leave it at that. There would be another occasion to press the point.

He pulled into the recess in front of the almshouses and Mavis bent down to gather the plastic bag of goods she had bought in the city.

'There. Quite a morning, eh? At least Dorgy can now rest in peace.'

'I 'ope so, Mr Mitchell, I certainly do 'ope so.'

She got out with some difficulty, dragging the bag behind her. She then bent down to thank him for the lift and he gave her a little wave in acknowledgement. The door slammed shut and he carried on up Fore Street.

'I 'ope so too, Mavis,' he mimicked, but somehow he suspected that it might be some time before Dorgy would be giving him any lasting peace.

CHAPTER 16

'Morning, Catherine,' Walter Cartwright's voice boomed from the hallway, 'is Jack in?'

He didn't hear Catherine's soft reply, but within seconds the antique dealer was being ushered into his office.

'Thank you, my dear.'

Catherine smiled wanly at him and then disappeared into the kitchen.

'Come in, Walter. Something to report?'

'Got the valuations for you.'

'Sit down.' Jack swivelled in his chair. 'Catherine offer you some coffee?'

'Not for me, old boy. Just had breakfast.'

Walter reached into an attaché case and pulled out two sheets of A4.

'As we both suspected there's nothing to excite a beneficiary here.' He handed one to Jack. 'The most valuable item is, of course, the desk. It's early Victorian, solid, with a sound back and lots of nice little recesses. In an auction it might ...' he sucked on his teeth, 'it might fetch about a thousand.'

'Oh, that's not bad.'

'On a good day, mind. As I told you, the market's gone flat on these dark furniture items, but you never know who's going to be bidding. I once pulled in a four figure sum for a wind- up gramophone and that was because two collectors were vying with each other.'

'And the other stuff?'

'I got a second opinion on the watercolours and my chum says they could be worth another five hundred, especially if they're sold separately.'

'I assume they're by different artists.'

'Oh yes, but sometimes dealers try to buy a group as a job lot, hoping that the sum of the parts is greater ...' He spread his hands and left the sentence dangling.

'Of course. So, apart from that ...?'

'Junk. Might as well go to the skip ... or you could try eBay.' He slapped his thigh and let out a bray of laughter. 'I never cease to be amazed at what sells through that site.'

'You do any business that way?'

'Oh yes, but please don't ask me to offload Dorgy's detritus that way.'

'Don't worry, I wouldn't do that to you. But, what do you suggest we do now? Auction, or private sale?'

'Auction would be simplest for you. There'll be the auctioneer's fee of course, but it should be the easiest and most profitable way to dispose of the best items.'

Jack looked down at the valuation list. Somehow it seemed a trifling inconvenience compared with Dorgy's main prize, but it all had to be accounted for.

'Thanks for that, Walter.' He smiled at the antique dealer and tapped the paper. 'I don't suppose you want any of this?'

'Not just now, old man. I've got a house clearance coming up and need all the space I can muster. Anyway, what about the beneficiaries? Might they not want some of it, rather than the cash?'

'Somehow I doubt it, but I'll have to ask anyway. Sure you won't stay for a coffee?'

'No, got to get on.' He stood up noisily and zipped up the case. 'What do I owe you for this?'

'Just put a beer on the slate, old boy.'

Jack stood and saw him to the door.

In the hall Walter collected his battered fedora and shouted a farewell to Catherine to which there was no reply. Jack saw him out.

It would be Nathan Pascoe's call next regarding disposal.

'Would you like to go up to Nare Head this evening?'

Jack had found Catherine indulging in her current obsession: sorting out her wardrobe. As usual, clothes were scattered on beds and floor, with some draped haphazardly over the back of a chair. There seemed to be no order or system involved. Apart from his natural concern about this compulsion his only other observation was that women tend to own too many clothes. Only his deeper concern about her brittle frame of mind prevented him from saying so.

Catherine did not respond immediately. She had her back to him and was holding a short cotton dress up to the light from the window. It was pale yellow with a low neck line and what he called puffed sleeves.

'Do you remember this one?' she asked wistfully.

'Yes, I do. My God, that goes back a few years. You wore it at that fundraising party in Veryan, if I remember rightly.'

She looked over her shoulder at him.

'Did I?'

'Well, that and on a few other summer occasions.'

'No good now, is it?'

'Time and fashion move on, unfortunately. I try not to be sentimental over clothes.'

'You try not to be sentimental over anything, Jack,' she sighed and dropped the dress unceremoniously at her feet. 'But, you're right I'm too old for this now.'

He reached out to hold her, but she moved away and trod on the yellow dress as she closed the wardrobe door.

'Well? Would you like to go up to Nare Head ... if that's not being too sentimental?'

She spun round and put her hands on her hips.

'What for, Jack? What's the bloody point?'

'The point, my love, is to get some fresh sea air on a warm summer evening before the cliffs begin to swarm with holidaymakers. Also, perhaps to enjoy each other's company over a bottle of something chilled. Is that point enough?'

Her arms fell to her side and she closed her eyes tightly. This time she didn't resist when he moved in and pulled her close to him. Her head fell against his shoulder and he felt rather than heard the sobs that shook her slack body.

He stood like that for what seemed like minutes, stroking her hair and gazing out of the bedroom window at swallows swooping above the rooftops. Gradually the sobbing eased and he felt her trying to disengage. She had opened the valves and now the sump was drying. That was fine for the moment, but it was no long-term solution to what he now accepted as a case of chronic depression.

Mental health specialists analysed depression with different degrees of severity. He had looked it up. There was mild, moderate or severe depression, each requiring differing levels of treatment by mental health teams of psychologists, occupational therapists or specialist nurses. These people attempted remedies involved anything from cognitive behavioural therapy to simple counselling. A psychological disorder was now countered with a psychological solution: thankfully the days of administering electric shock treatment were long past.

Jack released Catherine and gently raised her head with a supportive hand under her chin. She smiled weakly at him.

'Sorry for being so feeble,' she murmured and ran a drying finger under her eyes.

'You shouldn't apologise for being feeble. I should be apologising for being uncaring.' He smiled into her damp eyes. 'Let's help each other, eh?'

She gave a faint nod.

'Do you still want to go up to Nare Head?' she asked.

'Only if you do. I don't want to go up there again on my own. It's not the same.'

'You'd better pick up the bottle then.'

She was trying hard, but he noted that her voice still held a resigned note of overwhelming gloom. Even with antidepressants this was going to be a long haul back to a positive view of life.

While Catherine changed into her walking jeans Jack busied himself filling a rucksack with a chilled bottle of Pinot, a few scotch eggs and a couple of bags of crisps. It gave him some satisfaction to close the door on a ringing telephone a few minutes later.

They drove mainly in silence, but it was the silence of unspoken communication. Jack felt that for the first time in several weeks he had reconnected with Catherine. She was sitting beside him, not just in body, but in spirit as well. Her mind might be scrambled under the cloud of depression, but there was at last a dim spark: one that he felt he could work on until it burst into flame. They were no longer completely alone with each other and he felt a glow of warmth in that knowledge.

Jack parked the car in the usual place and was pleased to see that they were on their own. He locked up and, with the rucksack slung over one shoulder he took her hand. They walked on until, finding a comfortable spot near the top of the slope, they settled down on the spongy grass and he opened the bag.

She turned away from the sea view as he uncorked the bottle.

'You've been very busy recently. Tell me about it.'

'Not very exciting really.' He poured out the wine. 'Different and in some ways interesting, but ...'

She took a glass from him and leaned back on her elbows.

'But what?'

'Oh, I don't know ... slightly troubling actually.'

'Tell me.'

He looked at her and smiled. She actually sounded as if she wanted to know.

And so, for the next few minutes he regaled her with what he now referred to as 'Dorgy's case': details of the inquest, Nathan's mercurial moods, Mavis's anxieties, Rachel's revelations, he spilled it all out with no thought to client confidentiality. This was therapy: something to deflect her from her own perceived problems.

When he had finished he replenished their glasses and stared out at the reflection of the lowering sun shimmering over the rippled sea below them. Catherine didn't say anything for a while and he glanced to his left to see if she was still awake. She was chewing quietly on a scotch egg, holding it delicately between thumb and forefinger. He watched as she ran her tongue across her lips to each corner of her mouth.

'Tell me about Mavis Harris,' she said and then licked her fingers.

'What about her in particular? Do you know her?'

'I know her slightly. I sat next to her at a WI meeting once and we've talked at village hall events.' She shifted her weight to one elbow and threw the remains of the egg to an expectant gull. 'What do think she was anxious about?'

'Well,' he took in a deep breath, 'there was the inquest. New territory for her. New territory for most of us in fact, but she was really wound up about it. She's an old lady, so that's understandable.'

'Hmm, she might be old, but she never struck me as someone who might easily be rattled.'

'You can't really tell, until someone is put into an uncomfortable or unfamiliar situation.'

'She was in the forces, you know.'

'No, I didn't.'

'Before she married, but that should show she's no wimp.'

'What is this?' He grinned at her. 'The notorious woman's intuition at work?'

'Maybe something like that.' She sipped at the wine. 'From what you've said, I reckon someone's got at her. Spooked her.'

'Really?' He looked up at the sky to reflect on that suggestion. 'Well, if you're right, then there's probably only one person who might have done that.'

'The person who stands to gain and lose the most from Dorgy's death.'

'Nathan.' He frowned. 'He's not the most amiable of human beings, Catherine, but it's going a bit far to suggest that he might have threatened an old lady ... and for what purpose?'

'Jack, has anybody asked him where he was on the night his father fell down the stairs?'

He laughed loudly and the gull flew off.

'My dear girl, I think that's a bit fanciful. He might be an uncouth layabout, but what I think you're suggesting is ... well, completely insubstantial.'

'Why? You told me yourself that anyone could walk into the almshouses at any time. The old boy next door is deaf as a post and Mavis was away at the time. All he had to do was force his way into Dorgy's flat.'

'Firstly, Dorgy kept his door locked and secondly he would not have let Nathan in. He loathed Nathan, even though he was his son.'

'Ah, Nathan loathed his father, because of what he suspected he had done, but was it true the other way around?'

'OK, even if Dorgy didn't actually hate his son, I reckon at least he was afraid of him ... *because* of what he had done. Either way, Dorgy would never have let him in. And, I repeat, the door was not forced. The police established that fact.'

'So now it's quite probable that no one will ever be able to prove where Nathan was that night.' She reached out and prodded his arm. 'I don't know anything about inquest procedure, but don't you think it odd that the coroner didn't call Nathan?'

'I was surprised actually, but I suppose he was heavily influenced by the police report. They found absolutely nothing suspicious.'

Catherine thought about this for a minute, swilling the remains of her wine as she watched a pair of butterflies dancing in the evening sunlight.

'I think you need to talk to her again.'

'Mavis?'

'Yes. Try to get her to tell you what she's afraid of.'

'I'll think about it.' He sat up and brushed some grass off his trousers. 'But she'll just have to join the queue. There's Kylie, who's got to be told her dad's not her dad. There's Rachel to find out what she's told her daughter. And then there's Nathan to find out what he wants to do with his father's effects and to break the news to him about the fortune he's inherited.'

'Half a fortune now.'

'Oh, God, don't!'

'Poor you. I hope he doesn't feel inclined to shoot the messenger.'

She laughed then and he cheered inwardly to hear a sound that had been absent for months.

Some time later Jack had reason to remember that laughter, because in the innocent euphoria of the moment he had joined in the merriment.

On the way home he had rested his hand on her leg. They both knew that she was a long way from escaping from her black place, but at least they were now fighting it together.

The recorded message was from a tense sounding Rachel Coweth, saying briefly that she and Kylie had had a talk and that the latter would be in the next evening if he wanted to come round. Jack opened his diary and saw that he was free.

'Why do they need to see you in the evening?' Catherine asked as she began clearing dishes from the kitchen table.

'I know, it's not convenient, but maybe they think there's less chance of me being spotted at that time.'

'But why the attempt at subterfuge?' She shook her head. 'It's not even dark, for God's sake.'

'Perhaps they're not at home during the day? I don't know, love.' He picked up his mobile. 'All I know is the sooner this is over and done with the better.'

'Well, I hope someone's going to pay you well for all your chasing around.'

'Don't worry, it'll come out of Dorgy's estate. I'll make sure of that.'

'Good.'

He kissed her lightly on the cheek and went to pick up the car keys.

'You'll be alright?'

'I should think so.'

'I hope to be back in about two hours, but I'll give you a call before I leave Redruth.'

'Good luck.'

The now familiar journey to Rachel Coweth's terraced house took under half an hour and he parked in an adjacent street as before. As he approached the front door he glanced up and saw that Kylie's bedroom light was on. A moving shadow behind thin curtains told him that the occupant was at home.

He knocked and the door was opened almost immediately. It was as if Rachel had been hovering in anticipation of his arrival. Her chubby features folded into a smile that didn't quite reach her eyes and she stood back to let him pass.

'She's upstairs.'

'Good, but I'd just like to talk to you first.' He dodged the clutter in the hallway and looked inquiringly towards the front room.

'Yeah, come in.'

She turned down the TV volume, but didn't invite him to sit. He noticed that the strawberry streak now had a twin, but the rest of her coiffure was still a tangled peroxide mess.

'You've told her?'

'Yeah,' she sighed. 'It wasn't the easiest thing I've ever 'ad to do and there was a lot of cryin' ... from both of us.'

'But, in the circumstances, it had to be done.'

'I know that, but I'll tell you something ... after all these years hidin' it away, I now feel a sort of relief. Got it off me chest.'

'And Kylie? How did she take it?'

'Well, like I said, she cried and locked herself away for bit and ...' She stopped abruptly. 'Oh, do you want to sit down?'

'No thanks, I'll go up and see her in a minute if I can. But, tell me, how does she now feel about you?'

'Well, I don't think she hates me or anything like that. She was shocked at first, but now I think she's just disappointed.'

Blimey, that's an understatement if ever there was, he thought. Jack had no pretensions at being a behavioural analyst, but disappointment seemed to him to be the very mildest of reactions on hearing that the man you thought of as your father was in effect your ... what? Your half-brother once removed?

'I see. Did you talk about anything else?'

'Like what?'

'Like her potential legacy, or anything else that came out at the inquest.'

'No, I did explain to her about Dorgy's death and that there might be something coming to her, but I've left the rest to you.'

'OK. I'll go up and see her now, shall I?'

Rachel cocked a thumb in the general direction of the stairs.

'She's expectin' you.'

He turned and made his way upstairs. At the top he stopped and looked back down. As he suspected, Rachel was watching, so he pointed enquiringly at the door on the left. She nodded. Nice touch, he thought.

Jack tapped lightly on the closed door and, when there was no response, he knocked louder. Still silence, so he turned the handle and pushed.

Kylie was sitting on what looked like a beanbag near the window with her ears linked into an iPod, her head bobbing gently to whatever was playing. The single ceiling bulb was shaded by strings of coloured beads hanging from a circular frame and the effect was to dapple the walls with fuzzy dots. Her narrow bed was made up as before, covered with the badger-patterned duvet. There was a bedside table and a flimsy chair, but no other furniture. Then there was *the* wall.

He stood in the middle of the room and waited for her to open her eyes. When she did it was with a jump and she scrambled to her feet.

'I'm sorry to startle you. I did knock.'

She took the ear pieces out and it was clear she hadn't heard him.

'I did knock,' he repeated.

'Oh. Right.'

'I'm Jack Mitchell.'

He held out his hand and she looked at it as if she had been presented with a soggy dishcloth, but, after a moment's hesitation she reciprocated. Her hand was clammy.

'Do you want to sit somewhere?'

She cast around vaguely for somewhere suitable.

'It's OK. I'll just sit here.' He lowered himself onto the end of the bed and smiled up at her.

She was taller than her mother and very much leaner. Her hair was cut short and was died jet black, to match her fingernails. She had a slim straight nose, which gave greater emphasis to the silver ring pierced through her left nostril and her thin lips appeared to have been painted mauve. All of that, together with the dark jeans and loose black top, presented a picture of pure Goth. Jack's thoughts were instantly thrown back to when Rowan went

through that stage, but that was when she was fifteen. This girl –
this woman – was nineteen.

She put the iPod on the bed and sat down again on the beanbag
as her dark eyes followed his.

'You like my wall?'

'It, ah … it certainly tells a story.'

'Yeah, it does that. And the story it tells is not a pretty one.
Death and cruelty to harmless creatures just so humans can assert
themselves as the dominant species.'

He appraised the wall and stifled an impulse to look surprised.
She was either much more articulate than he had expected, or this
was a well-rehearsed mantra. He turned to face her.

'It's obviously a passion of yours … animal rights I mean …
We could probably discuss the pros and cons all evening, but …'

'There are no pros, Mr Mitchell. What is being done in the
name of medical science is pure evil.'

'OK, Kylie.' He raised his hands in mock surrender. 'I'll just
stick to why I'm here. Alright?'

'Fine.'

She fixed him with a challenging stare that somehow did not
quite conceal a spark of intrigue under the heavy eye make-up. To
begin with he found the scrutiny rather unnerving.

'Now, your mother has explained about Dorgy,' he began.

'You mean his death, or his having it away with her?'

He suppressed a smile.

'Both, I suppose. Of course, at present I only have her word for
it, but it appears that the grandfather you thought was long dead is,
or was, your father.'

No point beating about the bush, Jack.

She gave a little snort and stared at her nails.

'And, as you can imagine, that has opened a can of worms.'

'Look, don't go thinking I'm heartbroken about Nathan not
being my biological father. He deserted my mum soon after I was
born and he's done next to nothing for us since.' She flicked her hair
back and added ruefully, 'I almost wish I'd known Dorgy now.'

'Yes, it's ironic, isn't it?'

217

'You know, of course.'

'About your demonstration with VAG? Yes, I know.'

'Do you think Dorgy ever knew it was me?'

'I'm sure not. The most he suspected was that VAG was targeting him because he held shares in a company that carried out animal experimentation. As far as I'm aware he didn't know you were involved with the protest group.'

'Involved! I practically run it down here. The rest of them couldn't organise a piss up in a brewery.'

Jack shifted his position on the bed and pursed his lip. He was clearly dealing with a prickly young lady here.

'Okay, but let me add that Dorgy … believe it or not … didn't even know that he owned a substantial holding in Gammarho. He seemed to have no idea that they had bought up Life Solutions years ago.'

She pulled a disbelieving face.

'It's true. Some people, even in the twenty-first century, are still that ignorant about financial affairs.'

'Even their own?'

'Even their own.'

Kylie thought about that for a while.

'It wouldn't have made any difference, you know.'

'What? If you'd known that he was your father? You surprise me, Kylie.'

'You know nothing about me, Mr Mitchell, so you're not in a position to be surprised or not surprised,' she said vehemently. 'He was just a shareholder in an evil company and he needed to be shamed as such. I can't help it if people are so ignorant about the assets they own.'

'Alright, this is getting us nowhere, but, for the record can you tell me if at any time you spoke to Nathan about your protest outside the almshouses?'

This sudden change of tack obviously took her by surprise. She opened her mouth as if to say something, but then turned away and picked up her phone instead. From her facial expressions he assumed she was reading her latest tweets.

'Do you have many followers?'

'Thousands.'

'Mostly VAG supporters, I assume.'

'Mostly, yeah.' She put the phone down.

'Did Nathan know about your involvement with them … if I can use that word?'

She almost smiled.

'Yeah, he knew. And he contacted me soon after we did the Fentonmar run. Said he heard about it on the news. He wanted to know if I was in the group.' She was examining her nails.

'And you confirmed it?'

'Of course. Anyway, he wasn't going to do anything about it, was he? Not thinking I was his daughter …'

'No, I suppose not.'

He stored this knowledge away for when he had his next meeting with Nathan. But now it was time to face the tricky bit.

'Kylie, it appears that Dorgy died without leaving a will and, if it is established that you are Dorgy's daughter, under the laws of intestacy his offspring are entitled in equal shares to inherit his estate. And that means illegitimate as well as legitimate offspring. So, if no valid will is found, once I have letters of administration granted by the Probate Court I'll be in a position to distribute that estate to you and Nathan.'

He paused, but she seemed to be following.

'Knowing your strong feelings about animal rights and your commitment to VAG, how would you react to inheriting a holding of fifty-five thousand ordinary shares in Gammarho? And, by the way, that's worth about £900,000 before inheritance tax is paid.'

He studied her closely for reaction, but at first there was very little. She rocked gently on the bean bag, clutching her knees and staring at a landmark on her VAG wall. Eventually she turned her intense gaze on him.

'That's a lot of money.'

'It is. But how do you feel about the source? You'd have to keep that information out of your tweets.'

She said nothing for a while and then a slow smile crept over her pale face as she stopped rocking.

'There's a way I could accept it and not be a hypocrite. I'd sell the shares and then use the proceeds to throw right back in Gammarho's face.'

'You mean by funding VAG?'

She opened her eyes wide and gave him an approving look. It suggested acceptance that he was not a complete idiot.

'Exactly that. No one need ever know and I would just keep quiet about where the cash came from.'

'You'd have to sell quickly, before your name appeared on the share register.'

'Or better still, you could sell them. As executor of Dorgy's will you have the power to sell his assets for cash, don't you?'

'Slow down now. You'll only own shares if I'm appointed to deal with Dorgy's estate and that can only happen if no will is found. And if we do find a will for me to execute you might not even be mentioned in it.'

She jumped up and went to review her wall. In her excitement it seemed that the possibility of her not having Gammarho shares to sell had been completely dismissed. She spun round and faced him.

'Then that's how we'll do it,' she declared. 'If I get the shares, that is.'

She was now quite animated. The cool had slipped away, revealing a more pragmatic Kylie.

'Kylie, there's a long way to go before we reach the distribution stage. Don't raise your hopes too soon.'

Jack felt some of her enthusiasm rub off on him, but for quite a different reason. He had fully expected her to rail and rant about the possibility of inheriting shares from the very source she was striving to destroy. Instead she had with only a few moments consideration turned the whole situation to her advantage, without compromising her commitment. He had to admit, it was simple, but brilliant.

She plonked herself back onto the bean bag.

Mission accomplished, he thought: it was time to go.

He stood and smoothed out the duvet. This simple and

instinctive act of domestic tidiness seemed to amuse her and she gave him a lopsided grin.

'Right, any other questions before I leave?'

She sat cross-legged on the bean bag, craning her neck up at him.

'No.'

'So, you're okay with all this then?'

'It's sinking in.'

Jack moved towards the door, but then stopped to look more closely at the wall. He pointed at the most recent newspaper cutting.

'Did VAG have anything to do with the university lab break-in?'

Her eyes took a slow journey to the cutting and then back to him.

'How would I know?' she asked sweetly.

Jack gave a small toss of his head and grinned back at her.

'Goodnight, Kylie. I'll be in touch.'

He closed the door behind him and walked slowly down the stairs. For someone who had discovered a new father and learned of a substantial inheritance all within a few days this young lady seemed to have taken it all in her stride and for some reason that bothered him: that and the fact that she had been in contact with Nathan, the deserter.

Rachel appeared at the bottom of the stairs.

'Everything alright?' she asked, in the manner of a waitress in a cheap restaurant.

'Yes, I think so. But I explained there's a long way to go before the estate's all tied up.'

'But, how did she react about what's comin' to her?'

Jack eased past her and rested a hand on the door knob.

'I'm sure she'll tell you all about it, Rachel.'

'Maybe,' she replied dubiously.

'Well, as I said to her, I'll keep in touch as to progress.' He opened the door and stepped out. 'Goodnight then.'

'Night.'

Jack stopped to let a young cyclist flash past and then crossed the road. The sun had long set, but the sky still held a midsummer glow as if reluctant to admit the lateness of the hour. There was mellow warmth in the evening air and a breeze with just enough puff to flutter the leaves on the roadside trees.

He rounded the corner and took out his keys. The car lights flashed their response as he pressed the remote control button. And then he stopped and stared.

Even though the car was parked close to the pavement there was no mistaking the angle at which it had settled. The front nearside tyre was flat.

'Oh, shit.'

He went closer and bent down.

'Bloody hell!'

He got up quickly and instinctively looked about him. The tyre was not just flat: it had been stabbed. There were unmistakable incisions an inch across clearly visible under the orange glow of a nearby street lamp. Jack swore again and clenched his fists.

He looked up and saw a man coming towards him, being tugged along by a large dog on a short lead. The man came alongside as Jack was about to open the car boot. He must have noticed Jack's anger, because he pulled the dog closer to him and quickened his pace as he passed.

It didn't take him long to jack the car up and remove the damaged wheel and fortunately the spare had recently been pumped. It took ten minutes to change the tyre, but he was still seething as he yanked open the driver's door and jumped in.

'What sort of bloody place is this?' he shouted at his rear view mirror as he pulled out from the pavement.

It wasn't until he was nearing the A30 that the thought slowly crept up on him that this might not have been a random act of mindless vandalism. This could have been a malicious and calculated attack aimed specifically at him. Either that or he was becoming paranoid.

He had time to relax and think more deeply as he drove down through Shortlanesend and into Truro. The previous time he had visited Rachel he had the impression he was being watched, but this time something had actually happened. He was still wondering about the who and the why when he arrived home and found Catherine on the telephone.

Jack put the car keys on the hall tray and waited for her to finish the call. He soon gathered that it was Rowan on the other end.

'That's nice,' she said after ringing off. 'She's asked me to go up and spend a couple of nights with her.'

'What, in her grotty student digs?'

'No, she's booking in at a hotel in the city. And don't pull that face. She has some money of her own, you know.'

'Then go for it.'

'I will.'

He followed her into the sitting room, where a drama was playing silently on the TV screen. She picked up the remote and turned it off.

'When are you going?'

'As you're busy at the moment I thought you wouldn't miss me if I went this coming weekend. I'll probably leave by train on Friday.' She made a show of plumping up some cushions. 'Will that be okay?'

'Yes, fine. You should enjoy the break.'

He had decided not to mention the tyre incident. She seemed to be in a relaxed and cheerful mood and he didn't want to burst the bubble. Rowan had played an ace.

'Oh, by the way, Jack,' she bent down to check something she had written on the hall pad, 'that unpleasant man rang when you were out ... Nathan Pascoe.'

'Oh yes? What did he want?'

'He says he wants to come and see you to check on how you're getting on.'

'Does he now?' Jack raked his hair. 'Well, I suppose he has a right to know. Did he say when he wants to come?'

'No, he just said he'd come by sometime this week.'

'At his convenience, eh?' He sighed. 'Most unprofessional.'

'Well, if you must have clients like that ...' She patted his arm and turned to go upstairs. 'I'm going to bed.'

'By the way, Catherine, I hope you didn't tell him where I was tonight.'

'No, I didn't. And he didn't ask.'

'Good. I'll be up soon. Oh, and I have to go to the garage early tomorrow. Let me know if you want anything in Truro.'

She carried on up the stairs shaking her head.

CHAPTER 17

The mechanic at the garage inspected the tyre closely and drew in breath through pursed lips.

'There's three stabs here. Looks like 'e wanted to make a proper job of it.' He straightened up. 'There's no way of repairing this one, Mr Mitchell.'

'I thought as much. What a bugger.'

'Yeah, there's some mindless morons about.' He spun the wheel around and prepared to roll it towards the workshop. 'I can fix you up with a new one by tomorrow morning. That be OK?'

'It'll have to be. I'll see you tomorrow then.'

'Word of advice.' He flashed Jack a lopsided grin. 'Stay away from the badlands of Redruth until you have a spare.'

Jack laughed at that and then bade the mechanic farewell. He could foresee a long and trying day ahead.

Jack rapped his knuckles even harder on the solid door. He was sure she was at home, because he had heard movement inside and they weren't sounds usually made by a budgerigar.

It had been hard enough getting in through the outer door since it had recently been fitted with a combination security lock and no one was answering the buzzer. He had forgotten to find out the four-number code, so had phoned Jane Stokes at the vicarage. She had been out, but Milo, once he had satisfied himself that it was Jack Mitchell on the line and after more faffing about, had managed to track down the number. Not before time the almshouses appeared now to be secure from intruders.

He knocked again and this time called out her name.

At last he saw a shadow appear from under the door and heard the lock turn. Half of Mavis's face appeared in the crack allowed by the safety chain and only then did she accept it was someone she could admit. She released the chain.

'Good morning, Mavis.' He stepped into the stuffy room. It smelled of orange peel and camphor. 'Can you spare me a few minutes?'

'I'm sorry about that, Mr Mitchell, but you can't be too careful these days.'

She seemed to him to have shrunk since they were last together, but of course that had to be an illusion. Or perhaps the stress of the enquiry and her own performance there had in some way unnerved the old woman. Whatever the reason, he sensed that she was more withdrawn than on past occasions and definitely shakier.

'You should feel safer now, Mavis, with the new locks downstairs.'

'It's so secure, Mr Mitchell, that sometimes I can't get in myself.' She let out a nervous gurgling chuckle. 'I keep forgetting the number.'

'How's Harry getting on with it?'

'He writes it on his hand.'

'Well, let's hope he keeps that hand in his pocket when he's out and about.'

She looked puzzled for a moment and then squawked.

'Oh, I see what you mean.' With a steadying hand on the back of a chair she turned towards her kitchenette. 'You'd like some tea?'

'Yes please, Mavis.'

She hadn't asked him why he was there or how long he intended to stay, but he sat and made himself comfortable. Physically that was easy: mentally there was far less to be relaxed about.

Jack sat and surveyed the old woman's domain as she rattled cups and spoons next door. No doubt she was comfortable, but he found the decor, the furniture and wall hangings oppressive and completely lacking in anything that might uplift the spirit. It was like the anteroom to oblivion. And the stale air merely added to the doom-laden atmosphere.

He was watching the little bird and wondering if it felt the same way, when Mavis shuffled back into the room bearing a plastic tray. She lowered it onto a table before he could get to his feet.

'Have you heard if Dorgy's room has been let yet?' he asked as she handed him his tea.

'Not that I've heard, but then we're the last to be told about these things.'

She sat down heavily.

'Well when it happens I hope it's someone you get on with.'

She grunted.

'I don't mind, as long as they're quiet. Would you like a biscuit?'

'No thanks.'

Two tired looking Garibaldis remained undisturbed on the tray.

'What exactly did you come about, Mr Mitchell?' she asked cautiously.

He took a sip of hot tea. This was the hard part.

'Mavis, we've seen a fair bit of each other over the past few weeks. We've shared the tragedy of Dorgy's death, been through the trying times leading up to the inquest and then the inquest itself.'

Maybe she sensed that this speech was the precursor to something more profound, because she lowered her cup and saucer noisily onto the table and then clasped her hands tightly on her lap. He held her moist red-rimmed eyes in his gaze as he continued.

'You've been through all that and at every turn you've been brave in playing your part, especially after finding Dorgy at the bottom of the stairs. That's something I'm sure you'll never forget. And then you dealt with the coroner's questions so ... so competently, when I knew how nervous you were. Through all that you managed to hold it together. Nervous perhaps, apprehensive maybe, but never downright scared. Not that I could see anyway.'

She had removed her glasses now and was rubbing the lenses with an embroidered handkerchief.

'But not now.' He had lost eye contact as the polishing continued. 'Now you're scared and I'm worried about that.'

She stopped polishing and looked up suddenly.

'Scared?' She was trying to sound defiant, but she was betrayed by the quaver in her voice.

'Yes, something or someone's frightened you. I can tell. So, let me help by telling me about it.'

Her eyes darted around like a cornered animal seeking some kind of refuge. She pulled on her glasses and missed one ear at the first attempt.

'Mr Mitchell, I think you should leave now.' She started to rise, but fell back into the chair.

He didn't move, but neither did she. It appeared that all of her strength had suddenly been sucked out of that fragile frame. She was simply an old lady stuck in an armchair.

'Please, Mr Mitchell,' she implored, 'I've nothing to tell you. You shouldn't have come.'

Jack leaned forward and clasped his hands together.

'Mavis, I want to help. If there's been any kind of threat by anyone you need to tell me. If you do that I can take steps to ensure no one harms you.'

She was shaking her head in a gesture of despair, but at least she was now looking him in the eye. He was now certain that Catherine's intuition had been correct.

'You have to share this with me, Mavis. If you bottle it up you'll only worry yourself to death.' Dramatically corny, he thought, but it might be language she would understand.

There was a long silence as Mavis wrestled with her private torment. Then the tears began.

She removed her glasses again and dabbed each eye with the small handkerchief. It was painful to watch her, but he knew that she was on the verge of some kind of revelation. He held his pose and waited.

'You don't know him, Mr Mitchell,' she said in a voice so small and muffled that he only just heard.

'Know who, Mavis?'

Another long hesitation.

'Nathan Pascoe.' She said his name as if she were enunciating the name of some deadly poison.

'Nathan Pascoe has threatened you? How?'

She half turned from her slumped position and pointed towards the bird cage.

'He said he'd ...' she swallowed hard and almost choked on her saliva, '... pull out all his feathers and boil him alive.' The sentence ended in a trill wail.

'What?' Jack jerked upright.

'There, I've told you.'

'God, that's awful. But you still haven't told me *why*, Mavis. Why would he threaten to do that?'

She was struggling to control herself and, to her credit, to a certain extent the poor stricken woman was succeeding.

'Because I saw him here. He said if I ever told anyone he'd do that to Tommy.'

Jack looked across at the bird, which was parading up and down on its perch, completely oblivious of the fact that his fate was currently under review.

'Saw him when?'

'On the day Dorgy was burgled. It was no burglar,' she growled. 'It was him. He got into Dorgy's flat when he was out and I saw him leaving. Trouble is he saw me too.'

'When he was burgled,' Jack repeated. 'So it was Nathan. And that's when he threatened you?'

'Yes. He came down the corridor and stuck his foot in the door before I could close it. He scared me, Mr Mitchell. I know his reputation.'

Jack's thoughts ran amok. Nathan breaking into his father's flat, but without stealing anything. How did he gain access? What was he looking for? And then suddenly he knew.

Dorgy's will.

Nathan must have been looking for Dorgy's will and nothing else. So, when they had both searched together he was simply going through the motions of pretence. And if he got into the flat after his talk with Kylie he would already have known about Dorgy's holding in Gammarho shares.

She interrupted his thoughts. 'Mr Mitchell, what shall I do now?'

'We, Mavis, what shall *we* do. Nathan won't know you've told me, so Tommy is safe. And now that locks are on the door downstairs, so are you. I'll work out what to do about Nathan and, if necessary, call in the police.'

'Oh, no.' The handkerchief went up to her mouth. 'If you do that then he'll know I've told you and then ...'

'Mavis, you've done the right thing in telling me and I'll do whatever is necessary to protect you ... and Tommy.' He thought for a moment and then added, 'Has he contacted you again since that day?'

'Once,' she said in a small voice. 'At the inquest. He passed me a piece of paper when no one was looking.'

'And, what was on it?'

'A picture of a budgie ... with a red line through it.' Her shoulders jolted with the spasm of renewed crying. Jack rose rapidly from his chair and, crouching beside her, held her hand.

'Mavis, it's OK. You've got an ally now. I'll deal with this. No one's going to get at your bird.'

It took some time and a lot of hand patting to calm her down, but eventually he settled the old woman to a state where he felt that he could safely leave her. There was no doubt that in her vulnerable position of elderly seclusion she had been genuinely frightened and probably not merely for the safety of her budgerigar.

Jack gave her further reassurances and advice as to the safety precautions she could take and then left. He had given her his land line and mobile phone numbers and told her, in an emergency, to use Harry's mobile to contact him.

As he headed for the stairs he heard the key turn in the lock and the safety chain slot into place. Before reaching the bottom step he had decided what to do about Nathan Pascoe.

Back in his office there was a phone message from Jane Stokes, so he rang her back. This time she was at home.

'Did you get in to see Mavis?' she asked abruptly.

'Yes, we had a long chat.'

'How's she bearing up? I've been meaning to visit her, but other pastoral matters keep cropping up.'

'She's bearing up.'

'Jack?'

'What?'

'Something's amiss. I can tell by your voice.'

'Yes. She was pretty low when I arrived. I think the whole things caught up with her and she's spooked, but I calmed her down before I left.'

'Are you sure? Do you think I should follow up?'

'Jane, this is what I signed up for isn't it?' He managed a laugh as he spoke. 'I'm a visitor to the needy of the parish, remember?'

'Alright, Jack, quite right. And thank you.'

'I won't leave it there, by the way. I'll keep an eye on her at least until after Dorgy's funeral.'

'That's good. The service will take place next week on Monday and then he'll be cremated at the Truro crematorium.'

Jack made a quick diary note.

'Whose decision was it that he should be cremated? It's usually a request made in a will.'

'Nathan contacted me. He's next of kin, so I have to go along with his wishes.'

'Probably because it's cheaper, I expect.' Jack said caustically.

'Now, now.'

He chuckled.

'Alright, Jane, I'm around if you need me for anything else.'

They rang off and Jack turned immediately to locating Nathan's mobile number.

'Yeah,' came the response after the sixth ring.

There was a lot of background noise that Jack couldn't immediately identify: voices, piped music and occasional laughter. Probably a pub.

'Nathan, it's Jack Mitchell. Can you talk?'

The voice went muffled as Nathan Pascoe smothered the phone to make some comment to a companion.

'OK. Give me a second while I go outside.'

Jack waited.

'Hello, you still there?'

'That's better, I can hear you now. Nathan, I've had the valuation of Dorgy's effects. It's not much, but I need to know what to do with them. You can sell them privately, auction them or you can keep them yourself.'

'There's nothing there I want to keep,' was his immediate and off-hand reply. 'Give it all to charity for all I care. I'm only interested in the big fish. Know what I mean?'

'I know exactly what you mean,' Jack said dryly. 'In which case I'll arrange to have the better items auctioned and give the minor items – kitchen equipment etcetera – to charity.'

'Yeah, you do that.'

'Right. Now, more importantly, we need to talk about what you call the big fish … but it probably won't be with me.'

There was a long silence, during which he could hear Nathan's breath coming down the line like a pair of bellows being pumped.

'What you mean, not with you? You're my appointed executor. I signed … we signed a contract.'

'We signed a contract in good faith, Nathan, but you have not been honest with me and as a result you've put me in a difficult position.'

'How?' He shouted and Jack pulled the phone sharply away from his ear. 'How 'ave I been dishonest with you?'

'For a start you didn't tell me that you already knew about your father's holding in Gammarho and for some reason you also tried to put me off finding a will that Dorgy might have left.'

'Who told you I knew about … who've you bin talkin' to?'

'Never mind who told me. The fact is I told you from the beginning that it was my duty to do everything I could to find out if Dorgy had left a valid will, so that's what I've been doing. If we'd found one then I would have done what was necessary to obtain probate. Now that it appears there is no will the whole process changes. I cannot execute what doesn't exist.'

'You've been talkin' to my wife. I know you 'ave.'

'What makes you say that?'

'When I called the other night your missis said you was over at Redruth.'

'I know you spoke to her, but I also know she didn't tell you where I was. Anyway, why do you think your wife … ex-wife … might know anything about Dorgy's affairs?'

'You tell me. You're the one who's been talking to 'er.'

'Look, there's no point carrying on this discussion over the phone, but I won't be leaving you in the lurch. I'll recommend a solicitor to you and if it's finally established that there's no will he or she will get you to approve and sign a letter of administration. They won't have the baggage of the background to any of this, so it should be easier for both of you. And don't worry about a fee. I won't charge anything for the work I've done so far. Does that sound fair?'

'So you think you can just walk away, do you?'

'I've explained why. I've never done this to a client before, Mr Pascoe, but I regret to say I do not approve of your methods.'

Jack was preparing to end this unpleasant exchange, but Nathan suddenly had a thought and cut in.

''Ere, you haven't been talkin' to that old bag as well, have you?'

'Who are you referring to?'

'Mavis 'arris, of course. She's poison, you know.'

'Of course I've been talking to Mrs Harris. She was your father's neighbour and the last person to speak to him. He might have confided in her about a will and, if so, she might even have been a witness to it.'

'And that's all?'

'What else would there be? Or is there something else you've not been telling me?'

There was a mumbled comment that sounded like *fuck you*, but he couldn't be sure, because the line went dead at that point.

Jack looked down at his hand. It was shaking. He had poked the hornet's nest, now he had to be prepared for the consequences.

That evening Detective Sergeant Clive Bray was sitting at the bar of the *Plume* sipping a pint of lager, waiting for his table partners to arrive. It was Thursday, quiz night, and only when he was on duty did Clive miss making up a table. He and his mates rarely won the weekly competition, but it was all good harmless fun and he could get a lift home afterwards from Alan, who drank only ginger beer.

He was hunched in a position of idle contemplation when Jack Mitchell sauntered in and went straight up to him.

'Hello, Clive, can I bend your ear for a couple of minutes?'

Clive snapped out of his reverie, glanced at Jack and then immediately peered over his shoulder.

'Hello there.'

Jack patted the policeman's broad shoulder and ordered a pint.

'Don't worry, I know it's quiz night, but your team's not in yet. I just need to clarify a couple of points of law.'

'Okay, try me.'

'Right. An inquest has been held, there are no apparent suspicious circumstances and the coroner declares a verdict of accidental death, death by misadventure, or whatever they call it. But, later on, something comes to light that, had it been part of the evidence in the coroner's court, might have produced a different verdict – what would happen then? Would the coroner reopen the case, or would it become a police matter?'

Clive gave himself time to think by supping a draft of ale. He then wiped the corner of his mouth and cleared his throat.

'Not really my area of specialisation, but I think if there's later evidence that suggests foul play ... if that's what you're suggesting ...?'

Jack nodded.

'... then it becomes a police matter and the coroner wouldn't be troubled again.'

'And then I suppose the police will build up a case to be presented to the Crown Prosecution Service?'

'That's about the size of it. The CPS will look at the evidence and decide whether to take the case to court, and this is one area of policing that really winds us coppers up.'

'You mean you do all the hard work to present a case and the CPS throws it out?'

'That happens far too often for our liking.'

'I can understand the frustration.'

'So, Jack, what's this about? Don't tell me something's come up after the Dorgy Pascoe inquest.'

Jack smiled conspiratorially. 'Let's just say it's not a hypothetical question. But here is a hypothetical question. If someone thinks he has sufficient evidence to warrant reopening a case, who should he report it to?'

'That's easy. The case officer would normally be your first port of call, or if it's a very sensitive matter, his senior officer.'

'Right.'

'You said there were a couple of points?'

'Yes, and this is, shall I say, a slightly sensitive one. Where should I go to find out if someone has a criminal record? I presume that's something that would be in the public domain.'

Clive's eyes narrowed as he tried to analyse Jack's motivation.

'Yes, that would be a matter of public record. Anyone we know?'

'*We*, as in you and me, or *we* as in the police force?'

The policeman made a *whatever* movement of the head.

'Okay, I'm referring to Nathan Pascoe.'

Bray's lips slowly creased into a broad smile and he started nodding like the bulldog in the insurance advertisement.

'Oh, yes. No need to go to police records for that one. Nathan's got form alright: breaking and entering, a bit of GBH and probably more besides. But that's when he was much younger. I haven't heard that he's been in trouble in recent times. So, Jack where's this leading?'

'Nowhere, I hope, but I just need to check that I've made a right decision.' He paused to take a drink. 'I've just ditched him as a client.'

'I see. Well, speaking off the record, be a bit careful. That boy's got a fiery reputation.'

'Thanks for the warning, but I think he's better off my books anyway.' Jack looked across the room. 'I believe this gang coming in now is your team, so I won't keep you.'

'Yes, those villains are my team. Let me know if anything comes up. Always happy to help.' He gave Jack a wink. 'See you later.'

Clive slipped off his bar stool and went to greet the other members of the *Quiz Kids*.

Jack stayed on to finish his pint and then made his way out into the warmth of a late June evening.

Catherine was in the kitchen preparing the evening meal when he returned home. He could smell fish.

'Ah, there you are,' she said, looking over her shoulder as she dropped broccoli into a bubbling saucepan. 'I've arranged my visit to Rowan and booked a train ticket for tomorrow morning. Can you take me to the station?'

'Sure. What time?'

'It's the ten something train, so could we leave here at about nine-thirty?'

'Ten something …?'

'Oh, I can't remember, Jack.' She slapped the saucepan lid on with a clatter. 'The ticket's over there by the telephone.'

He sauntered over to look.

'Yes, I'll take you at nine-thirty. You'll have plenty of time to buy a magazine for the journey.'

'Good. Supper in fifteen minutes.'

'Right. I'll just go and check my emails.'

Too late to phone Walter at the shop and he didn't have his home number, so he sent an email with news that Nathan wanted rid of his father's flat possessions. If Walter didn't want them for his stock, Jack had decided to put the best of the items up for auction. As for the rest he couldn't care a toss, but if Nathan wanted to take any of the stuff it would have to be under supervision. Mavis would be climbing up the wall with fear if she knew he was in the building unattended.

He pressed *send* and then joined Catherine.

'What do you plan to do up in Bristol?' he asked as he drew a chair up to the table.

'Rowan's taking me to a play – some avant-garde workshop production I expect – and then we'll probably just talk, walk and eat.'

'It'll do you good.'

'In what sense?' She regarded him suspiciously.

'To get a break away from here. Fentonmar can become claustrophobic.'

'And what will you do while I'm away?'

'Oh, keep busy I suppose. There's plenty on at the moment.'

'Including that nasty bit of work, Nathan Pascoe.'

'Ah, I forgot to tell you. I'm not acting for him any more. I told him earlier today. I don't trust the man.'

'Good. How did he take it?'

'A bit of effing and blinding under his breath, but I think he got the message. But, I have undertaken to do one last thing and that's to get rid of Dorgy's more valuable items. I've asked Walter to help me.'

'Next time try to be more discerning with your clients.'

He stopped eating to check her expression and saw that she was teasing him. A spark of the old Catherine was somewhere there behind the smile.

'They can't all be saints you know and we have to pay the bills.'

They didn't talk much after that and an hour after the meal Catherine went up for a bath and an early bed. Jack stacked the dishes and then went to his office to write a couple of letters before settling down to watch the news at ten.

Walter Cartwright lived in a flat above the antique shop. He had done so since the death of his wife three years earlier, when he had sold their four-bedroomed detached house in Tresillian. The house wasn't a big place, but the sloping garden needed a lot of tending throughout the seasons and gardening was not his forte, so he had sold and moved into the flat: compact and manageable, with only a small patch and a window box to cultivate. His two children had been pleased, because he made them the beneficiaries of a large chunk of the house proceeds. They were recently out of university and like thousands of others at that age keen to get on the first rung on the property ladder. The rest of the proceeds had gone into paying off the mortgage and making some reckless purchases for the shop.

That Friday morning he rose at ten to eight, pulled on a shabby flannel dressing gown and shuffled into the bathroom for a pee before going into the tiny kitchen to put the kettle on. While it was heating up he clumped downstairs and into his small office at the back of the shop. He cranked his computer into action and, hunched over the keyboard, went to the email inbox. After deleting a dozen spam messages – three offering some remarkable and improbable physical enhancement – he viewed his incoming mail.

There were four enquiries regarding stock, one from his sister in Perth and one from Jack Mitchell. His hand rasped over an unshaven chin as he read Jack's request and, after a moment's thought he typed out a brief reply.

Upstairs the kettle began to boil and soon a film of vapour spread across the window glazing.

Jack backed the car out into Dowr Row and then went back to collect Catherine's suitcase. It was remarkably light for her, but then, he reasoned, it was high summer and she was away for only three days. He put the case on the back seat and waited for her to come out.

The house opposite was still for sale: it had been on the market since early spring and the owners had moved out two weeks ago, tired of waiting for an acceptable offer. He could have told them, or the agent, that it was too highly priced for the location and they were also selling into a falling market. In due course no doubt it would be bought by someone from up country who wanted a second home or a buy-to-let in a Cornish village. Meanwhile the grass grew higher on the front lawn and a branch, snapped by a recent storm, hung forlornly from its cherry tree host.

Catherine came out looking flustered as she slammed the front door closed. She paused frowning on the doorstep and glanced back.

'Too late,' Jack called out. 'We have to go. Traffic will be building up.'

She came through the front gate and Jack held the car door open for her.

'God, I hope I haven't forgotten anything. It's so long since I've been away on my own.'

'Pills?' Jack shot her a sideways glance as he started the car.

'Yes, Jack, I've got my antidepressants,' she said with a sigh. 'You don't have to worry about that.'

He simply smiled and patted her knee as he pulled away from the curb.

In spite of being stuck behind a lumbering tractor they made good time to Truro station. Jack parked and then jumped out to check that the train was running on time. The board said it was.

'You've got ten minutes to kill,' he said as he took Catherine's case out.

'Don't wait, Jack. I'm sure you've plenty to get on with back home.'

'You sure?'

'Yes, yes, the case isn't heavy.' She leaned forward and brushed his cheek with a dry kiss. 'I'll see you on Monday.'

'Okay, darling. I hope you have a lovely time with Rowan. Oh, and give me a call about half an hour before you're due to arrive back here.'

'I will.'

They parted and within a minute Jack was on his way back to Fentonmar. This time he joined a convoy of vehicles trailing a pace-setting learner driver. The lanes offered no passing opportunities, so he sat back and enjoyed all that the hedgerows had to offer.

Leaving the car in Dowr Row he closed the garden gate and scraped a small clod of mud from his shoe before pushing the front door open against a delivery of post. He picked up the scattered items and carried them into his office, dumping them on the chair by his desk.

Calling up the emails he saw the reply from Walter and leant over the keyboard to read it.

Happy to collect the items as agreed. If this morning will suit I'll call up the lad who helps me hump things around and we'll get the desk out first. I've found room in a corner of the shop. Give me a call after you read this.

'Coffee first, old boy,' Jack murmured to the screen and wandered away to the kitchen.

Ten minutes later he was on the phone to Walter and they arranged to meet at the almshouses at eleven-thirty.

The *lad* turned out to be a hulking young man of about six foot four, who looked as if he was designed exclusively to be a rugby lock forward. He and Walter were standing by the almshouses yard door when Jack strode in to greet them.

'This is Paul,' Walter said with an expansive gesture, as if showing off one of his prize possessions.

'Hello, Paul.' Jack felt his hand being mangled by the giant's paw. 'I expect you'll be able to carry the old desk all on your own.'

Paul's laugh came from somewhere deep down in the barrel chest.

Jack turned and keyed in the code. There was a responsive click and he pulled the door open for his companions. Leaning in he pressed the stairwell light.

'Straight up and then half left. Door marked *Hawker*.'

'It's usually *no* hawkers, isn't it?' Walter quipped as he followed Paul up the stairs.

'Ho, ho. Dorgy was a fan of the Reverend Hawker of Morwenstow I believe.' Jack fumbled in his pocket for the key. 'It's going to be a hell of a job to get it down these stairs, don't you think?'

'We've done harder places, haven't we, Paul?'

'Yeah, much harder than this. Should be a doddle.'

In Dorgy's room Jack went straight to the desk and began pulling out the drawers.

'Nathan and I've been through this lot once and he says he doesn't want any of it, so ...' He tipped out the remaining contents of the top drawer. 'I've already taken most of it so we'll just pile up what's left to be sorted later.'

Paul was carrying out a circular review of the room, wearing an expression of faint distaste as he did so. Walter caught the look and smiled at his assistant.

'We all hope we don't end up in a place like this, old chap.'

'It's not that bad, Walter, it's just the smell ...'

'Airless and old men's socks,' he guffawed.

Jack had finished with the long drawers and now turned his attention to the small ones above the writing area.

'Don't forget the secret pigeonholes,' Walter said.

'I've already emptied them. A few of Dorgy's little secrets were in there.'

'I won't ask.'

The emptying completed, they manoeuvred the old desk towards the doorway and had a brief discussion as to who should stand where for the descent. In the end Walter went downstairs to act as navigator, Paul was designated to take the weight from below and Jack would hold up the top end.

'All set?' Walter called from the bottom.

'OK,' Paul replied and the desk began its slow descent.

Jack couldn't resist a quick glance at the door at the end of the hallway, but either Mavis was out or she had resisted the temptation to have a peek at what was happening. Her door was firmly closed.

There were a couple of pauses on the way down to rest and to assess progress, but the desk never once touched the sides and it was eventually settled gently on the concrete in the yard outside.

Jack's chest was heaving from the effort and perspiration coursed down the side of his face, but Paul had not even broken sweat.

'Now what, Walter? This won't fit in your Volvo, will it?' Jack wiped his face and leaned on the furniture.

'No, it's Shanks's pony for the rest of the way, I'm afraid to say.'

'What? All the way up to your shop?'

'It's not far, old man. Just halfway up Fore Street. Anyway, you're not doing anything else for the rest of the day, are you?' His head went back as he barked a hoarse laugh.

'OK, you and Paul can do that and I'll deal with the drawers.'

'Crafty bugger. Okay, Paul, let's go to it. Mr Mitchell here can then buy us drinks all round after we get it into the shop.'

'I'll want more than a drink for this load,' Paul replied shyly and grinned at Walter.

'Usual rate, old man, usual rate. Right, off we go.'

Jack trudged up the stairs again and carried the drawers down two at a time. He had decided not to bother with his car, so after locking up began to carry as much as he could at one time up the street to the antique shop. Three times he passed the desk carriers on his trips and each time he jokingly chivvied them along.

On the third pass they were resting. Paul looked fresh enough, but Walter's face was puce and his mutton chop whiskers stood out from his face like the tips of a fox's brush. Jack started to suggest that he have a longer rest when a motorcycle roared past, drowning his words.

'Wasn't that Nathan Pascoe?' Jack asked as he peered after the machine. 'If it was then he's spending a lot of his time in Fentonmar these days.'

'Friend of mine clocked him once.' Paul was grinning at the recollection.

'Really?'

'Yeah, he was coming onto his girl in a pub and Col gave him one in the kisser. Never saw him again after that.'

There didn't seem to be anything more to say about that, so the slow progress towards the shop continued. There were a few ribald comments from passers-by and it was nearly half past twelve when at last Walter unlocked his shop door and they were able to place the desk in its designated spot.

'What about the paintings, Walter?'

The antique dealer had slumped onto the padded seat of what the attached label called a mid-Victorian lady's walnut chair. It creaked alarmingly as he leaned back.

'If you don't mind, old boy, I'll trouble you to collect them later. Right now I'm bushed.'

'Finished with me for now then, Walter?'

Paul hovered uncertainly.

'Oh, yes, of course, Paul.' He thrust a hand into a pocket of his maroon corduroy trousers and pulled out a crumpled twenty pound note. 'Great help, thanks old lad.'

'Cool.' He turned to Jack and nodded. 'Nice to meet you.'

Walter watched him go and chuckled silently at some private joke.

'Seems like a nice young man,' Jack said.

'Very obliging chap. Plays for the Reds, you know.'

'Ah, maybe that's where he came across Nathan.'

'In Redruth, you mean?'

'Yes, I'm told he used to play for them.'

A telephone warbled at the back of the shop and Walter heaved himself out of the chair with a groan. While he talked animatedly with a prospective buyer Jack took stock of the eclectic array of surrounding items. Knowing little about antiques he tested himself to pass the time.

Was that dinner service a Derby set, or Worcester? Both now unfashionable. The young preferred something plainer, that wouldn't break in the dishwasher. And that was a punchbowl, but probably not very valuable. A glazed pottery jar: but surely not Ming dynasty? That chair could be Chippendale, but the seat was in a poor state. Then there was a fine brass telescope on a mahogany tripod.

He was staring up at a plain-faced wall clock above the back room archway when Walter returned. He followed Jack's gaze.

'Looks a bit out of place here, doesn't it? An old railway clock. Still works perfectly.'

'I was wondering about the four. Unusual for the Roman numeral to be four separate strokes, isn't it?'

'No, not at all. Most old timepieces show four that way. Have a look at the faces of the clock on the church tower when you next go through Gerrans.'

'Well, that shows my ignorance.' Jack stood up.

'Fancy a pint down the Plume, or have you got to get back to the missis?'

'Sounds like a good idea ... especially as Catherine's away for the weekend.'

'Come on then.'

Walter flipped over the closed sign on the shop door and pulled it open. The bell jangled above the door frame as he slammed it shut and they set off up Fore Street. It was to be a pint well earned.

If the morning was one of physical effort that Friday afternoon turned out to be one of mental ordeal.

Having had a sandwich and a couple of pints in the *Plume* Jack arrived home in mellow mood and fully prepared to enjoy the peace of an empty house by catching up with a few repair tasks he had been delaying for weeks. However, he had only been indoors for ten minutes when the doorbell rang.

Nathan Pascoe stood on the doorstep wearing a black leather jacket, jeans and a scowl that would have melted an iceberg.

'Nathan. I wasn't expecting you.'

'No, I bet you weren't. Well, can I come in? We 'ave some unfinished business.'

Jack hesitated and looked over the top of the leather jacket, but could see no sign of the motorcycle.

'Well, it's usual to make an appointment,' he stood aside, 'but come in.'

Nathan brushed past him and headed for the office. Jack raised an eyebrow and followed. He was about to offer his visitor a seat, but Nathan was already in a chair with his legs crossed. Jack sat at his desk chair.

'Right, so what's this about?' Jack asked in an attempt to regain the initiative.

'What it's about, Mr Mitchell, is unfinished business. You can't just call me up and say you've done with me ... that you're not acting for me no more. We have an agreement. It's too late in the day for me to go round trying to find a solicitor to finish what you've started.'

'Look, I explained it to you on the telephone. I know you're anxious to tie up your father's estate, but I have to say that I can't act for someone whose methods are not ... not entirely above board.'

'Oh, I see. I get it.' Nathan leaned forward and uncrossed his legs. 'You've been checking up on me as well. That's it, isn't it?'

'Checking up?'

'Yeah, someone's told you about my record, haven't they? And because I've done time you're suddenly too 'igh and mighty to take me on as a client.'

'Yes, I do happen to know your past record, but as you say you've done time for it. No, I'm referring to what you've been up to recently. I'm not happy about ...'

'Like what, eh? Like what?'

'You really want me to tell you?'

'Yeah, you tell me.'

This was new territory for Jack Mitchell, but he was on home ground and he knew he had the intellectual march on Nathan Pascoe, but there was a barely concealed menace about the man which he found unnerving. He knew he was now being forced into divulging what he knew, or suspected, but somehow he would have to do it brazenly without revealing his source.

'OK, I've already expressed surprise that you kept from me the fact that you knew about your father's shareholding and I have to ask myself why that might be. Also, why would you keep insisting that Dorgy left no valid will, when you should have been cooperating in trying to find one? Did you perhaps try to find a will before you asked me to act for you?'

Nathan's expression changed dramatically at that point. His mouth dropped open and he threw his hands out in a gesture of complete innocence. Jack had hit the bulls-eye.

'What're you suggestin'?' Saliva glinted on his lower lip.

'Well, did you?'

'You know I 'addn't seen or spoken to Dorgy for years.'

'I know that's what you told me, but you don't necessarily need to speak to someone to find out what they've got.'

Jack was going too far and he knew it. He was pressing this volatile man beyond his ability to self-control, but he felt a reckless urge to needle him into some kind of confession. He wanted a reaction and was spurred on by an irrational disregard for the consequences.

Nathan was breathing heavily and his lips were drawn tight with anger. But he was just about holding it together.

'You got no right to say things like that to me.'

'I have the right of someone who's been asked to settle a dead man's estate, but if there's been any sharp practice along the way I want no part of it.'

Nathan's lips curled into a contemptuous sneer.

'What a load of bullshit.'

'Not in my book, Nathan. People have been chucked out of my professional body for less. So, did you or did you not break into Dorgy's flat to see if you could find a will?'

The sneer slowly dissolved into a smirk and Nathan leaned back in the chair.

'I didn't *break* in, Mr Mitchell. Someone didn't close the door properly, so I walked in. Anyway it doesn't matter, does it? It doesn't matter a shit if I did or didn't do what you said, because it can't be proved either way. Can it, Mr Smart Arse?'

'So, if you're so sure of yourself, tell me why you've been following me around. What are you so afraid I'll find out?'

'Who says I've been following you around? I've got better things to do with my time.'

'I thought you were currently unemployed. Plenty of time to do what you want, I'd have thought.'

'Like I said, I've got better things to do.'

'Like sticking a knife into my tyre?'

Nathan made a sudden move as if to leap out of his seat, but then flopped back and stabbed his temple with a forefinger.

'You know what? You're fuckin' crazy you are? Paranoid. You need to see a shrink.'

Jack steadied his breathing and stared back at his increasingly excitable visitor. It was possible that he was wrong. It could have been a random attack. Maybe he had stepped over the line with the accusation. He suddenly wanted the man out of his house, but the only way was to placate him somehow.

However, beneath all the cross-fire, there was still an elephantine factor that he knew had to remain unstated. It was a cop-out, but there was no way that he was going to tell Nathan that the girl he regarded as his daughter was in fact his half-sister. That was one storm he was not man enough to face. It was one revelation that he would be leaving to a far stronger team to handle.

'Okay, Nathan, maybe I spoke out of turn. Maybe I'm wrong, but I was sure it was you I saw parked near Rachel's house when I visited her and someone did stab my car tyre. I was angry about that, but maybe two and two don't make four this time. In which case, I apologise.' He adopted a conciliatory face. 'Can I get you a coffee?'

Nathan's hostility was still transparently evident, but it seemed that the apology had produced a temporary diversion.

'No.' He shot a glance over his shoulder. 'Your missis not 'ere then?'

'No. Gone up to Bristol.'

'Don't blame 'er. Can't be much fun livin' with a nutter.'

'Look, it's not going to get you anywhere by sitting there and trading insults with me. I've told you that I'm not prepared to act for you any further and you're not going to persuade me otherwise. It's too late for that.'

'Right.'

Nathan's dark eyes roved around the room as he wrestled with the situation. Jack watched in fascination as the man's face went through a number of involuntary tics while he appeared to be seeking a solution as to what his next move should be. Eventually, realising that he'd hit a brick wall, he focused a stormy glare on Jack face.

'So what do I do now?'

'As I said, I'll fix you up with someone who will contact the coroner's court with a letter of administration. That's how it works when there's no will and therefore no nominated executor.'

'Okay, well don't 'ang about. Dorgy's been dead weeks and nothing's been done yet.'

'Well, that's not true. You can't rush this kind of thing. I've done my level best to find out if there's a will and you certainly haven't helped by taking matters into your own hands.'

'Look, don't start that again.'

Jack got out of his chair and moved towards the door. As far as he was concerned this unpleasant meeting was at an end.

'I'll get on with it as quickly as possible.' He held the door open and Nathan rose slowly to his feet. 'You'll be going to the funeral I presume?'

'I might.'

'And I presume Jane Stokes has discussed the arrangements with you?'

Nathan straightened his back and then strode past Jack to the front door.

'She did,' he said without turning.

Jack reached out and opened the front door.

'I'm glad to see your leg's better.'

It was meant to be a throwaway remark, a parting pleasantry, but Nathan stopped suddenly and spun around.

'My leg?' he rasped.

'Yes, when I saw you here last you were limping.'

'Yeah, well, I er … I came off me bike.'

'Did you? Not as nimble as you used to be then.'

It was a casually rhetorical comment, but even to his ears it sounded like disbelief.

Nathan stood there for far longer than was necessary, staring bleakly into Jack's face, before turning slowly and walking down the path to the gate. He left it swinging as Rowan had done and didn't look back as he went to wherever he had parked the motorcycle.

Jack watched him go until he was around the bend and then retreated into the sanctuary of his house, feeling a line of perspiration trickling down his back. A sudden numbing thought had overwhelmed him. Out of a hidden corner of his mind, the words of old Harry Charters gave life to that thought. *There was someone here that night.*

Those, as far as he could recall, were the old boy's exact words.

That evening was one of the hottest of the summer to date. Earlier Jack had stripped off to shorts and tee shirt and done some strenuous digging in the garden. It was partly his way of purging thoughts of Nathan's visit from his mind and, more practically, it was a bed that Catherine had been urging him to tackle for weeks. It might well have been something arising from her series of obsessions, but it did also need turning over.

With sweat running down his back he went back into the house soon after four and took a shower. While he was standing naked on the bathmat rubbing his hair vigorously the landline began ringing. Wrapping the towel around his waist he loped into the bedroom and picked up.

'Hello, Dad.'

'Rowan, darling, how's it going with Mum?'

'Fine. The train arrived on time and we're having a cup of tea now.'

'But, how do you find her?' He lowered his voice. 'Can you talk?'

The towel slipped and instinctively he glanced at the window before tightening it around his middle.

'Sorry, I missed that.'

'I said yes, she's gone to powder her nose.'

'Ah, so what's your opinion?'

'She seems much brighter than when I was last down. I don't know if it's the antidepressants, or if she's just come to terms with … well, whatever her demons are.'

'I'm so pleased to hear you say that, because that's my impression too.' He gazed across at the blank windows of the empty house across the lane as he talked. 'It was such a good idea of yours to persuade her to go up to Bristol.'

'I'm going to keep us busy while she's here, so that should help too.'

'Do you need any money? I don't want you draining your funds.'

'No, Dad. I'm fine. Don't worry about that. Ah, she's coming back.'

'That was quick for your mother.'

Rowan laughed and he could hear her say, *It's Dad*, as she held the phone away.

'Do you want a word with her?'

'Okay, but I'm dripping wet.'

'Why, is it raining there?' Catherine asked.

'Just got out of the shower. I've been digging.'

'The rose bed?'

'That's the one.'

'About time too,' she laughed. 'What else have you been doing?'

He told her, but made light of the visit from Nathan Pascoe. She said how much she was enjoying being with Rowan.

To Jack it all sounded very satisfactory. They talked on for a few more minutes until he called time so that he could get dressed.

That evening he cooked a pizza and ate it while listening to a jazz CD that Catherine disliked because she found it too excitable. After dinner he opened a sitting room window and played it again as he relaxed on a sofa drinking Glenfiddich and trying not to think about Nathan Pascoe. That was the hard part: the guy had spooked him.

He watched the ten o'clock news with another whisky and

then went to bed immediately afterwards. He drifted off to sleep with his most pleasant recollection of the day: that Catherine and Rowan had bonded anew and he held onto that fact as a positive step towards his wife's rehabilitation.

CHAPTER 18

It was well after midnight when Liam McCarthy crept up the lane and slipped through the gap where a gate should have been and then made his way around to the rear of the house.

He had been around the village for three days or so, sleeping rough in an open shed at the back of what he assumed to be an empty holiday cottage. He made that assumption because he had observed a woman coming in with cleaning paraphernalia during the mornings, without any sign of a resident. It could be that this cottage would remain empty for a week, maybe two, but then on the other hand it could suddenly have holidaymakers arriving unexpectedly. The cleaning woman gave the clue that an arrival was imminent, so this was not to be the place for overnight occupation for long: better a place that seemed properly empty.

Fentonmar was a sleepy sort of place, he deduced, and one where everyone knew everyone else. Certainly he had attracted a few curious stares as he patrolled up and down Fore Street. They were polite with their nods and greetings, but the unasked question always hung in the air. *Who are you and what are you doing here?* He fantasised that if this were a town in the old Wild West the questions would be more open and forthright: *You passing through, stranger?*

Still, it was a trusting sort of place and no one had challenged him as he wandered around the convenience store, slipping items from the lower shelves into the sagging pockets of his unseasonally heavy coat.

It had not all been scrounge and help-yourself though. He had tried to find employment of a manual nature and one lady had asked him to clear out the launders at the back of her house. For that task he had earned a fiver, two fresh eggs and a cup of tea. Apart from that, nothing. Just the polite brush-off.

But on his third morning in the village he had gone up a side street and seen a 'For Sale' sign outside a small but handsome detached slate-fronted house. The grass was long, there was a snapped branch on the tree at the front and the windows had that empty look of a gaping mouth with no teeth. It seemed perfect.

He walked past nonchalantly, turned at the top of the cul-de-sac and then strolled back, noting the name of the road at the end. He had then walked the three miles to the coastal path and followed it down a wooded stretch until he reached a beach. The tide was out so he found a quiet spot by the rocks and away from the nearest sunbathers, took off his clothes and plunged into the sea. After splashing around for a while he waded out and wandered up to the thin stream of water that oozed out from the base of the cliff. He scooped up the fresh cool stream water and splashed it over his thin white body until he had removed as much of the salt water as he could. It was the first bathe of any kind that he had taken for nearly two weeks and it felt good. He flicked back the sodden rope of hair that hung from the side of his head like the remnants of a dreadlock exodus. Freedom to roam was great for a twenty year-old who had been kicked out of the family home, but there were some comforts that he missed. However, now that he had found somewhere to sleep that night as well, things were really looking up.

He lay back on a smooth rock under the sun drying off and airing his clothes for two hours before dressing and starting the walk back to his new-found home. It wasn't until much later in the day – or night, to be precise – that he realised he had exposed himself to the Cornish sun for far too long.

Jack and Catherine had owned a dog for much of their married lives. The third and most recent of these had been a golden retriever: a lovely looking dog with a sweet nature. His name was Laity. When he looked at you with mouth open and tongue lolling there was a distinct smile on his face. Of course dogs don't actually smile in order to express pleasure, but to human interpretation that was how it appeared.

They used to walk Laity many miles along the coastal path and run him across the sands of the Roseland once the holiday season was over. After these walks Jack would brush him down outside the back door and then leave him in the kitchen until dry. Catherine had a thing about his white hairs on the furniture, and wet white hairs were the worst as they clung to the fabric.

All dogs have their particular traits and Laity was no exception. He was terrified of unexplained noise. Many times after a report from a nearby bird scarer, a backfiring car or, worst of all, fireworks at any time, he would seek comfort from his human carers. If the noise came at night after he had been settled he would slink out of his bed in the utility room and creep upstairs. Although the treads on the stairs were carpeted, Jack and Catherine invariably heard the soft pad of Laity's paws as he made his way to the sanctuary of their bedroom. Once he had settled at the bottom of their bed, that is where he stayed until morning.

Sometimes Jack and Catherine slept on during the stealthy approach to their bedroom. But on other occasions the smallest noise from the dog caused one of them to wake.

This night proved to be one of those occasions.

Jack had settled in bed just after eleven, had read for a while and then switched his light off after only three pages, the whisky having added to his drowsiness.

And then through the fog of a dream he had heard Laity's footstep and the creak of a stair tread. In his half-awake state he smiled and waited for the sound of the bedroom door being pushed gently against the carpet. He turned over to face the edge of the bed anticipating the snuffle of a wet nose against the duvet that would announce the dog's arrival.

But that didn't happen and in a lurch from semi-consciousness to full wakefulness Jack's eyes snapped open and his senses switched to high alert.

Laity was no longer with them. He had died two years ago: put down after contracting a liver complaint.

They had no dog.

In such moments of realisation the instinct is to freeze and to hope that it's a false alarm: that one has been aroused out of slumber by an imaginary dream-induced disturbance, that one has been the victim of a nocturnal hoax. But to freeze into inactivity is to become vulnerable in the event of possible danger, so against his natural desire to lie there and wish the sound away, Jack forced himself to roll silently from under the duvet and then crouch by the bed.

He rose slowly and stood for a few seconds, adjusting his bearings in the room he knew so well and strained to pick up the smallest noise. There was no other sound, but an animal instinct told him he was not alone. In the darkness the senses are sharpened, so was it an alien smell that reached his nostrils, or simply a feeling that a small part of his space had been invaded?

Then, just as he was thinking of moving towards the door, there was another noise. He knew that one: it was the third step from the top, about six inches in from the bannister.

Groping for his torch on the bedside table and praying not to knock anything onto the floor, he took a step towards the doorway. And then another step. Three more would bring him to the door, which he had left ajar.

The rubber-clad torch felt clammy in his hand as he reached the aperture and slowly manoeuvred himself into a position where he could peer around the gap.

The house was in darkness, except for a dim nightlight that they always left on in the sitting room. The sitting room! He screwed up his eyes in the moment of realisation that he had failed to shut the window before going to bed.

He tightened his grip on the torch and tried to regulate his breathing. In the absence of sight and in the ambient stillness of the room it sounded to him like an air pump in action. Breathe slowly! Breathe normally!

If there had been a foot on that step then its owner must now be at the top. There were five doors leading from the landing, so which would an intruder head for first? From where he stood, Jack would have had a clear range of vision across to all of the other four doors if he had not drawn the curtain across the landing window that night. But, he reasoned, that must be to his advantage. An intruder would not know the geography of his house, whereas he could walk around it blindfolded without touching any furniture.

He began to ease the bedroom door open as slowly as possible so as not to create a sound of wood against the carpet pile. Then he stopped suddenly as he detected the faintest of alteration in the density of blackness across the landing. There was a figure. Someone was moving towards one of the other bedroom doors.

What should he do? He would have the element of surprise if he rushed the intruder, but there was a distance of about fifteen feet between his door and the top of the stairs. By the time he crossed that distance the intruder would have been alerted. And what if he was armed? He had only a rubber-encased torch as a weapon.

The dark shadow was now pushing open the bedroom door, but stopped suddenly as there was a small squeak from a hinge. At that same moment Jack had taken a step out of the bedroom. He froze in mid-stride, with the ball of one bare foot barely brushing the carpeted floor.

Another small squeak and the intruder had the door sufficiently open for the bedroom's undrawn curtains to allow Jack at last to see him in silhouette and he felt a surge of anger. That had been Rowan's bedroom when she was a girl. It still was her bedroom when she was home and now some lowlife was daring to invade his daughter's sanctuary.

A sudden rush of adrenalin made him forget all about controlling his breathing. As the figure slipped into Rowan's room Jack took a few rapid steps across the landing, ready to meet the intruder as he re-emerged. He deftly skirted the Lloyd Loom chair that stood in a corner between the bathroom and a bedroom door, but in doing so trod on the one place he should have avoided.

It was the slightest of creaks, but it was enough. In the stillness of the night it sounded like a firecracker going off.

The figure shot back out of Rowan's room and for a second he and Jack faced each other in the dark. Only the faintest of grey filtering from Rowan's open door gave either of them any perspective of the foe they faced, but each knew that the other was an enemy.

Jack, having the slight advantage of surprise, acted first and lunged forward, swinging the torch in the area of the intruder's head. But the man – and there was now no doubt that it was a man – was quick and managed to parry the blow. It glanced off the side of his head and took Jack off balance. As the two bodies came together with a dull thud the man swung a right fist that connected with Jack's back between the shoulder blades. He went down on the floor just above the stairs and at the same time he lost his grip on the torch. In falling to the ground this somehow switched the beam on and it rolled up against a skirting board, reflecting its white light eerily back onto the struggling pair.

As he fell Jack had managed to grab hold of a leg and his opponent lost balance, crashing into the wall with a grunt of pain. Jack struggled to his feet and swung a long speculative hook in the direction of the man's head, but managed only to hit him in the shoulder as he also got up from the floor.

For a couple of seconds Jack was silhouetted against the open door and, with the reflected torch glow helping him, that was all that the intruder needed to find his range. He threw himself at Jack, reaching for his throat with both hands as he did so. They went down together, but this time Jack had the man on top of him trying cut off his life's breath. The man's hooded face was a mere foot from his and Jack could feel the energy being squeezed out of him as he thrashed around trying to ease the unyielding grip. Rancid breath and spittle seared down on his face as the man grunted and growled with his effort.

Jack released one arm and with his last resources of strength lashed out at the man's face, trying to reach his eyes. Instead he felt the flesh of his neck and instinctively made a claw of his fingers, digging in as deeply as he could. To his immense satisfaction the man cried out in pain and for a second released his grip. It was just sufficient for Jack to roll aside and, reaching out, he grabbed the torch. The man was on his knees as the blow thudded down on his head.

The man let out a yelp and staggered back, but it was only a rubber torch and not a truncheon and in any event the strike was cushioned by the thick woollen balaclava that he wore.

Jack got quickly but unsteadily to his feet, preparing for the next assault, but he was too late. Although he could see it coming, he was too slow to move and a solid fist struck him on the side of the head. The last thing he remembered before the world went blacker than the night was falling heavily against the banisters.

His assailant stood over him, his chest heaving with the exertion of the fight. Only when he was satisfied that Jack was unconscious did he turn and walk slowly down the stairs to where he had left the implements for his night's work.

'Fuck it!' Liam McCarthy swore as he sat up in bed. 'You bloody fool.'

He had found a comfortable single bed in a room overlooking the lane and, after a meal of sausages and beans that he had lifted from the shop he had settled down in a plush armchair to enjoy the two cans of beer he had found in the kitchen store cupboard. Once again he congratulated himself on finding this perfect place and began to debate with himself how long he could remain there undetected. The owners had clearly moved out, leaving no active alarm system in place. The electricity was working – although for security reasons he obviously could only turn on lights at the rear – and the water was still running for him to have a proper bath. There was even a towel left hanging in the airing cupboard. It was all as if they had prepared the house to welcome him. It would have been perfect had it not been for his own stupidity.

He had spent too long in the sun and now, with scorched skin and the heat of the night, he couldn't settle comfortably to sleep.

Liam swore again and padded naked to the bathroom where he stepped into the bath and turned on the cold shower. He squealed as the fine jets of water hit his raw skin like so many needles. Only when he was satisfied that he had done all he could to cool his tortured body did he turn off the tap. Stepping out onto the bare floor in the darkened room he reached for the towel and gently dabbed his skinny pink body.

As an afterthought he wondered if the house held any such thing as a soothing sun cream, but he dared not turn on a light to search the bathroom's medicine cabinet. To be discovered now and thrown out in the middle of the night would be an even worse fate than lying uncomfortable and awake on a soft mattress.

Miserably he trudged back to the bedroom and stood for a while staring unseeingly into the blackness, wondering what next to do.

It took him a while to notice, but eventually he saw that it wasn't totally black outside.

A faint orange glow sliced through the tiny gap in the curtains that he had not quite managed to close completely before going to bed. He stood there looking at the slit, not immediately knowing why, until suddenly it occurred to him that there were no street lights in the lane. He had noted that point as another plus for his choice of free lodging. Complete darkness was his friend in need on occasions like this.

He felt his way around the bed until he was at the curtains and gently pulled one of them aside to look at the street below. In that instant he forgot about the searing discomfort from his naked skin as, blinking rapidly, he reached up and yanked the curtains wider apart.

It wasn't a street light that he had missed. It was a bloody fire and it was blazing away behind the open windows of the house across the road. He stood for a few moments open-mouthed with fascination and then in one swift movement pulled the curtains closed again.

His thoughts ran amok. It wasn't his business. If the whole house burned down it wasn't his concern. Someone else would spot it soon enough. But then that would mean fire engines and maybe police. The later it was left the worse the situation would become and then perhaps the police would come knocking on doors. If they found him, a vagrant, they might even accuse him of starting it.

Shit! He groped around his pile of clothes, found his briefs and pulled them on as he stumbled back to the window. Opening the curtains wide he saw that the fire was spreading rapidly.

Having calculated the risks that arose from the options of either taking action or of not doing so, he plumped for the former and quickly pulled a mobile from his jeans pocket. A vagrant might not have a pillow to lay his head on, he thought, but he will always have a mobile phone. The emergency services would probably be able to trace the call to his phone, but that would be far safer than making a call from the house landline. He congratulated himself on clear thinking as he stabbed 999 onto the key pad.

The call was answered without delay and he took a deep breath before asking for the fire service. What was the address? Fentonmar is the village. The road? He slapped his forehead and closed his eyes tightly in an effort to remember. Ah yes, Dowr Row.

'And for God's sake be quick,' he added. 'It looks real bad.'

Having pulled the bedroom curtains fully back – the house had to look unoccupied when the firemen came – he finished dressing and then paced the room anxiously, occasionally glancing at the growing fire opposite.

Then, for the first time, he wondered if there was anyone in there. The upper curtains were drawn in one room, so that probably meant someone was sleeping up there. He clenched his fists and shouted into the darkened room, 'Why doesn't someone else see this? Where's the bloody fire engine?'

It seemed like an hour, but was probably no more than twenty minutes, but the sound of a powerful diesel engine and the squeal of brakes at the end of the lane sounded like music to him. A second later he saw the flashing blue light as the fire engine pulled up outside.

Then, quite miraculously, almost as soon as the firefighters jumped into action, lights began coming on in bedrooms and a few heads appeared out of windows.

'Where were you buggers an hour ago!' he yelled at the window.

A hose was being reeled out and one of the firemen was already attacking the front door. People were coming out of their front doors, sleepily wrapped in dressing gowns, and at the sight of them Liam realised it was also his turn to evacuate. If he mingled with the watchers on the roadside then it was unlikely that anyone would ask who he was and how he happened to be there. He gathered together his few possessions and felt his way down the stairs to the back door. Too bad about the broken window: there was no way of hiding that.

No one was watching *his* house as he crept around to the front, so he dumped his clobber under a bush and slipped through the gateway onto the road. It had to appear as if he had just arrived, so he sidled along the neighbouring hedges and fences, then turned at the end of the lane and walked back to stand near a couple who had their arms around each other as they watched the activity in awe.

'Are you sure Catherine and Jack are in there?' the woman asked anxiously.

'I think Catherine's away, but I saw Jack this morning. God, I hope he's not up there,' the man replied.

'The curtain's drawn.'

He looked anxiously at her, but said nothing and then noticed Liam for the first time. They stared at each other for a moment, but then the man returned his attention to the action.

A ladder snaked out from the fire engine bearing a fireman wearing breathing apparatus. The others had located the fire hydrant and were now hosing the blaze through the front door.

Liam was so intent on the scene before him that he only saw the police car when it pulled up alongside. Instinctively he stepped back further until he felt he was blending with the beech hedge behind. The police officers, a man and a woman, got out and surveyed the scene, before the male began talking into his radio. The policewoman crossed the road to talk to a fireman who appeared to be directing operations, but the conversation did not last long. She came back shaking her head.

The man at the top of the ladder had now climbed in through the open window and as he disappeared, a rush of smoke, or possibly steam, escaped and curled crazily into the blackness. The policewoman turned and addressed the couple who had not moved from their vantage point.

'Are you neighbours?'

'Yes.'

'Would you know how many people might be in there?'

'We think just one,' the man replied. 'Mrs Mitchell's away, but we think her husband is in there.'

'Only him then?'

'I think so, but I can't be sure.'

She nodded and then muttered something to her colleague.

Several people were now gathered in small groups along the side of the lane and the police began telling them to get further back. Liam moved along and joined one of the larger groups. Sooner or later he expected enquiries as to who had made the call and he had no wish to become a public hero, nor attract media attention. All he wanted now was some sleep, with or without the comfort of a bed.

An ambulance pulled into Dowr Row and one of the police officers jumped into the driver's seat of his vehicle and moved it further up the lane. The ambulance glided into the vacant spot and two paramedics jumped out.

There was a gasp from some of the onlookers and Liam raised his tired eyes to the bedroom window, where the fireman was emerging with a figure draped across his shoulders.

'Oh, God, it's Jack,' a man said in a hoarse whisper.

They descended slowly and were met at the bottom by the paramedics, who instantly took charge of the sagging figure.

'That was good timing, thank God,' a small woman commented, and then self-consciously wrapped her dressing gown more tightly around her.

After that events moved swiftly. The fire appeared to be well under control and two firefighters had gone into the house to ensure that there was no secondary blaze. Jack was on a stretcher and being wheeled up to the back of the ambulance, while one police officer followed closely behind. She spoke briefly with one of the paramedics and then turned to make a signal across the road to her colleague. He went back to the car, but she got into the back of the ambulance.

The ambulance doors were quickly closed and its engine fired into life.

'That doesn't look good,' Liam heard a man say.

'What do you mean?' the woman beside him asked.

'I think they only travel in the ambulance when there's . . .'

Liam didn't hear the rest as the ambulance driver revved the engine and began the reverse to the end of Dowr Row.

The police car followed and then one of the firemen began suggesting in a loud voice that it would be a good idea if everyone went back to bed now. Having satisfied himself that there was no one else in the house he started securing the front door.

Liam looked at his phone. It was twenty-five minutes to three.

Jack tried to sit up, but the paramedic eased him back and then adjusted the oxygen mask that had slipped to the side of his face.

'Take it easy. You'll be OK now.'

The paramedic glanced across at the police woman quizzically.

'He told the firefighter that he'd been attacked before the fire started. I was hoping to get a statement,' she explained.

'Well, he's not going to be saying much with this on his face,' the paramedic said protectively. He was a round-faced young man with close-cropped ginger hair wearing an olive green uniform that looked as if it belonged to someone a size smaller than himself.

'Perhaps in the hospital then?'

'He's not about to die, you know. He's had some smoke inhalation, so the humidified oxygen's just a precaution.'

The police officer leaned over to look more closely at the patient.

'Head wound too,' she observed.

'Looks superficial. The bleeding's stopped now, but there could be concussion.'

'So, he'll stay in A&E for the night.'

'Definitely.'

As they were discussing his condition, Jack slowly raised an arm and lifted the oxygen mask from his face. His mouth was as dry as cardboard, so he ran his tongue over his lips before attempting to speak. It made little impression.

'Could you give me some water?' he croaked.

Two heads jerked in surprise as if it had been a crash dummy speaking.

'Of course.' The paramedic leaned back and seized a bottle, which he unscrewed and then eased gently to Jack's lips. He gulped and a small stream escaped to run down his neck as the speeding ambulance turned a sharp corner. The paramedic dabbed the wet patch and then began to put the mask back in place, but Jacked stopped him.

'I want to make a statement,' he whispered, looking at the officer.

'I can take it later, when you're on the mend.'

'Now,' Jack closed his eyes for a moment. His head felt as if it had been pounded with a sledgehammer. 'It could be important.'

'Alright. Take your time.'

She took out a notebook and Jack opened his eyes.

'I was attacked. Did they tell you?'

'Yes the firefighter reported that to us.'

'I fought him on the landing of our house. He must have knocked me out, but I think I got a piece of him.' He stopped for a few moments as the thumping in his head increased.

'I think you'd better finish this later at ...'

'No! You don't understand.' Jack lifted his right arm and held it out to the officer. The fingers trembled with the effort. 'Look ... look under my nails.'

Both the officer and the paramedic leaned forward and peered at his hand.

'Ah,' the officer exclaimed and immediately reached into her pouch.

'Swab kit?' the paramedic asked.

'Yes.' She opened a small sample container. 'Looks like a good scrape sample there.'

She smiled approvingly at Jack as she carefully removed the dried blood and a sliver of skin from under Jack's fingernails. When she had finished she took Jack's arm and placed it back by his side. She returned the phial to her pouch and grinned at the paramedic.

'That should be useful,' the man said and then turned to look at his patient. 'Good job.'

But Jack didn't hear. The effort had knocked him senseless again.

When he woke the next day it took him some while to adjust his thoughts and to realise where he was. It was an open ward and every bed was occupied. The one next to his had a screen around it and there was a small but steady pumping noise coming from the other side. A nurse was bending over a bed on the far side of the room and a woman's intermittent groaning came from somewhere near the window.

He moved his eyes cautiously as if anticipating pain, but to his relief there was none. Perhaps he had been given a painkiller: he couldn't remember. Slowly he lifted an arm to feel his head and found a large wad of dressing there. It also seemed that they had shaved hair away from the wounded area. His hand travelled down the side of his face and lingered on a tender spot under the cheekbone.

He turned his head towards the window and wondered what time of day it was. The sun was shining brightly across the roofs he could see opposite, but that told him nothing. He lay in that position for a few minutes. When he turned his head back the ward door was closing silently and a slim young man in a shiny suit was being guided towards his bed.

The nurse accompanying him bent down, checked the bandage and offered Jack a drink of water. He took a grateful gulp and then the nurse turned and nodded knowingly at her companion before leaving them together.

The young man peered down at him for a few moments before drawing up a chair. He introduced himself as Detective Constable Slack, then sat down and smiled at Jack.

'Are you up to answering a few questions now, Mr Mitchell?'

'Yes, I think so.' Jack glanced back at the door again. 'Have you been waiting long?'

'No, they told me you should be coming round at about this time.' He took out a note pad. 'I don't want to tire you, so I'll be as brief as I can, sir.'

'What time is it, by the way?' Jack asked, with a note of alarm in his voice.

'Just after midday. You've been out for a few hours.'

'Midday!' Jack struggled to pull himself into a sitting position and he felt a sharp stab of pain from his ribs. 'I can't stay in here all day.'

'That's probably up to the hospital staff, sir, but meanwhile, if you could ...'

Jack turned to frown at the policeman, as if it were his fault that he was incarcerated in a hospital ward.

'OK, but I'm not staying in here a moment longer than I have to.' He rested his head against the pillow. 'Fire away.'

'Thank you. Now you made a statement in the ambulance on the way here last night and the officer took a scrape sample from under your nails. Do you remember that?'

'Yes, I do.'

'You said that the sample was from your fight with an assailant ...' he paused to look down at his notes, '... on the landing of your house. Correct?'

'Correct.'

'And as far as you are aware, that fight took place before the fire started?'

'Right again. I tackled an intruder, who had entered the house and come up the stairs.'

Slack wrote it down.

'Can you add anything to that?'

'Only that I know who the intruder was.'

The policeman looked up sharply and Jack smiled at his surprise.

'I recognised his aftershave.' His laugh at the wry joke ended in a dry cough.

'I'm sorry?' Slack looked at him as if he suspected his interviewee had suddenly entered a state of delirium.

'No, I'm sorry,' Jack said contritely. 'His breath ... stale tobacco ... and even if not for that I know of only one person who would want to murder me.'

This was clearly not what Slack had expected, but he remembered his training and tried not to stray from the interview routine. He rolled his pen between his fingers for a while before commenting.

'You believe that this was a murder attempt, sir?'

'Well, what else? The bastard tries first to throttle me, then knocks me cold and sets fire to my house. What else do you think his intentions were? If someone hadn't called the fire brigade I'd be toast now. And, by the way, do you know who did call them?'

Slack licked his lips and quickly consulted his notes.

'An anonymous call on a mobile phone. You were very lucky actually. Now, why do you think someone would want to murder you?'

Jack noted the scepticism in the policeman's voice and turned away. He was still too weary to face a long explanation as to what had led up to Nathan Pascoe's attempt to kill him. It was enough for the time being that they should simply know who and not why. And as for being *very lucky* that his house had been set alight ...!

He rolled his head across the pillow to face the policeman again.

'It's a long story, constable, and I really don't feel up to going through it all now. Your forensic chaps have the evidence from the scrape, so I suggest you take a sample from a man called Nathan Pascoe. I don't have an exact address, but he lives in Redruth, so he shouldn't be difficult to trace.' He closed his eyes for a second before adding, 'Unless he's done a runner you should be able to find him.'

DC Slack finished the entry in his pad and stuffed it back into a pocket. He then stood up and flashed the patient a look of approval. This reported statement had clearly made his day.

'Thank you, Mr Mitchell. You get well soon now.' He thrust his hands in his pockets and then glanced around the ward awkwardly, as if searching for the exit. 'We'll contact you for the full report when you're ready. Take care.'

Jack raised a finger and nodded. The policeman turned sharply on his heels and headed for the door, almost colliding with a nurse coming in.

Jack's eyes strayed around the ward again. This was obviously evacuation time. Bed occupants were gradually being led from the room, presumably to be dressed for departure, or maybe to be transferred to another part of the hospital. He eased himself further up the bed awaiting his turn.

He had decided to make it happen as soon as possible.

A member of the staff — he had no idea of her status — came bustling over to his bed after spotting his waving arm. He announced that he was discharging himself and was relieved that there was little objection to this decision. Even the problem of having no outside clothes to wear was solved when she told him that a neighbour had come in that morning with trousers, shirt and shoes. Then there was further welcome news in that Walter Cartwright had left a message: phone him as soon as the patient was to be discharged and he would pick the poor chap up. It gave him a warm feeling that friends had rallied around in this time of need.

And then suddenly, and for the first time since waking, he thought of Catherine. She would be completely unaware of what had happened to him, but then again nothing would be gained by contacting her and causing concern. Let her remain in ignorance, enjoying Rowan's company, until he was due to meet her at the station on Sunday evening.

The clothes, which he pulled on over his stained and torn pyjamas, were not a great fit, but presentable enough for the return journey. He phoned Walter and then went to wait in the hospital entrance lobby. While he was assessing his aches and bruises someone kindly brought him a cup of tea and a biscuit.

Walter must have been in the city because Jack saw the old Volvo pull up outside the hospital entrance less than fifteen minutes after the call. He rose stiffly and walked to the door with as much dignity as his limbs would permit.

'My dear fellow,' Walter shouted as he rushed around the car to greet his hobbling friend. 'What a shocking state of affairs. Get in, get in.'

Jack chuckled at the welcome as he lowered himself gingerly into the passenger seat.

'Yes, not a great way to start a weekend. But thanks for coming to collect me.'

'No problem. I was in town anyway.' He jerked a thumb at some items in the back of the vehicle. 'So, one more antique along the way ...'

'And ready stressed as well.'

They both laughed at that, but Jack broke off sharply as a pain seared through his rib cage. Walter started the car and they wound their way out onto the main road.

There was silence for a few minutes as Walter concentrated on negotiating the roundabout and then filtered into the single traffic lane. He then turned to Jack.

'Popped round to your house this morning after I heard the news. There's a police tape across the front. Seems it's a crime scene now. Anyway I asked if I could go in to get some clothes for your escape. Nothing doing, but then your neighbour – George? – said he'd rustle something up and take it over to the hospital. Decent of him.'

Walter shot another glance at his passenger.

'I looked through the front door from the front gate.' He pulled a long face. 'Place looks a mess I'm afraid, old chap.'

'I expect it is. I wonder what he used?'

'What's that?'

'The crime scene ... you know it was deliberate? I was wondering what he used to start the fire, that's all.'

Walter negotiated the next roundabout and then accelerated down the hill towards the city centre.

'Well, I expect the fire investigators will soon find that out. The important thing is that it was reported in time and the fire was doused before too much damage was done.'

'That's what makes my flesh crawl, Walter. If he used petrol and everyone in the road had been asleep ... well, I'd not be talking to you now.'

Walter frowned and bit gently on his lower lip, but didn't reply.

'It could have been lighter fluid ... lots of it ... a smoker would use lighter fluid, wouldn't he?' Jack mused.

Walter threw another quick glance to his left, wondering if Jack was still slightly concussed. The bulbous dressing perched on the side of his head told its own story: best to humour him, he thought.

'I expect you're right. Petrol would have ... whoomf!' He threw his hands in the air. 'By the way, who called the cavalry?'

'I don't know. Anonymous caller apparently. But he or she is a saint in my books.'

It was a Saturday morning and the traffic was thinner than on a weekday. The day was dry and warm, so many would by early afternoon have gone to the beach, or maybe having a leisurely lunch at a local restaurant. In any event they were soon out the other side of town and heading for the Roseland.

'I'm taking you into my place pro tem. It's small, but should be comfortable and you can stay there at least for tonight.' Jack opened his mouth. 'No arguments, old chap, I've already made up the spare bed. It should only be for one night. Catherine's coming back tomorrow, isn't she?'

'Yes, I'm collecting her from the station in the evening.'

'. . . if you're up to driving. Does she know yet?'

'No. I saw no point in telling her.'

'Right, so I'll take you directly to Dowr Row now and I'm sure they'll let you in at least to collect some essentials.'

'Thanks.'

Walter was right. The police tape was still in place, fluttering its blue and white plastic message in a light breeze, but they allowed him in. There was a heavy acrid aroma hanging in the air which raked his throat. The stairs were burned beyond safety, so a ladder to the landing had been wedged in place. He clambered up that with difficulty and, after he had gathered some clothes and toiletries, he passed them down to the officer waiting below. Meanwhile, a white overalled man from forensics carried on his work on hands and knees at the bottom of the staircase.

Before leaving the house Jack put his head around the study door and was greatly relieved to see that it all appeared to be intact. George's borrowed shoes squelched on the soggy carpet as he crossed the hallway. He glanced back ruefully at the sad sight of his wounded home before rejoining Walter in the Volvo.

'Did they say anything about getting back in?'

'No, but I didn't ask.' Jack put his hand to the head dressing and winced. 'I think it's got to be a hotel job for at least a week, Walter.'

'You're probably right there, old son.'

As the Volvo turned left into Fore Street Jack suddenly realised that he had said nothing to Walter, or to anyone other than the police, about the reason for the arson attack, nor his suspicions as to the perpetrator. And to his credit, Walter had not asked. All he knew was that he needed time to think and that whatever was decided had to be done quickly before Catherine returned. At the moment the only certainty was that he could not spend more than one night at Walter's place: that simply would not be fair on either Walter or Catherine.

Walter parked neatly in front of the shop and heaved himself out of the driver's seat.

'I'll put the kettle on,' he shouted from the pavement. 'Then I'll show you where to doss down.'

Jack followed him in, clutching his clothes and a wash bag, while Walter disappeared to the back of the shop. As he stood there looking up at the old station clock his thoughts turned to what might be happening in Redruth at that moment. Had the police taken his accusation seriously and not simply dismissed it as the delusional ramblings of a concussed victim? If so, had they traced Nathan and taken a DNA sample yet? Or had Nathan somehow avoided that test through some legal loophole? If he was right about Nathan, but the man somehow managed to produce a plausible alibi, what was going to stop him …?

'Sugar in the coffee?' Walter called from the back room.

'No thanks.'

The antique dealer brought through two steaming mugs and handed one to Jack.

'Sit,' he commanded, indicating one of the Chippendale chairs. He went to the shop door and flipped over the *closed* sign.

'I hope I've not done you out of any business this morning.'

'No, not at all. Paul was shop minding when I left, but I told him to push off and lock up in time for his match this afternoon. He's playing at St Austell.' Walter gave a sudden lurch and coffee slopped over the side of the mug. 'Oh! Talking about business, I forgot to tell you. Dorgy's desk. I sold it this morning.'

'Good heavens, that's quick.'

Walter pointed to a gap at the corner of the room.

'The buyer must have come to collect it when I was out. Good job Paul was here.' He took a swig from the mug. 'Yes, it was a quick sale and a good price too. But, I must confess that I jumped the gun a bit. I changed my mind and decided to put it on my website just after we'd shifted it over here. The buyer was on to me early this morning. Keen as mustard.'

'Well done.'

'I hope you don't mind, Jack.' Walter eyed his companion warily. 'Jumping the gun, I mean. You might have had other ideas for it and ...'

'Lord, no. You did the right thing. Anyway, if I'd decided to do something else with it you'd simply have withdrawn it from the site, wouldn't you?'

'Phew, that's a relief.' Walter wiped his brow in a stage gesture.

'Now I must arrange for you to be paid your commission.' Jack smiled and was sharply reminded of the bruise on his cheek bone. 'Did we discuss the rate?'

'I thought you'd quit as Dorgy's executor. Not your responsibility any more, is it?'

'Did I tell you that? Yes, I didn't like doing business with the son, but I did agree to finish off the asset disposals that I'd started.'

He closed his eyes as he felt the headache returning. Walter put the mug down hastily and got to his feet.

'What am I thinking of? Come on, old chap, you're just out of hospital. Come upstairs and have a lie down. If you're feeling up to it we can share a pizza tonight.'

Jack rose slowly to his feet and then stopped suddenly after taking a step towards the stairs.

'God, what am I thinking of, Walter? I've got to tell the insurance company what's happened before they close down for the weekend. I've got to go back to the house to pick up my file.'

Walter tried to dissuade him, but he said the short walk and fresh air would help clear his head. But he did follow his host up the stairs, where he was shown the spare bed and the bathroom. He changed into his own clothes, bundled the borrowed ones into a plastic bag and went down to the showroom again.

'I'll drop these back to George, but I shouldn't be long.'

Walter stood in the middle of the shop and wagged a finger at him.

'Now you take care crossing the road. The state you're in ...'

Jack laughed as he stepped out of the shop and the bell jangled behind him.

George was in the garden cutting the lawn, but his wife answered the door and took the clothes. She expressed her deep sympathy about what had happened and offered whatever assistance the Mitchells needed. He politely refused the offer to go in and have a cup of tea, explaining truthfully that he had to contact the insurance company and left the well-meaning woman wearing an anxious expression. It was clear to Jack that she was aching to have more details as to what had caused the fire.

He crossed the tape in his front garden and stopped at the door. It was closed and a temporary lock had been fitted. Being locked out of his house was not something he had anticipated, but as he hesitated on the step the door opened and a white-suited figure appeared.

'Ah, Mr Mitchell. We're just packing up.'

'Well, I'm glad you're still here.' He pointed to the lock.

'Oh yes, I have the key here.' The man fumbled in a pocket and then handed it over. 'Mr Cartwright at the antique shop told us you're staying with him, so I was going to drop it in.'

'Thanks. I need to collect some papers.' He stepped into the hallway and then looked back over his shoulder. 'I suppose nothing's working in here?'

'The electricity's off, but the telephone line's still connected.'

'And, any idea how long before we can move back in?'

'We've done our work here, so it's up to you.' He dipped his mouth and made a gesture into the charred interior. 'But if I were you'd I'd get it all repaired first.'

Jack sighed and acknowledged the advice with a nod.

The man gathered his equipment and plodded up the path to the waiting van. Jack tiptoed across the sodden carpet into his office and pulled out his insurance file. The room stank like the remains of a bonfire after chunks of foam-backed carpet had been incinerated: which, of course, was exactly what had happened. He brushed some debris off his chair and sat down to make the call.

After suffering the usual recorded caveats and playing the

numbers game he finally got through to a representative who dealt with household claims. It was while he was going through the details of the damage and determining what the next steps should be that he found himself staring through the window at the empty house opposite. And there right before his eyes was the short-term solution to their enforced temporary homelessness.

At the end of the call he stood up, went to the window and, peering at the agents' sign, noted their telephone number. He sat down again and dialled.

An eager sounding female voice answered and, after introducing himself, Jack explained their predicament and then launched straight into his proposal. There was some hesitation as this was clearly not a standard request, but he persuaded the woman to take it to a higher authority if she was not in a position to make an executive decision. She agreed to this and said she would ring back that afternoon. He gave her his mobile number.

He leaned back, arched his fingers under his chin and considered what he had proposed. The neighbours had been trying to sell their house for months and had moved out pending their change of home. He had no idea what this was costing them, but was certain that they would welcome a month's rent while the Mitchells' house was being repaired. Apart from anything else there would be the security that occupation would afford. If an acceptable offer came up while the Mitchells' were renting, he was sure there would be no problem in showing people around.

Jack swung his chair from side to side and congratulated himself on a brilliant plan. It was even possible that the insurance company might contribute towards the rental charge: he made a note to check the small print.

A few minutes later he was getting up to leave when the phone on his desk rang. It was Walter.

'Jack, I don't know when you're coming back, but I've got a copper here who'd like to speak to you. Shall I send him round to Dowr Row, or ...?'

'No, it's alright, Walter. I've had to make a couple of calls, but I'm just on my way back now. Hold him there if you can.'

'I shall make a citizen's arrest,' he declared.

Jack gathered up his insurance file and some other papers before leaving his damaged home.

A very sleek police officer with swept back hair and a neatly trimmed moustache greeted him in the shop, introducing himself as DI Grant. He flashed his warrant card and a perfect set of teeth appeared from under the hirsute upper lip.

'Mr Mitchell, I have news for you.'

'I'll make myself scarce, Jack,' Walter interrupted and gestured towards the back room. 'Make yourself comfortable in the office.'

'Thanks.'

Walter padded upstairs while the other two found seats in the office.

'You have news,' Jack repeated as he cleared some catalogues from Walter's desk chair.

'Yes, we've located Nathan Pascoe and although he wasn't happy about it we took a swab and the lab is checking for a match with your scrape.'

'How long will that take?'

'If there's a match we should know by Monday morning. The lab closes down at weekends.'

'But Pascoe will have been alerted now,' Jack said anxiously. 'What's to stop him doing a bunk?'

'Because we've already taken him in for questioning. We can hold him at least until the lab test is complete, then we can either charge or release him.'

'If you took him in for questioning then you must have explained on what grounds. Did he offer an alibi?'

'Simply said that he was somewhere else all Friday night, nowhere near Fentonmar, and then he asked for a lawyer. The usual.' The teeth appeared again as Grant grinned smugly.

'Well, that's good news, I suppose, but you didn't come all the way from Truro simply to tell me that.'

'Quite so. I've come to complete the interview you had with the DC this morning.' Grant's hands suddenly shot up as if stopping his own progress. 'I'm sorry, I should of course have asked if you're up to further questioning at this time.'

'I'm feeling much better, thank you, so fire away.'

'OK.' Grant settled down to business by producing a pad and a small gold pen. 'You seemed very certain that Nathan Pascoe was the person who attacked you and who then set fire to your house. Can you tell me why you think that?'

It had to come sooner or later. He had been given the choice and he could have postponed this outing, but it was best to divulge everything now, before Catherine came back. So, he began at the beginning: when Dorgy had asked him to help with his tax affairs.

By the time he reached the night of Dorgy's fall down the stairs his head was beginning to throb and even his vision was becoming slightly blurred, but he carried on through details of the inquest and subsequent dealings with Nathan Pascoe. Then he launched into the grey area of speculation.

He told Grant of Nathan's threat to Mavis and how this was clearly intended to stop her reporting her sighting of him on the day of the assumed burglary. Then he reported his rather strange telephone conversation with Harry Charters and how he now interpreted the old man's sighting.

At that point Grant stopped him.

'And you reckon that the person he saw on the street below the almshouses was somehow connected with Mr Pascoe senior falling down the stairs.'

'That's very delicately put, inspector, but yes, that's what I'm suggesting. Nathan Pascoe knew by then that his father was a very wealthy man. He was desperately keen to establish that his father had left no will, because he believed he would be sole beneficiary if Dorgy had died intestate. There was certainly no love lost between them before and then unexpectedly he had the motive to see his own father out of the way.

'After Nathan's last visit to me on Friday – God, is it only yesterday? – I could see in his eyes that he knew I'd guessed the truth. So ...' he searched the policeman's eyes for reaction, '... so, he had to deal with me as well.'

Grant's expression didn't change, but he stared at Jack for

several seconds before responding. He was clearly not a man to be influenced by an amateur's conjecturing.

'Now, by that time, yesterday,' he began slowly, 'you were no longer acting in a professional capacity for Nathan Pascoe. Is that correct?'

'That's right. I'd just told him why and he didn't like it ... but then I didn't care much for him either.'

'He took it badly.'

'Yes, he must have thought I was some kind of soft touch who would wrap the whole business up in short time and then hand the contents of the estate over to him. It turned out to be more complex than that. It often does with cases of intestacy. The irony is that under current legislation he probably wouldn't be entitled to the whole estate anyway.'

'I see.' Grant scribbled something in the notebook and then looked up under his thin black eyebrows. 'You realise that what you've told me is nearly all circumstantial? Even if the CPS were to accept the case it could be difficult to produce sufficient evidence at this stage that Nathan Pascoe was responsible for his father's death.'

Jack's hand went to the head dressing. It was beginning to itch.

'I know. It's such a pity that the coroner didn't call Nathan to give evidence at the inquest, or even Harry Charters. That might have made a difference.' Jack looked down at the floor. 'Too late now I suppose.'

'Possibly. On the attempted murder of his father anyway.' Grant slipped the notebook back into a pocket and then admired the gold pen before putting that away also. 'But, you never know what might come out after we get the lab report on Monday. Meanwhile, thank you for your time and for the data you've given me.'

He stood up. The ordeal of the interview was over.

Jack showed the inspector out and shortly after that he heard Walter's heavy shoes clumping down the stairs.

'Didn't buy anything I suppose?'

'What, on a policeman's pay?' Jack smiled ruefully. 'I'm not even sure he bought my story.'

'Any news on the DNA match?'

'He says we'll have to wait until Monday for that.'

Walter glanced up at the station clock.

'Look, it's nearly time for me to shut up shop. You can sort your stuff out upstairs and I've got a few bits of paperwork to deal with. Then how about a drink at the Plume, followed by a pizza back here?'

'Sounds like you've got it all worked out. Fine by me.'

'Then I recommend an early night for you. I can practically feel the cuts and bruises from here.'

Jack laughed, but the antique dealer was right. The few activities of his day were beginning to take their toll and he was only too happy to accept the sound advice.

He turned to go upstairs as Walter called from his office, 'Do you play backgammon?'

'Yes.'

'Right, I'll challenge you when we get back tonight.'

He smiled as he carried on up to his temporary quarters, reflecting on the extraordinary events of the past twenty-four hours. He suddenly had a feeling of emptiness and vulnerability. Stopping at the top of the stairway he looked at his hands: they were shaking. Whether this was the result of delayed shock or not, he recognised his need of someone close.

He needed Catherine.

CHAPTER 19

The evening worked out as Walter had planned, but, overcome by tiredness, Jack could manage only one game of backgammon. Walter gave him a glass of port and wished him a peaceful night.

Jack had no idea of the time during the night when the dream merged with subconscious thought, which taken together somehow crashed into the solution to an enigma.

He had once solved the clue to a crossword puzzle in his sleep and he had heard that a cryptographer at Bletchley Park had cracked a code in the same way. Some people have dreams that are based on recent experiences; some have fanciful dreams that bear no relation whatsoever to reality; and others dream all night long but remember none of it on waking.

With the beating he had taken, the subsequent mental effort over a simple game and finally the glass of port, Jack had no trouble in dropping off to sleep in the narrow bed under the eaves. But he did have dreams.

Like waves thundering over the shore, relentlessly they came. Mostly they were a jumble of recent events, but involving people he had never met, in a place that he had never visited. Then there would be a vivid discussion with a policeman about some nonsensical occurrence that seemed to have happened to another individual entirely.

And then suddenly he was in a large warehouse, surrounded mainly by pine furniture, but with the occasional fine antique. He was standing beneath a gallery haranguing with a man about the price of a gilt mirror, when suddenly a large round wall clock with a flat face fell from somewhere above and landed at their feet. The warehouseman leapt back at this occurrence and began to blame

Jack. The man called a colleague for support and they were about to attack him with broken chair legs that were lying about, when Jack pointed out that the clock was still working. It was still ticking and seemed to be intact, except for one strange phenomenon: some of the painted Roman numerals were gradually sliding off its face.

The three of them were staring down at this weird occurrence when a young woman, dressed in black, came from nowhere, clutching a tin of paint and a brush. She cried out that this had happened before and it was alright as she would paint the numbers back on. They watched and, as she did this, crouching on her haunches, the warehouseman kept sending customers away, shouting, 'There's nothing to see here. Go home.'

She had almost finished painting the last numeral, when Jack pointed out that she had done the four wrongly. It shouldn't be a one and a vee, but four ones. That, he told them, was how it used to be. But she was having none of it. One-vee was how she was going to paint it, as she had always done before. Jack began protesting loudly that she cannot have done that, because it was four ones when it fell and therefore she must have lied about painting it before.

And still the warehouseman kept shouting that the customers should go home. 'There's nothing to see, there's nothing ...'

Jack woke and flinched as he struggled into a sitting position. His head felt wet and the thin duvet was half off the bed. He reached over and turned on the light.

It wasn't sweat, it was blood. The head dressing had come away and the wound had seeped over the pillow. He swore as he stepped out of bed and reached over for the flannel that he had draped over the side of the small basin. He mopped his head and found that the blood had now congealed into a moist scab. The dressing was on the floor, so he picked it up and placed it back over the wound with one hand. With the other he opened the medicine cabinet above the basin and fumbled around until he found some sticking plaster. He peeled this off and tore a strip with his teeth. The roll of plaster dropped into the basin as he clumsily stretched the strip across the dressing and onto the shaved part of his head. He did this twice more and then stared at himself in the mirror.

When he began to laugh softly at his pantomime image, it wasn't the fact that that he looked ridiculous. Neither was it hysteria brought on by delayed trauma. It was the fact that the strange black-clad female figure in his dream had unlocked the enigma. She and his subconscious had solved a puzzle.

Only then did he check the time. It was ten past three, but he knew that sleep would now be almost impossible. There was too much on his mind.

He pulled the bloodied case off the pillow and let it soak in the basin. The stain had gone through the case, but there was nothing he could do about that. Fortunately there were no other signs of blood on the bed.

He took the duvet and a towel and settled down in the small padded chair by the window. With the folded towel behind his head he pulled up the duvet and closed his eyes. It was going to be a long two hours until daylight.

The curtains across the bedroom window were thin, as was the glazing, so it was not long after dawn that a combination of early sunlight and the occasional vehicle along Fore Street woke him from a febrile sleep. His back was stiff from an unnatural position in the chair and the folded towel had slipped behind his neck, but he felt more rested than he had a right to expect.

Jack stretched his legs and then felt the top of his head. The makeshift dressing was still in place. He drew his legs back in, rose cautiously and went over to the window to draw open the curtains. The street below glistened in the sunlight from a light shower that had fallen during the night. Further down the road the newspaper lorry was parked outside the convenience store and a man was pulling a loaded trolley across the pavement. Fentonmar was waking.

He picked up the sodden pillowcase and wrung it out before watching the bloodied water curl its way down the plug hole. The stain had gone from the sodden cloth so he carried it to the bathroom at the rear of the flat and hung it on the towel rail.

As he waited for the water to run hot he stared out of the bathroom window at what Walter might loosely refer to as his garden. It was a long strip of grass that ended in a Cornish hedge.

A bolted gate in the hedge gave access onto the village back lane. To one side of the garden another stone hedge, greatly infused with ivy, formed the northern boundary. On the opposite side there was a sturdy wooden fence. Immediately below the bathroom window he saw a corrugated iron roof under which Jack suspected there was a coal shed. By the look of the grass it was unlikely to house a lawnmower.

Someone had made an attempt to introduce some colour by planting climbing roses and these trailed around a precariously leaning arbour, which seemed to be supported by a birdbath on a stone plinth.

He shook his head, put the plug in the basin and prepared for a slow and painful shave.

Ten minutes later it was no surprise to find the small kitchen deserted and Walter's door firmly closed. He had to remind himself that it was Sunday morning and not long after six o'clock. But the impatience for activity was gnawing away. There was so much to be done before Catherine arrived that evening.

He made coffee and boiled an egg.

When there was still no sign of life from his host's room he went silently downstairs and the terrier raised its head from its blanket by the back door. He bent to pat the dog and then went to unlock the back door. Once outside he went to the gate, slid the rusting bolt back and stepped out into the lane. It was time to test the battered body, so he walked cautiously down the lane as far as the cricket ground. No one else was about. Turning left at the children's sand park he took the footpath along which they used to walk their dog and kept going until he was in a wooded area. It was good to breathe in the fresh morning air and to feel his legs functioning again.

It wasn't until he was well out of the village that he decided to stop. He still felt the bruised ribs, but his head was clear and the wound seemed to have formed a firm scab.

He looked round at the sound of pounding feet and then gave a cheery greeting to a passing runner. It was after seven o'clock and time to return.

Jack went back into the house the way he had left and found Walter padding around downstairs in his slippers.

'Good grief, Jack,' he exclaimed. 'I thought we'd had burglars. Couldn't you sleep?'

'Slept fine, Walter, but I thought an early walk would start the day right.'

'Excellent. Come on up and I'll make some breakfast.'

Jack followed him up to the kitchen, telling him that he had already breakfasted and then apologising about the pillow. Walter seemed unconcerned, but began chastising himself for failing to check the dressing before Jack went to bed. He shoved some bread in the toaster, promising to exercise his first aid skills after he had put on some clothes.

It wasn't until Walter had settled and was slurping coffee that Jack, leaning against the oven, put forward his plan for the day ahead.

He began with the request of a favour.

'Walter, do you have the name and address of the person who bought Dorgy's desk?'

'Yes I do.' Walter squinted at him over the steam. 'Why?'

'I need to see the desk again. There's something in there that I need to find.'

Walter put the cup down slowly and peered at Jack as if observing a person of unsound mind.

'My dear chap, we've done all that,' he began cautiously. 'You and I went through it thoroughly, as did you and Nathan before. Nothing in there. Empty.'

'You'll have to trust me on this one. I know we've checked it thoroughly and I also know that no one was keener than Nathan to check that it was empty, but I've discovered something since.'

'Secret panel is it?' His tone was mildly mocking. 'This sounds most intriguing.'

'Look, what I'm asking you to do is contact the purchaser and ask him if we can go and check it out to see if I'm right. I might not be, but I have to know.'

'What? Today?'

'Yes, this morning if possible.'

'But, what on earth will I tell them?' He shook his ungroomed head. 'That some bloke who's had a blow on the head thinks he's left something hidden in that antique desk you bought yesterday?'

'Come on, Walter,' Jack pushed away from the oven and sat at the table, 'it's not that difficult. Tell them it was an executor's sale which you made in good faith, but now said executor believes there's something secreted in the desk that he needs to recover. Surely, at the very least, he'll be intrigued to know what it is.'

Walter leaned back and munched on toast as he thought it through. A smear of marmalade clung precariously to his mutton chop whiskers. Eventually he straightened up and levelled his gaze at the madman opposite.

'And you reckon this is important,' he stated.

'I do ... and I'll explain how I reached that conclusion ... but not until we're in the car.'

Walter threw back his head and roared. A chunk of toast landed neatly in his cup.

'Bribery, eh! OK, Jack, I'll do it. I'm hooked.'

'Thank you.' Jack looked up at the clock. 'But perhaps you'd better wait until they're up.'

'I'll give him a call when I've prepared myself to face the day. Oh, and don't let me forget to deal with that crazy head of yours.'

Jack stood up and stared benignly down at his host for a moment before going to tidy his room. Walter carried on munching and slurping. In their different ways they both anticipated a protracted couple of hours ahead.

At eight-thirty Jack made a call to the White Hart Hotel in St Austell and booked in for a couple of nights. Even if he had positive news from their opposite neighbours, the Batemans, it seemed unlikely that he and Catherine would be able to move in before Tuesday. The hotel had a double room available, so he took it.

Walter went down to the store for a newspaper and on his return declared that it was a decent enough time to make the call. He went into his office while Jack paced up and down in the showroom.

Five minutes later Walter came out, shaking his head.

'No good?' Jack asked anxiously.

'I might have guessed. They live in St Mawes. They've gone for a sail.'

'But you spoke to someone ...'

'Yes, a house guest. Said she'd pass the message on.' Walter sat down heavily. 'Sorry, old man. Best I could do.'

'Bugger! I have to get to that desk today. Could you not try again in an hour? Did they say if it was a short sail before breakfast or an all-day job?' Jack was pacing again, thumping a fist into his palm.

'Steady on, Jack.' Walter replied calmly, opening out the newspaper. 'Why today anyway? Can't it wait until tomorrow?'

'Have you forgotten, Walter?' He stopped pacing. 'Dorgy's funeral's tomorrow. I have to know one way or the other before then. And now you say they live in St Mawes ... for all we know they're from up country and going back tonight.'

Walter's brow furrowed as he lowered the paper to his lap.

'Okay, I'll give it another try in an hour.'

Not long after that, while Jack was trying to concentrate on an article in the financial press about pensions, his mobile started warbling. He grabbed it and Walter put the paper down again to peer over the top of his spectacles.

To Jack's surprise it was Colin Bateman, responding to the request for the Mitchells to rent their house in Dowr Row. He expressed his sincere commiseration about the fire and their loss and went on to say that he and his wife had discussed his proposal. In view of the fact that there had been little serious interest at the current asking price, together with the security risk posed with an empty house and no burglar alarm, they thought it was a very acceptable idea.

Jack looked at Walter, smiled and gave a thumbs-up.

A fair rental price would be agreed with the estate agent, who would then draw up a short-term contract. The agent would also be instructed to contact the Mitchells with ample warning of any arranged viewings during their occupancy.

Jack thanked Bateman profusely and rang off.

'Well, something's gone right so far today,' Jack sighed. 'Now, come on St Mawes.'

There was another mobile call twenty minutes later, just as Walter had gone to get a second cup of coffee. This time it was Rowan, letting her father know what train Catherine was catching from Bristol. If it was running on time she should be arriving at five that afternoon. Apparently the visit had been a success and, according to Rowan, Catherine seemed rested and relaxed. Jack smiled ruefully: that might soon wear off when she heard what he had to tell her.

Walter returned with two mugs.

'Well, the hour's nearly up,' he said, going over to wind a carriage clock that stood on one of his bookshelves. 'You'd better think of something else if they're still not in.'

'At the moment there's no plan B I'm afraid.'

Walter took a couple of sips and then trudged across the room to pick up the phone. He consulted a scrap of paper and then dialled.

There were several rings and, just as he was expecting it to go onto message, someone picked up. Walter introduced himself and then spun round to give Jack a wide-eyed look of encouragement.

He launched into the rehearsed spiel, listened to the response, and then asked if it was convenient for them to go over before lunch.

'Excellent!' He dropped the receiver back and clapped his hands together. 'You're in business. We leave in fifteen minutes.'

Jack laughed. 'I never knew you could be so eloquent. But thanks for doing that.'

'I'm a salesman, old boy.' He waved a hand at his guest. 'Now come on, I've got to patch you up before we go. Don't want to frighten the denizens of St Mawes.'

The Volvo sidled out of the alleyway by the antique shop and into Fore Street. A few people were milling around outside the Congregational church and one of them gave Walter a wave as they passed. It wasn't until the car was lumbering up the hill outside the village that Walter turned to his passenger.

'Right, time to tell all.'

'OK, let's start with the day that you and I were evaluating the things in Dorgy's flat. The only items of any value, you said, were the antique desk and a few watercolours. And, of course, you were right. The fact that you were able to sell the desk so quickly proves the point.

'Now, when we were examining the small drawers inside the desk you pointed out the hidden compartments. They weren't difficult to find, just not immediately obvious. Each one is fluted vertically on its face and spaced equally apart. Do you remember how many there are?'

'Of course. Four.'

'Four hidden compartments. And do you remember you pointed out some marks scratched on the side of the compartments?'

'Yes, they're identification marks. It's a way of ensuring you replace each one in the correct slot. These were hand-crafted pieces and no one drawer space is identical.'

'We do the same thing with our drawers, but we tend to use letters instead of numbers. The ones in Dorgy's desk are probably Roman numerals.' Jack gave Walter a sidelong glance and was silently satisfied at his friend's puzzled frown. 'Now, Dorgy was not an educated man and, although we take these things for granted, it's my belief that he didn't know his Roman numerals. He might have been astute in other everyday matters and he was certainly sufficiently literate to do his job, but in other ways I reckon he was pretty rustic ... certainly when it came to his own financial affairs.

'But, when he lay at the bottom of those stairs, barely conscious, he had plenty of time to work out his priorities. Whether he fell, or was pushed, he ...'

The car gave a jolt as Walter's foot stabbed the accelerator.

'Pushed?' he exclaimed. 'Is there a suggestion that might have happened? I mean who ...?'

'It's only my theory, but that's another story and the police are looking into it right now,' Jack added hastily. 'But, back to Dorgy at the bottom of the stairs. Did I tell you what he said to Mavis Harris when she found him?'

'Pushed ...' Walter's mind was lingering on that thought.

'Walter?'

'Eh? Oh, yes, something about ivy, wasn't it? Made no sense.'

'Absolutely so. Said the way Mavis thought she'd heard it, it didn't make sense. But it suddenly came to me last night ... the marvels of the subconscious ... Dorgy actually did say, *tell Jack Mitchell 'tis in Ivy*, so the clue should have been in the lack of definite article. He never said *'tis in the ivy*.'

Walter changed down for the double bend in Trewithian and then cursed when a tractor pulled out from the Portscatho turning ahead.

'Call me dim, old man, but I'm buggered if I can see where this is going.'

'You will very soon.' Jack found that he was enjoying this: the realisation had taken long enough, so it was worth spinning out now. 'I mentioned Dorgy's priorities when he spoke those enigmatic words to Mavis. He might barely have been aware of who he was speaking to, but his overriding thought was not to say something that might condemn his only son ...' Jack held up his hand as Walter opened his mouth to speak. '... but to ensure that *I* knew where to look for something far more important to him.

'You see, Dorgy didn't say *ivy* at all. He said eye-vee.' He turned to Walter. 'Do you get it now?'

'Good God!' Walter crunched the gear down to third and swung the wheel to overtake the tractor. The old Volvo responded like an oil tanker as it gradually picked up speed to clear the slow-moving vehicle. 'Of course! Not only eye-vee ... it should have been one-vee ... Roman four, Jack!' He thumped the steering wheel. 'So, that's what the old devil was trying to tell you.'

Walter's whiskered head shot back as he roared with laughter. He reached across and gave Jack a thump on the shoulder.

'That's what he was trying to tell me,' Jack repeated quietly. 'And that's why we're on the way to St Mawes now.'

'So, what do you reckon you'll find tucked away behind the fourth column?'

'I know what I'd like to find,' he paused for a second, 'but it might not be behind. It might somehow be in the box itself.'

Walter shook his head. 'We looked in each one. I just don't see ...'

He indicated right by the old water tower and turned off the main road at the top of St Mawes.

'Upper Castle Road,' Jack observed. 'If your buyer lives down here the old desk's found a good home.'

'Better than that, old man,' Walter replied with a grin.

'*Lower* Castle Road!'

'The same.'

'Then you sold it too cheaply.'

Walter laughed and then braked to allow a Bentley to pull out of a driveway. He followed it down the hill until arriving at the sharp right turn by St Mawes Castle and then slowed to a crawl.

'Halfway down the road he said.'

Jack turned to admire the view. This was why houses along the short cul-de-sac of Lower Castle Road commanded such an enormous premium in their value. All of the properties along the road had an uninterrupted vista of the water where the mouth of the Percuil river met the vast natural harbour of the Carrick Roads, at the far side of which stood Falmouth and its docks. For a yachtsman this had to be the next thing to heaven.

'Here we are.'

Walter turned into a tarmacked driveway and stopped at the top alongside a Range Rover. The house itself was surprisingly ordinary in design and size, but the garden at the front was immaculately presented and the grass cut smooth enough for a croquet lawn. Faint sounds of merriment came from the garden at the back of the house.

They got out and Walter led the way to the front door.

It was opened almost immediately by a short balding man of about forty, dressed in faded jeans and an open-necked striped cotton shirt. He was barefooted.

They introduced themselves and were invited in. Although his manner was welcoming enough to be civil, Jack immediately got the impression that the sooner their business was done the better. There was obviously a party going on at the back. An aroma of grilling fish wafted through the hallway from somewhere.

The householder scrutinised Jack's face, but was polite enough not to comment on the bruised cheek and head wound.

He opened a door and guided them into one of the front rooms that overlooked the sea. The desk had found its niche to the left of a stone fireplace.

'May I?' Jack pointed at it.

'Carry on. Mind if I watch?'

'I just hope there's something for you to see.' Jack went up to the desk, appraised it affectionately and then rolled back the lid. He saw immediately that it was as empty as when it had been delivered to Walter's shop. Taking a deep breath, he glanced at Walter and then eased out the fourth compartment.

As he had expected, that too was empty. He turned it over and smiled.

'I need something long and straight,' he said eyeing the fireplace until he spotted a strip of kindling. 'Ah, this will do.'

Like a conjurer preparing for a trick he made sure his audience was watching and then put the stick into the slim box until it touched the bottom. With finger and thumb gripping the stick firmly where it met the top of the box he then withdrew it.

'Look.'

Jack placed the stick along the outside of the box. It was a good inch short.

'Good grief,' Walter exclaimed and Jack noticed that even their host's eyes were wide in anticipation. 'A secret compartment within a secret box.'

Jack turned it over and ran a finger along the edge until he found what he was looking for: a tiny notch in the bottom. He slotted a fingernail in and pulled gently.

It might not have been opened for many years, but the bottom of the box came away surprisingly smoothly. And as it slid out a folded sheet of yellow paper began to appear, rather like a slowly protruding tongue. Halfway along the yellow tongue of paper a small red blob of sealing wax came into view.

Jack took hold of the paper before it fell to the floor and then, with a look of triumph in his eyes, held it up to his audience.

'This, unless I'm very much mistaken, is the last will and testament of the late Dorgy Pascoe.'

'Well done, Jack,' Walter trumpeted and slapped his friend on the back. 'So, you were right after all.'

'You doubted it?' He turned quickly to the householder. 'I'm sorry about the mystery, but this is something I've been searching for during the past few weeks.'

'How exciting.' The man sounded genuinely pleased. 'You're the executor, I presume.'

'I am now. Until recently I thought I was going to be administering a case of intestacy.'

The white lie saved a long explanation.

Jack put the document into a jacket pocket and then pushed the false bottom back into place. He gave the box a reverential pat and slotted it into position number four in the desk.

'Would you like a drink before you go?' the man asked.

The question was posed in such a way that implied a reticent obligation, so they declined and once again expressed thanks. He showed them to the door and then went off to rejoin the party.

Walter heaved himself into the driver's seat of the Volvo and for several seconds simply sat back with a stupefied grin spread across his broad florid face. Jack looked at him and laughed.

'We'd better go, or they'll start thinking we're casing the joint.'

He started the car and backed away from the Range Rover.

'In the words of old Joe Gargery, *what larks*, eh Jack, *what larks!*'

He set off down the driveway still laughing.

'Well, thank God for that,' Jack sighed. 'I didn't look a fool after all.'

'No, spot on.' Walter cast a sideways glance. 'Aren't you going to look at it?'

'Not now. Wait until we're back.' He patted his pocket. 'You know this changes everything?'

'No more intestacy, you mean?'

'Exactly. Regardless of who the beneficiaries are it will be a damned sight easier to obtain probate on a valid will than going through the process of proving assets under intestacy laws.'

'But, you are rather making an assumption, aren't you?'

'That I might not be appointed executor? Yes, I know, there might be a named executor in the will. In which case I'll take a back seat. We'll see.'

'Anyway, you've quit. Have you forgotten that?'

'No, but it now depends on who the main beneficiary turns out to be.'

They lapsed into silence after that until passing the Fentonmar sign, when Walter asked Jack again when Catherine's train was due in.

Back at the antique shop the two men parted ways: Jack went to buy a pasty from the store before going back to Dowr Row to collect some more clothes and Walter dived into the Plume for a pint and a pie.

It wasn't until he was seated at his desk that Jack removed the faded document from his pocket and took a paper knife to ease off the sealing wax. It came away quite easily and he began to unfold the paper slowly in case the creases had perished the paper with age.

It was an A4 sized sheet, which had been folded eight times in order to fit lengthways into the box cavity. It had been typewritten, but the typeset was small enough for it all to fit onto the single sheet.

Jack spread it out on his desk and smoothed it with the heel of his hand before beginning to read.

THIS IS THE LAST WILL AND TESTAMENT of me Charles Pascoe of Fentonmar in the County of Cornwall. I hereby revoke all former Wills and Codicils made by me.

1. *I appoint my daughter-in-law Rachel Pascoe to be the Executrix and Trustee of this my Will.*
2. *In this Will the expression Trustee shall mean and include the person who proves this Will.*

3. *Subject to payment of my debts and funeral expenses I give the following legacies free of tax:*
a. *To my daughter-in-law Rachel Pascoe the sum of one thousand pounds.*
b. *To my daughter Kylie Pascoe the entire residue of my Estate.*

Signed: Charles 'Dorgy' Pascoe

It was dated just over eighteen years earlier and witnessed by two people, whose names were hard to decipher.

The will was short, but unequivocal and seemingly valid in every legal respect. But, most importantly of all, it officially recognised Dorgy's paternity of Kylie, just as Rachel had claimed. It was written as if Nathan did not exist. So, assuming he had no hope of making a successful challenge to the will, Kylie would get all but a tiny fraction of Dorgy's fortune.

Jack sat back and stared out of the window. A wagtail was jumping up and down on the garden wall, excitedly plucking insects from the crevices. Beyond that the sun cast tree-shaped shadows against the wall of the house that would soon be their home for the next few weeks.

It was nearly all over.

He got up, found a plastic folder and eased the will into it. He could no longer trust the security or integrity of his home, so he put the folder in his briefcase. Walter, he knew, had a safe in the back office.

The pasty was only just warm, but he sat there quietly contented and ate it as if it were a choice delicacy. A few crumbs spilled onto his lap. He brushed them off onto the carpet before leaving the office and going up the ladder to collect some clothes suitable for a funeral. Tomorrow they would be saying a final farewell to Dorgy Pascoe.

The train was only five minutes late and he saw Catherine leaving the quiet carriage before she saw him. He dodged a man who appeared to have spent too long in the restaurant car and gave her a wave. She spotted him and waved back.

He reached out and hugged her as if she had been away across the globe for several weeks, feeling the tension of the past three days leach out like the release of a pressure valve.

'Oh, Jack, you're crushing me,' she exclaimed through breathless laughter. 'Have you missed me that much?'

'Yes, I have.' He reached down for her case. 'Come, we have much to talk about.'

Only then did she notice his injuries and let out a surprised gasp as she put a hand up to his face.

'What have you been doing?'

'Come.' He took her arm and set off for the parked car. 'I'll tell you all about it on the way home.'

He put the case on the back seat, got in and started the engine. Catherine was staring at him intently and he turned to give her a reassuring smile. He waited for a taxi to pull out from the station forecourt and then followed it down the hill into the city centre. It was going to be a long story.

She cut in occasionally with exclamations and questions, but mostly she just listened in awe to what had happened to him since she left. His story finally ended as the car pulled into Fentonmar's Fore Street.

'Why didn't you call me, darling?' She put a hand on his knee. 'I would have come straight back.'

He changed gear to turn into Dowr Row. It was taking him a while to adjust to her buoyant mood, coupled with an apparent sincere concern for his well-being. It had been months since she had called him *darling*, such had been the degree of self-absorption.

'I know you would have and that's precisely why I didn't contact you.' He patted her hand. 'You needed the time with Rowan more than you needed to be with me. Here we are. Now prepare yourself for a really sad sight.'

He got out of the car, unlocked the front door and pushed it open, watching closely for her reaction. At first there was none. She simply stood and stared. Then she took a step forward and peered up at what remained of the stairway.

'Mind the floor,' he said, 'the carpet's still sodden.'

Then, to his utter surprise, she turned to him with a stern face and said, 'I never liked the bannisters on those stairs. Will the insurance company cover the whole loss?'

'I don't see any reason why not. It's all covered at current replacement value.'

'Then I'll really enjoy designing a new staircase with more attractive bannisters ... with perhaps an elegant curve halfway up. What do you think?'

'I think that sounds like an excellent idea.'

And he really did.

How odd life can be sometimes, he thought. Out of a potential disaster comes a therapeutic opportunity: a project to enthuse and absorb his wife and give her a sense of purpose that for so long seemed to be lacking. He stepped into the blackened hallway and hugged her from behind. 'An excellent idea, which I think you'll do brilliantly.'

She smiled at him over her shoulder and tiptoed towards the ladder.

'Is it safe to go up? We'll need to collect clothes and other essentials.'

'It should be secure, but I'll come up behind you.'

They spent half an hour upstairs, gathering enough clothes and toiletries for two nights in the hotel and then, coming out of the bedroom, Catherine paused by the broken bannister rail.

'Is this where ...?'

'Yup, that's where he put my lights out.'

He saw her shudder.

'Thank God someone saw the fire, Jack. Do they know who made the call?'

'No. It was from a mobile, but the police haven't been able to trace the owner.' He took her elbow and directed her to the ladder. 'Maybe just someone passing by. Let's go now.'

They piled their possessions into the car and Jack drove the short distance to the antique shop. Walter was at home and was treated to a generous hug from Catherine. His large brown eyes bulged with pleasure and he gave her a wet kiss in return. Jack collected his things from the room upstairs, but declined Walter's offer of a drink.

'If you don't mind I'll leave the document in your safe for the night,' Jack said as he opened the door.

'No problem, old chap. Then perhaps you'll tell me who won the lottery.'

'I'll tell you after the funeral. By the way, are you going?'

'I'll be at the church, but probably won't go on to the crematorium.'

'No, I think that part is family only.'

'Right, see you tomorrow then.'

It was a twenty minute drive to the hotel in St Austell. They settled into the double room and then went for a drink at the bar before dinner. Catherine gave him a full account of her short stay with Rowan, including details of places they had visited and meals they had eaten. Clearly it had been a thoroughly worthwhile trip and certainly a morale-boosting fillip for Catherine.

For the first time in many months, that night he went to bed with his wife.

Immediately after breakfast Jack called Jane Stokes to get some details of the service and to ask if there was anything useful that he could contribute. No, she said, all was organised, and then she immediately launched into a series of questions about Jack's welfare. She apologised for not visiting in hospital, or calling over the weekend, and asked how he was feeling now. Jack tried to make light of what had happened, but said they could talk about it once the formalities of the funeral were over.

Catherine was deliberating over a choice of suitable clothes when the mobile started warbling. It was Detective Inspector Grant of Truro Police.

'Mr Mitchell, I know Mr Pascoe's funeral's taking place this morning, but I thought you'd like to know the result of the DNA tests.'

Jack stopped fumbling with a shirt sleeve button.

'Yes, I certainly would. Thanks for calling.'

'Well, it probably won't surprise you to know that there was a perfect match.'

'With Nathan Pascoe …?' It seemed an unnecessary point of clarification, but he just wanted to hear the policeman say the words.

'Yes, with Nathan Pascoe. The forensic evidence is that he was the person who attacked you and probably the person who set fire to your house. The gouge on his neck adds to the evidence against him … not that we need any more.'

'So, presumably he'll be charged with arson and attempted murder?'

'That's not for me to say, but something like that.'

'And that's all you'll be charging him with?'

There was a pause and Jack wondered if he had overstepped the mark.

'At this time, yes. Any further charge will only arise if after further investigation there's sufficient evidence to convince the CPS.'

'I understand.' Catherine came out of the bathroom and stood beside him. 'Er, just as a matter of interest, will Nathan be permitted to attend his father's funeral?'

'We gave him the option – under supervision of course – but he declined.'

'In the circumstances, probably just as well.'

'We'll be in touch, Mr Mitchell, to let you know how the matter is proceeding.'

Jack thanked him again and rang off. He turned to Catherine.

'Did you catch any of that?'

'Only the bit about Nathan not coming to the funeral. Was that the police?'

He gave her the news as he finished dressing and then complimented her on the smart formal linen suit she had chosen.

Ten minutes later, as they were driving away from the hotel car park, the phone rang again. He turned on the speaker to hear a hesitant voice from the estate agent's office.

'Just to let you know we've heard from Mr Bateman and we're drawing up a short-term contract for you and Mrs Mitchell.'

'That's excellent news. We're staying at a hotel in St Austell at the moment. Is there any chance that we might be able to move in tomorrow?'

There were sounds of nervous dithering, followed by a rustle of paper before she replied.

'Yes, I'm sure that will be in order, but I'd better check with Mr Bateman first.'

'That would be good.'

'Um, there's just one small thing I ought to mention ...'

'Yes?'

'We went to check the house first thing this morning and it seems that there's been a break-in. A rear window's been broken and they must have got in that way.'

'Oh, I'm sorry to hear that. Seems as if Dowr Row is currently the crime hot spot of Fentonmar.' A strangled giggle came down the line. 'Was anything stolen?'

'Not that we could tell, but the shower had been used and ... well, it looks as if someone had been sleeping in one of the beds.'

'Not so bad then. Presumably you'll arrange to have the window repaired before we move in?'

'Yes we'll certainly be doing that, Mr Mitchell.'

'Thank you. And you will contact me again with Mr Bateman's reply?'

'Yes, I will.'

Jack looked at Catherine and pulled a face.

'Whatever next?' she said, checking her hair in the visor mirror.

The ancient church was full.

People who had worked with Dorgy over the years were there, together with more recent village friends and drinking companions. Catherine and Jack were shown to a seat near the back and to right of the aisle. She turned to nod at the old woman beside her and Jack cast his eye around for familiar faces.

Mavis Harris was talking softly to a younger woman four pews in front and Walter sat awkwardly at the end of another near the vestry door. The organ was being tortured by an unrehearsed pair of hands and Jack could just make out a piece that would have sent Bach screaming into the graveyard. He stretched his neck to see who the culprit was and to his surprise saw old Harry Charters hunched on the organ stool. Jack smiled: last rights indeed.

Seated on their own on a front pew were Rachel and Kylie Pascoe. Rachel had a dark pashmina draped over her shoulders and for once Kylie, in her all-over black retro-Goth outfit, seemed appropriately dressed. A little way in front of them the pine coffin rested on its trestles, with a simple wreath of mixed wild flowers laid on top.

The doors closed with a thud and Harry stopped playing.

A few heads turned to see Jane Stokes in her white cassock wafting up the aisle. At the top of the nave she turned and greeted the congregation and then the service began.

It was a short and uncomplicated affair. Dorgy had not been a religious man and only an occasional churchgoer, so no one really knew what might have been appropriate music for his send-off. Rachel had selected a popular hymn and Mavis chose one that she thought he would have liked. There was no long eulogy, but an old friend from his inseminator days had tottered up to the pulpit to say a few words of farewell. Jane read a couple of prayers and then it was all over.

The black-suited pallbearers went forward deferentially, assumed their stations, and then heaved the coffin onto their shoulders. They were followed out by Rachel and Kylie and, to Jack's surprise, the latter was weeping. She was in her twentieth year and was now saying goodbye to the father she never knew. He lowered his head respectfully as they passed.

Outside, under a cloudy sky, Jack took Catherine's arm.

'I've got to have a few quick words with them. Be back in a minute.'

He hurried over to the waiting hearse and called Rachel's name just as the door was being opened for her. She turned and gave him a grim little smile.

'Thank you for coming, Mr Mitchell.'

'It was the least I could do for Dorgy.' He looked at Kylie. 'This isn't the time or place, but I do need to talk to you both as soon as possible. You have my number. Give me a call.'

'It's important?' Kylie had dried her tears.

'It's very important.' He winked at her. 'It's to do with carrying out your plan.'

A faint sign of animation flashed across that pale face as she said quietly, 'We'll call you.'

The two women got in, doors slammed and the hearse set off for the crematorium. Jack watched it for a few moments and then went back to find Catherine.

The clouds began to spit thin droplets as they arrived at the car and Catherine hurried into the passenger seat.

'Back to the hotel now?' she asked as Jack fastened the seat belt.

'I think so. I don't know about you, but I don't feel like socialising any more today.'

'A quiet lunch in then.'

He started the car and then turned to smile at her.

'A first class idea.'

They didn't say much after that until they joined the A390 by Hewas Water. Then Catherine suddenly said, 'You know your theory that Nathan pushed his father down the almshouses stairs?'

'Yes, but I reckon it's a bit more than a theory. What about it?'

'Well, I've been thinking. If there was such deep animosity between Dorgy and Nathan, surely he would never have opened his door to him that night.'

'Nathan could have tricked his way in. After all he got in to burgle the place before.'

She turned to face him.

'I still don't think Dorgy would have opened that door in the middle of the night to his son, but . . .'

'But what?'

The rain was falling a bit harder now and Jack accelerated the wipers.

'. . . but he might have opened the door to his daughter.'

She stared at him for a reaction. At first there was none. Then his lips parted slightly, before closing again firmly and his knuckles swelled as he gripped the steering wheel tighter. But he didn't reply.

'It's just a thought,' she said and turned back to watch the road.

They sat in silence for a mile and then, as he slowed behind a lorry, up ahead Catherine saw a bedraggled figure walking towards them on the opposite side of the road. He was wearing a shabby coat and a rucksack rode high on his shoulders. As they passed she caught a glimpse of a sun-reddened face and a single lank knot of hair dangling from his shaven head.

'Oh dear,' she said sadly, 'I do hope he has somewhere to lay his head tonight.'

Jack glanced at the figure in the rear view mirror and grunted as he overtook the lorry, but his mind was elsewhere. It had drifted to a dark landing at the top of a flight of stone stairs and then on to a door marked *Hawker*.